'UPSTAI

(WYSKOCH
Выскочка

JB. Woods

Book 3 of the Hunter series

Conversations written in 'Harrington font' are when the characters are speaking in a foreign language mainly Russian.

Books in the Hunter franchise:

1) **REBOUND** – formerly **'George Barrington Hunter'**
2) ~~**He's Behind you! formerly**~~ **'Below the Belt'**
3) **UPSTART**

2022

This novel is a work of fiction. Names and characters are a product of the author's imagination and any resemblance to actual persons, living or dead are coincidental.

This book contains a quantity of language and innuendo that some people may find offensive.

ISBN: 9798573354545

Cover design: Brian Platt
Lounging Model: Iain Powson

Prologue

Under the blurred streetlights at two 'o clock on a miserable September morning, the rain was sweeping over the Canal Bridge like a fine misty curtain when a silver Audi A4 approached. Ignoring the red traffic signal it moved slowly and manoeuvred across the bridge to the mini-roundabout before turning into the narrow cobbled alleyway which served both as a footpath to the ancient night entry gate of the Roman City walls and the exit of the car park behind the shops.

It swung in a wide arc and stopped parallel to the footpath close to the Wall. There was a dull clunk when the boot release was activated and the driver waited, watchful for any observers from the windows above the shops.

There were none and the driver dressed in black and wearing a hoodie slid out into the pouring rain and went to the rear of the car. Easing the boot open he fussed around twisting and tugging at a large object and pulled out a pale-coloured trenchcoat which he put on.

Grunting and breathing heavily with great effort he eased a body in a light grey suit out of the boot and onto his shoulders and drooping under the weight staggered towards the gateway. He struggled through the narrow arch before he humped the body off his shoulders and dropped it with little regard to how it lay. He hitched his collar up and ran back to the car and drove off into the cold murky early autumn night.

~~~~~~

Chapter 1

Since the day General Josef Bazarov received the call to drop everything and present himself at a dacha in the north of the country his life had improved. Gone were the long boring days of retirement watching TV and reading biased and controlled newspapers. He kept his fitness by taking long walks and he enjoyed the newly opened pedestrianised banks of the Moskva River all year round even in mid-winter when everything was frozen rigidly in its place but recently he had fostered the thought of ending it all.

Until that day when a messenger had presented himself at his apartment and left a letter telling him to be ready in civilian clothes the following day, a Saturday, at 0600 hrs and be prepared for an overnight stay. It was signed by a familiar hand he recognized from his KGB days.

On the stroke of six, a nondescript taxi picked him up and took him to Moscow Vnukovo International Airport where he was whisked through check-in and straight onto an internal flight to St Petersburg. Once there he was met by a uniformed FSA officer who drove him across the airport to a waiting helicopter. He was no sooner on board and they took off and minutes later they were headed northeast across a large lake. He wasn't a lover of flying and in a helicopter, over water, he felt distinctly uneasy but he steadfastly looked straight ahead until thirty minutes later a large island came into view and they landed on a helipad by a large modern wooden-clad dacha. As they hovered before touchdown he could see the expansive roof of a grass covered hangar and wondered who or what would require such camouflage so far north in the middle of a lake.

He was relieved when he saw the dacha, which meant he wasn't being transported to a high-security prison. The hangar was a concern as he was still unaware why he was there.

A golf buggy transported him to the dacha and after they had taken his bags and coat and he had changed his shoes which was the custom in Russia, he was ushered into a spacious living room furnished minimalistically. By a log fire and waiting was a face well known to him.

After the customary Russian welcome, he was shown to his seat, which was one of a pair close together. The uniformed servants were dismissed and his host who wasn't known for his drinking poured them both a glass of vodka and switched on a DVD player that played classical music not loud enough to inhibit close conversation.

'Welcome, Comrad General Bazarov, I see you're looking after yourself.'

This from a man well known for his love of sport and fitness was indeed a compliment and Josef wondered what was coming next, before he replied, 'I try to keep moving, comrade. I walk every day by the river at the statutory military pace although it gets harder.'

'Good work, and your brain, is that functioning well?'

'Yes.'

'We will drop the protocol, Josef. What I am about to disclose stays in this room. I want to take advantage of the turmoil our Crimean annexation and war in Eastern Ukraine is causing. Because he has less than two years to go Comrad Obama is not fully focused on world affairs. The need to prepare his country for the coming election is helping us and the U.K. is in a bit of a muddle at this time with its Scottish referendum and split government. Are you with me, Josef?'

'Yes, comrad, but where do I come in?'

'Josef, I have a list of people like yourself who operated under the old system. As you well know, I am not a fan of that system but in some areas the expertise was good. I want you to vet them and assemble a team, quickly mind you, and come up with a diversion while they are in turmoil, possibly 'Dirty Bombs.' big enough for us to retake some if not all of the countries we lost. That is countries like Ukraine, Estonia, Lithuania, Latvia, Belarus etc... We will do it under the guise of protecting our country.'

'Are not some of these countries covered by a defence pact with Nato?'

'They will do nothing but talk and you will create at the

same time fake news about a thwarted attempt on Russia.'

'Like someone else had an agenda involving both sides? How long have I got and do I get an office or something?'

'You, Comrad General, will be a Government executive without portfolio and answerable only to me. You will use the FSB with its security and international aids to assist you and your team and a country house in Zhukovka as your operational headquarters. That dacha is fitted out with the latest electronic aids and will be disguised as a tourist attraction and will appear on the European Tripadvisor website but it will always be full. The FSB will provide protection and transport. You will take your wife to the dacha and use your family as cover. Your operation will be called 'Wyskochka' (*Upstart*).'

'Why, *Upstart*?'

"*Upstart* is a series of movements a gymnast does on the parallel bars to reach a position to begin a routine and this is the beginning of a series of activities by which we hope to achieve a positive result for our future in the world. As soon as you have a plan and set it in motion discreet troop movements towards our borders will begin. Collect the briefcase from my secretary. In it is all the info you need. Destroy it when you are familiar with it. You are booked in to the tourist Nevsky Hotel in St Petersburg tonight and fly back to Moscow tomorrow. Don't forget—the future of Russia is in your hands.'

At that point, the door opened and a security guard entered and waited. They stood up together and after the complimentary goodbyes Josef was ushered out but his personal feelings were disguised. He wasn't sure he wanted the responsibility.

—

When Bazarov arrived in his chauffer driven Skoda Octavia at the dacha west of Moscow in the district of Zhukovka on his first day in charge of the '*Upstart*' Committee he was surprised that an alleged tourist dwelling should be a gated complex with an armed guard. He remained silent as the car progressed up the drive. If this was what his 'Nachal'nik' (Chief) had ordered so be it. It would be a few days before his wife moved in and commuting by chauffeur-driven car suited him.

The chauffeur cum armed guard carried his bags upstairs to his living quarters and after waiting an appropriate time Josef made his way to the meeting room and stood at the head of the table and surveyed his team. No one would sit without permission and they waited while a uniformed waiter delivered the customary round of vodka shots.

They raised their glasses, and said steadfastly, '*Zazdarovje.*'

Josef immediately gave the nod and they sat equally on either side of the long table and all but Fyodor Serov took a drink of water to wash the vodka down. Serov called the waiter and demanded vodka instead.

Josef took note and mentally thought little of the bunch of mixed military and political what he called 'has-beens' from the cold war era who had been foisted on him but he kept his thoughts to himself. They were after all on the list given to him by his nachal'nik and in their day experts at what they did. Moscow ex-police chief Fyodor Serov looked a little worse for alcoholic wear and Mafia boss Vlad Kryuchkov who had done time in a Cyprus prison for arms smuggling only thirteen years previously was bored.

The other four were Professor Ishak Akhmerov a nuclear physicist, Nikolai Arapov a U.S. and U.K. political specialist, Yuri Zablonsky and Yakov Krilov who were ex-KGB International agents who had been attached to various overseas Embassy's and whose expertise was infiltration and smuggling.

Standing at the head of the long table Bazarov picked up his briefcase as he viewed the assembled company sat in front of him. He withdrew six envelopes and passed them around, before announcing, 'Gentlemen, welcome to 'Operation *Upstart*'! The basis of this operation is to cause disruption and distraction in the West. In those envelopes, comrades, you will find your brief. You have five minutes to read them and then we will formulate a plan of action. I can tell you that this may mean digging up old connections etc...'

Serov picked up his envelope, gave it a quick glance and ripped it apart which suggested he'd had had enough of instructions and just wanted to get on with it while the others were more circumspect and did it aware that their leader would be watching and taking notes.

Five minutes seemed to pass quickly before Josef rapped the table, and said, 'What do we think, gentlemen?'

Prof. Akhmerov was the first to raise his hand. 'Yes, Professor?'

'Comrad General—I gather from these instructions that there is no limit to what we do so long as it's not total destruction and it covers both the U.S. and Great Britain?'

'Correct.'

'So what is euphemistically called a 'dirty bomb' could be used?'

'Yes, a disruptive dirty bomb. Collateral damage must be small and the evidence must point to someone else. Have you anything in mind, Professor?'

'A small nuclear device close to or in one of their recycling plants. One that is isolated or in a less populated area. This would cause minimum physical damage, maybe an area of sixteen kilometres but would give a wide radioactive fallout. We would have to manufacture it and then import it somehow but if my fellow Comrads can organise that I can design the device.'

Josef walked back and forth across the room a couple of times rubbing his chin thoughtfully and when he stopped he confronted Prof Akhmerov. 'Stick with the 'dirty bomb' plan, nothing bigger. Can you do it, Professor?'

'Yes.'

'How long would it take,

'Three or four months, maybe six.'

'Too long, Professor, we need to do it quickly while the political unrest is in our favour.'

Ex-Police Chief Serov raised a hand.

'Yes, Fyodor?'

'Sorry to interrupt, Comrad General, but in my spare time which I have lots of these days I browse the English newspapers on the internet and one called the Daily Mail reported that North Korea is experimenting with small nuclear devices carried in backpacks by suicide ground troops if their country is invaded. Would this be what the Prof was suggesting?'

Everybody immediately took notice and Prof. Akhmerov nodded vigorously. 'Very much so,' he said, 'even better as we could then lay the blame directly on that defunct regime.'

Josef looked askance at Serov. 'Fyodor, they are 'dirty bombs' and not the full-blown nuclear devices?'

'Yes, or you would not be able to move on to that territory for years which would be no good.'

Josef directed his next question to Krilov and Zablonsky. 'If we get our hands on these devices can you organise the import/export of them?'

They stood and walked to the end of the room and talked amongst themselves in low tones before Krilov stepped away and approached Josef, and said, 'Comrad General, we have contacts in North Korea who can obtain these packages and we can transport them if you can get the necessary funds to obtain them. Bribery will be involved but North Korea would welcome the income. Comrad Zablonsky runs the sleeper 'October Legion' in the U.K. with branches conveniently close to nuclear sites around the U.K..'

'Remind me, Comrad, what is the 'October Legion'?'

'They are sleeper agents left over from the Cold War spread around the U.K. and the U.S. They are still operational and meet up from time to time but mainly swap stories of the old days but they only need switching on.'

'Set this up. But remember—it must look like North Korea or Ukraine is doing this and when the time comes we will release fake news suggesting we have anticipated an attack on us and are moving to protect ourselves from further outrage.'

—

After the meeting, Krilov and Zablonsky travelled together and they had only gone a few kilometres when Krilov ordered the car to stop.

Zablonsky looked enquiringly at Krilov, and said, 'What is the matter, Yakov?'

'I want to talk but not in the car. Join me while we walk together.' He leaned forward and had a quick word with the driver before joining Zablonsky at the roadside and they began walking at a brisk pace as the car followed.

Krilov spoke. 'Yuri! You are aware that these Korean bombs are the real thing and not the dirty bombs that our Leader wants.'

Zablonsky nodded, 'Yes, and I wonder what we are going to do about it. What do you suggest?'

'It occurred to me, Yuri, that regardless of how big the devices are what we are about to do will cause International havoc anyway so why don't we import these proper nukes and say nothing. I mean, pretend they are dirty bombs.'

'My thoughts entirely, Yakov, what's the damage area of these devices?'

'Akhmerov says an area of about sixteen square kilometres.'

'And the fall out area?'

'Who knows? It depends on the wind.'

Krilov stopped and turned to face Zablonsky. 'We are agreed then that we organise two of these Korean pack nuke devices and say nothing?'

'Yes, Yakov.'

They shook hands and walked back to the car.

~~~~~~

CHAPTER 2

It was dawn on a Monday and in the office overlooking the Mall, 'C' peered over his glasses at Senior Agent Gus Thomas and demurred over his next words. 'This should be fives job but they don't have available staff and neither do we?'

'In a word, yes, sir. With the cutbacks and the increased activity in the Middle East, the Russians in Ukraine and Syria and the latest terrorist orientated activity here, there is no chance.'

'Any idea what they're up to in Syria?'

'We're concentrating on the terrorist threat, mainly the IS.'

'So who have we got to investigate this Chester affair assuming it's something to do with this increased activity.'

'You're not going to like this but I suggest we get Hunter back.'

'C' stood up and wheeled toward the window and standing with his back to the room looked up the Mall through the dispersing gloom towards the floodlit panorama of Buckingham Palace pondering the unlikely alternative he was presented with.

He pivoted around, and said, 'He's burned isn't he?'

'He was out of line, sir, which was understandable under the circumstances but this is a caretaker role.'

'Is he fit?'

'A lot fitter than me with a brain to match.'

'And his roll will be?'

'Local Field Controller.'

'Okay, Gus, get on to it.'

They shook hands and Gus left with the knowledge that he had already set the wheels in motion.

———

Hunter threw his antiquated Nokia mobile phone onto the dining table, 'The bastards want me back,' he said to himself, 'well, they'll have to beg.'

He picked up his mug of tea and wandered through the spacious conservatory and oblivious of the blustery wind and the miserable damp conditions he went out onto the patio to watch Tess their

German Shepherd dog investigating her new territory. Hunter liked their new house but he missed the open view across the Rec from his old bungalow.

The bungalow had been in the Hunter family for three generations and he and Jacquie had expanded it to fit their needs but reluctantly because of the invasion into their lives they had to move and this five-bed roomed house in Thornton was Jacquie's choice. It was roomy and in a peaceful location with easy access to Jacquie's Garden Centre chain and definitely no chance of sharpshooters taking advantage of open recreation grounds, which was almost the cause of his early demise but luck had been with him and he survived.

He had given up his part-time job to supervise alterations to the property, which they had been occupying for two months and he was enjoying his early morning cuppa before waking Jacquie and the children when his phone buzzed for a second time.

Although he missed the excitement and the adrenalin rush of MI6, he didn't want to give them the satisfaction of knowing it. He ignored it again and pondered the thought that throughout his life the dawn had played a big part and the dawn he remembered fondly was in Northern Ireland when he had first seen Jacquie. She had been an undercover agent for MI5 who had infiltrated the Provo IRA but her position became untenable and she was extracted by the SAS.

He went back inside and meandered up to the small bedroom, which he had made his Manhole. Three walls were covered with books that he used as research for his new hobby of writing. On the other wall he had his computer desk. He had written children's stories for Lesley and Iain when they were small but he was branching out and writing a novel.

He sat down at his desk and reluctantly returned the call. It was answered after three rings, and Hunter said, 'A bit early for you, Gus?'

'I'm going back to bed after this, don't you worry.'

Hunter grimaced, a lie-in was something he'd love but with the habits of a lifetime ingrained into his psyche, they were not to be. He exhaled noisily and replied, 'Go on, tell me, Gus, you want me back? Well, you're going to have to be nice.'

He could hear the audible sigh before Gus replied, 'George...'

'That's not a good start,' said Hunter.'

There was a pause before Gus spoke again and then it was forceful. 'Hunter! You're on the payroll and your permits are on the way. Have you got an android phone?'

'No, they're a pain in the arse, but Jacquie has.'

'Okay, I'll send your e-I.D to her phone. That will suffice until your hard copy arrives. Right now get yourself to Chester and link up with a Detective Sergeant Newlove.'

'Where?'

'One moment.' Hunter could hear the rustle of paper in the background and Gus muttering to himself as he searched, before he replied, 'By the City walls close to the Canal Bridge.'

'What's it all about, Gus?'

'I can't give you the full details over the phone but suffice to say you are now our Local Field Controller and it's about one of our GCHQ operatives. I'll have the office message you the details and Newlove will fill you in about the local scene.'

'Who am I working for?'

'You're on our books. It should be fives job but they don't want it because they're undermanned so we've called a truce and we're doing the job for them but your backup will be five. Got it?

'Okay, Gus, but I still have to get permission from the boss?'

'I don't think you'll have any trouble there she'll be glad to see the back of you.'

'Carrying permit, Gus?'

'And that. Now get off the phone and get yourself fixed up. Your permits will be with you shortly.'

'Gus, I want new plates for the car.'

'Can't you use one of ours?'

'And be recognised a mile away.'

'Leave it with me.'

Hunter put the phone down and conceded to nature before he put in his contact lenses and got himself ready for the day ahead and completed his morning ritual making Jacquie's statutory morning mug of tea. While it was brewing he swapped the Sim cards in their phones which she wouldn't be happy about and that done he poured the tea and went upstairs to the bedroom.

He knocked gently on the door and crept in but Jacquie was awake, and she said to him. 'Who were you talking to at this time of the morning?'

'Gus Thomas. He wants me for a job in Chester. Is that okay?'

'Do your own thing, H? You know you're fed up so just go.'

'Just for a day I need your posh phone as my I.D until the hard stuff arrives. I've changed the Sims already.'

'One day only, Hunter. I see you're dressed, do they want you now?'

'Yep, give us a kiss and I'll get going.'

—

As he approached the Uniform guarding the crime scene Hunter pulled his collar up as protection against the cold north westerly as it blew driving drizzle down the Cheshire gap. The crime scene was the narrow gateway under the red sandstone Roman walls of the City and was only wide enough for one person and much to the chagrin of the locals it had been closed off which meant a considerable detour.

He flashed his I.D but instead of lifting the tape, she said, 'Sorry, sir, you'll have to get togged up before you can enter.' She pointed to a nearby police van. 'Coveralls, shoes and gloves in there.'

'Thanks,' he said, 'It's been a long time.'

He went to the van and was given the desired articles and after he had togged up he returned to the scene and the tape was lifted without question. As he approached the gathered forensics and SOCO team, he said aloud to no one in particular, 'Okay, what have we?'

Everyone turned to face him and a familiar face, Detective Sergeant Effie Newlove a striking tall blonde about thirty-ish with short hair layered in the sixties DA style and suitably zipped up in a fashionable copper coloured quilted jacket over pinstripe boot-leg trousers with polished brown boots underneath her protective coveralls came forward to greet him.

Knowing Hunter's distaste of hugging she pushed out a latex covered hand. 'Morning, Hunter, it's been a long time...' They shook hands, and she continued, '...are you from MI5?'

'MI6.'

There was no immediate reaction but she looked puzzled.

'What's the matter,' he said.

'I don't understand,' she said, 'we were told MI5.'

'That's me, Effie. Just call me Hunter. Like your hair, lass, a bit longer than when we last met.'

'Thank you,' she said, 'back to the present. We have the body of a man in his late twenties who was found by...' she pointed to a young man in a high viz jacket over jeans and boots both covered in mud or plaster, '...that chap there on his way to work.'

'What time was this?'

'Five-thirty.'

'Time of death?'

'First estimate Doctor Kerr puts it between eleven and two last night.'

'And the ID, Effie?'

She held up a GCHQ ID tag. 'In a pocket in the lining of his jacket was this. That's why we called you lot.'

'Okay, Effie, let's take a look at him.'

'Just a minute, Hunter,' she pointed to the witness. 'I need a statement from him.' She called out, 'Farmer!,' and a young man with a №1 hair cut about six foot tall looked across. She waved for him to approach which he did in a manner that Hunter thought was a little disrespectful.

'Yes, Sarge?'

'Take a statement off our witness, Farmer, and then let him go.'

'Yes, Sarge.'

'Right, Hunter, let's go,' and she led the way towards the narrow opening in the wall.

The assembly parted to let them through but only as far as the wall and because the passage was too small for both of them Effie stood to one side. Only the feet of the body in polished casual shoes were visible at the far end of the passage and the rest of the torso was lying twisted against the wall on the cobbled ancient footpath leading up to Abbey Street on the other side. Hunter stood by the feet and looked down at Doctor Kerr who was examining the body in more detail.

Kerr glanced up and with a look of surprise on his face, he said, 'Well, well, Hunter, I thought you'd retired. Fully recovered are we?'

'Yes, Doc, with all my ribs intact.'

'They must be getting desperate.'

'You know how it is, Doc, you can't keep a good man down.'

'They didn't waste any time getting you here and I'm sorry to drag you out in this weather but there's no telling when these things are going to happen.' He stood up and groaned as he flexed his shoulders and stretched his legs, before continuing, 'I'm getting too old for this. As you can see, Hunter, we have a Caucasian male twenty-five to thirty years old who had a GCHQ ID and he's wearing a shoulder holster but there's no gun. Did he draw a gun from the stores and is he one of yours?'

'No, Doc, he's not a field man and I'll check with the 'Firm' about the firearm. Cause of death?'

'He was stabbed in the left side of his chest directly into his heart by a narrow instrument something like an ice pick. It was thrust very hard as the hilt has left a mark on his clothing and bruising on the flesh so definitely intended to kill in my opinion. I'll know more when I get him to the mortuary.'

Hunter rubbed his chin. 'Wearing a suit which was wet but no coat and armed. I wonder what he was up to. Okay, I'll leave you to it, Doc.'

He retraced his steps back through the passage and spoke to Effie. 'Where are we operating from?'

'We've been allocated an office in the Chester Police HQ out in Blacon.'

'See you there.'

———

Newlove stood by a whiteboard which apart from a picture fit of the victim had very little else on it when her Smartphone buzzed.

'Hello, Doc, any news?'

She listened for a couple of minutes and acknowledged the Doctor before she put the phone down and spoke to DC Farmer. 'Time of death fits. One-hundred and eighty centimetres, Caucasian. He has a fading tattoo on his right arm of some sort of trident symbol. We are looking that up. Apart from that, no other distinguishing marks. He could be American.'

'Why does he think that, Sarge?'

'His shoes were made in the US.'

'He could have bought them online.'

'Could be, Farmer. When we get the DNA results we'll forward them on to the U.S. Authorities.

'Shouldn't we tell that guy the toffs sent?'

'That guy is called, Hunter, Farmer, and don't cross him, you may live to regret it.'

'Huh, he's an old man and I bet he colours his hair.'

'I've got news for you, Farmer—he doesn't, and his field ID with the SIS is GBH. You have been warned. Did you get anything from the house to house?'

'No, Sarge, and nobody heard anything but we've put out an appeal on the local radio and TV channels plus the newspapers with a photo-fit of the victim.'

'Good. Add it to the board, and we have that hair off the wall. It could be bloody Roman but whoever it was will have sandstone and plaster scrapings across their shoulders where they rubbed the opposite wall of the tunnel. I'll leave you to it, Farmer, I've got a load of paperwork to sort out.'

———

It was some time later when Effie put the landline phone down and leaned back in her chair with a sigh. 'Nothings bloody easy.'

She picked up her Smartphone and dabbed her finger down on one of the contact apps.

It was answered immediately and a distant voice smothered by office hubbub in the background answered. 'Yes, Sarge?'

'Farmer, get yourself to the office.'

'Be there in a few, Sarge.'

She didn't have long to wait before there was a knock on the door and without waiting Farmer stepped into the room.

'Come in, Farmer,' Effie said sarcastically. Farmer sat down opposite her and slipping a piece of notepaper over the desk, she continued, 'I've just had info from uniform that after our radio appeal a local guest house has reported a missing person. Get your coat we're going up there now to check it out. Bring a photo and if it's our John Doe we go through his effects.'

———

Effie squeezed her car into the last parking space outside the large pleasant Victorian building which allowing for the time of year had a good selection of flowers and shrubs in its gardens. Grabbing her bag and with Farmer in tow, she walked towards the entrance when her inquisitive nature made her glance at the number plates of the other cars. She stopped at the third one and she knew this was not going to be straightforward. She kept an open mind and went directly to the reception desk and rang the bell.

Two minutes later she was about to ring again when a busy lady of around sixty came through the door at the end of the hall and approached her.' I'm sorry, miss, but we're full,' she said.

Effie held up her ID. 'Detective Sergeant Newlove, ma'am, and DC Farmer. You reported a missing person?'

'Oh, yes, sorry, come through into the parlour. I don't want to alert the other guests.'

Effie and Farmer followed her through into a homely, what Effie could only describe as what she thought was a nineteen-fifties style living room.

'Now, what can I do for you, miss?'

'Can I have your name, please,' said Effie, 'It makes for better communication?'

'It's Mrs Charters.'

'Okay, Mrs Charters, tell me about your missing guest?'

'He registered on Friday afternoon and I had just given him a discount on my last double room when a young couple turned up.'

Farmer showed her the photo of their early morning victim. 'Is that him?'

'Yes.'

'What was his name again?'

'He signed in as James Bond.'

Effie scribbled in her notebook, and continued, 'Since Friday, Mrs Charters, what did he do?'

'Friday, after dinner he enquired about *Dixie's Bar.*'

'The pub by the Town Hall?'

'Yes.'

'And he went out?'

'Yes, and came back after midnight by taxi.'

'And over the weekend?'

'Saturday he went out after breakfast and came back in time for dinner and said very little, not even to my other guests. I never interfere. It's up to them if they want to communicate.'

'And after dinner?'

'He went out again and he never came back.'

'Did he have a car, Mrs Charters?'

'Yes, Miss, it's the black Vauxhall in the car park but he never used it.'

Effie's worst fears were realised. It was a Government registered vehicle. She made a quick note, and said, 'Have you got a spare key, Mrs Charters?'

'I have a master key.'

Effie and Farmer followed her upstairs to a back room. Like the outside, the interior was immaculate and uncluttered, almost military. Every picture and ornament was perfectly placed and in line.

Mrs Charters opened the door she went to step inside and Effie stopped her. 'Sorry, Mrs Charters, it's off-limits. It's not a crime scene but connected. Neither you or your staff must go in there until we release it. I'll put some tape across the door to remind you.'

'Can I ask a favour, miss?'

'Yes, what is it?'

'Would you mind not putting up any tape? I don't want to frighten the other guests and then there's this social media thing. I don't want that kind of publicity. I'll keep it off-limits, I promise.'

'I'm putting my job on the line here but okay.'

'Thank you, miss. I'll be careful.'

They entered the room and closed the door behind them and began a search. After half an hour's digging around, they left and Effie flicked the '*Do not clean this room*' sign that Mrs Charters had hung on the door handle. 'Nice one!'

———

It was late evening when Effie put the phone down and pushed herself back from the desk. 'Farmer!' she said, 'that was the Home

Office and they delicately told me officially from now on the case is no longer ours. They checked out our vic and that car which is logged out to the security services and they will be taking over.'

'Does that mean we drop everything, Sarge?'

'Not quite. We will still be part of the team but it's their call and Agent Hunter, is in charge.'

~~~~~~

Chapter 3

It took him a couple of minutes to park his Golf GTi at the Police HQ and he was walking towards the entrance when an oversize Jeep 4 x 4 pulled up in the visitors bay and DS Effie Newlove got out and without looking left or right she headed for the front entrance.

Hunter stood a few paces behind her at the reception desk but said nothing, instead when it was his turn he enquired which office was theirs and made his way into the red brick matrix that was the Blacon HQ of the Cheshire Police. It was only one storey and he chose the stairs and at the top he followed the long corridor to the last door and went into what he thought was the next best thing to a storeroom.

He stood in the doorway and it was several seconds before she spotted him and walked across to greet him. 'Hunter, welcome to our humble surroundings. '

He shook hands with Effie and she took him by the arm and led him forward.

Hunter dragged up a chair and sat opposite Effie who took up her position behind the desk and when they were settled, she continued, 'Hunter, I take it you are now our Commander?'

'Yes, Effie, but I see no reason why we can't work together and up to now you know it all.'

'Good,' she said, 'we'll start with a quick recap. Our victim, as you know, was found yesterday morning stabbed through the heart. There is no evidence to say who did it but we know the weapon was a thin spike, an ice pick or something similar. Death was instantaneous.'

'A robbery gone wrong?' said Hunter.

'It could be, but I think the perp was being followed and he ducked behind the wall and waited until the victim caught up with him. There is more, Hunter, one moment.' She picked up the landline phone and dabbed down on a number and a mumbled voice answered and she responded, 'Farmer, get in here.'

Seconds later Farmer poked his head around the door. 'Sarge?'

'Farmer, what was the other name the vic used?'

'James Bond, Sarge.'

'Okay, Farmer, that's all.' She waited until he left. 'Not very original, Hunter. Do you know his real name?'

'The info I was given with this morning's update suggests it is Agent Rhys Owen as shown on the ID you found.'

Anticipating a cock and bull story authenticated by the 'firms' brass, Effie scribbled vigorously on her pad before she spoke, 'What was he doing in Chester, Hunter?'

Hunter didn't hesitate. 'I don't know. He's an I.T. specialist from GCHQ. Definitely not a fieldman.'

'And you've no idea what he was investigating?'

'I'm advised that he was last seen in his office with the other I.T. guys over a week ago and they've been looking for him ever since. Effie—you said his lodgings. You've been searching the effects of a security service agent?'

'Hunter, when a crime is committed it's our job to sort it and it was an unexplained death.'

'Sorry, Effie, you're right, but it's still my case.'

Effie flipped open her notebook and read for a moment, before she said, 'We found nothing other than a laptop in his room and a Sat-Nav device in his car which SOCO are now investigating.' Hunter held his hand up. 'Yes, Hunter.'

'Have you sealed off his room, Effie?'

'Yes.'

'Good, we'll go there when we're done here.'

She pushed her chair back and stood up. 'This meeting is over. The desk in the corner is for you, Hunter. You know the drill. We'll meet here every morning at eight-thirty. Farmer will keep you in the loop as will I.'

'Okay,' said Hunter, 'It may be my case but investigating crimes is more your scene so I'll sit back and let you get on with it and as you put it—keep me in the loop. Meanwhile, Effie, let's go to that guest house. We'll use my car.'

———

They sat outside in the parking area admiring the well kept but much modernised Victorian Building when Mrs Charters walked across and Hunter lowered the window.

'Can I help you?' she said.

'We're from the Police,' said Hunter, 'and we want to look at Mr Owen's room again.'

'We don't have a Mr Owen.'

'You may know him as, Bond, Mrs...?'

She finished the sentence for him. '...Charters. Would you like to go in now? The sooner you get in and done the sooner I'll get my room back.'

Hunter nodded. 'Okay, Mrs Charters, we'll do that—thank you.'

They followed her inside and upstairs to Owen's room. 'Nice place you have here, Mrs Charters,' said Hunter, 'but shouldn't you ask for my identity?'

'Thank you for the compliment and you look the part. Show me if you like but I know the lady from the last time.'

Hunter flashed his I.D. as she unlocked the door to Owen's room, 'It's not taped off, Mrs Charters as is usual.'

'I asked your Sergeant not to,' she said, 'in case it worried my other guests. We rely on return business you see. I haven't touched anything like she asked.'

'Good logic.'

Once inside he closed the door behind them and stood for a minute surveying the room. Hunter whistled. 'Wow! He didn't mind splashing out the dosh. I wonder did he put it on the books?'

Although Owen's clothes were spread around and the bed unmade the decor was immaculate. It was large with typical Victorian high ceilings with a Queen size bed and the basic cream colour was toned down with good quality pictures and a bevelled mirror, a smart TV and coffee making facilities.

'Where should we start,' he said to Effie.

He walked across to the wardrobe and opened the doors, 'I don't know what you expect to find,' said Effie, 'We went through this place with a fine tooth comb.'

'A new set of eyes,' said Hunter, 'and if we find nothing today we can let Mrs Charters have her room back.'

Effie tipped Owen's rucksack onto the bed and began searching for a second time while Hunter went through the clothes in the wardrobe. There wasn't much but he checked every seam and crease and the lining of the only coat in there but he found nothing.

'I think that's it, Effie, lass. Call it a day and let's give it back.'

Effie agreed and between them, they packed everything ready to take with them. That done Hunter slung the bag over his shoulder and went towards the door when something caught his eye. 'Carry on, lass, I'm going to the loo. See you by the car.'

Effie said one word. 'Men!' and left the room but Hunter didn't go to the bathroom. Instead, he waited a few seconds and climbed onto the bed above which the centre portion of a black and gold three-section set-piece was slightly skewed. It was barely noticeable but in Hunter's mind worth checking.

He eased the picture away from the wall and slid his hands around the back and—Bingo! It took him a few seconds to pluck away the tape but when he did a slim package dropped into his hands. Sitting back on his heels he centred the picture and satisfied he put the package into his pocket and went down to the car.

At the bottom of the stairs, he was met by the landlady. 'Mrs Charters,' he said, 'can we talk for a minute?'

'Why, yes, what is it?'

'Can we go somewhere private? It wouldn't do for your customers to see us.'

She took him to a small office at the end of the hall and he closed the door behind them.

'Take a seat, Mrs Charters.' She sat at the office desk and Hunter remained standing. He showed her his I.D. 'I'm not police, I'm from the Security Services and we're looking into the movements of our Mr Owen. When did he get here?'

'Late last Friday. I remember as only moments later I had a couple turn up and I'd given him the double room at a discount.'

'How was he?'

'What do you mean?'

'Was he flustered, dishevelled anything like that?'

'No, he was smartly dressed and well-spoken.'

'Since Friday, what did he do?'

'I told your Sergeant. On Friday, after dinner, he enquired about *Dixie's Bar*.'

'And he went out?'

'Yes, and he came back at midnight by taxi.'

'And on Saturday?'

'He went out after breakfast and came back in time for dinner and said very little, not even to other guests.'

'And after dinner?'

'He went out immediately and never came back.'

'What was the weather like on Sunday evening?'

'Bit like yesterday. Blustery wind and drizzle.'

'Did he wear a coat on Saturday?'

'A new cream trench coat.'

'A new coat?'

'It looked new and he wore it Colombo style, that's open.'

'Thank you, Mrs Charters, you can use the room now and sorry for the mess.'

She stood up and they shook hands and Hunter left. In the car park, he was met by an irate Effie. 'How long does it take to have a piss, Hunter?' she said abruptly.

'When you're my age quite a long time,' he replied, and then added, 'I spoke to the landlady about our friend.'

'And?'

'The only thing new interestingly, on Saturday night when he went out he was wearing a new trench coat.'

'Why would a perp take a coat, Hunter.'

'My thoughts also, to keep dry maybe?'

'Let's go and look at that passageway.'

———

Hunter was sure that SOCO would have covered all aspects of the scene but more in hope than anything else he took the torch out of the glove box and went to the crime scene which was still cordoned off. Effie joined him and they flashed their I.D. and the constable on duty lifted the tape and allowed them through.

Hunter held Effie by the arm to stop her, and said, 'Follow the path up to the wall and keep your eyes peeled although I expect they've covered everything,'

They edged forward covering ground already checked by SOCO and at the tunnel entrance Hunter switched his torch on and on a hunch he checked the roof inch by inch and was about to give up when something caught his eye. He called Effie and pointing upward, said, 'What do you make of that, lass?'

She looked hard at where he was pointing and took the torch from him to look closer. 'I'm not sure, Hunter but it looks like a light scrape like something brushed against it. You can see where the moss has been pulled.'

'I'm thinking Owen was carried here on someone's shoulder and when he humped him off the body touched the roof. Which means...'

Effie butted in, '...He was killed somewhere else.'

'That probably explains why there's no blood. Let's go to the lab and look at those clothes.'

Stepping carefully they backed out of the passageway and under the tape and on a whim, Hunter studied the tarmac on the car park for signs but saw nothing as they made their way to the car.

———

In the mortuary lab, Doctor Kerr stood alongside Hunter who was checking out Owen's suit. He put the jacket back in the basket and acknowledged there were scrape marks from the tunnel roof on them.

'So what do you think, Doc? He was taken there with his coat on and because it was raining the perp took the coat?'

'It looks that way, Hunter. I'll get the team to re-check the car park. Whoever it was must have driven there.'

'Sergeant Newlove and I gave it a quick once over but it's probably too late because of the weather. What about the lack of blood, Doc?'

'Death was instantaneous and because of the fine weapon the bleeding, what there was of it, was internal, but there would likely be traces in the car or original crime location.'

Hunter turned to Effie, 'Come on, lass, let's go and get something to eat and then we'll pop back to the office before we get ready for a night on the town.'

'One more thing,' said Kerr, 'Owen's tattoo is the Ukraine Coat of Arms.'

'Why would he have that I wonder?' He shrugged and followed Effie out.

Outside in the car park, she pulled on Hunter's arm and stopped him. 'Hunter, why do you keep calling me, lass?'

He let out a small sigh, 'It's an endearing north country term for a female partner, friend or helper, even a wife, that's all. You've lived up here long enough.'

'I don't like it. My names, Effie.'

'Ooooh...! Hark at you.'

When they reached the car he stood by the driver's door and looked across at her and with an emphasis on her name but smiling, he asked, 'Where shall we dine, Effie?'

She stuck her tongue out, and replied, 'I don't know. I'm going back to the station so it'll be the canteen likely.'

'I'll drop you off. I'm going to the Garden Centre. I get a free lunch there.'

'Charlotte says you don't.'

It clicked that she was referring to Jacquie's P.A. 'Silly me, you two are an item.' He laughed. 'Caught out. I'll have words with her, giving away my secrets. Are you pair getting married?'

'It's never crossed our minds, Hunter. We just like being together.'

———

Hunter pushed his plate away and leaned back from the table. Business was good but he had secured a quiet table close to the windows where he could observe the intermittent rain and squally showers that had been a feature of the last few days.

He checked his issue i-phone that had now become an element in his life since HQ had dragged him out of retirement. He didn't like them but modern methods required that he used it.

There were no updates concerning his current case and while considering the next move, he fingered the package in his inside pocket. On impulse, he took it out and using his Swiss Army knife eased it open and tipped the contents onto the table. The first thing he picked up was a driving licence.

'Hmm,' he mused, 'so you are, Owen.' He checked the details and did a mental calculation, 'Aged twenty-five,' and came to the conclusion he couldn't have been long out of University but the two items which intrigued him were the passports. A UK one in the name of Owen and another issued in Ukraine.

'My, my, Mr Owen who is Andriy Ivaskin? Are you Owen with the pseudonym Ivaskin or the other way around?'

He unfolded a sheaf of A4 paper and the first two pages were a host of words and numbers in columns and written in a language he recognised but couldn't interpret what he thought was —Russian. One column looked like GPS locations but the other just figures and letters. Written underneath were a couple of paragraphs of plain writing. The other two pages were written in some Middle Eastern script and what looked like Chinese and appeared to be identical in content.

Also enclosed was a motorway map of the UK issued by the CND and eight Sim cards. 'Eight,' he said mentally, 'one for each day and a rollover maybe? What were you up to?'

He separated the I.D. and driving licence plus the Owen passport and returned the rest to the package and slipped it into his inside pocket as a familiar voice assailed him, 'Hello, Mr Hunter.'

He'd been so involved in what he was doing he hadn't spotted Jacquie's P.A. approaching. Without undue haste, he gathered the remaining items and put them in his pocket. 'Hello, Charlotte, have you got time for coffee?'

She sat down opposite him, and replied, 'No, thanks, I've only come to pass the time of day. I hear you're back in the big time?'

'So much for the Secret Service. Who told you, Charlotte?'

'Effie.'

'I should have guessed. How are you pair getting on?'

'Effie's moving in this weekend, that's if she's not working.'

'That'll save you a few bob. Where's Jacquie, Charlotte?'

'She's out at the new place. It wasn't in bad nick but you know your Jacquie, she likes it just so with her stamp on it. Is she planning any more?'

'I don't think so, Charlotte, she said four was enough.'

'Okay, I'd better be getting along. Take care,' she said with a smile.

He watched her as she walked across the restaurant. He liked Charlotte with her long chestnut hair immaculately groomed in a business-like but feminine way. She ran the business when Jacquie was hospitalised and had shown then that she couldn't be messed with. He just hoped she had made the right choice with her life.

He pondered his next move before ringing Effie and arranged to meet her at the City Centre Police Station and while walking through the Garden Centre to his car he sent a quick message to Jacquie and before he could settle she confirmed that the security arrangements to pick up the children from school was all in order.

He smiled to himself, as he knew that in her business way things would be on the button and beware anyone who didn't fall into line. He was always in awe of her personality. A soft but firm mother, tactile wife and lover and a good friend but back at her desk she was a different animal but her staff loved her. He considered himself lucky as he had always worked with women who were both attractive, personable but also on top of their game.

—

Sergei Golovin sat stony-faced on the tarmac of Moscow airport in his heavyweight fork-lift vehicle observing the overcast weather beginning its wind-up to the winter storms. He was also watching the progress of the Air Koryo Ilyushin Il-76 Cargo plane as it taxied towards him.

He wasn't anxious about the instructions he had been given by a tall nameless man in a leather coat, who, along with his boss had taken him to one side and in a low tone conversation had told him what to do.

Ten years in the military had taught him not to query instructions from your seniors and after all, picking up a couple of suitcases wasn't that difficult although getting out of his warm cab and into the light drizzle blowing across the airfield was annoying.

The aircraft-parking guide finally crossed his paddles and the engines deprived of fuel went into a prolonged deepening whine but Sergei waited as his counterparts rushed forward to start unloading. He watched as steps were put into place by the front exit and moments after they were secure the door opened and the pilot twice walked uneasily down the steps carrying a brown leather suitcase which was obviously in the excess weight category. He left them alongside the steps before returning to his cabin to finalise the shutdown.

Sergei rolled forward as close as he could to minimize his discomfort from the weather and hurried across to pick up the cases and was surprised at the weight but with a little extra effort, he loaded them one at a time behind his seat and returned to the warmth of his cab.

Two hours later he moved on to his next job. Loading a Russian military II-76 bound for Sevastopol in the Crimea but this time he carried the suitcases up to the cabin and handed them over to the pilot. Job done, he carried on with his duties eight-thousand roubles richer.

The handover at Sevastopol went equally smooth but this time the cases were loaded into a nondescript white van of indeterminate age and driven away from the airport by two unkempt peasant-like men who it was hoped would raise no suspicion as they posed as refugees fleeing back into the Sovereign State of Ukraine. In the back of the van cuddling, two children was the wife of the elder, the others being his family who were now rich enough to migrate.

At the dockside in Odessa, they were met by a fisherman who swapped a large brown envelope for the cases and without a word he turned away and headed for his vessel which put out to sea immediately to progress overnight to Constanta the opening port to the Danube and the start of the transport link into Europe.

At Constanta, the cases were loaded onto a small handcart and pulled through the streets to a backstreet carpenters shop and after a hurried check right and left they were swiftly carried inside and the doors locked. This was a rush job as they had to be ready for the next part of the journey by breakfast the next morning.

—

Parking slots were at a premium outside the City Centre station house and Hunter doubled up in the same slot behind Effie who was waiting in her Jeep. He had no sooner switched off and she was holding his door open.

'Afternoon, Effie,' he said, as he clambered out, 'everything okay?'

She closed the door behind him and as they walked side by side the short distance to '*Dixie's Bar*' she said conversationally, 'Did I hear you groan?'

He glanced sideways at her and she kept a straight face. 'You did. Getting in's okay,' he said, 'but getting out is a bit of a haul.'

'You'll have to get something higher like a Jeep.'

He opened the door of the pub and held it open for her. She said nothing but she quietly liked his old-fashioned courtesies. At the bar, he ordered himself a half a lager and Effie settled for tonic water with a twist before Hunter pushed his i-phone over the counter at the barman. On it was a photo of Owen. 'Do you recognise this guy, mate? He was in on Friday night.'

'Who wants to know?'

Effie was quick to respond and slid her ID over the bar. 'Police!'

'Oh... Err... No. I wasn't on then.' He turned away and called to his fellow barman. 'Eddie, got a minute?'

Eddie strolled down to them with a look that said enough before he opened his mouth. 'Yeh, what is it?'

Hunter rested his elbow on the bar and dangled his ID. 'Civility first.' He pushed the phone towards him. 'Do you recognise him from Friday night?'

Eddie looked and shook his head. 'No, I went off at seven.'

'Okay, now get me the names and addresses of those who were on duty Friday night.'

'Err...'

Hunter leaned forward to emphasise his next words. 'Now would be useful, matey.'

Effie looked at this person beside her with a side hitherto unseen by her. She was willing to let Hunter do the talking and said nothing but looked at Eddie and with a slight movement of her head indicated that he should comply.

'I'll have to speak with me boss. Hang on.'

He disappeared through a swing door and Hunter thanked the barman and indicated that it was okay for him to carry on. A few moments later Eddie returned followed by the manager, a thickset man with a beard whose body stature said he was not to be argued with.

He stopped in front of Hunter and Effie, and said gruffly, 'Who wants to know about my staff?'

Both Hunter and Effie held up their ID, and Hunter said, 'We do. It's part of an ongoing investigation and once they have ID'd...' he pointed to the phone, '...that guy and who he spoke to we won't trouble you again or them except for a pint maybe.'

The manager looked at the picture. 'I remember him. He met up with a foreign-looking guy. You know, one of them as come here from Europe. He pointed down the long bar-room. 'They were sat on those stools right up there at the end of the room.'

'The guy he met, is he a regular?'

'No, but he had a tattoo on his neck. The tips of three swords or sommat were sticking up above his collar.'

'Was he wearing a suit?' said Effie.

'No, an open-neck white shirt with a black leather jacket but he did have a posh pair of shiny white Nike trainers.'

'Thanks,' said Hunter, 'have you got CCTV?'

'Yep, but it only covers twenty-four hours and if there are no problems we re-use it.'

'We'll need to speak to your other staff to see if they can add anything. Have you got their details?'

'Hang on, I'll get it for you.'

He disappeared into the back and came back a few minutes later with a slip of paper with two addresses on it. 'There you are, boss. They're not in trouble are they?'

'No, just a quick word and then we're done.'

———

Hunter rang the front doorbell and stood back. They waited a few moments and he was about to ring again when the door opened a crack and a weary head with straggly curly hair and bloodshot eyes peered out at them.

'Yeh, what is it,' the face moaned.

Effie held up her ID. 'Police! Are you Willy Nelson?'

'Yeh!'

'We'd like a word. Can we come in?'

'If you must.'

He pulled the door open and turned away to walk down the hall. Effie and Hunter followed the bedraggled figure wearing a T-shirt and leisurewear shorts and a pair of worn grey socks. He stopped by a door and pushed it open. Go in,' he said, 'I'll pop some clothes on.'

He joined them in the living room a few minutes later looking much refreshed and his hair combed. 'Have I time for a caffeine fix?'

Hunter nodded, and said, 'Have you got two spare mugs one black, one white and no sugar?'

'Yep, won't keep you a minute.'

He ducked out of the room, which was pleasantly furnished, and not the home of a young bachelor and five minutes later he returned with three mugs of coffee.

'Sit down,' he said, 'and what can I do for you?'

Hunter plonked himself down in an armchair and Nelson sat opposite but Effie preferred to stand and stood between them and the door and she asked the first question.

'We have just come from your place of employment Mister Nelson, and we understand you were on shift on Friday night last. Is that right?'

'Err... Yes,' he said.

Hunter held out his i-phone and Effie continued, 'Have you seen this character before?'

Nelson took the phone and studied it for a moment before replying, 'Yes, he was in the pub on Friday with one of them eastern looking guys. I remember him. He didn't drink much.'

Hunter butted in. 'By eastern do you mean Asian?'

'European. You know, Polish or something. You can tell by their swarthiness, sort of, and he spoke with an accent.'

'Was he Polish?'

'I dunno. I only speak English and a bit of French from school.'

Effie stepped up to the plate. 'Did he have any distinguishing marks or clothing?'

'Only a posh leather jacket. It was good quality you could tell and the guy in the picture was wearing a light coloured mack. Sam, my mate, he was amongst the tables more than me. Maybe he heard a tad more. Is it something big?'

'No, Mr Nelson,' said Effie, 'and we shan't be bothering you anymore. Thanks for your time.'

They stood up and Hunter and Effie were about to leave when Nelson said, 'There was one thing which might be nothing.'

'What's that,' said Hunter.'

'When they came in they ordered a beer plus vodka and before they paid they said that Russian thingy for 'cheers' and drank the vodka.'

"*Zazdarovje*',' said Hunter.

'Summat like that.'

'Are you sure? '*Nasdarovje*' is the Polish version.'

'No, it was the first one.'

'Thanks,' said Hunter, 'we'll see ourselves out.'

—

Effie and Hunter sat outside in the car and she couldn't contain herself. 'Alright, Hunter, where did you learn that?'

'It's a long story, Effie. I did a tour behind the Iron Curtain in the eighties and my partner taught me a lot.'

She had a feeling he was being modest but slipped the car into gear and drove off. Fifteen minutes later they were outside an unpretentious sixties house in the district of Lache and Hunter knocked on the front door and stood back to let Effie make the first approach.

They didn't have long to wait when a woman of mixed race opened the door.

'Excuse me,' said, Effie, 'does a Sam Khan live here?'

'Who's asking,' said the woman.

Effie held up her ID. 'Police! We would like a few words with Sam. Is he in?'

'I'll go get him.'

'Can we come in,' said Effie, 'it wouldn't do for the neighbours to get nosy.'

'If you must.'

She stood to one side to let them in and pointed to a door just inside the hall. 'Wait in there I'll go get him.'

They pushed the front room door open and the woman went upstairs and they could hear muffled conversation and some cursing before she came back down and spoke to them.

'He won't be a minute, he's getting some clothes on. He works late you see and the lazy so and so stays in bed. Can I get you a cup of tea or something?'

Effie looked at Hunter who shook his head and they both declined. Ten minutes later a tall well-dressed young man of mixed origin with smartly trimmed facial hair and wearing tidy but fashionable leisure style clothing entered.

'Alright, who wants me,' he said sourly, 'and before you start I'm a Christian and my Mum and Dad come from Guyana.'

'Whoa, steady on, lad,' said Hunter, 'it's nothing to do with that malarkey.' He nodded towards Effie. 'This is DS Newlove and I'm her assistant and we only want to know...' he shoved his i-phone forward, '...what you can tell us about this guy on Friday night.'

Sam studied the picture for a moment before rubbing his chin while collecting his thoughts when he suddenly burst out, 'Him and another guy were sat up in the corner and the tight bastards only had a half the whole time they were in there. I tell lies, they had a vodka when they came in.'

'Your mate said you were collecting glasses near them. Did you overhear anything?'

'Nah, they were speaking in a foreign language.'

'Which one?' said Hunter, 'do you know?'

'One of them eastern thingy's.'

Effie stood quietly observing during the conversation her trained eye wandering around the room but she saw only a pleasant family home with many photographs and a couple of pictures to remind them of their ancestral background.

Meanwhile, Hunter continued, 'And there's nothing else?'

Sam shrugged. 'No. They scribbled a few notes between them and that was it. Hang on though, there was one thing. I was cleaning the tables outside when they left and that fellow...' pointing to the identity photo, '...was being directed to a club. I remember now as it was the only English spoken.'

'Where was it, Sam?'

'*Bar 69*.' Effie suddenly took an interest as Sam continued, 'it's a gay club down Boughton Road. It's a long hike so he said what I think is 'cheerio' and went to the taxi rank.'

'The other chap,' said Effie, 'what did he do?'

'He wandered off towards the bus station or the car park down there.'

'Have you seen him before?'

Sam shook his. 'Nah, I'd know him. We have mainly regulars with just a few tourists looking at '*Dixie Deans*' old place.'

'Oh, I see. There's nothing else?'

'No, that's as much as I know, sorry!'

Hunter picked up his phone. 'You're okay, Sam, you've been a great help. Thanks. We'll see ourselves out you can go back to bed.'

'Huh! I wish,' said Sam, 'now I'm up Ma will have me working.'

Outside in the car Hunter and Effie exchanged notes.

'Effie,' said Hunter, 'can you chase up the street cams?'

'And what are you going to do, Hunter?'

'I've got a date in a funny bar.'

'Hunter, be careful what you say. Not only is it sexist but...'

'Effie, I'm sorry. I didn't think. I'm old school and can't get out of the habit.'

'It's okay, Hunter, I'm used to it. Anyway, you need me along. I have friends in that club including the manager.'

Hunter checked his watch. 'It's getting on a bit, Effie. Let's call it a day and meet up later at the club, say, eightish?'

'I'm going back to start on those webcams, Hunter, but I'll be at the club. Just one thing, Hunter.'

'What's that?'

'There are certain dress codes in these places most of them pretty smart and if you don't want to be fending off admirers come in your working clothes, that is, like you are now.'

Hunter flicked his leather jacket. 'Doesn't this qualify?'

'It's tat, Hunter, but I'm told the beer's good. Take me back to my car.'

He grimaced and turned the ignition key.

—

A tall sun-tanned man with thinning grey hair in a silver-grey suit and open-necked striped maroon shirt who obviously enjoyed his food came through the door alongside the bar and approached Effie. 'Hello, Effie, it's business tonight is it? Who's your friend?'

Effie turned to face her enquirer with a smile. 'Hello, Warren. Yes, it's business but we won't keep you long. This is my colleague,

Hunter. He's on attachment.'

Warren nodded his acknowledgement to Hunter who did likewise. Hunter had already decided to take a backseat as this was Effie's territory and her explanation of his presence was ambiguous.

Effie slid her i-phone with the photo-fit of Owen along the bar to Warren. 'We know this guy was here on Friday night, Warren. Can you tell us who he met or left with and can we have your CCTV records?'

'You can have the CCTV, Effie, but as for who met him, I've no idea and I don't suppose the crew have either as Friday is one of our busy nights.'

Hunter interrupted. 'Excuse me,' he said, 'but is your CCTV on a twenty-four-hour loop?'

'No, Mr Hunter. I run a tight ship and keep a fortnightly loop.'

'Could we have the coverage for the weekend?'

'Yep, you sure can. What's he done this guy?'

'He's dead,' said Effie. 'It's who he met we're interested in.'

'Okay. Have a drink on the house and I'll go and get 'em.' He called over one of the staff. 'Give Effie and her mate what they want, Oré, and put it on my bill.'

While Oré took their order, they made themselves comfortable on the bar stools and surveyed the scene around them and Hunter had to accede to Effie's suggestion about his dress. Regardless of inclination they were well groomed.

Hunter put his glass down. 'You're right, Effie,' said Hunter, 'this reminds me of my youth.'

'Ha! Can you remember that far back, Hunter?'

'Watch it! What I mean is, in my day we had Teddy boys and you never went out scruffy. Always had your shoes polished and a suit that was in fashion with your trousers pressed and not a hair out of place. The girls weren't bad either.'

'You're sexist, Hunter.'

Warren returned and put six video recordings on the bar. 'There you are, Effie. Everything from Friday night to six a.m. Monday inside and out.'

Effie scooped them up. 'Thanks, Warren, we'll have them back asap. Cheerio, and thanks for the drink.'

'You're welcome. I hope you get the guy.'

'We will,' said Hunter nodding as he walked past Warren, 'we will!'

It wasn't what Hunter said that made Warren think but the way he said it.

Outside Effie and Hunter stopped for a moment to say their goodbyes. 'What now Hunter, another pub?'

'I'm off home, Effie. I have a wife and family. I'll see you in the morning, and you?'

'I'm staying with Charlotte tonight, I'm knackered and I want an early start on those tapes. See you.'

———

Hunter tested the security of their new home with a hint of satisfaction. The electric gates swung open silently and the halogen lights lit up the front of the house but putting his car in the garage was a step too far and he left it parked out front.

Before he could put the key in the front door, Jacquie, with Tess at her side, alerted by the internal alarm, opened it and teased him. 'Welcome home, Mister Hunter.'

He was used to it and when he reached her he wrapped his arms around her and with a hand on each buttock pulled her towards him. She didn't resist and pressed up against him. 'Glad to be back, Mrs Hunter. What's for supper?'

They kissed disregarding anyone who may have been passing and Tess did her best to wriggle between them. As they turned to go into the house, Jacquie said, 'Single malt for starters and then if you're good I've made a pepperoni pizza.'

Her pizzas were made from a recipe handed down through her family with the modern western items added. He gave her a squeeze, 'One or two slices?'

'It's late, Hunter, it's one only.'

'Meannie,' he said, as he let go of her and swung off into their newly converted lounge/diner while she continued to the kitchen. The original lounge they had made into a workspace for the children because they were now in a private school for security reasons which meant they had more homework.

Jacquie joined him a few minutes later and she noticed with a frown that his whisky was more than two fingers but said nothing as she handed him the tray with his supper on.

She plonked herself down alongside him on the rich leather sofa, 'Okay, Hunter,' she said, 'tell me what you've been up to. You're working with Charlotte's partner?'

'Yep, and she's keen to move in with Charlotte but this case is stopping her.'

'What is it exactly?'

He spent a few minutes giving her the details and ended, '...and that's as far as we've got. Tomorrow it's camera watching.'

'Will you be doing that?'

'Technically, no, but I've nothing more to follow up so I'll muck in. How are the kids?'

'They're doing very well considering the short time they've been there. Iain's loves the sports and has taken up rugby union while Lesley has added dancing to her repertoire.'

'Blimey, an artist and a dancer and all this happened today? I thought Iain was doing footy.'

'He was but he said it's too poncy. That's his very words. He wants to do a manly thing.'

'Huh! On that note, I'm going to check the locks and go to bed.'

'I'll be right behind you, Hunter.'

~~~~~~

Chapter 4

Hunter, with his obligatory cup of black coffee, entered the office at eight-thirty and was greeted by a crowded room. There was a mixture of plain clothes and uniform stood around but over to his left, DC Farmer was slumped in Hunter's chair. Hunter walked towards him but said nothing instead he stood in front of him and with a quick jerk of his head indicated in no uncertain terms that he should go.

Farmer didn't move instead he looked across at Effie who was stood by the whiteboard. Her body language was enough but with a flick of her thumb, she indicated that to move was the practical thing to do.

Farmer sneered his protest but gathered his things and shuffled to one side muttering to his compatriots while he did so.

Hunter nodded, and said quietly, 'Good thinking,' before he put his cup on the desk took his jacket off and put it over the back of the chair and plonked himself down.

Effie gave a couple of urgent taps on the whiteboard to get their attention and said to the assembly, 'Good morning all,' and to the new bodies, 'what a welcome sight you are. For the benefit of the new arrivals, we will go over what we know and then I will allocate your jobs.' She looked across the room towards Hunter. 'But first, let me introduce Agent Hunter who is representing the Security Services and is in charge of this investigation...' Hunter stood up and there was a murmur of 'Hi's' and other comments before he sat down but as he did so he looked across at Farmer who blushed slightly but nodded his acknowledgement, and Effie continued, '...and now we've been introduced let's get down to business. DC Farmer? What do we know about the Owen case?'

Farmer gave them a quick rundown of Owen's movements up until late Friday night, '...and that's all we know. He met two men. One in the *Dixie Pub* and another in *Bar 69* neither of whom we have ID'd yet so the first job this morning for all of us is to check CCTV. Split into two groups. One will do the street cams and the other the videos from the club. Any questions?'

A uniform female police officer stuck her hand up. 'Yes, constable, what is it?' said Effie.

'Sarge—I've collated all the house to house stuff from around the crime scene. What should I do with it?'

'Anything useful in there, constable? What's your name?'

'Jones, Sarge. There's nothing. They're old houses around there and soundproof and nobody saw or heard anything. I don't have anything from the local CCTV yet.'

'Jones,' said Effie, 'you've just become our filing clerk,' Jones face dropped, 'I know you want to be in the front line but this stuff is just as important. You will liaise with all groups and collate all the data and facts and keep the board up to date and then prepare a useful speech with a minimum of info to give out to the press and as head of this investigation you will also keep Agent Hunter in the loop.' She stepped away from the board. 'Meanwhile, the rest of you have now got a third set of cams to check so get to it. Whatever you find give it to Jones and nothing is to go outside this room without permission. Got it!'

There was a rumble around the room but no response and Effie said louder, 'GOT IT?'

There was a collective, 'Yes, Sarge,' and they began filing out but Effie stopped Jones. 'What's your first name, Jones?'

'Fiona, Sarge.'

'Come with me, Fiona.'

She led Fiona across to Hunter. 'This, Fiona, is, Hunter.'

She looked puzzled, but said, 'Morning, Mister Hunter.'

'I can see your dilemma, Fiona, he is a problem to all of us but he's harmless.'

Hunter stood up and stuck out a hand. 'Morning, Fiona. Ignore her, just call me, Hunter. It's a long story so you don't want to know.'

They shook hands and she liked the firm but gentle grip.

'Okay, Hunter,' continued Effie, 'is it alright for her to share your desk until we can sort something better for her.'

'By all means and does she need to wear a uniform while she's on attachment. She'll feel more like one of the team then.'

Fiona's eyes widened but she said nothing and looked at Effie, who said, 'I don't see why not. I'll clear it with upstairs.'

Hunter stepped to one side and bowed as he swept his arm across his body and directed Fiona into his seat. She was beginning to like this man and she smiled as Hunter joined Effie and they walked down the room towards her desk.

'You're making an impression on our juniors, Hunter, not planning on stealing another are you?'

A reference to Carrie Long who had transferred to the Security Services after working with Hunter.

'No, but I see nothing wrong with encouragement.'

'About the case, Hunter. Have you learned anything more from your people?'

'No, but they're searching his flat in Cheltenham and have confiscated his laptops.'

'Laptops, plural?'

'Yep! His personal one, and his work Tablet not to mention his desk. I should know later today or tomorrow morning. What about our situation, Effie?'

Effie opened her notebook but didn't use it, 'You heard the debrief, Hunter. We're checking street cams around the town for Saturday and Sunday. That's it. We're watching videos today.'

'You didn't find a phone or a weapon?'

'No.'

'Talking of which, Hunter, was Owen assigned a weapon?'

'No!'

Effie glanced at her notebook. 'We haven't traced his wallet but he did use his debit card in *'Club 69'* on Friday and we're checking receipts for the weekend.'

There was a knock on the door and DC Farmer came in waving a photograph and joined them at the desk. He nodded to Hunter as he pushed the picture over.

'A bit of luck. We found an old friend on the first reel from *Club 69*.'

Hunter looked at the photo and gave it to Effie and they said at the same time, 'Who is it?'

'It's Billie Bonar. How shall I say this... he's... he's an adult rent boy known locally and he's seen chatting to our vic. We're checking the outside cam now to see if they leave together.'

Effie gave the photo back. 'Give this to Jones and then we'll pick him up.'

Effie spun away and went to her desk to collect her things. 'Okay, Farmer, let's go.'

———

An hour later Hunter joined Effie in the corridor and walked with her to the interview room where Bonar was being held. 'I won't come in, Effie, but can you transmit your chatter through to me?'

She looked at him and screwed her nose up at his humour before she said, 'Stay by the one-way visual panel. There are speakers along the side or you can plug in headphones.'

When they reached the cell door she pointed to the panel a couple of metres further along. 'That's it and the controls are just at the side.'

'Thanks, Effie. Best of luck but I have a feeling he won't help much.'

She didn't reply but pushed the door of the cell where DC Farmer was waiting and went in. Hunter wandered down to the window and switched the speakers on.

She plonked a file down on the table and sat opposite Bonar while Farmer stood behind her in an aggressive no-nonsense stance with his legs apart and his hands folded in front of him. Effie pressed a switch and spoke into the recording machine at the head of the table. 'Interview with Billy Bonar 13th October 2014.' She looked at her watch. 'Time is thirteen-thirty-five hours. Present are Detective Sergeant Newlove and Detective Constable Farmer...' She opened the file and took out some pictures that were face down, '...and before we start can you say your name aloud for the tape, please?'

He nodded, and said, 'Billie Bonar.'

'Thank you,' said Effie. 'First question, Mister Bonar. Do you want a solicitor?'

He shook his head, and said,' No, I ain't done nothing.'

She flipped over the first photo. 'This is you in the *Bar 69* and you're talking to Rhys Owen. Is that right?'

Bonar nodded. 'Yep, but he said his name was James Bond. I guess he didn't want his secret out.'

'What did you talk about?'

He looked at Effie and smiled. 'Do you really want to know?' She nodded and he continued, 'Sex mainly and where, how, what and how much.'

Effie scribbled into her notebook. 'Nothing else, like what he was doing in Chester. His business etc...'

'No, just things like the weather, football and respective managers but he stopped when it got to politics. That was it for the rest of the evening. Pretty boring really.'

'You went home together?'

'Yes. My place.'

'How long did he stay?'

'A couple of hours and he caught a taxi back to his digs.'

She was holding another photo but never turned it over. 'Did you see him again?'

'Yep! Saturday night same place. He had a very posh mack on. He never took it off all night.'

She flipped the photo over. 'Like this,' she said.

Bonar nodded. 'That's us. I was wearing that new white shirt and my light blue jeans.'

She looked at the photo and the clothes fitted the description and the time and date. 'And what time did you leave?'

'Just after ten. It was early but he wanted to go.'

'Did he say why?'

'No, but it was about half an hour after some swarthy guy came over and whispered to him and after that, he was a bit disturbed. He wouldn't say why. I put it down to a dumped boyfriend.'

Effie pulled another photo from the folder and flipped it over. 'Was it him do you think?'

What Bonar was looking at was a street cam picture of the Eastern European stranger who had met Owen on the Friday. He looked at it from different angles before giving it back and Effie said, 'Well!'

'It could be. He's got a similar leather jacket but I can't say accurately as I can't see his full face.'

'One last question, Billie, what time did Owen go home on Saturday?'

'We had a quick session which wasn't as good as Friday and he left by taxi at twenty-five past eleven.'

'Whose taxi was it, Billie?'

'You've got me wallet. There's a card in there. I use the same guy all the time. He's very discreet.'

Effie looked back at Farmer, and said, 'Can you fetch his wallet from the holding room?'

'Err... Will you be okay?'

She nodded, 'I've got the best back-up in the world outside. I'll be okay unless Billie here feels like committing Hari-Kari.'

She spoke into the recorder as Farmer left, 'DC Farmer leaving the room,' she checked her watch, '1415 hours.'

Farmer glanced to his left as he closed the door and saw Hunter and knew what she meant. Five minutes later he was back and gave Effie Bonar's wallet and after the necessary preamble she handed it to Bonar, and said, 'The card, give it to me.'

Bonar opened the wallet and fiddled amongst debit cards and pulled out a tattered business card and pushed it over.

'Thanks, Billie, that's us finished but we're keeping you in overnight.'

'Why, I ain't done nothing.'

'That's for me to decide, Billie. You see, James Bond is dead.'

Billie's eyes popped wide, 'Fuckin' hell, and you think I did it? It wasn't me, I only screws 'em.'

Effie found it hard to keep a straight face as she switched off the recorder and removed the CD's before repacking the folder and leaving the room with Farmer in tow and a uniformed PC took their place. Outside she handed Farmer the CD's, 'Give these to Jones and then chase up our foreigner. See if you can get a car plate as he leaves the car park if that's where he went and also check the street cams outside *Bar 69* on Saturday night again.'

'Right, Sarge, will do.'

'Farmer!' said Effie.'

'Yes, Sarge.'

'Thanks.' She turned away and as she walked down the corridor Hunter fell in beside her. 'What do you think, Hunter?' were her next words.

'He's innocent, of murder that is.'

They laughed together as they entered the office and Hunter took a half pace back, 'After you.'

When they were sat down by Effie's desk, she said, 'Other than being a one night or rather a two-night stand with Owen I think he's not guilty. He did ID our other suspect in a fashion insofar as they, that is Owen and Bonar, were approached by our Eastern European mystery man in the *Club 69* but he only whispered a few words to Owen and left. After that Owen became agitated.'

'And no positive ID,' said Hunter.

'No, just that the figure from the street cam was wearing a similar leather jacket to the guy who approached them in the bar. The build looked right though.'

'And we're no nearer identifying the perp?'

'In a word, No!' said Effie, 'but you know all this.'

'You may as well let Bonar go, Effie, but put a tail on him...' he saw Effie stifling a giggle and shook his head, '...not literally, you chump,' and joined in the merriment at his *faux par*. When things returned to normal he continued, 'So what's your next move?'

'I'm going to join the gang looking at CCTV, and you, Hunter?'

'I'll get in touch with the 'Firm' to see if there are any updates on Owen but before I go, Effie, can you get another desk for Fiona? I think she's going to be busy and I'd like to do this without someone listening in.'

'Already in hand, Hunter.'

'Good, I'll be in my other office aka '*Garden Aspects* №1'.'

—

In a dingy smoke-laden, one-bedroom flat above a Polish cafe in the district preferred by the Polish and other Eastern European population of the city, a greying six-foot Theodor Fabianski wearing a blue pinstripe business suit and rugged workmanlike Janis Ragozin stood face to face in a manner that could not be described as friendly. The living room furniture was sparse with springs visible through the cushions on the sofa. The backs of the 1940's dining chairs creaked when pressed and matched the tea-stained table in shabbiness. The springs on the single bed along one wall in the bedroom were sagging ominously from the punishment they had received over the years. The doors of a WW2 utility wardrobe were sagging in protest and the new trench coat hanging on it looked oddly out of place. The only things close to modern were the electric stove and the toilet facilities across the corridor.

All this was ignored by the two men arguing in a dialect that was closer to Russian because of the high Russian population in the Crimea during the Cold War. Tempers were most getting frayed and voices raised when there was a loud knocking on the door and a short stocky man in clean working clothes burst in and remonstrated in broken English.

'Shut Up!' he bellowed, 'We hear you in the cafe. You want to rent my flat and you shout like this then I say, NO!'

'Fryderyk,' Fabianski replied in unaccented English, 'We're finished now.' He pulled out his wallet and retrieved several large denomination notes. 'Here, something extra for the flat.'

Fryderyk took the money. 'Okay, you stay but you make noise and you go. Use back door, okay?

He stuffed the money into his back pocket and in defiance of his 'be quiet' order he slammed the door behind him.

Immediately, Fabianski, said belligerently, 'Ragozin! You do it tonight!' and walked out.

—

Hunter was busying himself taking photo's of the items in Owen's package when a hand rested on his shoulder and a voice whispered, 'Got ya!'

He looked up and saw Jacquie and ignoring customers around them they kissed before she slid into the seat opposite him. 'Is this the stuff you told me about, H?'

'Yep! It's too busy in that tiddily office they gave us and I want this material to stay private so it's going in this gadget until I can put it on my computer at home. When I'm finished here I'm going over to Williams place to see if Tanya can translate it.'

'Have you been in touch yet?'

'No. HQ tells me that Duncan is in Moscow but it's Tanya's knowledge I want.'

Jacquie picked up the typed list and Owen's Ukraine Passport and studied them. 'What do you think. He's spying you reckon?'

'It looks that way, Jacquie, but for whom? He's not a fieldman, he went awol...' he shuffled his hand through the paperwork on the table, '...and he's got all this. It looks like he came across something and is trying to make a name for himself or he's a sleeper and has been wakened or he could be being blackmailed. He was funny Ha! Ha! by the way...'

'Shssh...! Hunter, you can't say that.'

'Why not? It's a free country.'

Jacquie groaned inwardly and shook her head. 'He's going to cop it one day,' she said mentally.

'That aside,' he continued, 'blackmail sounds most likely.'

'Any ideas?'

'I'm hoping Tanya can help, if she's in I'll be on my way.'

'Okay, H, be careful.'

She got up from the table and gave Hunter a peck on the cheek and he watched as she walked across the restaurant still mesmerised by her symmetry.

———

Tanya opened the door before he could knock. 'Good day, Mr Hunter?'

He squeezed her hand, and said, 'Hunter will do just fine, lass, and how are you?'

Pointing to her head, she said, 'As you say in England, Hunter, touch wood, we're all fine,' and as she turned to lead the way into the kitchen, she continued, 'What can I do for you?'

He took Owen's papers from his inside pocket and spread them on the kitchen table. 'What do you make of that lot, Tanya?'

'I'll make a drink first,' she said, 'tea or coffee?'

'Coffee, please.'

Sat across the table from him five minutes later she pulled the papers towards her and studied them. When she lowered them, she said, 'It's not true Russian, Hunter, but Crimean Russian and I'm not much on geography but it is a list of places with GPS and map references from UK Ordnance Survey maps. The other two pages appear to be identical but one is I think Korean and the other, Arabic?'

'And the bumf across the bottom?'

'That's instructions on how to read the maps and also use the Sim cards and the last paragraph although it looks a lot is a note telling whoever it is to destroy after memorising although how you're meant to remember all those numbers I don't know.'

'Probably put them in your encrypted smartphone, Tanya. Can you translate them into English for me?'

'Yes, come through and I'll do it on the computer.'

He followed Tanya to the small back bedroom that Williams had made into an office and ten minutes later she had it all done and printed. Handing Hunter the folded sheets of A4 she said, 'I'll keep it on file in case you lose it. Will you be calling on Duncan to help you?'

'It depends how it pans out, Tanya. Why?'

'Because we might see him more often. He's been away for three months.'

'I can't promise but I'll have a word.' He held up the copies and said, 'Thanks for this, Tanya, I've got to go. I have some map-reading to do.'

———

The phone conversation with Effie verified that the only progress had been finding the taxi driver who took Owen back to the Guest House on Saturday night. He had confirmed that he had dropped Owen at the gate before driving off.

'What you're saying in essence, Effie, is that someone was waiting for Owen at the guest house.'

'Got it in one, Hunter.'

'So we're no further forward?'

'Yep, right again.'

'Okay, Effie, see you in the morning.'

He hit the red symbol on the Bluetooth facia and drove home only stopping long enough to get a cold lager from the fridge he went directly to his 'Manhole' and more notably a brown leather box stool in the corner. From it, he pulled a collection of one inch to the mile Ordnance Survey maps and from the list he began searching references.

It wasn't long before he realised what the list was all about. He had in effect the location of every Nuclear establishment in the UK including the local plant.

'Why Capenhurst? It's only a waste plant,' he muttered.

He delved wider and noted that the Naval base at Rosyth was on the list and was a location on the CND map also. 'They've got it all covered, but why? I'd better chase up, Gus.'

He put the maps away and called Gus Thomas at his office in Vauxhall House.

'Yes, Hunter, what can I do for you?'

'Have you got anything from GCHQ yet,' replied Hunter.'

'Nothing yet but it's early days. Being an IT specialist Owen has devised his own encryption and other security on his computers etc... It's taking time to crack them but they'll get there. The theory is that he uncovered something and wanted to make a name for himself and he got out of his depth. Have you found anything?'

'Yes, Gus, I have. He had two fake ID's. One as James Bond and...'

'You what?' exclaimed, Gus, 'James Bond? What the hell was he playing at? Who's the other one?'

'A Ukrainian passport in the name of Andriy Ivaskin.'

'Anything else?'

'Yes, he was gay.'

'Oh!' There was a moment of reflection before Gus continued, 'How did you find that out?'

Hunter went on to explain about Bonar and that they thought he had no connection with Owens death and they were looking into the Eastern European who had so far eluded them... 'And they are trawling through hours of CCTV videos at this moment.'

'Okay, Hunter, keep me posted. Are you managing on your own?'

'Yes, Gus, no problem. There is one thing though.'

'What's that?'

'Mrs Williams is complaining she hasn't seen hubbie for three months.'

'I'll look into it. No promises but she knows his job.'

'On that, Gus I'll say, cheerio!'

He swiped the 'off' app and sat back pondering his next move and came to the conclusion that until they discovered this mystery

European there was nothing he could do. A quick check of his watch told him the kids would be home from school soon and he retreated to the kitchen to prepare and indulge his passion—Cold Premium lager.

———

On the outer limits of the parish of Greater Sutton two miles south of the Hunter residence, six-foot Theodor Fabianski dressed in his usual very English style business suit with the brogues and tie parked his car on the short drive outside a modest two-bedroomed bungalow in a quiet cul-de-sac. As he swung the driver's door open the front door of the bungalow opened and he was greeted by an attractive black lady from a local Estate Agents.

'Good afternoon, Doctor McRae,' she said cheerily, 'did you have a good trip?'

With only the slightest trace of an accent which could have been mistaken for a Scottish burr Theodor replied with the lie already on his lips, 'Yes, thank you, I stayed in Chester overnight and today I've been learning the lay of the land for what is to be my home for the next few months.'

She led him into a small hall and closed the door behind him. 'Is it a business trip, Dr McRae?'

'Yes, it will be about six months.'

'The owner of the property is in Dubai and feels a six-month contract will be ideal. What do you do, Dr McRae?'

He was feeling a little irritated by the questioning nevertheless he replied, 'I'm a specialist in nuclear safety and will be working in your local site to try and improve things so that they can operate until 2031.'

She took him into the lounge and pointed to a door at the far end. 'Through there are two bedrooms and the bathroom and the way to the conservatory. The property also comes with a garage that is behind those high gates you saw when you came in. The owner is a bachelor and so the furnishing will probably suit you. All he asks is that you look after the garden.'

'I'll take it. When can I move in?'

'If you follow me to the office we can do the paperwork and tomorrow I'll arrange for the facilities to be switched on. The TV, telephone and broadband are already operating and included in the rent. You will of course have to use your own passwords to set it up for a second user but I think next Monday will be good.'

Theodor Fabianski aka McRae wasn't interested in broadband as all his work would be done on his encrypted Apple tablet.

———

A buzzer sounded which told Hunter the gates were opening and a quick glance at the CCTV confirmed it was the kids arriving home and followed eagerly by Tess he went to the front door to greet them.

Tess dashed ahead as he walked to the car while Jamie the driver opened the rear passenger doors and released Iain and Lesley into Hunter's custody. Hunter liked Jamie who was an ex- Parachute Regiment Sergeant who had been struggling with PTSD since his tours of Afghanistan. Hunter was aware of Jamie's problems because of his own experience with the illness and had employed him through the 'Help for Heroes' organisation.

His main job was the protection of the children and when he wasn't doing that he worked for Jacquie in the Garden Centres. Because of his illness, his first marriage had broken down but since working for Jacquie he had met a new partner in *Garden Aspects* №1 and he was recovering.

Hunter greeted him. 'Hi, Jamie, any problems?'

'No, Boss, only that the motor has to go in for servicing.'

He was referring to Jacquie's Range Rover that he used on the school run.

'I'm sure herself has that organised, Jamie.'

Lesley was jumping up and down in front of Hunter waving her latest artistic masterpiece so Jamie got back in the SUV and left them to it.

'Daddy, daddy,' she shouted excitedly, 'look what I did in art class today.' She shoved forward a landscape drawing the centrepiece of which was an old Oak tree drawn with charcoal with a baby shoot sprouting some metres away painted in colour like the countryside around it.

Hunter took the drawing, rolled it up, and as they turned to go into the house he put his arm around Iain's shoulders, 'Hi, lad, okay?'

Iain nodded and replied with a solitary, 'Yep!' before Hunter led them indoors.

Inside they sat around the kitchen table and while the children tucked into a sandwich and a fruit smoothie Hunter unrolled Lesley's picture and studied it before he read the note written on the back by Lesley's teacher.

'Lesley's image of **'New Life'** *is excellent and shows wonderful foresight. It is hard to believe that she is only eleven.'*

He lowered it and looked at Lesley and mentally acknowledged that moving to a bigger house had been a good move as they had been rapidly running out of wall space to hang Lesley's work in the bungalow.

'Well done, Lesley, I'll get this one framed.'

From the corner of his eye, he saw Iain surreptitiously sliding his android phone out. 'Not now, lad, it's homework first,' and to show no favouritism, he added, 'how did rugby go today?'

Iain shoved the phone away before he spoke, 'Alright, I scored a try, and Mr Howard wants me to play on the wing in Saturday's game against the High School. He says with my speed it's the right position. Can you come?'

Hunter took a deep breath, 'I don't know, lad. I'm on this new job. I'll try, but I'm making no promises, okay?'

'Is it like the last one, Dad, when we was kidnapped?'

'Were kidnapped, Iain. No, I'm just observing and advising on this one but I have to be there. Right, you pair, if you're finished run along and do your homework. Mum will be home soon.'

They slid off their chairs and Lesley in her usual energetic manner skipped out of the door and down the hall to the living room that Hunter had converted to a study. Iain trudged steadfastly behind.

Hunter had only just finished clearing up when the gate buzzer sounded and he opened the front door to welcome Jacquie and regardless of who may have been looking, with Tess weaving between their legs, they kissed on the doorstep before going indoors.

—

Dinner over and the children tucked safely in bed Jacquie was sat enveloped in a deep leather armchair enjoying a glass of *Malbec* and Hunter was sat on the sofa with his legs outstretched onto the coffee table. The TV was on but neither was paying any attention. They knew that Iain would be reading but she didn't mind and his current interest was Stephen Hawkins *'A Brief History of Time.'* They were both amazed by their son's sudden interest in quantum physics.

They were instead discussing recent events in the Owen case when Hunter's in-house smartphone began a demented Morse code signal.

'Hells bells, Hunter, what's that?' said Jacquie.

'That,' said Hunter, 'means it's urgent.'

He picked up the phone and slid his finger down the 'accept' app and shoved the phone to his ear. 'Hunter!'

He listened intently and Jacquie watched as he nodded his head and muttered replies before he switched the device off and threw it on the coffee table.

'Shit!' he said aloud.

'What now, H?'

'That chap Bonar I was telling you about has been murdered and his house turned over. They want me there and they're sending a car. Sorry, lass, I gotta go.'

He got up from the sofa and did a few loosening exercises before he left the room. He came back a couple of minutes later and he had changed into his cavalry twill trousers and desert boots. He bent over and kissed her.

'Night, lass, don't wait up.'

'You're not going like that. Where's your coat?'

'Stop nagging woman.' At that moment there was a beep of a car horn. 'Gotta go.' He blew her a kiss and slid out before she could reply.

When she went to bed she saw that he had picked up his green Barbour wax jacket and she had a little smile to herself.

~~~~~~

Chapter 5

Effie was waiting for him at the front door of the apartment in the suburb of Blacon and as the lift doors closed behind him, she said, 'Welcome to chaos, Hunter.'

'Thanks, Effie, what have we got?'

'You'd best come inside and see for yourself. Our friend Bonar has been killed by the same MO as Owen.'

She handed Hunter coveralls some overshoes and surgical gloves and when they were ready-made to go into the flat. 'Lead the way, Effie.'

She pushed open the front door and immediately Hunter could see the chaos that Effie had mentioned. Coats had been pulled of hooks in the hall and after the pockets had been searched dumped on the floor. The drawer of a small telephone table had been pulled out and its contents strewn around before the intruder had moved into the living room that was virtually upside down. The sofa had been pulled out and two armchairs tipped on their side surrounded by clothes, CD's and papers and pictures which had been pulled from the wall and some photos had been ripped from their frames and dumped with the rest of the detritus.

Kneeling amongst this was Dr Hale and his SOCO investigators from the Forensics department.

Hale looked up as they entered. 'Evening, Hunter, no peace for the wicked.'

'Evening, Doc, what have we?'

'As I told Sergeant Newlove we have a Caucasian male of about twenty-two with a stab wound through the heart. The same MO used on your Agent. Very neat and precise with little blood.'

'How long, Doc?'

'A couple of hours at the most.'

Hunter turned to Effie. 'Who called it in?'

'We don't know. It was somebody local who didn't leave a name or number. They tend to keep themselves to themselves in this part of town.'

Hunter squeezed his chin and nodded. 'It figures, I take it the rest of the flat is like this?'

'Everything, Hunter, including the waste bins. They were looking for something but I can't imagine what a rent boy could have. Maybe drugs?'

He could see there was nothing else they could do there and Hunter lead the way back into the hall and out of the front door to the landing by the lift before he spoke. 'Effie, I didn't want to say anything in there but I think we must look beyond the locals here. I'm thinking that whoever did this was looking to see if Bonar and Owen were... how should I say this? Working together.'

'You mean in a business way?'

'Yes.'

'Your lot?'

'Exactly or maybe checking that Owen never passed anything on accidentally.'

'I never thought of that.'

'Don't worry, Effie, carry on with your police enquiry until I can link it up. Just keep me posted, okay?' Hunter had his misgivings, but said, 'And if you don't mind, Effie, I'm going to look over the rest of the flat just in case whoever it was left a sign that they had found something.'

'Hunter, don't you think SOCO are capable?'

'Different eyes. I'm looking from a spooks angle.'

'Go ahead, we'll meet at the office later.'

He followed Effie back into the flat but went down the hall to the first bedroom and what met him was more of the same. The large king-size bed stripped, drawers emptied, wardrobes bare and clothes strewn around and more pictures and photos ripped out and dumped.

'My, my, they were thorough,' he muttered.

Taking care not to disturb too much he tentatively searched amongst the chaos for anything untoward but found only occasional smudges of cigarette ash which surprised him because there were no implements in the place that a smoker would use. He looked for an ashtray without success but after some careful searching amongst the debris, he found a cigarette butt.

Whoever the smoker was had not been worried about the

outcome as they had dropped a lengthy one and it had scorched a mark across the carpet before it was extinguished. Using the tweezers from his Swiss army knife, he picked it up and carried it into the front room and holding it up he spoke to Effie. 'Have you got an evidence bag, Effie?'

She fished one out of her jacket pocket and held it open while he dropped the butt in.

'I found it in the bedroom amongst the debris. Did Bonar smoke? There's no ashtrays or suchlike.'

'I don't know,' she said, 'I'll ask the doc.' She sealed the bag before, she said, 'Doctor Kerr?'

He looked up, 'Yes, Sergeant.'

'Did the victim smoke?'

'There's no outward visible sign. We'll know more when we get him back to the lab.'

'Thanks, Doc.' She held the bag out to Hunter. 'It's your case, do you want it?'

'No, Effie, put it with the rest but I want the results of the DNA asap.'

'Will do,' and she slipped it into her pocket.

'There's nothing else we can do tonight, Effie, so after I've given the backroom the once over I'm heading home. See you in the office in the morning.'

'See you there.'

In the backroom, he found more traces of cigarette ash but nothing else and after five minutes he gave it up and went down to his car where he sat for a moment pondering before he put a call through to Gus Thomas.

The phone was about to change over to 'voicemail' when a weary Gus Thomas answered, 'What is it, Hunter?'

'Sorry to bother you this late, Gus—there's been a development and we need to talk.'

'Can't you tell me now?'

'You know better than that.'

'You're right, Hunter, I wasn't thinking. When can you get here?'

'I've got to stay on top of it here.'

'Okay, Hunter, I'll use the chopper first thing. Where will you be?'

'Tell me when you're half an hour from Broughton airfield and I'll come for you.'

'Okay, can I go back to sleep now?'

Hunter didn't answer, instead, slid his finger over the 'End Call' app.

—

The morning brought the usual meeting and the crew with extra members drafted in from other districts assembled in the tiny space. People were sat on desks, the lucky ones on seats and the latecomers leaning on the walls but one seat remained empty until the door was pushed open and Hunter reversed into the room with a coffee cup in each hand. He swung around and let the door close behind him and made his way to the empty seat that Fiona had been guarding.

He sat down and offered her one of the drinks. 'Thanks, lass, it was tea wasn't it?'

'Yes, sir.'

'Ooh, I've gone up in the world...' Fiona laughed and he continued, '...just plain Hunter will do, lass, but you made me feel better.'

Effie, stood by the whiteboard waiting patiently, coughed, and said loudly, 'When you've all done!'

Hunter winked at Fiona, 'Herself has spoken.'

He took a swig of his coffee and nodded to Effie and she continued, 'Morning all, just a quick update of where we're up to after last nights incident and then we'll move on.' Hunter held his hand up. 'Yes, Hunter?'

'I'm expecting an urgent text so I apologise beforehand for the interruption. If and when it comes I'll have to leave.'

'Thanks for that. Moving on. We are now looking for a double killer of Eastern European origin and we still have no ID of any sorts. We are awaiting DNA results from last night and those of you working on the CCTV expand your search to cover the roads out of town towards Blacon two hours before the estimated time of death. We are looking for a silver Audi A4 similar to the one seen coming out of the Market car park.'

DC Farmer raised his hand. 'Yes, Farmer?'

'Is there any connection to the Owen incident?'

'We don't know but it is likely.'

Looking directly at her with a hint of irony, he said, 'It's not just another queer basher?'

There was a snigger around the room which Effie stopped. 'DC Farmer! This is a warning! You will not use that term and treat all LBGT as required by law. What you think privately you keep to yourself, understood?'

'Yes, Sarge.'

'Good, and Farmer, you're with me this morning so don't go.' She put down the marker she had been holding. 'That's it, we'll reconvene at four-thirty this afternoon.'

Hunter thanked Fiona and walked down the room to Effie and with a tilt of the head he steered her away from the others.

'What is it, Hunter?'

'My SIS boss is on the way up,' and he told a little white lie, 'and I don't know why. He said something about an update. I'll keep him away from here.'

'Okay, Hunter,' she nodded towards Farmer, 'I've got your stand-in and he's in for some serious updating.'

'It's young blood now is it?'

She smiled at the implication. 'Hunter—you know better than that.'

Hunter's phone did its impression of a doorbell and warned him a message had arrived. He acknowledged Effie and turned away to check it out as he walked towards the door.

—

An hour later settled down in the corner of the restaurant in *Garden Aspects* №1 Gus Thomas said, 'Alright Hunter, what is it?'

Hunter picked up a leather document holder from the side of his chair, plucked out some paperwork and spread a copy of Owen's papers and the info downloaded off the net onto the table in front of Thomas. 'There was second killing last night by the same guy that did for Owen. I have since been informed that we have a likeness for the assailant from CCTV in the club that Owen frequented but more disturbing, Gus, is this stuff.' He pointed to the coded map references. 'This was in Owen's room and I had it translated and from it, I got all this bumf.' He spread the results of his O.S. map search and the route map from the Manchester CND.

Gus studied them for a few minutes before he sat back. 'Are you thinking the same as me, Hunter? We could be onto a plot to plant a dirty bomb or something like.'

'It looks that way, Gus.'

'You've ringed Capenhurst.'

'It's less than two miles from here. What have they got from Owen's flat and his workspace in GCHQ?'

'Very little at this moment. He was definitely on top of his chosen career and it would have taken Bletchley Park most of the war to break it. Everything was first coded and then encrypted. We will get there but it's very slow. More worrying, Hunter, having seen this. Is it the latest Russian code because if it is we're in a mess.'

'I don't think you need worry on that score. My contact was able to read it with no problem and from there I got the rest of the info from the net.'

'Have you any ideas, Hunter?'

'For what it's worth I think Owen came across something in his searches at GCHQ and he was trying to boost his CV by tracing the culprits and got killed for his pains. He obviously thought there was nothing to it hence the silly alias.'

'Or he was a mole and passing security info to them.'

'No, I think he was sussed and they topped him and did for Bonar because they thought Owen may have passed info to him as a contact or accidentally during their, and I use the term loosely, lovemaking.'

'Okay, Hunter, assuming that's what it was it's now looking more like a National security issue and one for MI5 or Special Branch.

Hunter picked up his phone. 'One moment, Gus.' He quickly dialled a number and uttered a few words before he put it down and said to, Gus, 'It's already ours and I want to keep it. The police are running a parallel murder enquiry and are working with me and I'm not interfering, I'm leaving it to them. We could just have a gay stalker in which case we hand it back but if it is as I suggested a security issue then we take it over completely and call in Special Branch.

'Right, Hunter, be it on your head. Do you want help?'

Just then, one of the baristas from the restaurant brought over two cups of coffee and picked up the dirty ones. Hunter slipped her a coin. 'Thanks,' he said, 'put it on the Bosses tab.'

'Will do, Mr Hunter,' and she turned away and wended her way through the tables back to the service counter.

'Where were we,' said Hunter. 'Ah, yes, as for help, Gus, I'm okay at the moment but it would be good to have someone on back-up.'

'We've recalled Williams and we'll get him primed. I'm informed he's found his forte. Did you know he's a polyglot and speaks fluent Russian along with all the other Slavic languages?'

Hunter nodded, 'Yes, he told me earlier this year on our last job. That's what you get when you marry a Russian.'

Gus scooped the paperwork from the table. 'I'll keep these, I want to show 'C' who will no doubt want to impart your knowledge to the JIC (Joint Intelligence Committee) or the Home Office. Take me back to the chopper.'

As they stood up to leave, Gus said suddenly, 'One more thing, Hunter, I don't know if it's of any significance but we had it on the grapevine from the Cousins that they have reliable info from Japan that Russia has been making enquiries in North Korea about field mini nuclear bombs. So small they are carried by suicide troops'

Hunter parked his car in time to see Effie and Farmer dashing out to her SUV at the same time a Patrol car drove off with lights flashing and sirens whining.

'Hunter!' shouted Effie, 'Get in!'

He didn't hesitate but ran over and levered himself into the back seat just as Effie drove off at speed. With a flick of a switch, she turned on hidden blue lights behind the grill at the same time a siren began wailing.

'What's going on?' said, Hunter, breathlessly.

Farmer turned in his seat and said over his shoulder, 'We've got info on the car seen coming out of the car park on the CCTV Friday night. It's registered to a Ralf Jenkins out in Upton near the Zoo.'

Effie weaved a way through traffic on a roundabout cursing deaf or stupid drivers while flinging Hunter around in the back as he struggled to fasten a seat belt with the buckle catch hidden between seats. The manoeuvre at the next roundabout went smoothly and onto the 'B' road towards Upton their destination. Effie cursed the traffic calming obstacles and occasionally disregarded them altogether which left Hunter clinging on for dear life with everything braced. They did a final right-hand swing into a quiet 1930's suburban street and skidded to a halt only seconds behind the Patrol car. After alighting from their vehicles Effie, Hunter and Farmer waited until a Police bus turned into the road and as it pulled up half a dozen armed Police tumbled out and spread themselves around a beautifully presented bungalow with its trim gardens. One of them with impressive build prepared to hammer in the front door just as it opened and a neat grey-haired lady stepped out and demanded, 'What is going on, and why are you trampling all over my garden?'

Effie held up her ID and hurried forward. 'Detective Sergeant Newlove, ma'am. We're looking for a Mr Ralf Jenkins. Does he live here?'

Peering over her glasses the lady looked sternly at Effie, and said harshly, 'And what if he does?' An armed officer came down the hall behind her and she looked over her shoulder and shouted hysterically, 'What are you doing? Get out! Get out!'

'Sorry, ma'am,' he said, 'but the Sergeant here will have to come and see for herself. We won't keep you long.'

He indicated that Effie should come inside. The obvious relaxed attitude of the officer told Effie all was not well, and she said quietly, 'I'm sorry. Are you, Mrs Jenkins?'

She nodded, 'Yes, and can you tell me what's going on?'

'Can I come in and I'll explain.'

Mrs Jenkins stood to one side and let Effie through and the officer said, 'Follow me, Sarge, something's not right.'

She followed him down the narrow hall and he pushed open the second door and standing to one side ushered Effie through. She took one step forward over the threshold, stopped and inhaled sharply as her hand went to her mouth. She stood speechless and then uttered quietly, 'Oh, my god, what have we done?'

Before her propped up in bed with a heart monitor, drip tube and a breathing tube attached was an elderly man in obvious distress. She shook her head and turned away and left the room and almost bumped into Mrs Jenkins who was stood behind her. 'I'm sorry, Mrs Jenkins, there must be some mistake. Is that your husband?'

Still looking very annoyed, she said stiffly, 'Yes, and now can you tell me what's going on?'

'I will, Mrs Jenkins just as soon as I chase this lot and I'll make sure they leave no mess. Shall we go into the lounge?'

When Mrs Jenkins was settled into a chair Effie asked if it was okay to make some tea. She said, 'Yes,' and Effie asked a uniform policeman if he could oblige and then went out and called Hunter to join her. She sat on the sofa and Hunter stood just inside the door as Effie went on to explain the situation and finished by holding out her smartphone and asking, '...Does your husband own an Audi with that registration?'

Mrs Jenkins nodded, and said, 'Yes, and it hasn't moved for over six months. It's too big for me.'

'Can I see it?'

'Yes, the keys are in the hall.'

Hunter interrupted, 'Stay there, Effie, I'll go.'

The flower petals and cobwebs hanging around the garage lock were evidence enough but to make sure he pushed up the door to reveal a shiny Audi Q3 with the dodgy registration. He squeezed himself around the car and opened the doors just wide enough to push his arm in, sniff and then try the ignition. Many dim lights came on but he could see that the battery was low and it was obvious it hadn't moved in months. He stood upright and did a quick check of the tyres on the driver's side and saw that the front offside tyre was at a very low pressure and with that he returned to Effie.

'That car, Effie, hasn't moved this year let alone in the last six months. We've made a boo-boo.'

Effie sighed, 'I'm sorry, Mrs Jenkins, but it appears someone has duplicated your car number plates,' Effie fished a card out of her wallet and gave it to Mrs Jenkins. 'Call that number and we will arrange for the house cleaners to come around and make a note of any damage which will be fixed. We are very sorry for the disturbance and I wish your husband all the best but it doesn't look good does it?'

'It probably brightened his day, Sergeant. He only has days to live. He should be in a hospice but he wanted to pass away at home and the MacMillan nurses are excellent.'

She stood up and was collecting her things when Hunter said, 'Mrs Jenkins, I couldn't help but see that your car has done less than 1000 miles. If at any time you want to sell it...' he handed his card to her, '...call me, I would be interested in buying.'

She took the card and gave it a quick glance. 'Thank you, Mr Hunter, I'll do that. It's much too big for me.'

She made to rise and Effie stopped her. It's okay, Mrs Jenkins, we'll let ourselves out and I'm sorry for what we've put you through.'

'That's life, Sergeant. Where would we be without you?'

—

Hunter threw his coat over the back of a chair and walked down the room to Effie. He stood nonchalantly waiting with a hand in his pocket until she finished talking on the phone and then butted in, 'What a fine mess etc, etc... Do you have the description of the vehicle seen coming from the car park?'

Effie plucked a file from her briefcase and opened it at the appropriate page and gave it to him. He browsed it for a few seconds and said, 'And the info from the DVLA?'

She pulled a single sheet from her briefcase and handed it to him. At the same time, she added, 'I know what's next, Hunter.'

'If you do, what was all that nonsense this afternoon? I may be sounding a bit glib here but from the screenshot, it's obviously an ageing A4 with a 2013 registration plate. Didn't that ring alarm bells when compared with the DVLA bumf?'

Effie blushed, 'Well... Yes, but we couldn't take chances.'

'A couple of watchers would have sufficed. We have the best in the world at that sort of thing. Let's move on. Whoever it is, is an amateur. Who uses false number plates of a car in the same city?'

'Good point, Hunter.'

'Get uniform on it, Effie. Scour them bloody streets. I'll see you in the morning.'

He walked towards the door in obvious dissatisfaction and as he scooped his coat up, he said 'Cheerio' to Fiona and left.

On the way out to his car, he stopped by the front desk, showed his ID and spoke to the desk Sergeant. 'Is there a district or ghetto in the city where the Eastern Europeans hang out?'

~~~~~~

Chapter 6

Captain Franz Jubert eased the eighty-metre barge **GCS Jenny** from the lock and took his hat off and wiped his forehead with the back of his hand. It had been a long ten days threading his way up the Danube from Constanta the busiest part of the journey. Low water levels didn't help and after Budapest, the increased tourist vessels had hindered him. He always felt that they were given priority through the locks and the Danube-Main Canal and going upstream was always slow at the best of times but what made it worse was his special cargo in the storeroom. A lead-lined coffin. His crew thought it bad luck to carry such a thing and he couldn't wait to offload it. 'Only one more day,' he said to himself.

He cursed as he had to wait while a cruise boat did a three-point turn in the entrance to the docks and then reversed to its mooring on the other side of the canal before he could nudge into the first bay. Unloading wouldn't take long and then he could take his wife into town and celebrate her birthday.

Early the next morning he nudged out of the dock and started on the quicker part of the trip and he expected to be in Frankfurt-am-Main by mid-afternoon. His orders were peculiar. He had to stop but not dock at Mulheim where a boat would meet him and the coffin unloaded. It was not a difficult job as the ships onboard crane could manage it easily and if they were willing to pay a little extra all well and good. Someone's loved one must be worth it, he surmised.

Franz stopped the ship by the kilometre marker as instructed and held it steady with expert use of the engines and propellers and breathed a sigh of relief when a motorised dinghy pushed out from the small jetty and drifted down to them. He was told that the deceased was a tall heavy man and the coffin was about 1.90 metres in length and weighed a hundred and ten kilograms. His crew were prepared and the changeover took only seven minutes and checking his radar and a quick visual he was on his way again as the dearly departed was ferried toward their last resting place but what surprised him was the camper van on the jetty and not a hearse. He shrugged, it wasn't his problem anymore and a party was already planned when they arrived in Rotterdam to use some of the cash handed over on the exchange.

—

The nights were closing in and it was quite dull and grey when Hunter alighted from the taxi outside the railway station and after he paid the driver he wandered inside. He stopped by the newsagents and pretended to check his change as he watched the taxi pull away. He counted to ten, left the station and turned right to walk towards the town.

A few minutes later he crossed the major junction at the bottom of the bridge and he began concentrating on what was his real mission. It was pure speculation but worth a try as evidence in the case was leading them nowhere. It was also a nostalgic walk for him as he looked at the old buildings and how they had changed over the years and he was very much surprised when he stood opposite an Asian Supermarket. It looked familiar but it was some moments before he recognised the Dance Hall where he had learned to dance as a young man.

'Whatever next,' he muttered.

Under the glow of the streetlights, he studied faces which was hard to do without attracting attention as it was the practice of Eastern European men folk to stand in their ethnic groups and correct the world. At the end of the street, he crossed over and began walking back when on a whim he went into a Pub only to leave fifteen minutes later after drinking half a mediocre pint of what should have been one of his favourite lagers.

As he left the premises his phone broke the silence. He stopped to check it and saw it was Effie and slid his finger up the green symbol. 'Yes, Effie?'

'Hunter! Where are you?'

'Bourn Street.'

'That's handy. Someone has just used Owens debit card at the Post Office Cash Point in that street.'

At that moment he was jerked around and a pale skinned spotty youth with a doubtful southern accent waving a fish slice knife with a six inch blade, said viciously, 'Give us ya phone or you get this.'

Hunter heaved a distinct sigh and shook his head before he held his hand out, and said wearily, 'Give me the knife, lad, and go home.'

The youth waved the knife angrily. 'Give us da phone.'

'I recommend that you do as you're asked,' said Hunter.

'PHONE! You bastard!' screamed the lad, while making a thrust towards Hunter's stomach.

Some say it was so quick they never saw it but Hunter stepped forward one pace and grabbed the youths right wrist with his left hand, spun inward on his left toe, put his right arm over the youths and curled it under the elbow and jerked upward at the same time thrusting down with his left hand.

The crack and the scream were heard the length of the street as the elbow dislocated and the knife fell to the floor. Hunter let the arm go and spun back the opposite way and his rigid right forearm struck the youth down the side of his neck and he collapsed in a heap at Hunter's feet. For good measure, Hunter kicked him in the groin and leaned forward and spoke into the lad's ear, 'Pick on someone your own age, you prick.'

He picked up the knife with his handkerchief and someone returned his phone that was still broadcasting.

'Hi, Effie, you still there?'

'Yes, there's a car on the way, what's going on?'

'Some idiot tried to mug me. What was that about a debit card?'

Effie sat back and looked at the phone and shook her head. 'Is he real?' she muttered before telling Hunter the original message.

'Got that,' said Hunter, and he rang off. In the distance could be heard a Police car siren and he turned to the man who had returned his phone and held up his ID. 'Police! Take the knife and give it to the guys in the car that's coming.'

The man hesitated and Hunter shook it at him, 'It's clean,' he said.

He handed the knife over as the police car turned into the end of the street and Hunter crossed the road and walked purposely towards the Post Office. He tried to blend in at the same time doing a visual on everything and anything that moved and in the distance he spotted a light coloured raincoat walking away. His intuition made him follow and he lengthened his stride and stepped into the road away from other pedestrians but he had eyes on his quarry for only twenty seconds before it turned into an alleyway. He increased his pace but when he turned into the alleyway his prey had disappeared.

Disappointed he made his way down the alley and fifty metres later it opened into a back entrance to the shops and down to a suburban street but no sign of his objective from which he assumed that whoever it was lived locally.

He gave up the chase and turned back towards the High St when his phone delivered its call again. He glanced at it and as soon as he zapped the slider he said, 'Yes, Effie.'

'Hunter, where are you. Uniform have been left with an A & E case and a knife. Witnesses said you did a runner after claiming you were Police.'

'I'm invisible, Effie. I'll see you in the morning but what I can tell you is that I have a slender lead on our posh mack.'

He rang off and walked to the railway station and flagged a taxi.

—

Recently retired Moscow Police Chief Inspector Alexei Savitsky pulled the flaps of his ushanka down over his ears and drew his overcoat tighter around him as he fought to keep out the early Siberian north-easterly wind blowing across Moscow. 'The last time winds this cold blew so early it stopped a whole invading army,' referring to the winter of 1941.

Undaunted he made his way to the Bar frequented by other police retirees and the warmth that surrounded him as the door closed behind him was a relief. He stamped his feet as he hung up his coat and hat and made his way into the almost empty bar. He would have stayed away himself but his wife was entertaining other ladies living in the commune flats where he lived and a bit of cold wind wasn't a big sacrifice.

Vodka was his first choice followed by a cold imported lager, a drink he had come to like while working briefly alongside a UK SIS agent some fourteen years earlier. The vodka warmed him but the lager soothed him and he wondered how Hunter and his partner were doing.

He emptied his glass and he ordered again when an unsteady

Fyodor Serov staggered against him and he spilt a drop of the liquid nectar. Serov tried to make amends by ordering vodka for both of them and another lager for Alexei.

Alexei could see that Serov was under the influence something he was well known for since his wife had died and Alexei ever the gentleman accepted and soon they were deep into conversation albeit a one-sided one as Serov burbled on about the world and modern politics.

Alexei was looking for a way to distance himself when Serov in his drunken burbling, muttered, Operation '*WYSKOCHKA*' and the nuclear destruction of something which Alexei didn't catch. He quickly ordered more vodka and plied Serov with it and enquired casually, 'Sounds like some of that false news we keep hearing on CNN, Fyodor. Where was it you said?'

Serov grabbed Alexei's arm and pulled him around face to face and said, slurring his words until they all ran into each other, 'It's true, I'm telling you. I was on the committee. We are going to send Korean dirty bombs to the 'October Legion' in England and America.'

Serov's arm slipped off the bar and Alexei caught him. 'I think it's time we went home,' he said, and looping one of Serov's arms around his neck and pulling him up with the other he half-carried him to the coat rack and then helped him to a taxi. In the taxi, Serov continued with his ramblings despite Alexei trying to stop him as the information may get to the driver.

After making sure Serov was safe inside his apartment Alexei went home with a conundrum. It all sounded scrambled but if it was true what should he do? Patriotism was one thing but nuclear bombs?'

The following morning Alexei was disturbed by urgent knocking on the apartment door and when he opened it he was confronted by two men wearing leather coats and black ushankas and he took a pace back when they flashed FSB ID at him.

FSB, NKVD and KGB? He didn't need to see the ID. The dress code over the years had not changed and they stood out like the proverbial sore thumb. 'Yes, what is it?' he said irritably.

'Comrad Inspector Savitsky?'

Alexei nodded. 'That's me.'

'Get dressed, you're coming with us.'

'Am I under arrest?'

'No.'

'Why are you asking me to go with you?'

'We only obey orders.'

'Step inside, I'll be five minutes.'

At the FSB Headquarters, he was lead into a sparsely furnished side room, not an interrogation suite he noted, and waiting for him was General Bazarov. The door closed behind him and Bazarov said, 'Comrad Chief Inspector Savitsky, take a seat. This shouldn't take long.'

Alexei sat by a worn office table while the General remained standing and spoke as he walked backwards and forward across the room. 'Comrad Inspector? Last night you met and talked with Comrad Police Chief Serov. Is that correct?'

'Yes, General.'

'What did you talk about?'

'The Comrad Chief was drunk and burbled on about politics, religion and the world in general.'

'Is that all?'

'He was depressed and mumbled something about being dumped from a job which gave him relief from his loneliness in retirement. He lives on his own since his wife died.'

'Did he say what the job was?'

'No, General. He collapsed and I took him home. I left him slumped on his sofa with the television on and I went back to my wife. Has something happened to him?'

'He was taken into hospital this morning. I'm assured it was alcoholic poisoning.'

Alexei knew what that meant but said nothing and the General continued, 'That will be all, Comrad Inspector. I'll get them to take you home. Ah! One more thing, Inspector. When you were in the force what did you do? Did you have any foreign contacts?'

'I did my last years working with Interpol underground

chasing the mafia and gangsters who were doing drugs and money laundering. I did work alongside foreign agents but only in an official capacity on the same case.'

'Oh, I see. You didn't run agents?'

'No, General, I left that to the FSB. I was a policeman in the MUR.'

'Thank you again, Comrad Inspector.'

As General Bazarov left the room Alexei stood and acknowledged him, 'Comrad General.'

———

Irritated by his constant pacing up and down and muttering to himself Alexei's wife told him to go for a walk and in an instant, he had made up his mind. He sat at his workplace and scribbled a note put it in an envelope and after searching the draws of his desk he retrieved a piece of paper with a number on. He wrote a few more words on the outside of the envelope and the number before he grabbed his coat and ventured out into the cold again.

After the morning's incident, he knew he would be watched and he did nothing to arouse suspicions. He stayed in plain view at all times and walked to the nearest Metro station where he deliberately mixed with the crowds but didn't do anything out of the ordinary. There was a surge when the train pulled into the platform and he went with the rush and was able to grab a seat inside the doors. When the train pulled into Revolution Square he didn't make a move instead he waited for the signal that the doors were closing before he banged his fist on his knee in mock frustration, jumped up like he had made a decision, and darted off the train.

He didn't hurry away instead he stood for a few moments rubbing his chin pretending a moment of indecision and glancing to his left he saw a man hurriedly turn away and pretend to look for his phone. 'Amateur,' he thought before he made his way to the main entrance where he hoped tourist sightseers would be gathered looking with awe at the architecture and frescos.

His luck was in and he tagged on the back of a small English party listening to their guide and worked his way around until he came upon a middle-aged couple. He stood behind for a full minute before he turned sideways as if to walk away and as he did so, his inside arm now hidden, he dropped the envelope into the ladies open bag before sidling off and back to the trains. Still in open view, he travelled to the river and enjoyed a chilly walk along the embankment and finally into a bar and a warming vodka.

———

After two nights of blending in with the locals in and around Bourn St speaking his best imitation of broken English, Hunter was no further forward finding the suspect wearing what appeared to be Owen's stolen coat. He knew someone was in the area as Owen's card had been used a second time but frustratingly when he wasn't there. Downing the dregs of his pint he was about to leave when his phone pinged. Ignoring the dangers on the street he waited until he was outside before he checked it and saw it was a message from Gus Thomas. 'What does he want at this time of night,' he muttered before he read it... **SMS: Get down here asap. Gus.**

Over the drink-drive limit, he said to no one in particular, 'No chance, matey,' and typed a reply to that effect before making his way to the taxi rank.

———

It was just after midday when he entered Gus's office with a coffee in one hand, a ham roll in the other and his briefcase tucked under his arm. He lifted the roll as he acknowledged Gus, and said, 'Sorry about this. I've come straight here and didn't snack on the way down.'

Senior Agent Gus Thomas waved a hand in acceptance. 'Take a seat, Hunter.' He waited until Hunter was settled before he passed a letter with a note attached over the desk to him. 'Take a look at that and tell me what you think.'

Hunter picked it up and read the letter and the note, and said, 'I think this is genuine. It's a bit scrawly but I recognise the writing. How did you get this?'

'It was found in the bag of a tourist and they got in touch with us. It's a disused contact number which you must have given him on the Cyprus job. He says it's urgent and wants to meet but no subject.'

'He's retired now but the way I read it, Gus, is that whatever he's got is tying him down. He's being watched. Get someone from six to feed him an Apple i-phone plus an English throwaway sim with only one contact—me, and set up with *Whatsapp* which is all he must use to contact me. I also need a device set up the same way.'

'Put me in the know, Hunter. Why *Whatsapp*?'

'Their messaging service is encrypted as is the Apple device which gives you double encryption.'

Thomas picked up his landline phone and pressed a key and after a few minutes conversation he put the phone down and said to Hunter, 'That's all set up they'll deliver yours shortly.'

'Good. Let me know when he's got the phone and I'll organise a City break to Moscow. I'll take Jacquie. She's still on the books isn't she?'

'Yes, but only as a sleeper.'

'Revive her status to 'live.''

Gus scribbled on his pad, and then said, 'Before you go I have more on Owen. He was detailed to follow up on some intercepted encrypted messages coming from Eastern Europe thought to be an illegal immigrant smuggling gang. Triangulation by GCHQ along with our other listening stations traced the source this end to a place near Aldermaston and instead of handing it over to the fieldmen he went off on a private venture and infiltrated this cell. He sussed it was something bigger and again instead of telling us he went off on a tangent to trace a newly formed sub cell in the Chester area. With his stupid alias, they in turn must have sussed him but not before he had that bumf you passed on to us. We have checked out those sim cards and they're dead. We have dissected them and like you, they were using *Whatsapp*. The other murders were a cleanup exercise in case Owen talked.'

'The Ukraine passport?'

'They're still following that up.'

'How come he had an official car, Gus?'

'That's under internal investigation. He must have told them some cock and bull story.'

'Have they deciphered those messages?'

'We have applied to both Microsoft and Apple for help in decrypting them but they gave us some bull about customer privacy so we are taking it to court which could take some time. Owen was ahead of his game and found a way to do it which doesn't help us.'

'Meanwhile?'

'You're on your own.'

'Pull in Williams.'

There was a knock on the door and a bright, smartly dressed secretary came in carrying a small package. She waved the package towards Gus. 'Sorry to interrupt,' she said, 'but here is the phone and one time you asked for, sir.'

She carried it across the room and laid it on his desk. 'Thank you, Elaine. We were just finishing.'

She left the room and Gus gave the package to Hunter. 'Best of luck with that. We'll let you know when Savitsky has his and then it's your move. Have you been to Moscow before?'

'Nope.'

'You need, Halfpenny.'

'No thanks, Gus, the last time I worked with her it almost ended in divorce.'

Gus laughed, 'Ha, ha, if I remember, Hunter, you had a dirty weekend which is still small talk here.'

'Enough, I've got a train to catch.'

Hunter dropped the package into his briefcase and headed for the door.

———

Alexei Savitsky was idly pushing a shopping trolley around the local supermarket following his wife Malika who was studying her list at the same time muttering unflattering comments about prices. A lone male shopper wearing a worn blue scarf and his head buried in his i-phone swung around the end of the aisle and bumped into him and knocked the bag of flour he was holding to the floor and spraying some of the contents over him.

The man was prolific with his apologies and made desultory attempts to brush off the fine white powder spread over Alexei at the same time he pushed something inside Alexei's coat as he did so he said in a low voice, *'Skroyte yego I otkroyte, kogda vy doma.'* ('Hide it and only open it when you're home.')

He snatched a new bag of flour off the shelf and shoved it into Alexei's hand before continuing on his way apologising profusely with his eyes once more glued to the phone. Alexei watched him referring to a list in the phone while grabbing items off the shelves and as they turned to go into the next aisle they saw him cross to the checkouts.

Fearful of the FSB watchers who had become a feature in his life since the demise of Serov, Alexei shrugged and circulated his shoulders and arms trying to ease stressed aching muscles and make his heavy coat more comfortable at the same time he slipped a hand into his coat and made the package secure in an inside pocket.

Ever watchful, at the end of the shop they went to the bag lockers, an anti-shoplifting security element in all Moscow stores and while transferring the shopping into their bags he surreptitiously looked around but no one made any move or showed the slightest interest and feeling somewhat relieved they left the store.

Outside, Malika said to him, 'Are you alright, Alexei, you're very quiet.'

'It's nothing,' he replied, 'just a bit stuffy in the shop and I'm glad to be out in the fresh air.'

The fifteen-minute bus journey home was endless but at last, he was able to close the apartment door behind them and leaving Malika to unload the bags he went to the bedroom and took out the package. With shaking hands he tore at the wrapping to reveal the latest Apple i-phone switched on and fully charged with its attachments and operating instructions and a note written in Russian telling him code words and what to do. '*Milk*' meant go to the supermarket, '*water*' meant go to his local bottle shop in each case carrying a blue '*avos'ka.*' No '*avos'ka*' the contact was off. His contact would be wearing a blue scarf. No scarf, no contact.

He dropped it on the bed and removed his coat but before he could hang it up the device tinkled out its first incoming message...
SMS: Arriving Friday p.m. Will contact. Hunter.

Android phones were now widely available in Russia and so he was familiar with them but this was the latest superfast Apple and in English. He picked up the instructions but before he could read them Malika entered the room.

'What was that noise, Alexei?'

'Malika—It's best you don't know.'

'Where did you get it?'

'From that man in the supermarket.'

'Why?'

'Malika, I make contact with an old friend I met in Cyprus. Anymore you don't need to hear but over the next few days I may be out in the town and then it is finished.'

'It's not criminal, Alexei?'

'No, but secret from my police days.'

'Okay, I prepare dinner. Be careful, Alexei.'

He studied the instructions and to show that he was *au fait* with the device sent a reply. **'OK'** was all he put and later as they cuddled in bed he told Malika about Hunter.

———

Hunter put the tray down and handed a coffee to a weary Duncan Williams and the ever-vibrant Jacquie sat around a corner table in the restaurant of *Garden Centre* №1 Hunter's preferred location for an SIS meeting. What they talked about was outside the police remit and therefore safer.

Putting the tray to one side, he said, 'What's the matter with you, Dunc?'

'I only put a foot back in Blighty last night and I'm called out to you lot this morning. I've not even had time to see my kids. In short, I'm knackered.'

'Let's get to it, Duncan and then you can nip home. Jacquie is sitting in for two reasons. One—to give the impression of a business meeting, and two—just to keep in the groove so to speak. This is the case so far...' He brought Duncan up to speed on both the police case and the SIS case, '...and you'll be my eyes and ears while I'm away in Moscow with Jacquie.'

'What does that mean exactly?'

'Be yourself. Dress in your scruffiest and mingle in and around Bourn St.'

'Are you suggesting I'm shabby?'

'I didn't say that.'

'What am I looking for?'

'A guy in a posh light coloured Burberry trench coat so a rainy day or night would be good and hang out near the Post Office. He's been using Owens card in the ATM there.'

'And you pair are off on a dirty weekend in Moscow.'

Jacquie smiled, she liked Duncan, and Hunter replied, 'We're going to meet Alexei Savitsky. You remember him from our Cyprus gig. He got in touch with the 'Firm' on an old contact number.'

'I gave him the package with the i-phone in just before I left. He didn't recognise me though. It's the real business then?'

'Yes.'

'When?'

'We leave Thursday night. My sister and Jamie are looking after the kids and hopefully, we'll be back Tuesday evening.'

'Who's Jamie?'

'Ex paratrooper sergeant we hired for security.'

'Got ya! And the police?'

Hunter shoved a piece of paper over to him. 'This is your contact. Use your code name. She has your details. More coffee anyone?'

~~~~~~

Chapter 7

Friday

The BA Flight 1783 landed at Moscow Domodedevo International airport on time and progress through Passport control went smoothly and living up to their reviews Lingo taxis were waiting to transport Jacquie and Hunter to their final destination, the five-star *art nouveau* Metropol Hotel just a long walk to Red Square and close to the city centre.

Using Hunter's long-standing pseudonym of Byewater they were shown every courtesy as rich foreign tourists. They had booked a superior Grand suite and when they finally stretched out on the king-size bed with a complimentary glass of champagne, they fell about laughing. 'I didn't think Russia had evolved this much, Hunter. Do you think there is any need for subterfuge these days?'

'Very much so, lass. The FSB is just another name for the KGB just not communist. Anyone who believes that your free Wi-Fi and Internet goes unchecked is on another planet.'

'This will keep them occupied, I'm going to call the kids before we go down to dinner.'

'Give it plenty of that and pictures on Twitter and Facebook when we're out. Which reminds me. I must make it up to Iain somehow. I said I'd go and watch him play on the wing for the school tomorrow.'

Jacquie stood up and made a short video of their suite before tweeting it to her friends and although they were three hours ahead she made a call to Iain and Lesley to wish them goodnight and she promised Lesley she would bring home some genuine Russian dolls. All done they showered and got dressed ready for dinner.

Wrapped up against the cool October nights they went for a walk after dinner. Jacquie had added a full fur Ushanka to her wardrobe and played the part of a trophy wife and if there was any watchers about they took every chance to be noticed. After dinner, standing on the doorstep of the hotel Hunter held a map up and pointed to his right then Jacquie had a look, turned the map upside down and pointed to her left before Hunter asked the doorman who gave them directions to Red Square.

While they strolled towards the Square away from any detection devices in the hotel Jacquie held onto Hunter's arm and leaned against him to cover Hunter's covert actions as he typed out a short message on *Whatsapp* to Alexei.

Their movements could be tracked but with the combined encryption of Apple and Whatsapp, the favoured communication of criminals and terrorists any message was safe. In the square, they were fascinated by the illuminations and they made a couple of short videos and took numerous photos some of which they tweeted and messaged before making their way back to the hotel.

—

About the same time as Hunter and Jacquie were returning to their hotel, Effie was stood at the breakfast bar while Charlotte finished preparing the evening meal when her i-phone jangled. She picked it up and read the message… **SMS: Ernesto on station.**

She put the device down and Charlotte said, 'Work?'

'In a fashion. These security bods are certainly on the ball. That was Hunter's sidekick telling me he was on the job already.'

'Who is it, Effie?'

'Some guy called Williams but we only use his code name.'

'Does he look Latino?'

'I don't know, I heard him mentioned by DCI Fearn earlier this year but I never met him. Do you know him?'

'Hunter used the Garden Centre as a meeting place then and I was briefly introduced. He looked a bit like Che Guevara but he seemed nice enough.'

'They're taking this case pretty seriously. What I thought was a homophobic hate crime appears to be something bigger. Have you heard anything?'

'No, Effie, Mrs Hunter never talks about Hunter's job and he doesn't either. Did you know she was one of them?'

'I heard it on the grapevine. Apparently, that's why she was targeted earlier this year. Let's eat before I get called out.'

—

Unshaven and wearing his old suede gardening shoes and a raggy pair of jeans with a worn gilet under an old navy blue fleece and a battered NY Yankees cap, Williams dawdled along Bourn Street familiarising himself. He was taking no chances and unlike Hunter, he was armed.

The main area of his surveillance, on Hunter's instructions, was the Post Office and the ATM. This was also the meeting place for many of the Eastern Bloc immigrants who would stand around in groups and put the world to rights. After fourteen years living with Tanya he spoke fluent Russian albeit with a Crimean accent but he didn't let on.

He mumbled something unintelligible as he pushed through them to the ATM and withdrew some cash and then went into the Polish supermarket that was also home to the Post Office. He was quite impressed by the array of imported goods mainly from Poland but he settled for a tin of Tyskie beer and ignoring the City bylaws he opened it and drank from it as he continued his wanderings up and down.

It didn't take him long to survey the length of the street and he wondered what he was going to do for the rest of the evening when the smell of a good Indian curry wafted down to him. He'd eaten before he left home but decided that a takeaway cafe was a good place as any to get to know the locals so a Madras curry with fried vegetable rice was the order of the night.

While waiting for his order he spoke to a man standing beside him in his version of broken English. 'Hello, I new here. Where I get work?'

'I no can help,' the man replied. He pointed out of the door and to the left. 'You go to the pub at end of the road and find Janis.'

His order arrived and as he left the shop he looked at the man and gave him a nod, and said, '*Spasibo*.'

Leaning against a wall eating his curry he watched the street paying particular attention to the crowd around the P.O. but nothing untoward happened and the weather was clear so no raincoats and when he finished his meal he wandered down to the *'Cheshire Arms'* pub with which he immediately found an affinity. It was still an old-fashioned public house not modernised for the eating only fraternity but for drinkers with a local jazz band playing in the main room.

He had long been a convert to Hunter's favourite tipple and at the Bar, he ordered a pint of 'Stella' and as he slid his money over the bar, he said to the attractive blonde barmaid, 'I want to speak to Janis.'

She laughed, 'Which one? We have many Janis.'

'He shrugged, 'I don't know, I want job.'

'Oh! You want that Janis. He's not here. Maybe later.'

Williams picked up his drink and as he turned away, he said, '*Spasibo.*'

'You Russian,' she said.

'He put his drink on the bar and continued speaking Russian, '*Yes, I'm from Russia.*'

'*That is not Russian accent.*'

'*I'm from Crimea. We're still Russian.*'

'*Ooh! You run away from fighting?*'

'*Yes, I want money for my family. In Crimea, there is no work for Russians.*'

'*There is plenty of work here. Have you friends here?*'

'*I'm looking for friend he has a new raincoat. He'll help me get work.*'

'*That is Janis. Come back later or tomorrow.*'

'*Okay. What's your name?*'

'*Lani, what's yours?*'

'*Ivan, Ivan Andrejev.*'

'*I'll tell Janis you're looking for him.*'

He turned away from the bar and being right-handed he chose a seat in a corner where he was covered by a left-hand wall and where he could observe the comings and goings of the other patrons. He sat for a minute taking a few sips from his glass and then pulled a folded copy of a newspaper from his pocket and pretended to read while surveying the movements of the clientele but with no sign of Janis after half an hour he gave up. He sent Effie a quick message and called it a day.

—

Saturday

On Saturday morning after experiencing the sumptuous breakfast buffet they adopted their fluffy tourist attitude and with Hunter clutching the map made their way outside. The doorman called a taxi that whisked them away to the Krymskaya Embankment a recently converted four-lane highway on the South Bank of the river now a year-round park with Artist Studios, cafes and restaurants with facilities for both cyclists, pedestrians and dog walkers as the streets of Moscow weren't designed for animals.

At the Gorky Park end, they paid off the taxi. Wrapped up against the cutting October breeze with a blue scarf wrapped around Jacquie's neck, they began the leisurely walk along the kilometre-long attraction and were pleasantly surprised by the easy-going attitude and display of friendliness by the locals many of whom were young mothers wheeling pushchairs giving their offspring a relief from Moscow's eternal traffic overload.

Occasionally they stopped and pretended to look at the map and passing river traffic while surreptitiously checking for any obvious watchers of which they saw none but they didn't relax their stance of being 'in love' tourists. Halfway along they saw ahead of them a large triangular concrete bandstand low enough to sit on with steps at the back to drag up your instruments.

There was a hardy trio of modern jazz players with a small group of listeners around them but on one corner sat on his own with a Labrador dog on a short lead watching the river was Alexei Savitsky a man of medium build but showing a bit of weight around his middle since they had last met. Alongside him, he had his blue '*avos'ka.*'

Hunter and Jacquie ignored him while they surveyed the river and using his map Hunter pointed to different things and Jacquie appeared to be arguing with him and after a moment deliberating they walked across to Alexei and showing him the map they asked him directions.

Alexei gestured that they should sit down and taking the map from Hunter studied it and began pointing here and there at landmarks and while taking precautions that no one was in the line of sight and able to lip-read, he said, '*Dobroye utro*, Mr and Mrs Hunter.' Changing to English, he continued, 'It's a pleasure to see you after so long. How are you?'

'Enjoying the sights, Alexei, how goes it with you?'

'Old and bored. There is nothing to do here.'

Jacquie began fussing with the dog. 'What do you call him, Alexei?'

'*Pekc*, that's Rex in English. He belongs to a neighbour.'

She played and talked to Rex while Hunter enquired, 'What have you got, Alexei?'

'I've put the whole story inside your map but I simply overheard an old comrade talking in his alcoholic stupor about planting diversionary dirty bombs in England and America and I don't like it. I helped him home and in the taxi, he told me more but since then my comrad has disappeared and the FSB now watch me.'

'Okay, Alexei, hang on to that phone, I'll be in touch.'

Hunter stood up and took the map off Alexei and shook hands with him before helping Jacquie up and with a wave and a loud, 'Cheerio,' they went on their happy go lucky tourist way.

Within minutes, they were aware of someone following them as they made their way along the Embankment to the landing stage where they made a show of buying tickets and boarding the next tourist cruise along the River Moscva. They enjoyed the scenery but spent much of their time in the bar laughing and joking and drinking bubbly but consuming very little while Alexei's notes were transferred to a secret compartment in Jacquie's bag.

Saturday evening.

It was a dirty night with drizzly rain and Williams delayed his sortie into Bourn Street in the hope that those who wanted to come out would be out by nine-thirty only this time he walked the length of the road and ventured into the pub Hunter had used previously.

He wasn't impressed. He tried to engage the bar staff in conversation but was ignored even when he complained that his beer was mediocre, to say the least. After trying to connect with a few of the locals he pulled his hood up and moved onto the Supermarket and bought himself a can of beer and hung around the fringes of the small crowd gathered there.

Not a lot was said as they were more interested in sheltering from the weather when a tall guy hunched inside an expensive branded coat with his hood up and his hands stuffed deep into his pockets stepped back and bumped into him.

'*Vybachte!,*' he uttered, and as he turned to face Williams, he said in English, 'Sorry, are you okay?'

Williams patted him on the shoulder and keeping to his broken English, he said, 'Is okay, I must watch better...'

The rain had stopped and the man pushed his hood back to reveal a tall greying fifty-year-old man wearing underneath his coat a blue pinstriped business suit and there was a whiff of a familiar brand of aftershave, and he replied, 'You speak not so good English. Where are you from?'

Williams pushed his hood down and put his hand out and spoke in Russo Crimean, 'Ivan *Andrejev from Crimea?*'

The man shook William's hand and replied. 'Theodor Fabianski. You speak Russo Crimean, Ivan.'

'Yes, Theodor, I only want to work for my family not fighting and so I come to England where they say there is plenty. I have been told to look for a man called, Janis.'

'Did you vote for Russia to stay?'

'Yes, the Ukraine don't give work to us.'

'What do you do, Ivan?'

Williams had to think fast and chose the most common employment in modern times in the area where his wife came from. 'I work in I.T. in Dzankoy.'

'Up north. I know it and Ivan, I'm telling you, that Janis is no good. Come and have a beer and we talk.'

'Okay, Theodor.'

Williams turned towards the '*Cheshire Arms*' when Theodor stopped him and pointed in the opposite direction. 'Not that one, Ivan, come with me, this is a real English ale pub we are going to.'

They only walked a short distance when Fabianski pulled on William's sleeve, 'In here,' and he led them into a cosy snug in a genuine Olde English Pub.

Williams was surprised as he had walked the street a few times and never noticed the pub. It was an eighteenth-century building moulded into the other old buildings around it and inside the atmosphere was warm and you could feel the friendliness as you eased yourself to the bar.

'Ivan,' said Theodor, 'in here we speak English, okay? What will you have.'

'Stella.'

'Ivan! You must try the special beers. I'll pick one.'

The barmaid approached. 'Hello, Theodor, back again?'

'Yes, Julia, I want to introduce a friend to real beer. Two pints of Olde Speckled Hen, please.'

'Coming up.'

When they had their beer, they found a seat in the corner of the Bar and discarding their topcoats sat down and before they spoke they enjoyed their first taste of the renowned English Ale.

Williams put his glass down, and said, 'Wow, that is good, but it cool. I always think English beer is warm. Why we speak English?'

Theodor leaned towards him, 'Because it is polite in their country and you learn quicker. Tell me, Ivan, how did you get here?'

'In a lorry.'

'You're illegal?'

'Yes.'

'Are you married?'

'My wife, she died when they bomb Crimea.'

Theodor plucked a business card from his wallet but before he gave it to Williams he drew a criss-cross star on the back. 'This is a card for my agents.'

'Why you draw on the back?'

'They know my sign and will give you the best help. Go there but first, you must dress yourself better. Have you got money?'

'Only a little. I leave all for my Mother and Father.'

'You have somewhere to live, Ivan?'

'Yes, I have a room in Hoole.'

Theodor took out his wallet and peeled off some notes and offered them to Williams. 'Take this and you buy good shoes and not too expensive clothes from Marks and Spencer and after you have a haircut you go to my agent.'

'I cannot take money.'

'It's okay I have plenty and you can give it back when you're working.'

Williams took the money and estimated there was two hundred pounds. 'Thank you, Theodor, what you do?'

'This and that, Ivan.' He didn't expand and continued, 'Have you got a phone?'

'Yes.' Williams dragged his coat over and searched through the pockets until he unearthed an ageing 'Samsung Galaxy Note.' 'Here it is. I put English Sim card in.'

'Give me the number.'

'Why?'

'I am also a Russian voter from Sevastopol and we stay in touch in a foreign country and maybe I find you work.'

Williams fiddled with the phone and then read out a number and Theodor wrote it down on an old receipt.

'Thank you, Ivan, I'll be in touch. Do what I say and you will get a job in no time. Right now I have to go. I am meeting a friend.'

He got up from his seat and plucking his coat from the bench he threaded his way through the tables and made his way out leaving Williams to mull over what had happened and wondering what the consequences might be.

There was a couple of things that troubled Williams notwithstanding the money side of it. On impulse he counted to ten and followed Fabianski out. It was raining again and he flipped his hood over his head and looked up and down the street. He couldn't see Fabianski but his attention was drawn to a light coloured military-style raincoat approaching the Post Office.

Because the rain was heavier the groups had dwindled to a couple of hardy souls which gave him little option but to pretend he was sheltering from the weather. Hunched up with head down he crossed the street and took refuge in a shop doorway. He kept his head low enough to hide his face but still observe. His suspect drew level with the three guys outside the P.O. and he muttered a greeting and went straight to the ATM, withdrew some cash and set off back the way he had come.

Williams eased himself out of the doorway and shielding his

face with his hood and with his hands stuffed deep into his pockets he wandered across to the P.O. and followed at a discreet distance when suddenly he had to pick up his pace as his quarry turned down an alleyway. He reached the corner and cautiously looked around, but too late, the alley was empty.

Did he hang around or did he leave it? He decided to take a chance and check it out and he ventured into the passage. Twenty metres down on his left there was a door with the number 1A, which he took to be a sub flat of the main building and making a mental note he continued walking and a hundred metres further down the alleyway opened out into a rear access road for the houses and shops. Still no sign of the raincoat but as he followed the road around he saw parked in the back yard of the flats an old Audi A4 with a familiar number plate.

He continued until he came to a main road running through the local housing area but saw nothing untoward. He reckoned he had been close enough for his quarry to be in sight when he reached the alleyway and concluded that he must have gone into 1A.

Too late to do anything without concrete evidence. A raincoat was no reason to go knocking on doors and he wouldn't do it without backup. It was a job for the specialists and he called it into the 'Firm' as he walked back to his car.

They were quick to respond and on their instructions, he drove around to the access road at the rear of Bourn St. and parked in such a way that the whole of the alleyway was visible through the rear-view mirror and pretending to sleep he settled down for a long wait. It was not ideal as anybody with the slightest knowledge of undercover security would sus it but the best he could do in the circumstances. At least now they had eyes on a suspect.

It remained quiet and two hours later, he was relieved by the pro's of 'A' Branch of MI5 or the 'Watcher Service' recognised around the world as being the best in the business.

—

On Sunday morning, Williams called a meeting in Garden Centre №1 and was surprised when only Effie turned up.

'Where's Inspector Fearn, Sergeant?'

'What do I call you? Agent Williams or Ernesto? Anyway, I've been promoted, it's Inspector Newlove now and DCI Fearn has moved on to greater things.'

'Oops,' he said mentally, 'this isn't going well,' and then aloud, 'I'm sorry, I'm not up to date. I've had more serious things on my mind and, Yes, Inspector Newlove, I did mean DCI Fearn.'

'Fearn has taken up the vacant post of Superintendent in head office and I'm number two to Hunter.' She took a deep breath and as she breathed out she relaxed a little. 'Mr Williams, we got off to a bad start. Call me Effie and is it okay to call you, Duncan?'

'Thank goodness. Yes, Inspector Effie, you may and I'm sorry if I'm a bit clumsy. I usually work at the business end and leave all this to you know who but him being on holiday an all, you got me. Let me get the coffee. What's yours?'

When he came back with the drinks he congratulated Effie on her promotion and then told her all that had gone on over the weekend and that their suspect was now being looked after by the 'Watcher Service.' He neglected to tell her about Theodor and finished with, 'And I located a car with that reg you were on the lookout for but don't do anything yet.'

He pushed a folded page of A4 across the table.

'What's that?' she said.

'That's a list of call signs and agent incognitos of the MI5 guys. You notice that they use only initials and you can follow their movements on Band 6 on your radio. If you want to contact them, call their leader Alpha 1 or me, and Hunter when he comes back. They will keep you informed regarding 'BURBERRY' and the car.'

'Err... what's BURBERRY?'

'Oh, sorry, didn't I say. That's the code name given to our suspect. It may not come to anything or he may lead us somewhere like the guy who gave him the raincoat or bumped off Owen, who knows? He could be innocent and have bought a new coat but this one does stand out. It's in the wrong place if you get my meaning. They don't wear stuff like that in that part of town. BURBERRY is the coat connection. Do you have anything for us, Effie?

'No, we've no extra leads and because of a manpower shortage, we've given the legwork over to you lot. Hunter said before he left we must use code names. Do you know why?'

'I'm in the dark too, Effie, it seems that things took a step up from a police liaison to a full-blown security job in the middle of last week and I'll be the last to know but be ready to respond.'

'Well, if that's it, Ernesto,' she said with a smile, 'I'm off. I've got some paperwork to catch up on. How about you?'

He stood up and gathered his things, 'I've done my bit for now so I'm off home to see the kids. Take care, Inspector Effie.'

She could detect the humour in his voice and thought, 'He's been working with Hunter too long.'

Monday

Sunday morning aware of their 'watcher' Hunter and Jacquie kept up their fluffy tourist act. They went on guided Metro tours and other touristy things organised by the hotel. On the Monday morning they went to the GUM store to buy Lesley's Matryoshka stacking dolls and on a whim, Hunter bought Iain a book by a Russian scientist translated into English called '*Non-dual perspectives on Quantum Physics.*'

'That should keep him quiet,' Hunter remarked, 'although I suspect it's more or less the same as Mr Hawkins.'

He had read Hawkins books when Iain had first shown an interest and concluded that Quantum Physics was ordinary physics applying Murphy's Law.

On time, the Lingo taxi picked them up and whisked them away to the airport and although there was a 'watcher' with them right up to Passport control they were not held up and their BA flight took off on time allowing Hunter the first genuine opportunity to study Alexei's notes.

He gave them to Jacquie, and said, 'This is serious. I think we need to get Alexei out of there.'

Jacquie studied the notes and replied, 'How much do you know already, Hunter?'

'Not enough. It looks like Owen was onto something and we've had to cover two murders since. The damn fool should have reported this from day one.'

He sat silently contemplating and at the precise moment the

flight attendant placed his meal in front of him he uttered aloud, 'Jeezus!'

The attendant jumped back in surprise and knocked over Jacquie's wine. Hunter jerked back in his seat and his hands came up in a position of surrender and he stuttered apologetically, 'I'm... Err... I'm... I'm sorry. Oh Hell!' He looked appealingly at the attendant, 'I'm sorry, I was having a Eureka moment. There's nothing wrong—honest!'

Jacquie gave him a quick elbow. 'Hunter—shut up!' and to the attendant, she said, 'I can't take him anywhere.'

The attendant laid a consoling hand on Jacquie's shoulder. 'It's alright. We get worse. I just hope his ideas are practical. Give me a moment to clear it up and I'll get you another drink.'

'Thank you,' said Jacquie, 'much appreciated,' she turned to Hunter, 'That's going to cost you.'

Minutes later after it had all calmed down Jacquie leaned towards Hunter, and said quietly, 'What was it?'

Hunter bent his head towards her, 'Owen! He's a double agent. That Ukraine passport is genuine.'

'Why would they kill him?'

'They sussed him.'

'The Ukes are anti-Russian aren't they?'

'Jacquie, you're right. He was a Uke sleeper and he latched onto a Russian plot. What do you think?'

'I think you're onto something, Hunter, but do show a little less enthusiasm at your age.'

He patted her hand, 'I'm sorry. It was one of those reality moments. I'd give you a kiss but for the audience.'

'You can make up for it later.'

~~~~~~

Chapter 8

Manhandling a lead-lined coffin up a flight of slippery wooden steps onto the landing stage at *Mulheim am Main* attention was quite a feat for the three men and a woman reception committee. They managed it without too much fuss and within minutes had it hidden inside the UK registered Bessacar E660 campervan where they quickly stripped off the coffin outer woodwork to reveal two leather suitcases that were lead-lined to prevent Geiger counter detection.

They manoeuvred them into the storage space below the double bed and surrounded them with extra blankets and duvets to hide them from anything but the most rigorous inspections. Matt and Maria Dewey formerly Rogov allegedly from Aldermaston shook hands with their two helpers and watched as they sped upriver in the inflatable boat.

It was getting late and they programmed the Satnav for the pre-booked camping site in Thionville, France and set off on the long circuitous journey which would take them to their fantasy home in the U.K. They survived the rush hour traffic around Mulheim and were waved through the France - Germany border control and after four hours travelling they turned off the Motorway and made their way north to the Camp Moselle on the outskirts of Thionville.

It was after dark when they arrived but the lady on reception made them welcome and directed them to the hard-standing site they had been allocated and after giving them directions into the town left them to it.

Half an hour later they took a pleasant walk along the river and made their way into the town to sample the bars and restaurants like the pretend tourists they were.

A little after nine o'clock the next morning they set off again and after suffering long delays on the Paris circular a little over eight hours later they made it to Rennes and because the ferry from Roscoff was late the next evening like good tourists they took advantage of the local night life. Shopping in Rennes took up most of the next day and just after tea they set off on the hours drive to Roscoff to catch the overnight ferry to Cork.

The thirteen-hour crossing was uneventful and they disembarked in Cork a little after ten a.m. where they were questioned about their route. Their explanation that they were on a circular tour of Europe starting in England was viewed with dubious looks and a discussion and a search of the vehicle was ordered.

Matt handed over the keys and they stood and watched while two officers searched through the vehicle. After two minutes one of the officers called Matt and asked for the code of the combination lock on the bedroom storage compartment.

'I can't give you that,' said Matt, 'but I'll do it for you.'

The officer watched as Matt twiddled the dials on the combination lock. It clicked open and Matt was signalled to step back. He did so and the officer lifted the lid and ran his hand inside and ruffled the top duvet and then closed it again before he stood up, and said, 'Carry on, Mr Dewey. Sorry about the holdup. We were tipped off about a camper van smuggling immigrants but you're good to go.'

Matt locked up while Maria collected the passports and they drove off the docks not quite singing but feeling quite euphoric after the pangs they suffered earlier. Satnav switched on they made their way to the M8 and on to the Camac Tourist Camping site on the outskirts of Dublin where they again engaged in frivolity paid for from the back-hander they had received for the job in hand.

At midnight a BMW MINI Countryman pulled up by the motor home and one of the cases was loaded into the back and minutes later it set off for Shannon.

—

Tuesday morning

Gus Thomas dropped the file onto his desk and looked across at Hunter and Jacquie. 'It's all Russian to me, Hunter. What's it about?'

'It outlines a plot that Savitsky overheard from an alcoholic old comrade who was an ex-Moscow Police Chief and who has been abducted by the FSB. Since that time he is being watched.'

Thomas picked the papers up again, and continued, 'On receipt of your message we've already ramped this up to an AMBER job and if these are anything to go by it will soon be RED. Do you think there's anything to it?'

'Yes, Gus. We know Savitsky and he is solidly Russian so it would take a lot for him to betray his own.'

'You don't think he's a plant?'

'No, and when you tie it to what's gone on here with Owen etc... You can see the link...'

'Hunter did, right in the middle of lunch,' chipped in Jacquie, 'but we won't go there.'

'Okay, Hunter, I'll get these papers translated before I hand them over to 'C'. Are you fixed up for tonight?'

Hunter had already made copies and sent them on to Tanya so he nodded his affirmation, 'Yes, we're going home but one more thing, Gus. I think we should get Savitsky out of there.'

'Why's that?'

'The Russians aren't keen on treason especially from an ex-police Inspector and if he's found out it's curtains for him and his family.'

'I'll pass it on and while we're here—Welcome back, Jacquie. Are you sure you wouldn't like to return full time?'

'I've too much on my plate already...' she hooked a thumb at Hunter. '...what, with him and two kids...' she shook her head, '...no chance.'

—

Wednesday Morning

Hunter gave Williams the once over and was surprised to see him with a short haircut and trimmed beard in a smart office type shirt with a polo neck sweater over newly washed and pressed jeans and he couldn't help but frown when he saw the smart office-type shoes although he wasn't a fan of the light tan look.

'Must be turning a new leaf,' he thought.'

He, Duncan and Agent Dan Walker the leader of the 'A' team watchers, were sat facing the whiteboard and Effie was stood alongside it twiddling her marker while she waited for the team to sort themselves out. She decided enough was enough and she gave a loud cough and when she finally had their attention she said, 'Morning, gentlemen, have we anything to add besides the update I had from Agent Ernesto over the weekend?'Walker raised a hand and Effie responded, 'Mr Walker isn't it or do I call you, Alpha 1?'

'It's Dan Walker, Inspector, but please, in the present company call me Dan.'

'What have you for us, Dan, and call me Effie.'

Walker hesitated and half turned and nodded towards Fiona who was quietly going about her business at the back of the room, before he said, 'I think, Effie, this should be kept in-house.'

'One minute, Dan.'

Effie walked down the room and spoke quietly to Fiona who nodded the affirmative and scooped up her things and acknowledging the team she left the room.

Back at the board, Effie said, 'Carry on, Dan.'

'Well, Effie, since we took over from Agent Ernesto in the early hours of Sunday morning we have monitored that flat in Bourn Street and I'm sorry to say that we have nothing to report. There has been no sight of BURBERRY or anyone else coming or going. As for the car, we have that tagged and it hasn't moved.'

'By tagged you mean GPS?'

'That plus a hidden mic and camera.'

Hunter chipped in, 'You're still on it though?'

'Yep!'

'Effie! Dan! With no progress for sixty hours, I think it's time we made a move. Effie, can you organise a raiding party asap, and Dan—as soon as they move in you can stand your team down. Any problems?'

They looked at each other in turn and all agreed that all was okay and Hunter gave it the nod. 'Right, let's go!'

Dan went to the other side of the room and started talking into his shirt collar in low tones while Hunter walked over to Effie. 'I've got a few calls to make so let me know when you're ready. Williams has a dental appointment so he won't be coming, and Effie?'

'Yes, Hunter.'

'Just blues, no sirens.'

'Thanks, Hunter. I'll get things on the move.'

———

Hunter stuck close to the tail of the last vehicle in the Police convoy as they made their way to Bourn Street. At the junction by the bottom of Railway bridge two police cars and a mini-bus went straight ahead to come in by the access road at the rear while Hunter followed Effie and her two CID compatriots one of whom was DC Farmer down Bourn St. and pulled up at the entrance to the alley. He ignored the double yellows and followed Effie down the alley and hung back while the uniform did their stuff.

The unseen 'A' team watchers melted away while a six-foot-six bulky constable all of two hundred pounds used his body mass and a metal battering ram to hammer the door. Four blows, two to each hinge was all it took and he stood back to let the team in. He dropped the battering ram and pulled out a hand-gun and followed his colleagues.

Outside they heard two shouts, 'Clear! Clear!,' and moments later they were repeated and then silence. Hunter said under his breath, 'That doesn't sound good.'

They waited and after a couple of minutes, the Uniform Inspector in charge came out and spoke to Effie who in turn called Hunter forward.

Being on the job he called her by her rank. 'Yes, Inspector?'

'It's turned into a crime scene, Hunter. We have a body. Give them a few minutes to tape it off and we'll go and have a look. SOCO and the Path Lab have been called. Meanwhile, Farmer can look over the car around the back.'

They hung around and fifteen minutes later the Uniform Inspector came over and ignoring Hunter, said to Effie, 'We're clear to go, Inspector Newlove. Put your stuff on and follow me and don't touch anything.'

Effie gave him a look to kill, and said, 'I know the drill and while I'm at it let me introduce Agent Hunter, Field controller of MI6. It's their case. Give them all the help you can.'

The Inspector covered his mouth and coughed slightly with embarrassment as he spoke to Hunter. 'I'm sorry, sir, I... I didn't know. Have you got gloves etc...?'

'You're okay, I'll pinch some off the Inspector here. Thanks anyway.'

'You're welcome.'

He took the proffered articles off Effie and when they got to the door of Flat 1A they put them on and followed the uniform upstairs making sure to stay in the middle although clomping size tens had earlier run up them with complete disregard and only one intent on their minds.

At the living room door, they could smell the odours of early decomposition and the uniform held his arm out and told them to tread carefully as they circulated and when they were level with the table he pointed down. One of the dining chairs was lying on its side. Wedged between it and the sofa was the body of swarthy Caucasian male wearing white trainers with a pool of dried blood staining the threadbare carpet. Under the table close to the body was a glass and an empty bottle of vodka the contents having poured out over the carpet.

Hunter glanced around the room and saw the trench coat hanging on a hook behind the door and nodding in the direction of the body, he said, 'That explains the three days inaction but Williams said he was watching the flat and saw no one leave.'

There was a knock on the door and Doctor Kerr stepped in. 'What have we got?...' Effie pointed to the body, '...I thought so, I could smell it. I'm sorry folks I'll have to ask you to leave. I'll call you when the team is done.'

'Doc,' said Hunter, 'can you take a quick look and give us an idea.'

'Wait outside.'

They filed out and Hunter stopped and sniffed. Was there a mild smell of cinnamon and citrus in the air? He shrugged and thought nothing of it and stood in the small hallway with the others. The Uniform Inspector said, 'Goodbye,' and left them to it.

It didn't take Kerr long and three minutes later he poked his head around the door. Attracting their attention with a small cough, he said, 'Primary cause of death was a 9mm calibre bullet in the back of the skull and because of the lack of powder marks probably fitted with a silencer and the fatal shot I think was too precise to be any further away than two feet.'

'And the time of death, Doc,' said Hunter.

'At first guess, I'd say a minimum of forty-eight hours. I'll know more when I get back to the lab. One more thing.' He held up an evidence bag and in it was a ten-centimetre long thin metal spike

with a removable wooden handle of the type used on engineering
files or screwdrivers. 'The vic was holding this in his right hand out
of sight underneath him.'

Effie took the bag off him and Doctor Kerr disappeared back
into the room before another query could come his way. Hunter said
to Effie, 'Was the tele on when your lot went in, he was facing that
way.'

'I don't know, Hunter, but I don't think the TV was his priority
with this clutched in his hand. I'll find out when we get back for the
de-brief. Is it important?'

'I'm not sure. Was he being quizzed and then shot or was it a
casual walk behind job and done without his knowledge? The
position of the shot suggests an execution but that weapon does
suggest he was getting ready to defend himself and there was only
one glass.'

'One may have been taken to remove DNA evidence, Hunter.
Whatever, we won't know any more until SOCO and the Doc have
finished. Let's go and see what Farmer has found.'

Outside Hunter took a deep breath and puffing his cheeks blew
it out again loudly. 'Thank goodness for that. The smell was getting
a bit much in there. I don't know how those guys do it.'

Effie laughed. 'You're getting old, Hunter. They get used to it.'

They walked together side by side down the alleyway and when
Hunter glanced at Effie who in her heels was level with him he
instinctively pulled his shoulders back, stomach in and stretched to
his full height, and said mentally, 'Behave yourself, Hunter, you're
old enough to be her Dad.'

They got to the back entrance of the supermarket as DC Farmer
was stepping back from the car and he wandered over to join them
and nodding towards the car, he said, 'It looks promising. There are
signs of blood in the boot. We'll know more when the SOCO boys
have done. We're waiting for a pick-up truck to take it away.
Anything indoors?'

'We have a body, go and have a quick look and report back.'

When Farmer rejoined them, he said, 'That's BURBERRY,
boss. It fits the description left by your man and the coat and trainers
say it all.'

'We're going back to base,' said Hunter, 'join us.'

Back on the street, Effie climbed into her Jeep, wound the window down, and Hunter said. 'This has gone 'Code Red' now, Effie. Keep it close.'

'Roger that. I'll see you at base. Do you need a blue light?'

'No thanks, I'll use our Steel Badge protocol if I'm in a hurry.'

'What's that?'

'You don't want to know but it does your insurance no good.'

She slid the window up and manoeuvred into the traffic and Hunter followed.

Alerted to the police activity Fabianski walked down the street and into the English Cafe opposite where he ordered a pot of tea and took a window seat and with an i-pad set on camera he lifted the net curtain and at the same time as he took pictures he made notes.

The proprietor, a grey-haired lady wearing a pristine pinafore came over, and said crossly, 'Excuse me, sir, what are you doing? Leave my curtains alone. If you want pictures go outside.'

'Oh! I'm very sorry. I work for the local newspaper, you know, the Chester Chronicle, and I want to get the story before the big boys.'

'All very well,' she said, 'but I want to maintain standards so leave the curtains be. Is that another pot of tea you want?'

'Oh, err... Yes, that will do nicely, thank you.'

He maintained a watch long enough to sneak a few more photos and to drink two pots of tea and see who was talking to who while making a note of vehicle numbers. The tall guy in the VW Golf and the tall blonde in the Jeep appeared to be the centre of attention.

Back at the Blacon base Effie and Hunter stood looking at the whiteboard and after scribbling a few notes Effie stepped back and using the Americanisation that had crept into MI6 terminology while MI5 still used the more familiar English terms, she said, 'Now that things have gone 'Code Red' in your words. How are we going to play this, Hunter?'

Hunter paused for a brief moment before he answered and then as if he had made a snap decision, he said, 'Very much like we are now, Effie. I want you to pursue the local incidents like it was your case. Collect what evidence you can while I concentrate on the wider issue presented to us.'

'Hunter? What happened to make this a Code Red?'

'Effie? What is said in this room stays in the room, okay?'

'Yes.'

'One moment.'

He walked over to Fiona who was beavering away collecting details for the next media release and he dropped a five-pound note onto her desk. 'Get yourself a coffee or something, lass,' he said, 'take your phone and I'll call you when it's okay.'

She smiled up at him. 'Thank you, Mr Hunter. Chucked out twice, I'll have to change my perfume.'

He patted her on the shoulder. 'Keep up the good work, lass, it's nothing personal.' As she grabbed her jacket off the back of the chair he rejoined Effie. 'Now where were we?'

'Code Red?'

'Ah, yes, that. The 'Firm' have had info from our Cousins over the pond that Japanese security have knowledge of Russians making enquiries about field nuclear devices and we have reliable facts from a Russian contact about a plot to use dirty bombs sometime in the future both here and in the U.S.'

'What are dirty bombs, Hunter?'

'It's an RDD. That is a radiological dispersion device. A mixture of conventional explosive that is used to spread radioactive material over a large area but without the mass destruction of a nuclear bomb. It's sometimes called a Weapon of Mass Disruption. Its primary purpose is area denial to the civilian population and the panic it would cause not to mention the economic damage which would be considerable. Death by contamination would be very small and after a year ineffective and a lot depends on which way the wind blows on detonation.'

'So what's the point?'

'Distraction is my guess. While everybody is looking into the why's and wherefores somebody else is using the turmoil to achieve their purpose.'

'I see, but why here?'

'I can't expand on that, Effie. We don't yet know where or how or even if it's a fact but we do know that it hinges around Owen.'

'So you think he was silenced because he knew too much and might have said something to Bonar during their fling?'

'Yes, Effie, but this latest one puts another twist to the saga.'

'Like what?'

'It may seem a bit presumptuous, but who killed the killer?'

'Aah! I see.'

'Keep that quiet, treat this as an associated murder without the dirty bomb factor but I'll keep you informed.'

'Thanks, Hunter, I'll call Fiona.'

She put her phone down and sat on the end of her desk looking at the board. 'What did Williams tell you, Hunter? I've not had a chance to speak with him.'

Hunter repeated what Williams had said about his movements over the weekend, '...and now you know as much as me, Effie.'

'Thanks for that, Hunter, do I tell DC Farmer?'

'No, Effie, he's probably wild on social media and the fewer people that know the better.

'Got that.'

Hunter's phone buzzed and he fished the device from his pocket. He glanced at it and saw it was Gus Thomas, and said, 'Sorry, Effie, gotta take this.'

As he began walking to the other end of the room he slid his finger up the answer symbol and acknowledged his Boss. 'Hello, Gus, what can I do for you?'

'Where's Williams, Hunter, his phone's off.'

'That's contrary to orders, Gus. He left us downtown saying he had a dental appointment. Why?'

'Get hold of him, we're short of a blind courier to meet up with Savitsky so we want him back on the job in Moscow asap.'

'Okay, Gus, I'll chase him up.' He snatched his jacket up from his chair and called to Effie. 'Effie! Put an all-points call out for Williams and bring him in.'

She waved a hand in acknowledgement, 'Okay, Hunter, I'm on it.'

—

Outside the Dentist trying to rub some life into a frozen jaw, Williams looked up and down the alleyway and mentally tossed a coin and enjoying the new smart Ernesto he decided to take the passage leading through the Rows and down into Eastgate and the shopping centre.

You can only drink so much coffee and bored with window shopping he made his way on foot towards Bourn Street where a decent pint of lager awaited and a chance to integrate into the Slavic community but his plans were thwarted as he prepared to cross the City circular and into Bourn Street proper. A police car with blues flashing braked hard and the door flung open and a voice shouted, 'Agent Ernesto! Get in, you're wanted.'

—

General Josef Bazarov stood up and walked around his desk as Nicolai Arapov entered the room. They met with the customary Russian embrace before Josef said, 'Join me, Nicolai, I am prepared.'

He turned and picked up two glasses of vodka and they raised them with vigour, and said together, *'Zazdarovje!'*

Niceties over Josef returned behind the desk and Nicolai pulled up a chair undid his briefcase and pulled out an A4 envelope from which he tipped a collection of photographs across the desk. 'These arrived this morning from the Propaganda department and I thought you should see them before we send them out to the media.'

Josef started sorting through them occasionally holding one up to the light and he used a magnifying glass on one and studied it closer. 'Are those the International nuclear symbols I see, Nicolai?'

'Yes, comrad, they are.'

'And the other writing on the label, is that Korean?'

'It is.'

'And these troops lugging these packs around, are they Ukrainian?'

'No, we enlisted the aid of our Infantry fighting in the Ukraine conflict and manufactured the uniforms ourselves but as you see the pictures are blurred as if taken discreetly from a distance except for the labels and there we zoomed in of course like you do.'

'And they were allegedly taken by our special forces?'

'And drones.'

'I see, very good. You have the bumf that goes with them?'

'It is all prepared and we will release all this on the social media after the diversionary event in the U.K. and USA.'

'Good, work, Comrad. I will keep these. Now I have an interesting request from Comrads Zablonsky and Ponomarev.' He opened a drawer and took out a handful of photos and gave them to Nicolai. 'These came in from our man on the ground in the U.K. and he wants to know if we have them on our books. Pass them on to our friends in the FSB and your Propaganda department and see if we can trace them.'

'Are they involved?'

'Things are not going to plan over there and our man is having to reorganise and recruit a new team of helpers.' He picked up one of the photos and pointed at two of the characters. 'We're interested in this man and woman in particular.'

'I'll get on to it right away. What about the progress of our delicacies?'

'The U.K. package is on track and currently in Ireland making its way towards the Northern Irish border but the U.S. is proving awkward.'

'In what way, Comrad Josef?'

'Getting it onto a flight for the U.S.'

'Can we not go via Canada? The border checks are minimal between the States and Canada. A bit like the Irish borders and the U.K..'

'A good concept, Comrad Nicolai. I'll have Zablonsky and Ponomarev work on that and see what Kryuchkov can come up with. His connection with arms smuggling may help there.'

'Better still, Josef, send both packages to England and then ship the U.S. one from there from an obscure airfield and you won't have the bother of loading in Shannon only refuelling and doing U.S. immigration paperwork. No one will notice which will save you hours waiting on the Canadian border.'

'You're wasted, Nicolai.' He picked up his i-phone. 'Wait one moment while I speak to Comrads Yuri and Yakov.' After a two minute conversation, he put the phone down. 'Nicolai, you will work with Zablonsky and Ponomarev and comrad Kryuchkov. Outline your plan and then get propaganda services to give you the paperwork. Now I must get on. Goodbye, Nicolai.'

They stood up simultaneously and shook hands before Nicolai did a smart about turn and left the room.

—

Nicolai, Zablonsky, Ponomarev and Kryuchkov sat clustered around a desk in a back office of the FSB Headquarters. In attendance was an FSB Agent who preferred to stand as he pointed to an array of photographs spread around the desk but in particular to the one in the middle.

'For this one,' he said, 'we had to go back into cold war KGB records. He is, was, a retired fieldman for MI6 called George Hunter middle name Barrington and our GCHQ contact confirms he has been brought in as temporary local controller to link up with the police in their investigations. The woman is a Detective Inspector from the police investigating the associated crimes.'

Ponomarev chipped in. 'Does this mean they're on to us?'

Nicolai stepped in before the conversation went further. 'This calls for a discussion.' He stood up and walked around to the FSB man and took him by the arm and began leading him to the door. 'Thank you, Comrad, for all you've done. We will take it from here. Give our acknowledgements to your staff.' He shook the man's hand and held the door open for him. The message was clear and the man left before Nicolai returned to the desk. 'Collect your things, Comrads, we must speak to our Leader and find out the reason why all this has come to our attention. Like you, I'm worried that we may be blown. Why are MI6 in that area?'

The Skoda Octavia was waiting and whisked them the twenty kilometres across the Moskva to the villa in Zhukovka. General Josef Bazarov was waiting and the traditional vodka was welcome before he asked them to sit at the long polished table.

'Right, Comrads, I understand you have some concerns, tell me.'

Nicolai who had been nominated as spokesman said, 'Comrad General, it has come to our notice that MI6 are in attendance near our primary U.K. target. We cannot plan further until we know why. Are they on to us?'

Bazarov raised a hand palm outwards towards them. 'Comrads, be calm. What has happened will not interfere with our plans. MI6 are helping the local police because a GCHQ operative was found murdered in that town. That is all.'

'Is this a coincidence?'

'Yes and no. My informant tells me that the GCHQ man was acting on his own. He had suspicions about our man on the ground when he worked in the Aldermaston branch of the 'October Legion' and when he moved up to our target area as part of his investigations he was silenced. It did get a little out of hand but that has now been suppressed but our man has to recruit a new team so a slight delay.' There was an audible sigh around the table at the same time the i-phone on the desk pinged which Bazarov ignored, and he continued, 'Comrad, Nicolai?'

'Comrad General.'

'Have you made progress with your suggestions?'

'We have and on Comrad Kryuchkov's advice, we are going to use his Mafia smuggling outlets. It was suggested that the package could be dropped offshore and picked up by local fishermen but this activity is mostly on the West coast for drugs shipped from Columbia and difficult to organise so we have determined that his other suggestion is the best.'

'And that is?'

'Disguise the package in an air ambulance taking a chronically sick person or child back to his, her, home state and the only delay at this moment is finding a patient and forging the appropriate documents.'

'Will they not query why we are going via Canada. Why not fly directly?'

'A reaction to low pressure will affect the patient.'

'Well done, Comrad Nicolai. In fact, "well done!" all of you. Push the packages onward and hopefully, we will get a solution by the time they are in the U.K. That's it. Good day, Comrads.'

They all stood and Zablonsky, Ponomarev, Nicolai and Kryuchkov acknowledged their leader and left. As the door closed behind them General Bazarov picked up the i-phone and checked the message and immediately made a call. It was answered on the second buzz and standing to attention he spoke quietly into the phone. '*Gaspadin, Nachal'nik.* '

He immediately took a deep breath and blew it out noisily as the reprimand came into his ear and he apologised instantly, '*Ya prosha proshcheniya.* I must remember to put this ageing brain in gear before I speak. How can I help?...' he listened for a few seconds before continuing, '...it is going very well. We have come up with a new plan for the U.S. which will delay us for a few days but otherwise as the Americans say—ay Okay!'

There was a short rapid response and feeling ill at ease addressing his senior in a friendly manner and not with the Russian formalities he was used to, he said, 'I think you can begin moving things anytime.'

Two seconds later with a sigh of relief, he slid his finger up the 'Off app' and dropped the phone on his desk before reaching for the vodka bottle and slumping into his chair. 'I'm too old for this,' he muttered.

———

That same night the BMW MINI Countryman returned to the Camac Tourist Camping site outside Dublin and the heavy package was transferred back to the campervan ready for its onward journey.

~~~~~~~

Chapter 9

When Alexei came out of the bottle shop carrying his Vodka in the blue mesh *avos'ka* he was confronted by a down at heel bearded old soldier well wrapped up with a scruffy blue scarf around his neck and holding his hand out asking for small change. Alexei wasn't prepared but the man was wearing a blue scarf as he had been warned and always the sucker for ageing veterans he offered some cash.

The man grasped his hand, shook it, and said gruffly, '*Spasibo, priyatel', spryach'te eto.*'

(English, 'Thanks, buddy, hide this.')

Alexei felt something slide through his hand and up his sleeve and using both hands he continued to robustly shake the old soldier's hand and answered so that anyone could hear, 'Take care, comrad, and the best of luck for the future.'

Bowing his head and mumbling to himself the old soldier walked unsteadily away and Williams thought he should qualify for the part of *Tvye* in *'Fiddler on the Roof'* after that.

It was difficult for Alexei to concentrate and do nothing that would alert his watcher but he continued with his shopping in plain sight before making his way home and it was only when he was indoors that he pulled a rolled-up envelope from his sleeve, excused himself and retired to the bedroom.

He closed the door behind him and with shaking hands he eased the envelope open and took out the contents and spread them on the bed before he sat down and perused them one at a time.

After five minutes reading, he sat back and wondered how he was going to explain this to Malika. 'Did she want to leave Russia and would she be able to keep up the pretence?'

Malika disturbed his thoughts as she pushed her way in. 'What are you doing, Alexei? Why are you hiding and what are those papers?'

He wasn't sure how to approach the matter and stuttered

slightly, 'I... err... Oh, Hell, they want us to leave Russia for our own safety.'

'Who does?'

'The English.'

'Why? Alexei—what have you done?'

He stood up and placed his hands on her shoulders and looked her directly in the eyes. 'Malika, I had a drunken conversation with a comrad about a plot to send nuclear bombs to England and America and I didn't like it so I passed the information to my old English friend from many years ago and now we are being followed by the FSB.'

'Have they found out what you did?'

'No, but my drunk comrad has gone missing and since then they follow me.'

'The rumour must be true then. They are plotting bombs do you think?'

'Yes, there would not be such security over mere drunken babble.'

'What must we do?'

'Prepare to go on a weekend trip to St. Petersburg next week. Carry on as normal so that everyone knows but we won't be coming back. Only pack clothes for a weekend and there are instructions to meet and identify a courier at Vnukovo airport when we leave. From there I don't know and what we don't know we can't tell. Are you okay with that?'

Malika stood on her tiptoes and kissed him. 'Alexei, I want peace and if what you did saves the world I am behind you. What will be, will be. What's England like?'

'I was there on MUR business and I didn't really meet the people but I have a good friend there and he will guide us.'

'Alexei, put that stuff away and come and get your dinner and I have to plan what I need to take but I shall miss all this.'

He gave her a squeeze and kissed her on the forehead. 'I love you, Malika.'

———

Matt & Maria Dewey showed little concern for urgency making up for their disturbed sleep by lying in until ten o'clock and taking their shower before strolling over to the site restaurant for a late breakfast. There was time to do some washing and then they took a taxi and made their way into Dublin for some window-shopping and some light refreshment. They had their evening meal in the site restaurant and at eight o' clock they set off for their trip up to Belfast.

They followed the ring road around Dublin to the M1 which would take them through the border with Northern Ireland and onto the A1 main road into Belfast and the ferry port where they had time to spare before the last ferry over to the Scottish port of Cairnryan.

The weather was fair and they landed on time at one-thirty in the morning when checks were more courteous than curious and they were soon on the short drive to the Caravan Park where arrangements had been made for their late arrival.

—

Hunter and Effie stood on either side of Dr Kerr looking through the windows separating them from the main forensic Lab were laid out covered by a sheet was the body of Janis Ragozin.

Hunter was the first to speak, 'What have we got, Doc?'

'An Eastern Caucasian male and the primary cause of his demise as you know was a bullet in the back of his skull. We're waiting for forensics to come up with the make.

I put him in his mid-fifties and he's been through the wars as he has many scars and one of them is definitely a bullet wound. He has a tattoo similar to our man Owen. That is a Ukrainian trident the national symbol. However, this one is newish. I mean it was only done this year.'

There was a light knock on the door and they paused as Mark Chapman the SOCO Unit manager entered the room and joined them.

'Sorry I'm late,' he said, 'but criminals are very inconsiderate and don't keep to timetables.'

'Don't worry, Mark, we have the same problem and have only just started. You've met Inspector Newlove. Let me introduce MI6 Agent Hunter whose running this case jointly with the Inspector.'

Hunter and Chapman shook hands and Hunter said, 'Morning, Mark, what have you got for us?'

'My, my, you don't waste time do you, Mr Hunter?' He put his briefcase on the table and withdrew a sheaf of papers and after a moment checking them he continued, 'Our vic over there,' he said nodding out into the lab, 'we can only identify as Janis Ragozin from his driving licence and from the Border Agency who says he is Ukrainian but I have my suspicions. Any other identifying papers were removed from the flat. Passport etc... We have sent his DNA, photo and the Border Agency details to the Ukrainian authorities to see if they can help.' He turned towards Effie. 'Have you anything to add to that, Inspector?'

Effie flicked open her notebook. 'What we learned from his landlord who is Polish confirms that but he did say that he's sure he heard him arguing in Russian.'

Hunter who was writing all this down chipped in, 'All the Slavic languages sound similar. Did he say who with, Effie?'

'No, but we'll follow that up. Anything else, Mark?'

'The blood in his car we have identified from the DNA as Owens and also material off that raincoat which is also Owens. DNA off that cigarette butt from Bonar's place matches Ragozin.

'That confirms our multiple killer. Was there anything in the flat to suggest who killed him, Mark?'

'None whatever! Whoever it was, did a thorough job in the short time they had. I'd say they came prepared and probably wore gloves.'

'Nothing on the vodka bottle?'

'Only Ragozin's fingerprints.'

'Phone.'

'Nothing. They are pulling up the floorboards as we speak.'

Hunter looked at Effie and shrugged. 'There's not much we can do here, Effie, I'll see you back at base.' He picked up his coat and briefcase. 'Mark, Doc—Thanks! I'm going to confer with the 'Firm' and I'll be in touch.'

———

Hunter threw his pen onto the table alongside his notebook and leaned back in his chair and surveyed the greenery out in the *Garden Centre* №1 as he spoke to Gus Thomas on his i-phone. 'And that's it, Gus. The police are continuing their investigation but we've come to a dead end. Can't you grab a couple of eleven-year-olds off the street to crack Owen's computers, they'll do it in no time.'

Gus sighed while he continued his doodling and it was a few seconds before he answered. 'Hunter, are you thinking like me that whoever did this latest killing has wiped out a cell? Plugged a leak so to speak?'

'It did occur to me, Gus. I'm guessing that now they may have to employ some new faces...'

'...Hold the line, Hunter,' said Gus, 'I've got a message coming in from the Ukraine security in Kiev. I'll get back to you asap.'

Hunter held the phone away from him and was left looking at a flashing red phone symbol which he immediately swiped. 'Hold the line, he says and hangs up. He's getting old.'

He put the phone down and stood up and after a quick stretch he made to go and get himself a coffee but before he could move he was anticipated by Jacquie walking towards him with a loaded tray.

'Too late, Hunter, I'm mind reading.' She put the tray down and ignoring onlookers she gave him a peck on the cheek. 'Okay, tell me how it is,' she said plonking herself down opposite him and sharing the coffee out.

Hunter shook his head. 'I dunno,' he said, 'What? with Gus in London and you here, a man can't win.'

Jacquie, her eyes laughing leaned forward and rested her chin on her hands and she smiled in the way that turned him to jelly since the day they first met. 'You don't like my company?'

'Err...' He flushed slightly and screwed his face up and to save himself he picked up his coffee and took a sip. 'You're evil,' he said, 'It's a good job there's a crowd around as it is you'll have to wait 'til I get home.'

She laughed, 'Promises! Promises! Now tell me all about it.'

He filled her in on the latest developments, and finished, '...Gus and I are both thinking on the same lines, that whoever did this latest killing has closed down a leaky cell.'

His phone rang out with that distinctive tone from phones long gone. He picked it up, swiped the app, and said, 'Yes, Gus?'

'Hunter, the bad news is, Ragozin doesn't exist. He was a fake. The real Janis Ragozin died thirty years ago.'

'And the good news, Gus?'

'Owen is Andriy Ivaskin. He's one of theirs and was working undercover. The latest info they had was that he had uncovered a Russian cell.'

'And they never told us?'

'That's right. There's going to be repercussions but they have acknowledged their *faux pa* and are sending a specialist to help with Owen's computers.'

'Well, that's something. Gus! Before you snatched Williams away he said he had made a contact in the local Eastern European community here. When can we have him back? His language skills besides anything else are a big help?'

'I'm coming to that, Hunter...' Hunter felt Jacquie touch his free hand and looked up and she signalled she would have to go. She blew him a kiss and stood up as Gus continued, '...we are extricating Savitsky this weekend and I want you to meet and greet at Paris Charles Le Gaulle Airport so get yourself down here asap. After that, you get Williams who is on the job from the Moscow end.'

Hunter's shoulders visibly drooped as his plans for the weekend were dashed. He had promised Iain again to come to his rugby and was taking the family out to their favourite pub restaurant for Sunday lunch later.

'Got that, Gus. I'll ring off now. I have to make arrangements. Cheers!'

He put the phone down and grabbed his notebook and scribbled his to do list before he went to Paris. His first priority was to his family that evening before he drove down to London and his next was a phone call advising Effie.

—

Hunter stepped out of the shower carrying his towel instead of wrapping it around his waist and was stunned to find a naked Jacquie waiting for him. Mesmerised by her symmetry and the gentle six-pack visible under the flawless skin his first action was to pull the towel in front of himself. His eyes wandered to the bullet wound scar on her left thigh which was still plainly visible but it did not detract from her toned athletic figure. They had been together fourteen years and she still sent his primaeval senses into overdrive and left him weak at the knees. There was something, not a skill but a mystifying allure about her which had saved her life a few times in her undercover career during the Northern Irish Troubles.

She approached and draped her arms around his neck and he couldn't stop the uplifting feeling that came over him. 'Hunter,' she whispered, 'thank you for a wonderful evening and I want to show you my appreciation before you go.'

She manoeuvred him towards the bed, as he uttered, 'Jacquie, what about the kids. It's early.'

'Mmmm,' she mumbled flirtatiously as she kissed his neck and her hands wandered freely around his torso, 'Try dragging Iain from outer space and her from her art.'

The back of his knees touched the bed and she pushed him backwards and so began the seduction of her willing partner. Her breathing became heavier as she teased him to almost the point of orgasm when he pushed her back and rolled her over. While his hands caressed, searched and fondled his tongue flicked and massaged the tiny lobe that led to heaven. She sighed and writhed, her breath coming in short gasps. She pushed her hips upwards to meet him and pulled his head into her. Throwing her head back, she dug her fingers into his shoulders and groaned.

'Quicker,' she urged but he teased and held her at the peak until she could hold it no longer and the writhing human volcano erupted with a loud sensual groan.

She waited for a few seconds breathing heavily her breasts rising and falling with the exertion before she pulled him down and into her and devoured him with her passion.

As they lay breathless wrapped in each other's aura she whispered in his ear, 'Now you've got to come home.'

Before he could answer, their peace was shattered by a plaintiff cry. 'Mummy! Mummy! Help me!

Jacquie slid off the bed and grabbed a dressing gown and as she left the room, she said to Hunter, 'Get yourself dressed. The sooner you get away the quicker you get some sleep.'

A few minutes later as he stood in front of the mirror doing up his tie Jacquie returned. 'Hunter, you've got a job to do before you go.'

'What is it, Jaq's?'

'Lesley's bedside lamp isn't working.'

'Okay, that won't take a minute.'

'I'll make some coffee while your fiddling.'

He straightened his tie and gave his hair a quick comb and went to see what the problem was. As he entered Lesley's room lit up by the glaring centre light he was greeted by an enthusiastic, 'Hello, Daddy, I thought you had gone already.'

'I'm just getting ready, lass, what's the problem?'

'My lamp stopped working. It just went—POP!'

Okay, let's have a look.'

He went around the bed and one look was enough to tell him the bulb was knackered. 'I'll be back in a jiffy, lass, you need a new bulb.'

Two minutes later he was back with a new bulb and after he had screwed it in firmly he pushed the switch and nothing happened. He glanced at his watch and time was moving on. 'Oh, dear,' he said, 'that doesn't look good.'

'What's up, Dad?'

'I think the fuse has blown. I'll go and get a new one. Hang on.'

He met Jacquie on the landing. 'You're taking a long time, Hunter. You'd better get going.'

'Give me five minutes. The fuse has blown. I've got some new ones in my room.'

She left him to it knowing that once he started something he wouldn't let go until it was finished especially where the children were concerned and he returned two minutes later with a Tuppa box marked 'Electrical' and with a sigh started moving furniture and the bed to get at the hidden wall plugs inherent with built-in furniture.

Mission accomplished he was now able to reach the plug and get to the real business when a voice from the door said, 'What's up, Dad?'

It was Iain and Hunter stopped and without looking around said, 'Come here son, you might learn sommat.'

Iain knelt beside Hunter and watched as he removed the plug and replaced the fuse before screwing the cover on and firmly pushing it back in the plug and flicking the switch.

'Tra! Laa!' sang Hunter as the light came on, 'That's it, Iain, now you can help me with the furniture.'

Iain pulled a face but did as he was bid and as they were leaving the room, Iain said, 'Dad? What happens if the light doesn't work after you change the fuse?'

Hunter stopped and put his hands on Iain's shoulders and looked down at him. 'Iain, lad, I haven't got time right now, but grab me when I come back and I'll tell you, okay?'

'You're on, Dad, take care and no shooting.'

With that, he skipped across the hall and into his room.

Downstairs in the kitchen Hunter swigged the dregs from a mug of coffee and plonking the mug down walked around to Jacquie and gave her a hug. He could feel her nakedness through the thin material and the urge to linger intensified but after a long passionate kiss, she pushed him away.

'Enough, Hunter, and take care. I want you back in one piece.'

'I will—Love you, lass.'

He grabbed his bag, spun around and headed for the door.

~~~~~

Chapter 10

With nervous expectation, Alexei and Malika had been waiting fully dressed in their apartment for almost an hour when the doorbell rang. Malika jumped visibly and Alexei checked his watch before grabbing their hand luggage and stepping out into the long balcony passageway outside. While locking the door he fumbled and dropped the key and when he reached down to pick it up he deftly pushed a second key under the foot scraper by the door. He locked the door and holding hands he and Malika followed the Lingo taxi driver down to the car.

The early morning traffic was light and didn't hinder the black Skoda following them and Alexei took great pains not to look around to confirm its presence. They arrived at the airport and went through the preliminary checks at the entrance with plenty of time to spare.

St. Petersburg was a popular destination and check-in took a little longer. Following their instructions, they meandered around the shops on the way towards passport control and security taking care not to look around. When they were close to the access gate leading to Passport control, Alexei, began to wonder if something had gone wrong when behind them there was a scuffle and a cry of dismay as a careless young woman preoccupied with her android device in one hand and a carton of coffee in the other careered into a man in a leather coat.

The loosened lid on the coffee sprang off and the contents splashed all over him and the woman was devastated and made such a fuss grabbing tissues and sobbing while she tried to clean him up bent on a mission of total distraction.

Sidetracked by the scuffle Alexei and Malika turned to watch as a middle-aged couple wearing blue scarves moved in and skilfully took over their hand luggage and whispered, 'Follow, as they wheeled away towards their respective gender toilets. Inside they quickly exchanged coats and scarves and did a swift about-turn and left.

Outside, the couple moved unhurriedly towards Passport

Control while Williams wearing a blue football scarf with the French 'coq gaulois' motive emblazoned on it approached them and as he walked past he instructed them in Russian to follow.

Holding hands nervously Alexei and Malika did as they were told and they went out through the main exit and were guided to a large extended saloon with French Diplomatic number plates and before they knew it they were on their way. To where? They didn't know, but in the car, Williams introduced himself as Bernard and he gave them valid French Passports and flight tickets to Paris and when they read the tickets they realised they were on their way to Moscow's Domodedevo International airport as French citizens who had been on a Governmental Cultural visit and who were now going home.

Bernard turned in his seat to speak to Alexei in Russian and called him by his new French name. 'Monsieur Massot, do you speak any French?'

Alexei shook his head. 'Not one word.'

'Okay,' said Bernard, 'pretend you have a heavy cold and blow your nose a lot when someone speaks. What about you, Henriette?' Malika's new name.

'A little from school,' she replied.

'Not to worry,' said Bernard, 'when they check your boarding card just say 'merci,' and nod. I'll be right behind you.'

With their diplomatic immunity and Alexei's fake head cold keeping people at a safe distance there was little hold up and they were soon waiting in the VIP lounge for their flight to be called. A little after midday they boarded an Air France flight to Paris and two Savitsky's flew from Moscow Vnukovo to St. Petersburg and checked into the four-star NashOTEL Hotel but never checked out.

To ensure there was no record of them arriving from Moscow at Paris Charles De Gaulle Airport Williams walked on ahead across the bridge from the aircraft. Hunter acknowledged him before stepping forward to intercept Alexei and Malika. They shook hands and he guided them through the staff side door and down the steps to a waiting car with CD plates and they were driven across the airport to the Private Owners Park. A civilian twin-engine **Beech G58 Baron** waited and they were no sooner boarded when they were given clearance and took off for the short flight to Earls Colne Airport in Essex, England.

On the flight across the English Channel, the atmosphere was solemn as Alexei and Malika contemplated what they had done and what their future would be. In the limousine from the airport to the safe house in Camden Town, a place Hunter was familiar with, the mood was equally sombre but now they were mesmerised by the countryside and the English way of life to which they would be inducted.

Hunter introduced them to the resident housekeeper Mrs Amy Archer and her ex-SAS husband and only when they were settled in and on their own did Hunter step forward and grip Alexei by the arm and shake his hand vigorously and then gave Malika a hug before he said, 'Welcome to England, Alexei. It's been a bit of a rush and I'm sorry I can't stay but after the debriefers have done their thing we'll go out to dinner. It'll be a cracker I promise and then we'll move you up North to my part of the country. You must be tired so take advantage of Mrs Archer's hospitality she has a wide knowledge of international cuisine even with the meagre allowances the powers that be allow her. Have a good sleep tonight, cheerio.'

He left the room feeling relieved that they had got out safely but sad about what they must have left behind.

—

In Moscow, moments after they left with their 'watcher' in tow an innocuous dirty van pulled up outside the apartment block and two men and a woman in working clothes unloaded a mass of flat cardboard boxes and went upstairs to the apartment. One of the men stayed behind and fiddled with the lock and the other two returned to the van and brought up the rest of the boxes. In less than a minute entry had been gained and choosing a room each they set to work.

In ninety minutes the apartment had been minutely searched and every moveable personal object that may assist any future search by investigating authorities including computers, photographs, bedding and more delicate items together with small pieces of furniture were loaded into the van. Taking the key with them when they had finished loading, in plain sight, the crew lounged around the front of the van chatting and smoking. The woman indulged herself on her android device until one of the men who was the driver looked at his watch and tapped the face of it and with urgent hand gesticulations and muttering something unintelligible urged them to get in the van. They nonchalantly dropped their cigarettes and stood on them before jumping in and driving off.

Their destination was a small yard with a rusty metal shed at one end in a little-used industrial park abandoned after the Cold War era when communal Nationalised industries were gobbled up by wily entrepreneurs and reorganised into more efficient money makers.

They drove the van into the shed and the doors were closed behind it. Then the transformation began. The van was washed and dried and different number plates fitted. New symbols and lettering were pasted on.

Two hours later a van with the logos of a well-known International delivery company left the premises to disappear into the teaming traffic of the metropolis its destination the warehouse of the company close to Domodedevo International airport.

~~~~~~~

Chapter 11

Hunter, Effie and Williams sat around the table in *Garden Centre* №1 Hunter's preferred meeting place. After their refreshments had been delivered to the table and Hunter had suitably rewarded the member of staff, he said, 'Let's get down to business. Effie! Is there any progress from your side?'

She flicked open her notebook. 'We have been notified by your people about Ragozin's false identity and the Ukraine authorities can't identify him from photos either but on the other hand there is enough positive evidence to ID him as the killer of Owen and Bonar. Also, he has been identified by the staff at *'Dixie's Bar'* and the *'Club 69'* as the man who met Owen. Last but not least we are looking for a smart guy who Ragozin's landlord said was a frequent visitor to the flat.'

'Hold it there,' chipped in Williams.

Hunter who was about to take a sip of coffee paused with the cup halfway to his mouth. 'What's up, Duncan?'

'That's Fabianski my contact in that community. It's a no, no.'

Hunter looked at Effie. 'Did you get that, Effie?'

She nodded. 'And?'

'He's off-limits, get your crew to make a note of everything they hear about him but do not approach him or make any open enquiries about him.'

'Why?'

'Williams here is working undercover in that community because as you know our enquiries are seeking something bigger and we don't want any distractions that may scare Fabianski or his associates. If you come across Williams who will be known as Ivan Andrejev you may check his ID and when you do he may pass on info or *visa versa*, Okay? Make sure and tell your comrades.'

Effie scribbled furiously before she banged her pencil down on the table. 'Are you freezing us out, Hunter? I thought we had a deal.'

'We still have but now the 'Code Red' has priority. I will keep you informed and when our case is done you may make your move, until then—Hands off! And Effie, tell your crew if there are any breaches whoever it is will have made the wrong career choice.' Hunter leaned towards her slightly, and said firmly but not aggressively. 'Do I make myself clear?'

Effie sat speechless looking at this new character in front of her, before she nodded, and said, 'Hunter! I don't like your attitude, but yes, I'll do as you ask. You will keep me in the loop?'

'I'm sorry, Effie, and yes, I'll keep you informed and if we learn anything concerning the murders we'll pass it on.' He leaned back fiddling with his pen. 'If you need anything or learn anything contact me on your closed line only.' She nodded and he continued, 'Now Effie, let me tell you what happened this weekend.'

He told her of the connection with Savitsky and how he was their source of the limited information concerning the 'Code Red' operation. Coupled with the Owen debacle it made it likely that something covert was going on but because Owen was gone, they had to start from scratch so to speak... 'In other words, Effie, the operation has to be allowed to flow free of interference until we have a positive lead. Effie, I'll go further and stick my neck out and promise that if we apprehend anyone at the end of this we will pass it on to you to arrest them and charge them before Special Branch steal the glory, okay?'

She leaned back in her seat and crossed her legs at the same time tapping her pen on the table. 'Hunter, you're a diverse character. One minute you threaten my job and the next you're improving my career prospects. It's a deal. I've got to go now.'

She stood up and gathered her briefcase and coat and stopped to shake Hunter's hand. 'Best of luck, Hunter. I know what Jacquie sees in you.' She turned and looked down at Williams, 'And you, Ivan, we'll see you around.'

She left and Hunter sat down, and said, tongue in cheek, 'Do you want more coffee, Ivan?'

'No, Boss.'

'Okay, Duncan, listen up. From now on you're on your own. You inveigle yourself into the local community and see what you can pick up. You know the drill. Only contact us with your phone with

Whatsapp. Set up a dead letter box and keep a GPS tracker on you at all times. Last but not least, the operation from now on is called 'Trenchcoat.' I know, don't ask. Go home and back on the job tomorrow and I'll fill you in when I get more info. Best of luck.'

They stood up simultaneously and shook hands before Williams grabbed his coat and left through the long window that led out to the outdoor section of the Garden Centre and he took the long path back to his car.

~~~~~~

Part 2

Williams

Chapter 12

Williams plonked his holdall down on to the doorstep of a Victorian terraced house converted to bed-sits and looked back at a run down ten year old Skoda Fabia he had parked half on the pavement on double yellow lines but this was no ordinary Skoda. Underneath the bonnet was a 1.4 Turbo engine and to complete the upgrade it had modern suspension and disc brakes.

He rammed his finger onto the bottom doorbell, which, like all the others had no name. He waited for around twenty seconds and tried the next one up.

He did this three times before a voice in broken English, said, 'What you want?'

Williams replying in broken English, said, 'I want to come to my new apartment but I have no key.'

'What your name?'

'Andrejev, Ivan.'

'You in number two. I let you in.'

A buzzer sounded and there was a click and the door eased back slightly. Williams pushed it and dragged his holdall after him into a dimly lit hall. On the right-hand side was a staircase and coming down to greet him, breathing heavily, was a greying overweight man with a weeks growth of facial hair. A distinctive Eastern European wearing a collarless shirt over baggy jeans held up by a pair of red braces with his sockless feet pressing down over the back of well-worn slippers.

He made no offer to shake hands instead he held up a fob with two Yale keys attached, and said, 'Me, Boris'

He squeezed past Williams and led him to the door at the end of the hall and after a moment fiddling, pushed it open and went inside to an open plan lounge/kitchen.

Williams followed and once inside was surprised. The place exceeded his expectations. Instead of the tatty run-down hovel he was expecting the furnished one bedroomed flat had been modernised and redecorated right down to the digital 32" TV and was spotlessly clean.

Williams let out a low whistle and dropped his bag both in admiration and surprise.

Boris said, 'You like?'

Williams nodded, 'I like, and the bedroom?'

Boris beckoned and shuffled over to a door on the other side of the room. After he had pushed it open he stood to one side and let Williams in and he was not disappointed. The room with Victorian proportions had been modernised and although the furnishings were sparse they were new as was the duvet and sheets. Built into one corner was an en-suite unit in which was a single shower, toilet and a modest size sink unit and shelves tactfully placed for convenience and the towels looked new.

'Boris, I was not expecting this.'

They went back into the front room and as Boris was about to hand over the keys, he said, 'The Master say you late. Why?'

Williams had his answer ready. 'My landlord, he not give me my money back as I leave early so I stay until the end on my time. Now I am here I will call Mr Fabianski, okay?'

Boris mumbled something unintelligible, shoved a note and the keys into William's hand before he shuffled out banging the door behind him.

'Nice to meet you too, Boris,' muttered Williams.

He picked his holdall up and placed it on the single armchair before he read the note. He ran his fingers through his hair and breathed out noisily. 'My, my, work already. That's a bit of a comedown, bloody car washing and a seven 'o clock start.'

He threw the note onto the coffee table in front of the sofa that ran along the back wall and went out to his car to bring in the rest of his belongings. Testing the kettle was his next priority and tasting the first mug of tea in his new abode, he set about putting his things away at the same time writing a shopping list of things he needed.

An hour later he surveyed his work and then grabbed his coat to go shopping but before he could leave his ancient Samsung Galaxy chimed. He picked it up, and answered, 'Hello, Theodor, what can I do for you?'

'Ivan, Where have you been?

'My landlord kept my cash until I finish contract.'

'Okay, Ivan, go to work tomorrow and I see you there and we talk.'

The connection went dead and Williams held the device away from him and looked at it quizzically. 'Hope the pays good, matey.'

He retrieved a canvas shopping bag from a cupboard in the kitchen area and chose to walk instead of driving to Bourn Street to sus out his future workplace.

As he dawdled past the car wash pretending to read his phone he was surprised to see the quality of cars that used it. The City Valet & Car Wash Co. was no ordinary car-wash as the Ferrari and 500 Series Mercedes parked in a holding bay testified and a couple of local Taxis were lined up also. He closed the camera and carried on into Bourn Street that would be his local shopping area with its large array of ethnic outlets mixed with cafes and good English style pubs to which he could already testify were good except maybe one that lacked the oomph in its beer.

As it was lunchtime, he chose the *'Cheshire Arms'* while chatting to the lovely Lani and she was willing although a little perplexed when she couldn't identify him straight away.

'I know you,' she said, 'have you been before?'

He nodded his affirmation. 'Ivan, I was looking for Janis.'

'You have changed. Before you wear old clothes and have long hair. You have work now?'

'Yes, Lani, I work in City car wash tomorrow.'

'I know the boys and Anna from there. He makes them work hard.' Williams face dropped at the thought but he cheered up when she added, 'but he pays well.'

'Huh! That's something. Do you know the boss?'

'Mr Fabianski, he has many houses here also but he mixes with the people. Nice man.'

'Has he been here long, Lani?'

'You ask a lot of questions, Ivan, and you not drinking.'

'Oh! Sorry, Lani, I just want to know my new boss. Give me a pint of Stella and one of those cheese and onion batches, please.'

She served up his pint and batch and as she took his money, he said, 'What time do you finish, Lani?'

She smiled, and said, 'You too late, Ivan, I have boyfriend.'

He picked up his items and as he turned away, he said, 'One can but try.'

He was a bit disappointed because relations with Lani would have given him good insight into the latest gossip. Undeterred he sat on the bench within hearing distance of a group of five men who were talking in Polish ~~one~~ and with one ear tuned he got stuck into his cheese batch and beer and read the local free newspaper which someone had left on the table.

He heard nothing untoward and after twenty minutes he folded the paper and was ready to move when the android device of one of the group jangled out its 'answer me' chimes. Williams paused and listened to the garbled phone conversation and heard the word Russia and soldiers a couple of times and he decided it was time to become friends with the group.

The guy put his phone down and with one of those wide-eyed facial expressions which was neither fright nor surprise he spread his news.

It was then Williams intervened. He stood up and took the one pace to the table and with an apology in their mother tongue, said, 'Sorry, brothers, I'm Ivan. I couldn't help but hear the phone call and your frantic conversation about Russian soldiers. Is there something wrong at home?'

The five sat silently and stared at him and it was full thirty seconds before the guy who had taken the phone call, said, 'Hello, Ivan, where are you from?'

Williams put his finger over his lips before he replied quietly, 'Ukraine.'

'Sit down, Ivan.'

They shuffled their chairs around to make room and Williams squeezed in before the guy with the phone, said, 'I'm Illya, and me and my friends are Polish. I come from Lublin and I just speak to my sister who says she had a message from our cousin who is living in Donetsk that there are reports of Russian troop movements along the borders with Belarus and Ukraine. Have you family there?'

'Yes, my parents.'

'What do you do now, Ivan?'

'I can't go back yet, there is no work in Dzankoy. That is why I come here.'

'Well, Ivan, as they say in England—Fingers crossed.'

'Thank you, Illya. I go now and I phone my father. Cheerio!'

Williams wriggled his way out from the table and with a quick nod around he left the pub with droopy shoulders and a disgruntled look on his face. Outside he straightened up and with a curse he made his way back to the supermarket to replace the frozen items he had purchased earlier.

With his shopping stored, half an hour later he sent a message and a photo of the car-wash to Hunter and arranged a rendezvous for that evening.

—

Williams parked his Skoda and walked across the car park and spotted Hunter's Golf but it was the car parked next to it that made him look twice. 'That's ours,' he said under his breath and he perked up his pace as moved towards the entrance. Once inside he didn't have long to find out as Tanya called out to him and hurried across the room to greet him with a kiss and a hug.

He held her at arm's length and grinning from ear to ear, said, 'What are you doing here?'

She hooked a thumb over her shoulder. 'He called me.'

He looked across the room and he saw Hunter indulging his hobby sampling cold lager. Hunter acknowledged him and called him across and went to the bar and indulged his younger partner before they began talking.

Williams spoke first. 'Explain, Hunter, what's Tanya doing here?'

'After I got your message I mulled things over and I came to the conclusion that you need a girlfriend and we need a messenger and Tanya fits the bill. Same language, same accent. Perfect, and when I spoke to her she agreed. I've fixed it with the authorities not to call on her services until further notice so don't worry on that score.'

'And my kids?'

'We have arranged for Agent Carrie Long to do it. You know

her from the last job. The convert from the police. Apart from the evenings or knowing you pair, nights, when she is with you, Tanya will be at home. If anyone asks, you met on Facebook.'

'Is Tanya on the books?'

'Yes, and her ID docs will be here soon

Williams reached across the table and held her hand. 'Okay, boss, tell me about this car wash.'

'It's a legitimate business and gets five-star ratings. It's owned by, Fabianski, your contact and he allegedly employs EU immigrants.'

'Sounds alright but he seems pretty well established for someone who hasn't been up here long.'

'We're looking into that. Tell me about this conversation you overheard.'

Williams gave him the lowdown on the encounter he'd had at lunchtime, '...and that's as much as I know. Troop movements along the Russian borders but they did seem a bit anxious about their relatives and mine of course.'

Hunter picked up his smartphone and stood up. 'Give me a couple of minutes while I pass that on to the 'firm.'

He left Williams and Tanya holding hands and chatting while he went outside to make his call. He was back five minutes later and before he spoke he took a long swig of his lager. He put the glass down. 'Alright you pair, have you worked out some sort of plan?'

Williams gave Tanya's hand a squeeze. 'Yep! I'm going back to the pub which I have made my local and I'll drop the hint about my new girl friend and then we'll introduce her maybe tomorrow or the day after. I met her on the Internet and she lives up the Wirral and stays over now and then so no long breaks from the kids or me.'

'Good. My apologies, Tanya, no offence meant but I won't expand on 'Trenchcoat'.' The less you know the safer you are. In fact, forget you ever heard it, Okay?'

Tanya picked up her glass and finished the last drops before she concluded, 'That's alright, Mr Hunter, I'll go now.' She grabbed William's hand, and said, 'Come on, you, you can give me a long goodbye.'

They stood up together and left the pub while Hunter indulged himself with another pint. A long goodbye it was and it was ten minutes before Williams returned.

'I was just going to send a search party,' quipped Hunter, 'but back to business. Owen was a Ukrainian agent. He worked undercover in GCHQ and uncovered a Russian cell down south. He apparently wormed his way in but did not inform us only his Uke bosses and then he moved up to Chester. Why? We don't know but he was sussed and it looks like the Russians topped him and they, in turn, have made sure of no leaks by killing off their hitman Ragozin. Now he is or was posing we think as a Uke as he recently had the Uke traditional symbol tattooed on his neck but they have no record of him.'

'What you're saying, Guv, the Russians are pretending to be Uke's?'

'That's our theory. Why? We're not sure but put together with Savitsky's info and what the 'Cousins' passed on to us via the Japs something is going on. I want you, Duncan, to listen out for any mention of anything to do with, 'October', 'Upstart' or alternatively, 'Wyskochka.''

'What's all that?'

'October we don't know the connection but Savitsky said the other two were the names of an operation we think the Russians are planning. He heard of it through an old alcoholic compatriot of his who has since been, how shall we say this? Removed by the FSU.'

'Was there anything else?'

'Savitsky's informant said something about hitting the U.K. with dirty bombs. It could be in October. In which case we have to move quickly. That's as much as we know, Duncan, so now we have to join the dots. It's going to be hard work washing cars but look at it this way. You're getting paid twice.'

'I can keep my wages then? That's a first and this puts a whole new meaning to "working undercover." I'm working for real.'

'It's for a good cause. Wear your Yankees cap and keep a look out for the Yankee's symbol. That's us.'

'On that note, I'm off. How are you getting home, Guv?'

'Driving, why?'

'You've had two beers.'

'I'm going the scenic route.'

On the stroke of seven, Williams presented himself with his squashed Yankees cap and was greeted with little enthusiasm by the people who were supposed to be his work colleagues. He was put on the spraying and washing section and was immediately busy mainly with taxis and businessmen and women who left their cars to be collected later. Fabianski had seen to it that the ground behind the shops on the street was kept free and was used as collection parking.

They were a nine-man and one-woman team and it was an hour later when Williams was allowed a break that he was able to chat to the young woman whose job was interior valeting. He threw his cap down and slipped off his waterproof jacket and accepted the cup of black tea with a slice of orange in and spoke Ukraine which was the common language between them. 'Thank you, and what do I call you, miss?'

'Anna, and you are Ivan?'

'How do you know?'

'We were told you were coming by the boss.'

She offered him a black bread and krakowska sausage sandwich which he declined but readily accepted when she said, 'Take it, we share our food in here. Tomorrow you bring some and put it in the fridge with the others.'

'What about lunch?'

'We take it, in turn, to go over the road to the '*Cheshire Arms*' for half an hour. Tuck in as you will be last.'

'I will. Tell me, Anna, why are the boys unhappy with me?'

'Because we are a ten-man team and we worked with only nine and shared the extra man's wages between us and now you come. Don't worry, they will soon change.'

'I'm sorry but I need money for my family...' he went on to explain about his alleged family problems in Ukraine, '...and Mr Fabianski he give me job.'

'You are illegal?'

'Yes.'

'Oh!'

'What's the matter.'

'It is very hard but all of us here are illegal.'

He finished his tea and sandwich, grabbed his coat and went back to work wondering at her reticence and he found out at three 'o clock when he was called into the office and told to shut the door. Waiting for him was Fabianski.

'Sit down, Ivan.'

Williams duly obliged and sat on an old rough office chair across the desk from his new boss. 'What can I do for you, Boss, have I done something wrong?'

'On the contrary, Ivan, they say you work hard. But let's get down to business. You owe me two-hundred pounds,' Williams nodded, 'and you have moved into one of my flats which is four hundred pounds a month.' Williams jaw dropped but he said nothing. 'I want a deposit for the keys which is two-thousand pounds which means seven hundred pounds is coming out of your wages every month. I pay you the minimum wage less taxes but only six pounds an hour cash for overtime.'

Williams sat stunned mentally working out the income he was supposed to live on and it was two minutes before he spoke. 'But Mr Fabianski, that only give me eighty pounds a week to live on. What about my family?'

'You will have to work hard won't you, Ivan.'

'I'm going to complain. It is wrong.'

'Ivan! Who are you going to complain to? You are illegal. Now get back to work before I dock your pay.'

Stunned by the revelations he didn't argue and he wearily pulled himself up and left the office with eighty-four hour weeks awaiting him. He was determined to stop this slavery but it would put people out of work and possibly put them behind bars. A dilemma to be sorted out later.

———

He worked until seven-thirty that evening and then along with the rest of the crew they went across to the '*Cheshire Arms*' for a reviving drink before retiring for the night.

Inside at the bar as the new boy, he offered to pay for the first round and then he spoke in their common language to Anna who was stood alongside him and behind her was a tall black-haired man with three days growth of beard. Duncan looked at him and thought he would have been a good looking guy without the beard.

Anna,' he said, 'the Boss told me what he pays us today. It is bad I will not be able to send money home.'

She turned around to the man behind her and pulled him forward. 'Ivan, you meet, Alex Petrov. He is my boyfriend and our leader. You speak with him.'

Duncan looked up at Alex whose deep black eyes stared down at him. His quilted jacket was good quality as was his Levi jeans and he wore shoes instead of the usual trainers. He hadn't noticed this when they were working but Alex was the best dressed of all of them which was unlikely on the wages and made a note that Alex was Fabianski's number one and he immediately became wary of what he said.

Notwithstanding, Duncan shoved his hand out. 'I know we work together, Alex, but this is the first time as a drinking compatriot.'

They shook hands and Alex smiled showing a full set of glowing white teeth. 'Hello, Ivan, welcome to slavery. What can we do about it?'

'I will think of something, Alex, but we must not lose our jobs.'

'Do you know anybody, Ivan?'

He knew Alex was fishing so his answer was a short, 'No!—I come from Ukraine, Alex, where are you from?'

'I come from Kiev with Anna but you speak with Crimean / Russian accent. You steal our land.'

This was the confrontation Duncan didn't want and his brain went into overdrive as he tried to remember what he had told Fabianski and he replied, cautiously, 'No, Alex, I only want peace and to work for my family. I was lucky and had a job in I.T. but when the Russians come the business closed down. It was hard before but there is still no work in Dzankoy so I run away.'

'So you think England is better, Ivan?'

'I was told by my agent that they give you money here when you not work but this is not right is it?'

'Only EU citizens, Ivan so you must work and keep quiet.'

'But I must find more money for my family and I meet a new girlfriend last night.'

'That's nice, Ivan,' chipped in Anna, 'Is she from Chester?'

'No, but she has a car.'

'English?'

He shook his head, 'No.'

Williams decided this had gone far enough and after a glance at his watch plonked his glass down on the bar. 'I'm tired and we start early. I'm going to bed. Cheers, goodnight.'

He left them looking slightly bemused at his sudden departure but not for long as Alex bought the next round and the drinking continued. Outside the autumn weather had taken over and the continuous drizzle was blowing in waves along the street and the street lighting dulled by the rain was in misty cones.

Williams pulled his collar up and crossed the junction and walked toward the car wash. He stopped and sat on the low brick wall across the front of the forecourt as a cautionary check for stalkers and then while re-assessing his workplace he sent a short message to Hunter and a longer one to Tanya and arranged to meet her the following evening after work.

His first day at work had been a busy one and he'd had no time to learn the layout. The yard with a low wall across the front of it had been a former petrol station with the office at one end which had been converted into the customer waiting room, employees restroom and toilets and storeroom for their equipment. The fuel pumps and the overhead awning covering the forecourt had been removed and the raised platform levelled to make it into a long yard but what intrigued him was the black-painted cargo container in the corner against the back wall behind the office and it had never been used all day.

He waited until the road was quiet and checking that no one was looking out from the buildings opposite he slipped into the yard and behind the office. With his back to the wall, he moved along to his target and then along to the end of the building where he waited for a few moments to make sure it was still quiet. A couple of cars went by and one stopped at the 'Red Dragon' Chinese takeaway a few doors along but no one was paying any interest in the car wash.

Bending low he went around to the doors and holding a small torch examined the lock and he let out a low whistle when he examined the large heavy yellow padlock which held a fitted hasp and staple fast against any interested lowlife.

'My, my,' he said to himself, 'who needs an Abus Granit Insurance lock.' His knowledge of locks told him that they cost around £150 and were mostly used by people with houseboats or yachts and were virtually unpickable and safe from bolt cutters. He made a note of the model number, and said under his breath, 'One for 'YouTube' methinks,' and as he switched off his torch he heard laughter coming from the road and he flattened himself against the doors and watched as a party of teenagers immune to the weather meandered towards the takeaway. Immediately they disappeared behind the corner of the first shop he bent double and ran to the front of the yard. It was all clear and he followed the youngsters along the road past the few shops which were hairdressers, a Leisure Wear shop, the 'The Red Dragon' Chinese takeaway and a newsagent come corner shop.

He stopped at the hairdressers long enough to look in the angled window of the doorway and double-checked to see that he wasn't being followed. Satisfied, he joined the young crowd in the takeaway and settled for a Prawn Curry and Fried rice before returning to the only rewarding consolation of his current position and that was the tastefully modern flat.

Inside he laid out a tray and grabbed a beer from the fridge before settling on the sofa and switching on the TV. He took little interest in the programme that was playing instead he finished his curry and dug out his laptop and went straight to 'You Tube' and searched for the *Lock Lawyer* and sure enough in the list of pickable locks was the Abus Granit. He watched the video four or five times until he had the routine firmly in his head and bookmarked it. Satisfied he had the tools for the job he sent another text to Hunter and got himself ready for bed.

———

The next day the car wash was busy and time passed quickly but he was glad when his lunch break came around and he was able to collapse onto the bench in the '*Cheshire Arms.*' When he had his breath back, he went to the bar where Lani had a pint of Stella waiting. 'Hello, Ivan, you look tired,' she said, 'You been busy today?'

'Very busy. Can I have cheese and pickle batch as well?'

'Yes, Ivan. On the tab or cash?'

'Cash.'

He slid the money over the bar and as he turned to go to his seat a scruffy man wearing glasses and a crumpled oily Yankees bomber jacket bumped into him and knocked the beer from his hand.

Williams cursed loudly in his pseudo mother tongue, *'Yoptel-mopsel! Idiota kusok!'*

'Ere, watch it, mate, I'm sorry,' was the instant reply, 'Let me get you another.' The man turned to the bar and said to Lani, 'Give me some tissues, love and we'll need a brush and mop around here.'

Lani handed a couple of table napkins over and the guy began wiping down the front of Williams at the same time mumbling, 'Open your jacket.'

Williams opened the top two buttons and the man crudely wiped a non-existent mess away and shoved something into William's coat. The charade went on until everyone was satisfied and he was able with a package wedged under his elbow to sit down and enjoy his lunch while the object of his disrupted lunch break made his way to the toilets and a few minutes later left the pub.

Transferring the package to the pocket of his jacket was easy and because the incident had taken so much time he hurriedly finished his lunch and went back to work a couple of minutes late. Nothing was said but he saw Alex checking his watch.

'Huh! That's me a couple of quid short this week,' he muttered.

He didn't have time to linger as the queue of cars was getting longer and there was no respite until after five 'o clock by which time they were all tired and looking forward to closing time.

—

Hunter wasted no time getting home and changing out of the grubby clothing of his disguise and after a brief hold up at the gate while they checked his credentials at three 'o clock on the dot he was ready for a meeting with the MD of Capenhurst Nuclear Services.

Julia the MD's PA, a person of comfortable proportions, picked up the phone and pressed a button and a male voice answered, 'Yes, Julia?'

'Mr Hunter is here, Mr Drummond.'

'Send him in and hold any calls, Julia.'

'Will do.' She put the phone down and looked up at Hunter. 'In you go, Mr Hunter. Would you like a coffee or something?'

'Thanks, but I'll wait and see what Mr Drummond is doing but if the call comes it's a strong black with no milk or additives.'

'Got that.'

He picked up his briefcase and knocked on the office door and didn't wait for an answer as he entered a clean modern unfussy office. Lionel Drummond stood up and came around his desk to greet him. They shook hands and Hunter put his briefcase down and sat on an easy chair, one of two in a discreet corner of the office with a coffee table between them.

Drummond sat on the other and opened the conversation, 'It is not often we get to meet with the security services, Mr Hunter, what can I do for you?'

'It's like this Mr Drummond, we have a situation or rather a possible scenario where we think someone may be planning to carry out some sort of terrorist or sabotage attack on this plant or even the country in general.'

'Like what?'

'We think that they plan to detonate a dirty bomb in or near this plant and we wondered if you could give us some idea of the possible damage we could expect.'

'By dirty bomb, you mean an RDD?

'Yes.'

'An RDD would not have much effect on the plant at all but would be toxic to the immediate surrounding area. Not from any contamination from here you understand but the bomb itself.' He stood up, 'One moment,' and he walked over to the door and stuck his head out. All Hunter could hear was a mumbled conversation and inside a minute, Drummond had rejoined him and stood alongside him. 'Julia will have some documents shortly for me to show you. Would you like some refreshment? A coffee or something stronger?'

Hunter had noticed the bottles of spirits in a cabinet as he sat down and knew what the stronger element was. 'A whisky if you have it, please.'

Certainly, will single malt do?'

'Is there any other type? With water at this time of day though.'

'Precisely, Mr Hunter, my sentiments entirely.'

He went over to the cabinet and poured two glasses with a one finger measure in and when he gave Hunter his he proffered a water jug which he took and made a fifty/fifty mixture.

'Thank you, Mr Drummond, and while we speak can we use our more familiar first names? Most people call me, Hunter.'

'I'm Lionel, but what's with this Hunter. Is that a code name?'

'It's complicated, Lionel. Hunter is my former surname which I had to discard for security reasons but I still use it as my preferred known name tag.'

'Oh,' I see.' At that moment Julia came in carrying a folder which she was about to put on Lionel's desk, when he said, 'Give it to Mr Hunter, Julia, and, thank you.'

'You're welcome,' she said. She handed Hunter the folder and like all good secretaries, she drifted away like a feather on a breeze leaving only a slight whiff of her perfume to remind them of her presence.

Drummond sat down and took a sip from his glass. 'Where were we?' he said, 'Ah, yes, that folder, Hunter, is the UUK Stress report for this plant. It will tell you better than I can but basically, it shows all the safety aspects of the plant.'

He got up from his seat and went to the long-sealed treble glazed window and swept his arm across the plant that was visible outside. 'The population around here are one hundred per cent safe if an RDD detonation happened apart from the fallout from the device itself but a full-blown nuclear device might be different in as much it could crack a vessel or a pipe and then the chemo toxic risk from UF_6 could be an issue.'

'What's UF_6?'

'Uranium fluoride, to give it one of its names, is used in the Nuclear enrichment program which is in a solid crystal state stored in large steel cylinders and since the 1986 disaster in the U.S. we inspect and upgrade them regularly. Would you like to see them?'

'No, Lionel, we're not checking up on you I'm merely getting wise to what the outcome might be but going on what you've said even if it didn't do any real damage to the plant it would have a significant effect on the surrounding area.'

'Depending on the wind at the time we would be looking at an area of twenty square miles which would take you right over to Liverpool.'

'Lionel, could you increase the plant security and I will notify the 'firm' and they will speak to the right authorities and do the same for the transport system that's in place. When's the next delivery due although I suppose I've only got to look on Twitter for the CMD post?'

'We had an import from Europe only yesterday and we're not due another one until they've finished servicing the latest sub to return from its travels. About a month I'd say.'

Hunter took a card from his top pocket and shoved it over the coffee table. 'Call me if you spot anything suspicious and we'll keep you posted on our progress. At the moment we only suspect an operation is in place but we have no definite proof.'

They both stood and shook hands. 'It's been nice meeting you, Hunter,' said Drummond.'

'Likewise, Lionel, I hope it comes to nothing because if something does happen it will have international consequences.'

Hunter stuffed the Stress Test folder into his briefcase and went to the door accompanied by Drummond who opened it and showed him out before calling Julia into the office.

Hunter checked his watch and decided that this was a good time for an early finish. After going through the rigorous security checks he drove fifty metres to the main road, paused to let a vehicle pass before he turned left and up and over the railway bridge ignoring the tall figure of Alistair McRae better known as Theodor Fabianski with a borrowed dog, walking along the opposite pavement.

McRae made a mental note of the familiar face in the car last seen at the shindig in Bourn Street.

'What is our retired MI6 Agent doing here?'

———

Meanwhile, Matt and Maria Dewey who were drawing ever closer to their final destination were enjoying the delights of Wordsworth and Beatrix Potter in the Lake District.

—

Knowing he had thirty minutes before the kids came home, Hunter didn't waste any time changing but threw his jacket over the back of a chair and went straight to the fridge to retrieve a can of his favourite lager before going upstairs to his den to update his notes. It wasn't long before he heard the alarm as the gates opened.

He slurped the last dregs from his glass and got to the front door as Jamie his driver was putting the key in the lock. Hunter opened the door and welcomed him and stood to one side as Iain and Lesley, swinging their school bags pushed their way in. They didn't get far as Hunter grabbed Iain around the shoulders and held him back and snatched the phone from his hand.

He clicked the phone off and looking down at Iain, said, 'Whoa, there! Not so fast. Where's your manners? How about saying 'hello' or something?'

Surprised at seeing Hunter, Iain paused before he uttered, 'Err... Hello, Dad. Err... what are you doing here?'

'Funny you should ask that, Iain, I came home to see you pair, that's assuming you want to see me.'

'Of course, Dad, can I go now? I want the bathroom.'

'Off you go, I'll see you in the kitchen you can have your phone back then.'

Iain slid out of Hunter's grip and Lesley looked up at him. 'Hello, Dad, does Mum know you're home?'

'No, love, I'm still technically working but you can give me a hug if you like.'

He could see the twinkle in her eye when she said, 'Ooh... Dad, don't be soft. Can I get a drink and a butty and then I'll show you the latest masterpiece.'

'Give me five minutes to speak to Jamie and I'll join you in the kitchen.'

'Okay, Dad.'

Unlike Iain, Lesley ran upstairs to her room to dump her school things and change into something more leisurely while Hunter spoke to Jamie. 'Hi, Jamie, How's things with you?'

'Fine, boss, and they were studying their books all the way home. Have they got an exam or something?'

'I don't think so, Jamie, but since they joined their new schools they've been a lot more studious. Never mind that, how about you?'

'I'm fine, Boss, the doctor has reduced my tablets and he reckons I'll be off them in a couple of months. Lizzie, that's my partner, is doing me the world of good and I love this job.'

'Good, are you still confident with your set-up, you know, the tools in your possession?'

'Yes, boss, even better now. I feel like my old personality has returned and the self-doubt has gone. Just let anyone near those kids and they'll know what for.'

Hunter patted him on the shoulder. 'One more thing, Jamie?'

'Yes, Boss?'

'Would you be up to using small arms if you had to?'

'It depends on the circumstances. Looking after the kids or you and the misses, Yes! Back in the Forces, I don't know. Why? You expecting problems?'

'No, Jamie, but after the last ordeal I want to be ready that's all. I'll arrange for your licence. I won't hold you up any longer just let us know if you need anything.'

'Will do, Boss,' and as he made his way back to the car Hunter watched him and noted that he was standing taller and had lost some weight. 'Methinks he's down the gym,' was his last thought as he closed the front door.

In the kitchen, he found the kids already tucking into the snack and fruit drink left for them in the fridge by Jacquie and he joined them at the table with a cup of tea.

He returned Iain's phone, and said, 'Okay, what's happening?'

'Where's Uncle Jamie,' said Lesley, 'he usually has a cup of tea with us.'

'You've got me today. I've let him go home early. Would you rather have him?'

'No, Dad, silly, it's just... You know! We like him.'

'I get the message. He'll be back tomorrow. So, what's happening at school, Iain?'

'The Headmaster said that if I get good maths results in the end of term exams I'll be pushed up a grade after Christmas.'

'Wow! That's good. What about other subjects?'

'I'm top in Science but English is a bit ropey, Dad.'

'That'll come, son, keep it up. And you, Lesley?'

'Can't wait for my Art classes and Hockey but the rest is boring.'

'Oh, dear, why's that I wonder. Iain! Go and do your homework. Lesley, let me and you have a chat.'

They cleared things away and put the dishes in the dishwasher and Hunter had just sat down with Lesley when his phone buzzed. 'What now?' he uttered with a hint of frustration in his voice.

He looked at the caller I.D. and groaned quietly before he slid his finger up the answer app. 'Yes. Gus, what do you want?'

'Nice to speak to you too, Hunter. Just a catch-up call.'

'Can it wait until tomorrow, Gus, I've taken time out with the kids?'

'Okay, Hunter, ring me when you're ready. I'm in the office from nine in the morning.'

'Thanks, Gus, I owe you one.'

'Did you say one, Hunter? Never mind, speak tomorrow.'

He hung up and Hunter turned his attention back to Lesley. 'Right, lass, where were we? I know, you said you were bored at school. Why's that?'

'I don't know. I'm waiting all the time like I'm finished and I have to wait for the others to catch up. I asked the teacher for more work and she says I have to wait. Art classes are good though.'

'Oh, dear! Does your Mum know?'

'No, Dad, I haven't told her.'

'Okay, sweetie, you go and do your homework and I'll talk to your Mum tonight and see what we can do.'

'I've done my homework. It's easy.'

Hunter looked at his daughter while squeezing his face and rubbing his chin in perplexed wonderment. 'My, my, alright, off you go and play with your art. I know, let's go and see Iain. Come on.'

He stood up and put his arm around Lesley's shoulder and together they went into the children's designated workspace where Iain was beavering away in front of a computer doing his homework.

He stopped when he heard the door open and Hunter and Lesley entered. 'Hi, Dad, what's up?'

'Nothing, Iain, but I wondered if you could let Lesley read your school books and help her with any questions she has and show her your homework. Can you do that?'

'Aw, Dad! She's a girl.'

'Iain, do this for me just this once and it doesn't matter she's a girl. They're just as clever as you. Look at your Mum.'

'Okay,' he said grumpily. 'Come on, you,' he said to Lesley, 'drag your chair over and no messing.'

Hunter helped Lesley with her chair and left them to it as he went to put the kettle on for Jacquie coming home.

—

It was sometime later in the evening after the children had gone to bed and Hunter and Jacquie both flopped down with a glass of red wine when he brought up the subject of Lesley.

'What about her,' said Jacquie, 'she's doing okay at school by all accounts.'

'I'm not sure how to say this, Jacquie, but I think she needs to go up a grade or go to a special school or class.'

'Why do you say that, Hunter?'

'She's bored senseless. She told me this afternoon while she was having her snack. She says she has to sit around waiting for the other kids to finish and the teacher is no help. She just tells her to wait whenever she asks for more. Iain let her look at his homework and as it happened it was Maths and she was well into it. She's way ahead of her year.'

'Oh, she's never said and the school haven't mentioned it. I'll call in tomorrow and have a word.'

'Righty ho! I copied Iain's homework and kept the pad that Lesley used so you can take that in. Would you like another drink?'

'No thanks, Hunter, are you trying to get me tiddily?'

'Would I do a thing like that, Jay, or do I have to?'

'Oh, I don't know, a girl likes a bit of encouragement sometimes.'

'Mrs H, join me on the sofa and we'll talk about this.'

Jacquie unwound herself sensually from the armchair and

snuggled up alongside Hunter on the soft leather sofa and whispered in his ear. 'It's Mrs R and I'm looking for encouragement.'

Hunter twisted and threw an arm across her body and pulled her lengthways down onto the sofa and leaned across her.

'Mind the hip, lover boy, but be inventive,' she said breathlessly.

———

Williams patted his pockets as he searched for his keys and remembered the package hidden deep in the lining of his coat before he twisted the key in the lock. Picking up the plastic bag containing a six-pack and some frozen meals he was in a hurry to get into the freezer he was surprised to be met inside the door by Boris.

Speaking Ukraine, he said, 'Hi, Boris, what is it?'

'You have a visitor, Ivan. I let her into your flat.'

'What's her name, Boris?'

'Tanya.'

'That's okay, she's my new girlfriend.'

Boris shrugged and turned towards the stairs as Williams went down the hall to his flat. He didn't try to open the door, instead he knocked and waited. He heard the locks turning and the door was flung open and Tanya, wearing the erotic leather outfit she had worn when she first captured him during their Cyprus fling only waited briefly before she flung herself at him with open arms.

He could feel her athletic figure through the material and the effect it had on him and it was a full minute before he could get his breath back. Holding his bag in one hand he lifted her and pushed her back into the room and kicked the door closed behind him.

He lowered the bag to the floor and lets his coat drop from his shoulders before he grabbed her again and they continued to kiss and fondle. Breathing heavily he had to hold her away, and he said, 'What are you doing here?'

She took his hand and led him over to the kitchen area. 'Here is better, *zolatka*, and we can have dinner together,' and squeezing his hand and smiling, she added, 'and maybe talk or do something later besides I've cooked our dinner already.'

'I can't argue with that,' he said, 'but tell me, Boris let you in, that means he has a key to my flat?'

'Yes, and did you know he's Russian?'

'No, we didn't talk much. Pour me a beer, gorgeous while I take off this work gear. Tomorrow I buy a new lock.'

He kicked off his boots and picked up his coat and as he went towards the bedroom to shower he put Hunter's package on the table while Tanya picked up the bag with his goods in and after storing the borderline frozen food she poured his beer.

Later as they snuggled together on the sofa they began talking about his work. 'First of all, my Duncan, Hunter has nothing to add to what you already know and was the lock he got you the right one?'

He unwrapped the package on the table to reveal the yellow Abus lock. 'Yep, that's the right one.'

'That reminds me,' she said, and she got up from the sofa and went across to the armchair where she had left her bag and withdrew something wrapped up in cloth. She flopped down beside him and gave it to him. 'Check it, see if I've brought the right one,' she said.

He had no doubt she had as she knew his equipment inside out after nearly fourteen years together and many hours watching him practice his lock picking. He set the package on the coffee table and unwrapped the cloth to reveal a shiny oiled padlock barrel-unlocking tool and a selection of stainless tapered flat metal strips with different sized lobes on the end.

'That's them, precious.' He gave her a squeeze and wrapped them up again. 'I'll practice tomorrow night. Tell Hunter it was the right one and he owes me some wages as I was late going back to work after his clown performance.'

'You were late? How long?'

'Only five minutes but our supposed team leader is an arse licker and the boss a tight bastard and he stopped me an hours pay. Would you like some more to drink?'

'No, *I'vionachik,* I want to make love.'

She pulled him to his feet and led him to the bedroom.

~~~~~~~

Chapter 13

While the car wash crew were contemplating working a man down on the busiest day of the week, ~~while~~ Alex their foreman was parking his car outside the business premises of the 'Starlight Vehicle Designs' in a business park in the Rossfield area of Ellesmere Port close to the M53 Motorway. Shielding off the cold northwesterly wind he pulled his coat tight around him and hammered on the metal customer entrance door.

He didn't have long to wait until Fabianski opened the door and hurried him inside and after taking his coat showed him into the warm welcoming office and when they were seated he addressed him in his mother tongue which on this occasion was Russian.

' *Dobroye utro,'* Alex, 'how are you this morning?'

'*Dobroye utro,* to you, Comrad Colonel, I'm okay, but this English weather gets me. In Moscow you are cold or hot here you are wet also. You never know what to wear.'

'It won't be long, Alex, preparations are going well and I expect to be out of here in a month. The packages are safe in the English Lake district tourist area and we will be moving them here in a few days. The U.S. part of the plan is not so easy and I cannot understand who came up with the silly idea of doing it from here when doing it from Shannon was the obvious choice.'

'Colonel, Sir, should we worry about that? Have we got the equipment for the road ambulance ready for when the Air Ambulance arrives?'

'Yes, Alex, come, I'll show you.'

They stood up simultaneously and Fabianski led the way through a side door and into the main workshop and he immediately stood to one side and waved Alex forward. Before them stood a shining ex-NHS Mercedes Sprinter ambulance.

'There you are, Alex, think you can handle it?'

'Not a problem, is it loaded?'

'Not yet, Alex, you will stay here today and tomorrow to take delivery of the necessary equipment to make it believable.

This place has all the accoutrements you need like a toilet, a fridge, a TV and a kitchen and you can use the nearby shops to get food etc...'

'This includes all the sedatives and drugs that, Anna, needs as a nurse for reality?'

'Yes, she gave me a list and it was simple to order it online so no need for secrecy. It's all above board.'

'What about wannabe customers, Colonel? What do I tell them?'

'If you get any enquiries about our work or future bookings tell them we are not ready and the Ambulance is just for you to practice. Is that it?'

'Have we made any moves to get our prospective patient?'

'That will be simple enough. I have something in mind as we need to get the paperwork organised. That's it, I'm going.'

Fabianski didn't stand on ceremony. He went through into the office, picked up his coat and briefcase and without any acknowledgement, left. The look on the face of Alex said enough about this arrogant treatment and the unintelligible mutterings as Alex inspected the premises should have made Fabianski's ears burn or even encouraged a rise in temperature.

—

Work eased in the car wash around lunchtime. They were all able to take their break. Williams first port of call was to the local hardware store where he purchased a new Yale lock barrel before a hurried sandwich and a half pint in the pub before going back to work.

He knew Alex was away but he didn't trust Anna so he was back on time and for the rest of the day things became easier as the weather changed for the worse and come six 'o clock they closed shop and went home early.

Back at the flat, he checked to see if the small piece of broken match was still wedged out of sight between the door and the jam. It was, and once inside did a double check of his other security traps. People scoffed at hairs across doors and draws but these little things did work and alerted you to breaches of your privacy although a practised spook would check for them.

While the kettle boiled, he spent five minutes changing the lock before he had a welcoming cuppa as he stripped out of his work clothes and showered ready for an evening practising with his Abus lock.

After dinner, he spread his tools and the lock on the coffee table and with his back resting on the sofa he sat on the floor with his legs stretched out underneath. First, he inserted a thin flat tensioner strip and turned it clockwise until it would go no further. He took that out and fitted a telescopic disc detainer pick and because he had the keys he didn't need to waste time finding the correct size disc lever. Keeping tension on the lock with a lever extension fitted to the device he carefully tested each disc, twisting some and leaving others and after seven minutes of fiddling, he opened the lock.

He did this repeatedly until he had the time down to three minutes. He didn't think it could be done any quicker so he left it at that and settled back for a beer and an hours TV before going to bed.

He didn't think anything would come of his search around the car wash and mixing with the other 'illegal's had revealed nothing except an elaborate cover-up job to make money for Fabianski. Deep down he had misgivings about revealing this as it would mean hardship for the others and they weren't stealing jobs from UK nationals. The only people willing to do that type of work on minimum wages were immigrants legal or otherwise.

With that thought in mind, he tidied up and went to bed with a book that helped him to get to sleep.

—

Fabianski, meanwhile, was entertaining a local lady and things were getting intimate when his phone jangled. He dismissed it at first but the caller was insistent and cursing quietly in his mother tongue he picked it up and noticed it was Boris. 'Yes, Boris,' he said in English, 'what is it?'

Boris spoke his first language and addressed Fabianski by his official GRU rank. 'Comrad Colonel, sir, I have to tell you that the new guy has changed the lock to his flat.'

Fabianski stifled a curse. 'What made him do that? Okay, I'll be there in the morning. Don't call again, I'm busy.'

He switched the device off and threw it on the floor by the bed and as he rolled over, he said in his best English, 'Now Rosebud, where were we?'

Fabianski didn't waste time when he confronted Boris the next morning. 'What happened, why did he do it?'

'I did not think. The day before I let his girlfriend into his flat and he's put two and two together.'

'You did what? You let someone into his flat?'

'Yes, Comrad Colonel, I did it as a joke.'

'We may have a problem, Boris, did you get his girlfriend on CCTV?'

'Yes, Comrad Colonel, I have everything, even him changing the lock.'

'Good, let me see it.'

He followed Boris up the stairs and he screwed his nose up as the mixed smell of sweat and spicy sausage assailed him. He said nothing but waited patiently while Boris retrieved the video of the last two nights and looked closely at the pictures of Tanya. He handed Boris a small USB drive, and said, 'Hold it there, Boris and get me a copy of her close up and Andrejev if you can.'

Boris complied and two minutes later he sat back when he returned the USB drive to Fabianski. 'Is that all, Comrad Colonel?'

'No, did you get into his flat?'

'Yes, Colonel, but he is a trained man, he leaves little traps but I did not forget my KGB days. I have a master key and inside I found them.'

'What else did you find?'

'Not a lot but he has a heavy padlock in his draw with a funny looking stainless steel barrel thing and false keys. I took photos to make sure I put them back correctly.'

Fabianski turned to leave but as he did so he said over his shoulder, 'Get this place cleaned up and open some windows and use your KGB talent to smarten up. If you want to live like a gypsy I'll put you out on the street.'

He didn't wait for an answer but hurried downstairs away from the cloying atmosphere of vodka, cigarettes and bodily functions.

From there he paid a quick visit to the carwash where he spoke with Anna and then went directly to 'Starlight Vehicle Designs' to consult with Alex and using equipment installed there he sent a 'Whatsapp' photo of Tanya and Williams to the team in Moscow.

All done he put his coat on, and said to Alex, 'I will be away for a few hours as I'm going to do another reeee of the Nuclear plant. You stay here Alex and contact me immediately if we get an answer. I have a feeling that our Mr Ivan is not who or what he says he is and tomorrow our packages are being delivered. Got That?'

'Yes, Colonel.'

Before he drove off Fabianski changed into his English facade of Dr Alistair McRae and ten minutes later he was knocking on the door of his next-door neighbour and borrowed Bailey the Golden Retriever for his next excursion around the Nuclear Plant.

—

It was a little after two 'o clock when Hunter pulled into the car wash. He ignored Williams and gave his order to Anna before putting his coat on and walking off in the direction of the station.

Williams picked up the pressure soap spray and as he went around the exterior of the car spraying the wheels and lower panels he noticed the seat belt dangling below the driver's door. He put the spray down and opened the door to replace the belt at the same time surreptitiously exchanging sunglass cases in the driver's door. He stood up and slammed the door disdainfully and carried on with his spraying before using the power jet to clean off the surface dirt.

Hunter returned half an hour later and after paying his bill drove off without giving Williams a glance but he only went two hundred metres to a parking space outside the railway station.

He opened the sunglass case Williams had left and read the latest information. There wasn't much but what did interest Hunter most was the info from Tanya that Boris was Russian and Williams thought that the Ukrainian symbol tattoos worn by the other carwash workers were false. They were too new ~~ones~~ and on two of them, they had definitely changed position.

'My, my, what have you uncovered, matey?' he said mentally, 'time for some pickies methinks and no mention or connection with October other than the month.' He sat pondering for a few moments and as he slipped the car into gear, he added, 'I wonder if Alexei could help on that one?'

He did a U-turn and headed towards the City Circular intent on going to the Blacon HQ when the sudden urge for a caffeine fix came over him and did a speed dial on the Bluetooth hands-free device to Inspector Effie Newlove.

She answered immediately. 'Yes, Hunter, what is it?'

'Good morning, Effie. Are you busy?'

'Hunter, we're always busy. What is it?'

'Can we meet up for coffee somewhere?'

'Only if it's the Grosvenor Hotel and you're paying.'

'You're on. Fifteen minutes?'

'See you there, Hunter.'

He stabbed at the off button, and muttered, 'Women! Always five star.'

They met in the entrance of the classic 19th Century hotel and as they entered the building the doorkeeper acknowledged the Military Veterans badge that Hunter had pinned in the collar of his coat as he followed Effie into the plush lounge.

She paused and habitually, like all policemen and women she had a quick look around before settling for a quiet corner of the plush lounge. He helped Effie with her Burberry jacket and placed it over the back of a chair with his own and as he sat down on her immediate right so they wouldn't have to speak loudly the waiter came over and took their order.

Hunter looked at Effie, and said, 'Are you going the whole hog and having a scone?'

'Of course,' she replied and she looked up at the waiter and said to him, 'Can we have coffee for two, please, but only scones for one and two plates.'

The waiter nodded his affirmative, 'Certainly, madam, would there be anything else?'

'No, thank you.'

The waiter left and they sat back. 'Okay, Hunter, what is it you want to tell me?'

He gave Effie the note left by Williams. 'This is my latest info from our agent 'Ernesto.'

'That's Williams?'

'Yes!'

'How's he doing in the car wash?'

'He doesn't like it very much as he's got the shitty end of the stick and he's getting ripped off with the wages. Read that and I'll tell you what I want doing next.'

She took a moment to read the note and folded it up as the waiter delivered their order. She waited until he had finished and was about to speak when Hunter said, 'I thought you only ordered scones for one?'

'I did but in here you get two scones each complete with double cream and jam which is too much so help yourself.'

'Thanks, Effie, I'm looking forward to that. What do you think of the note?'

As she sliced her scone, she said, 'They are without doubt illegal and that gives uniform the right to pull them in but I suppose you think otherwise?' He was about to reply when she whispered, 'Jam first, cream second.'

He tactfully changed to her recommendation, before he replied, 'I think Williams has accidentally uncovered something which may tie into a wider plot. What? I don't know but we need to get pictures of this mob but without them knowing.' He took a bite of his scone and continued, 'therefore, I want your lot to do nothing but observe while we set up a 'watcher' team in the houses opposite. They will get the photos we want and hopefully we will get a trace on them from HQ. I have to square this with the 'firm' but that is the plan I want to put in place.'

She put her scone down, and said, 'Uum... These are delicious. Okay, Hunter, let me know when it's in place and we'll go from there. As for our investigation, we have made a significant discovery in the flat in Bourn Street and it's all down to a SOCO trainee. She found a discarded tissue and had it tested and we have previously unknown DNA with a Slavic connection. We have sent it to Interpol but as yet no luck and no other advances because of your situation as the suspect for the last murder would appear to be from the immigrant section of town.'

'We'll leave it there, Effie, and I'll be in touch. It's nice here, isn't it? A big change from the crèche called Costas in the Arcade. I'm surprised Jacquie's never dragged me in here.'

'Hunter, we women like to have our quiet time and I bet this is one of hers. Finish up I've got a job to do.'

'You go ahead, Effie, I'm going to hang on here awhile and speak to the 'firm' and I forgot to mention, tell your lot to look out for NY Yankee symbols, they're ours.'

He stood up and helped her with her coat and she held out a hand and as they shook hands, she said, 'Thanks for the update, Hunter, it's much appreciated as was the coffee. I'll return the compliment sometime.'

'I'll look forward to it, Effie, take care.'

He watched her for a moment as she left the lounge before he sat down and dialled a number on his phone and waited until a grumpy Gus Thomas answered, 'Yes, Hunter!'

'Good day to you too, you grouchy old bugger. You said you wanted a catch-up call well here it is. I want a 'watcher' team set-up opposite the car wash where Williams is working and get photos of the staff.'

'Why's that?'

'Tanya, William's wife, has discovered that the housekeeper in his block of flats is Russian and because of other discrepancies with the workers in the wash we believe they maybe also be Russian but posing as legal Ukrainians.'

'I see. I'll get onto that straight away. Was there anything else?'

'One more thing, Gus, get the debriefers to ask Savitsky if he can tell us any more about the October connection other than the revolution and the month. There is a connection there somewhere.'

'I can go one better than that, Hunter. A young crypto-analyst from GCHQ and I mean 'young', eighteen, in fact, has broken the code on Owen's computer and it appears he was investigating the 'October Legion."

'Who are they, Gus?'

'These are the leftover sleeper agents from the Cold War spread around the UK but it's beginning to look like Owen stumbled on more than he bargained for and uncovered a re-awakened 'October' team operating as Ukrainians.'

'Doing what, Gus? At the moment we only have a carwash which, with the murders, could be the start of something I suppose.'

'Get Williams to dig a bit deeper and I'll chase up the 'watcher' department to get on the job quickly. Do you need a hand up there, Hunter, or can you cope?'

'Thanks for the concern, Gus, but I'm managing at the moment. The hardest job is keeping the local fuzz happy. They're itching to make arrests and close the murder cases.'

'I'll get in touch with the Cheshire Chief Constable and make sure they don't spoil it.'

'Thank, Gus, and tell the watchers about our Yankees symbol, okay!'

The line went dead and he ordered another coffee and began writing in his notebook while pondering the new information and he made a quick grab for his phone as it jangled out in the cosy atmosphere and as he answered he looked around embarrassed but nobody was the slightest bit concerned. 'Sign of the times,' he muttered to himself as he slid his finger up the green tab. 'Hunter!'

'Agent Hunter?'

'That's me,' replied Hunter, 'in the flesh.'

'Mr Hunter, this is Dan Walker, we met a couple of weeks ago after the Bourn Street fandango.'

'I've got ya! How are you, Dan, it didn't take you long. I take it you're in charge of the 'watchers' again?'

'Got it in one, Hunter, we'll be back on the job in a couple of hours. We're flying up asap. Is there a likely place we could use for this job?'

'Yep! I sussed it out this morning. There's a small travellers hotel right opposite. I'll go there now and organise things. If they can't do it a couple of doors down they are refurbishing an old Georgian four-storey house and we could probably get in there.'

'Good, I'll be in touch as soon as we touch down at Broughton.' He rang off immediately.

Hunter sat back and looked at the phone in his hand quizzically for a moment. 'You don't hang around, do you, Walker,' he said as he swiped the 'off' app.

He slurped the rest of his coffee and dropped a tip on the table before paying the tab on the way out and making his way to his car.

Ten minutes later he drove past the carwash and the line of shops immediately after it and when he reached the roundabout he took the first exit and instantly left again into a narrow alley at the back of the shops. He progressed slowly until he came to the rear entrance of the hairdressers and pulled alongside a shiny red Mazda two-seater sports car. He left a 'Police' sign on his dashboard and rapped sharply on the back door of the hairdressers and waited. After a minute he banged with a bit more aggression and the door eased open and Phil the hairdresser looked out. 'Yeah! What is it?'

Hunter held up his ID. 'Mr Chadwick, is it?'

Phil looked closer at the ID before he answered, 'Yes, that's me, what can I do for you?'

'Can we go inside, Mr Chadwick?'

Phil stepped back and with a jerk of his head signalled Hunter into what was a snug kitchen and rest room at the back of the shop and waited while the door was closed behind him before he spoke. 'Mr Chadwick, I'm MI6 and I want to leave my car out the back and pass through. Will that be alright? I'll spare you the details but it will help us with our investigation.'

Phil handed Hunter one of his cards. 'No problem, what did you say your name was?'

'Hunter.'

'That's okay, Mr Hunter, there's my details but it'll cost you a haircut. You could do with a trim.'

'Got it,' he looked at the card, 'Phil. I'll let you get on and we'll see about the hair later. I'll keep you informed.'

Phil showed him into the shop with just one customer waiting and watched Hunter go out through the front and wander casually across the road and along to the Bourn Street Hotel.

Inside Reception at the desk he was met by a young girl who greeted him cheerfully, 'Good morning,' she glanced at her watch,' Yes, were still there, just!'

'And, Good Morning, to you too, young lady,' he showed her his ID, 'can I speak with your manager, please?'

'Yes,' she said, 'can I ask what it's about?'

'Err, unexpected business would be the best, I think.'

She picked up the phone and pressed a key and spoke quietly for a few moments and as she replaced the phone, she said, 'Mrs Minchin is on her way.'

'Thanks, lass.'

He didn't have long to wait when a smartly dressed businesslike lady came through the swing door at the end of the entrance hall and as she approached she held her hand out. 'What can I do for you, Mr...?'

He shook her hand and proffered his ID. '...Hunter, Can we talk somewhere private?'

'Yes, of course. Come through.'

He followed her through the hall door and immediately turned right into a well-proportioned and very organised office where she showed him a chair. 'Take a seat, Mr Hunter,' and she sat behind a modest modern desk.

'It's just, Hunter, Mrs Minchin. I'm the local controller for the Security Services and I want to hire a top floor front room for observation purposes. Have you got one?'

'Just a moment I'll check with young, Carol.' She spoke for a few moments over the phone before she continued, 'We have one on the third floor directly above the entrance. It's a twin room but I don't suppose that matters. Can I ask, what for?'

'It will be mainly camera work and probably two people in there at the most maybe two days.'

'When do you want it?'

'This afternoon so they can start immediately. Is there any other access beside the front door?'

'We have an entrance around the back with space for parking.'

'Good, that saves me annoying the hell out of Phil the hairdresser over the road.'

'Oh, he's okay. Who do I bill it to?'

'Speak to a chap called Dan Walker when the team arrives later today. It's just possible they may want another room beside that one. All good for business.'

'Very welcome, Hunter.'

He stood up and dropped his card on the desk before he held out his hand. 'Mrs Minchin, keep this under your hat and definitely—no social media. I won't go into all that 'Official Secrets' crap. I'll trust you.'

She stood up and shook hands. 'Thank you, Hunter. It's safe with me and I'll speak to the staff.' He was about to leave the room when he turned back. 'One more thing, Mrs Minchin, have you any Eastern European staff?'

'No, I have a lovely Guyanian couple and the chef is ex-Army. Very good too but we don't do fancy here only down to earth basic meals. Healthy ones mind.'

'Sounds good to me. I'll be in touch. Thank you.'

He didn't go back through the hairdressers but instead went to the end of the road and around the back of the shops and saw that Phil had pushed one of his business cards under a windscreen wiper.

'Now is that for me or to tell the neighbours?' He had a little smile to himself. 'Probably both. He's touting for business.'

Manoeuvring around the cars in the alley was tricky but once out on the main road he did a recce trip around the rear of the hotel. Satisfied by what he found he parked by the railway station and sent a *Whatsapp* message to Dan Walker with the hotel postcode and back entrance info and advising that a hire car would be there for them. That done he sent another message this time to Tanya and arranged to meet at Garden Centre № 1 in half an hour.

—

He placed the tray on the table and gave Tanya her Mocha before he sat down with his statuary Americano. 'Lunch is coming soon, Tanya. They'll bring it over when it's ready and would you believe it, she made me sign for it. I can see the increased expenses of the security services will soon be a debate in parliament. Now, where was I? I know, make a note, Tanya, and memorise it. 'Watchers' are in the Bourn Street Hotel taking photos and tracking movements during daylight hours. The Yankees is still the symbol to watch out for.'

One of the Restaurant staff came over, and said, 'Hi! Mr Hunter, lunch is served.' She placed a bacon batch in front of him and passed a healthier veggie wrap to Tanya, 'I'm sorry, Mr Hunter, but the boss cancelled your other batch, can I get you anything else?'

'No thanks, lass, I'm in enough trouble.'

'Enjoy,' she said, and she spun away and walked back to join her colleagues.

They didn't speak while they ate and then Hunter sat back and wiped his hands on a napkin. 'Was there anything else, Tanya?'

She pushed her plate away. 'Yes, you're my boss now, what do I call you?'

'Hunter! Is that it?'

'No, do you think it a good idea if I got a job at the car wash? I mean, I'm one of them and might fit in better. I know Duncan is good, but...'

'Don't worry, Tanya, I'm not expecting this to last very long. What I'm more afraid of is we might shut them down before we know what's going on. Did he tell you what he wanted that lock for?'

'No, but you know what he's like, he loves playing with locks.'

'I suppose so but that one was bloody expensive and I've no doubt questions will be asked.'

'I'll ask him tonight, Mr Hunter.'

'You're going to see him?'

'Yes, I've got my own key and I've cooked his favourite.'

Hunter waved a finger at her. 'Business first, Agent Tanya.'

She laughed. 'Of course, followed by dinner, what else?'

They stood up and he helped her with her jacket. 'Take care and we'll speak tomorrow.'

—

Williams checked the time on his mobile. It was 3 a.m. and he slid from the bed doing his best not to disturb Tanya but before he could move off the bed a hand reached out and she whispered sleepily, 'Be careful, *lyubovnik,*' and immediately curled up cuddling a pillow.

He tiptoed out and into the lounge area where his clothes were laid out ready. Dressed head to foot in black he jammed his Yankees cap on, picked up his phone and closing the door softly behind him went into the darkened hallway. It was then he noticed for the first time two-pinprick red lights in the smoke alarm. He dismissed them and eased the front door open and gently closed it behind him and with a quick look around to see the coast was clear he went out onto the pavement.

Keeping close to the buildings it took him two minutes to walk round to the junction by the 'Cheshire Arms.' The roads were clear and he crossed over to the carwash side of Bourn Street and sticking close to the wall walked slowly up to the entrance. Some sixth sense made him stop and he cautiously peered around the corner of the building and into the carwash and he saw the Dewey Mobile Home backed up to the open doors of the container and Fabianski and Alex were lifting a heavy package out. Williams ducked back and pressed himself tighter against the wall and slowly eased out just enough to see with one eye the transfer of the package into the container.

He'd seen enough and he melted into the shadows and retraced his way back to the flat and in ten minutes he was snuggled up behind Tanya.

—

Fabianski, Alex and the Dewey's stood around the two weighty brown suitcases laying on a board across trestles and Fabianski who liked everything ship shape nudged one into line with the other before he spoke in his native Russian. 'Were there no instructions?'

Matt shrugged. 'No, they're both the same and you can pick which one you use here or in the U.S.'

'You have the keys?'

Dewey pulled an envelope from an inside pocket and gave it to Alex. 'I forgot about them. There are probably instructions in there as well.'

Fabianski took the envelope, before he asked, 'What are you two going to do now?'

Maria spoke for the first time. 'We are finished with this and are going home to Aldermaston. What you do from now on is your business. If you've nothing else to add we'll be off.' She took hold of Matt's arm and eased him towards the door.

'One moment,' said Fabianski, 'you said home. Where is that? You're not going back to the Mother country?'

Maria stopped and turned and looked Fabianski straight in the eyes. 'We have lived here for thirty-four years in the service of our Mother country and this is our home now. We have family and grown-up kids. You may call on us as we swore we would do but we stay here.' She grabbed Matt's arm again, 'come, we go now.'

She pushed him through the doors and towards his side of the camper van before climbing into the passenger seat and within two minutes they were gone.

Fabianski looked at Alex and shrugged. 'I bet she nags him something rotten.'

'Don't they all,' muttered Alex, 'What's the plan now, Colonel?'

'Go to Starlight in the morning, Alex, and I'll see you there in time for the morning update from 'Wyskochka' base. I'm hoping for news of the next delivery of Nuclear Waste at Capenhurst and then we move.'

'Have you found a place to plant it?'

'Yes, and you will watch for the transport in a lay-by on the main road and detonate it by dialling on your mobile phone eleven minutes after it has passed you. I will give you the number later.'

'Will I be safe?'

'Yes, it's only a 'dirty bomb' and you will be gone before any rubbish spreads. Lock up, Alex, and off you go to bed. I'll be in touch.'

'Shouldn't we check them?'

'No, I have seen them and they are disguised and ready. The hand-operated suicide trigger has been removed and all I have to do is fit the remote mobile phone detonator, so, goodnight, or rather, morning.'

~~~~~~

Chapter 14

Hunter went to the Blacon HQ and saw they were coping and that the criminal fraternity of Chester was keeping them busy and instead headed for the rear entrance of the Bourn St Hotel. Inside he poked his head around the office door and said his 'Good mornings' to Mrs Minchin before dragging himself up three flights of stairs to Room 302. He pushed the door open and before the 'watchers' huddled over their equipment could move, he said, 'Morning guys, how's it going?'

The man peering through the day and night binoculars placed two metres back from the window turned his head and seeing who it was, replied, 'Morning, Hunter, it looks like a normal day over there but your man has his cap on back to front.'

'That means he has a message. How are the photos coming?'

The figure huddled over the camera alongside the binos stepped back and stood upright and a presentable young woman with the deepest of brown eyes shook her long dark brown curls loose. 'Very well, Mr Hunter...' she held her hand out, '...Alpha 3 reporting,' she flicked a thumb over her shoulder, 'and that's Alpha 2. Would you like a drink? Mrs Minchin is very generous with the extras.'

'A good strong coffee, Alpha 3 or should I call you, Penny? How are you and what are you doing with this lot?'

'I'm fine, thanks, but this department is busy and I volunteered as it's only a short job.' She stepped away from the camera and went over to the tray on the dressing table with the kettle and assorted packets on. 'Lavazza Americano do you, Hunter?'

'Very much, any ginger nuts?'

'It's Kit Kat or nothing.'

'I'll share one.'

'Suits me,' she said, 'gives me an excuse to indulge.'

While she was making the coffee, Hunter continued, 'I'm surprised they let you come, Penny, after the rumours.'

She laughed and shook her head. 'I think Gus Thomas is

winding you up. He was only too keen to get me up here.'

Penny finished what she was doing and when she handed Hunter his mug he threw his coat off and sat on one of the beds which had been pushed over to the side of the room while Penny stood by the camera. 'We have photos of all of them,' she said, 'but someone is missing. We were told there were ten but we only have nine and one of them is your man.'

Hunter stood up and went to the binoculars. 'Let me have a look.'

Alpha 2 stood to one side and Hunter after tweaking the focus knobs looked across the street and watched for two minutes and when he stepped back, he said, 'It looks like their supervisor is missing. He's been identified as Alex and he's been absent for a few days.'

'What's going on, Hunter,' said Penny, 'why the interest in a car wash?'

'Very briefly, Pen, we think they are cover for a Soviet plot which one of our GCHQ ops uncovered but we have no positive leads as yet.'

'I heard about that,' said A2, 'he went off on a loner instead of handing it over to 'A' Branch. Owen, wasn't it?'

'That's right, and his demise, which brought us in, lead to the deaths of two others. We are hoping that we might I.D. them from the photos.' He put his mug down and scooped up his coat, 'I can't do anything more here, I'll leave you to it. If a smart grey haired guy in a business suit about six foot tall turns up that's the boss. Make sure you get a good picky of him. Cheerio, see you around, Penny. If you get a chance come and meet, Jacquie, she's dying to meet you.'

'I bet,' she laughed, 'bugger off, Hunter.'

—

In the '*Cheshire Arms,*' Williams was sat with his pint and a sandwich when Hunter with his hair roughed up and wearing glasses and a Yankees bomber jacket crashed down on the bench beside him and haphazardly plonked his beer on the table.

'How you doing, boyo, you like it here?'

Williams replied in his best broken English, 'I like here but the work hard and you?'

Hunter picked up his pint and replied with his poor Welsh accent, 'It's okay, but I like my hometown better.'

While they were talking, Williams slid a note across the bench between them and under the jacket of Hunter. 'Are you working,' he said, 'because I know a good job.'

'I'm doing okay, mate.'

Williams finished his sandwich and took the last swig from his glass and stood up. 'Cheerio, see you around.'

Before Hunter could answer, he left without looking around. Hunter leaned back and while he was sipping the last drop from his glass he picked up the note with his other hand and slipped it into his jacket pocket before he too left the pub.

Back at his car, he read Williams' proposed break-in of the container on site but most of all his interest was the info that there had been a delivery by a camper van at three a.m. that morning. After that, he wasn't sure that Williams should go ahead with his plan and on the drive back to the Garden Centre which had become his HQ he played the likely scenario over and over in his mind.

'Should he or shouldn't he?' was the question that plagued him. In the end, he decided that Williams could look after himself.

—

Still drowsy after his early morning stint Alex was slumped across the desk in the back office of 'Starlight' with his eyes shut when he was disturbed by the i-pad in front of him ringing its alarm bells. Alex lifted his eyes and wearily reached forward and acknowledged the Whatsapp message before dropping his head forward onto his arms again. It was not for long as his i-phone penetrated the cloud in his brain and with a long sigh, he pulled himself upright, saw it was Fabianski and answered it immediately.

'Comrad Colonel?'

'Petrov! Have you had a signal or message?'

'Yes, Colonel.'

'And?'

'Sorry, Colonel, I was sleeping and have not looked.'

'Petrov, we do not pay you to sleep. Check it out and let me know if it has anything important. I am making my way back and should be with you in half an hour. Get to it.'

The connection went dead and Alex sat stiffly upright and sarcastically saluted, 'Ða ser!' he shouted.

He ignored the instruction and splashed his face and made himself a coffee before he addressed the issue of the i-pad and he couldn't believe what he read and went through the message again.

'Comrad Colonel, you will be pleased, I don't think.'

His musings were disturbed by the customer door alarm and he went into the reception office expecting Fabianski instead he found an attractive lady with long straight blonde hair dressed in black with a brand logo on the breast pocket and an I.D. label hanging around her neck.

She checked her watch, and said brightly, 'Good afternoon.'

Alex responded, 'Good afternoon, what can I do for you?'

She plonked her bag on the counter and pushed a business card over. 'My names, Julie,' she said, 'and I have my own candle business...' The door alarm jangled and she paused and looked over her shoulder to see who was entering as Fabianski closed the door behind him, '...and I want advertising logos on my car. Can you do that?'

'One moment, miss, I speak with my boss.' Alex spoke to Fabianski. 'Our suppliers have left a message for you, Boss. It's on the desk.' He turned back to Julie, 'I'm sorry, miss, we are not open for business yet. We are having problems with our suppliers.' He bent forward and scrabbled under the desk for a moment before he stood up and held out a business card to her. 'Here, miss, you go to these people and say we sent you, okay?'

'Oh!,' she said, 'I could have saved myself a trip, thanks for your help anyway.'

She scooped her bag up and wheeled out of the door displeased with the outcome. Alex waited until she had reached her car and then locked the door before joining Fabianski in the back office.

'Have you read it, Colonel?'

Fabianski nodded, 'I knew Andrejev had something to hide when he changed the lock on his apartment and see his girlfriend Tanya, who is his wife. She is a double traitor, first in 2001 and now. She is our diversion for the U.S. We wait until she stays with Andrejev overnight and then we deal with them both.

Is the ambulance ready?'

' Yes, Colonel.'

'Good, prepare, Anna and I will chase up the paperwork and passports needed in the U.S. for the woman.'

Williams stretched out on the sofa preparing for an evenings TV, a beer and his favourite Chinese curry when he heard a key turning in the lock. His first reaction was to swing his legs down and to reach over to his jacket hanging on the back of a chair where his Glock 17 was hidden.

He was slow and Tanya stepped into the room before he could reach it.' What the..., what are you doing here? Who's looking after the kids?'

She dropped her bag and opened her arms and let her *Barbour* quilted coat slide to the floor and she stepped in front of him and grabbed his sweater in both hands and pulled him towards her. 'Nice to see you too, *lyubovnik.* Kiss me before I do some damage.' She jerked him forward and they kissed passionately. After a few seconds, she let him go, and continued, 'Hunter sent me. If you find anything tonight, he thought you might want to get a quick message out and there you have it. I'm a messenger. Oh, and the kids, they like their new Auntie, she's not strict like me.'

'I know, Hunter,' he said, 'the old bugger is worried. He wouldn't have done this a few years ago. Have you eaten, Tanya?'

'I've brought my own.' She picked her bag up and went into the kitchen and set up her own Chinese takeaway and joined him on the sofa. 'Now tell me about tonight.'

In between forkfuls, Williams explained that after the previous night's discovery of a delivery it was his intention to find out what it was but he didn't see any reason for Hunter's decision to send Tanya but he looked forward to an early night together ready for his three 'o clock start in the morning.

On the stroke of the witching hour, Williams inserted the detainer skeleton key into the lock and when he had maximum pressure he fitted the detainer pick tool and began painstakingly moving the lever access tool backwards and forwards until he had raised all seven catches inside the lock and with a sigh of relief the lock popped open.

He put his tools away and eased the lock from the hasp and hooked it into the staple before he eased the door open. It was well oiled and opened easily and he slid in and closed it behind him. He switched on a small LED torch and shone it around and stopped when he spotted the two leather cases on the trestles. In the torchlight, he took a photo on his smartphone and then he checked the floor for obstacles before moving across to them. After a moments sizing up he unfastened the straps on one of them and with his basic lock picking tool he opened it. He lifted the lid and let out a low gasp at what confronted him. He quickly took another snap and posted both pictures on Whatsapp just a few seconds before the container door swung open. Fabianski stepped in with a Makarov pistol fitted with a silencer held two-handed in front of him.

He fired instantly. Williams spun and fell to the floor gasping for life and unseen in the shadows his phone skidded across the floor and came to rest against the wall.

Williams was still clinging to life with a look of determination in his eye when Fabianski walked over to him and calculatingly held the gun a foot from his face and unemotionally pulled the trigger. He put his gun away and began searching Williams pockets until he found his apartment keys and then went to the door where Alex was waiting and gave them to him, and said, 'Here's the keys but first of all give me a hand.'

Back inside Fabianski finished sorting through William's belongings and was surprised to find the handgun but what he wanted most of all was I.D. It took him a while but he found it in a concealed pocket in the lining of Williams coat along with the GPS device. He dropped the GPS on the floor and stamped on it. That done he fetched his SUV from the customer parking and gestured to Alex to take Williams upper body while he took the legs and together they carried him out to the SUV and loaded it onto plastic sheets in the luggage area and pushed it in as far as it would go.

'Alex! We are going to have to do it ahead of schedule. Help me load the packages I will take one and you take the other to put in the ambulance but first I want to check the contents.'

They lifted the lid of the one Williams had opened and while Fabianski studied the pack inside Alex stood back and watched but he took a deep breath and exhaled with his hand over his mouth when he saw the labels. He had heard of the suicide mini nuclear bombs carried by North Korean troops as a last ditch reprisal and this was one of them.

'That is not a dirty bomb,' he said to himself.

Fabianski closed and fastened the case and together they carried it out to the car and shoved it tight up against Williams body and closed the tailgate. Fabianski gave Alex the thumbs up, and said, 'Load the other package into your car and get around to the apartment and help Boris.'

While Alex hurried to fetch his car Fabianski dialled a number and as soon as it was answered he was sparing with his words. 'Five minutes,' was all he said and hung up and drove off taking the shortest route out of town back to his lodgings.

Alex meanwhile heaved the heavy bag into the trunk of his car and proceeded to lock up and a minute later he was on his way to the apartment where he parked at the rear of the premises alongside Williams Skoda. He didn't lock the car instead he eased open the rear doors and left them before treading carefully across the narrow space to the back door of the block.

It was open and Boris was waiting inside with a small plastic box and together they crept through the house and stopped outside Williams apartment and listened for a few seconds. Hearing nothing Alex slid the key into the lock and they entered and leaving the door ajar tiptoed towards the bedroom. They listened again and Alex nodded and together they eased into the room and without hesitation, they dived onto the bed and made a grab for Tanya.

Although half-asleep Tanya was quick to react and in her struggles she pushed her i-phone from under the pillow. She tried to scream but Alex had his hand firmly over her mouth and nodded to Boris who opened the little box and taking out a hypodermic syringe he pulled the duvet to one side and jabbed it into Tanya's thigh. It didn't take long for the *Propofol* to take effect and she slowly stopped struggling and eventually went into a drug-inspired sleep.

Alex picked up her phone and purse ~~table~~ and together they worked quickly and rolled her into the duvet. Nudging furniture aside, with unexpected tenderness they carried her inert body through the house and out to the car. When she was safely restrained across the back seat Alex left Boris to lock-up and departed into the night for the drive to the 'Starlight' premises where Anna was waiting.

Anna, in her nurse's role, took over. She did an overall examination of Tanya and then made Alex remove his outer garments and wear sterile gloves as they sprayed and sanitised the suitcase with its secret before securing it into a hidden compartment under the mobile patient transfer bed and then treating Tanya like any other patient in poor health they transferred her to the ambulance. Anna chased Alex out and began the precise fitting of the equipment to make Tanya comfortable and ready for her journey as a terminally ill comatose patient across to the USA while Alex went to the office and went through Tanya's purse mainly out of curiosity and he was surprised when he found her MI6 issue GPS device. He wasn't sure what he was going to do with it but he dropped it into his pocket with her phone.

—

While driving back to his bungalow Fabianski determined his next move. Plan 'A' he decided was to be discarded and instead everything would be brought forward on an ad-hoc basis.

Considerate of his neighbours, he quietly parked his SUV on the drive down the side of the bungalow. It was late but he made the effort to heave the package into the kitchen and spent the next hour fitting the simple adaption of a mobile phone as a trigger system. Planting the device and disposing of Williams would be done at the earliest opportunity. The planned flight out to the U.S. would be brought forward and take place in twenty-four hours.

That done he poured himself a stiff single malt whisky one of the finer elements of life outside Russia and then set about sending a message to his №1, General Josef Bazarov in Moscow who being three hours ahead would be waking from his slumbers.

Fabianski smiled inwardly although it was probably not the right occasion, and said to himself, 'That's going to spoil his breakfast.'

He emptied his glass and threw himself onto the sofa to grab some sleep.

~~~~~

Chapter 15

Josef Bazarov pushed himself back from the breakfast table and reached for his coffee cup but before his hand could settle on the handle the door burst open and his aide-de-campe pushed his way in his progress heeded by a security guard. The aide shook himself loose and hurried across the room while the guard stood to attention, and said aloud, 'Comrad General, I am sorry, I tried to stop him.'

Bazarov stood and wiped his mouth with his napkin and held out a hand to take a piece of paper being held out to him by his aide at the same time waving a dismissive hand at the guard. 'What is it, Captain, that is so important?'

He didn't wait for an answer but instead picked up his reading glasses off the table and studied the message. He read it twice before removing his glasses. 'When did this arrive, Captain?'

'Seven 'o clock, Comrad General, just as the night manager signed off.'

'Why didn't you bring it then?'

'I did not wish to disturb you during your ablutions and breakfast?'

'In future, Captain, just bring it. Right now though you will contact the committee and get them here a.s.a.p. We will meet in an hour. Leave me now I have a call to make. Oh! And take it easy on our security, they have a job to do so use the protocol and make him feel better by letting him ask my permission. Like a speeding car, the few seconds saved won't make any difference'

The aide saluted and left and Josef picked up his coffee cup and drank the dregs. He was about to go to his study when his wife came in. 'Josef, can I get you anything else?'

'Net, moya milaya, something important has come up. Can you send some more coffee to my study and don't disturb me. The committee will be meeting in an hour.'

'Yes, Josef, I will make sure the room is ready.'

He blew her a kiss as he collected his glasses and left the room. Two minutes later he was sat behind his desk and looking at the red phone with mixed feelings. 'How do you give bad news nicely and survive?' was a dilemma he could do without. He reached for the phone, picked it up and it was halfway to his ear when he shook his head and replaced it.

He was sat looking at the phone for half a minute when he took a deep breath and released it before reaching for the handset and dialled. His fingers drummed on the desk in a nervous tattoo until a voice answered. He stiffened in the sitting attention position and listened. 'Comrad Bazarov, what is so urgent that you have to call me on this line?'

'Moi iskrenniye izvineniya, gospodin, Comrad Nachal'nik, something very disturbing has happened and I need to warn you and take your advice.'

'Spill it, Josef.'

'The U.K. security has penetrated our plot. We have eliminated the infiltrator but we don't know how much has been uncovered. Colonel Fabianski (~~Fabianski~~) suggests we bring the timetable forward. That is—don't wait for the delivery of the radioactive waste and do it now. He is setting it up tonight and also pushing on with the U.S. plot.'

The line went quiet but in the background, Josef could hear muffled rantings and a fist thumping a table. After about ten seconds a calm voice, said, 'Do that, Josef, set up but hold the U.K. until you are in position in the U.S. or nearly ready to do so. I will bring forward the troop manoeuvres anticipating an outcome in a week. Keep me informed.'

Josef clicked his heels and replied with a stiff, 'Yes, Comrad Nachal'nik.' He didn't salute but his hand was hovering.

With a relieved sigh he put down the phone and prepared for the committee meeting which would be a brief affair following the directions of his leader and then he paused, 'They can wait, I must tell Fabianski.'

He scrabbled in his pocket for his mobile and after turning it around a few times cursing modern technology he got it the right way up and he poked a finger down on the *Whatsapp* symbol. The message was brief and to the point which left Fabianski in no doubt as to his next course of action.

—

It was eight 'o clock and Hunter was starting his second cup of coffee when his phone jangled. 'What now,' he muttered, 'at this time of the morning.'

He slid his finger up the answer symbol, 'Yes, Alpha 3, what is it?'

'Hunter, it's me, Penny! Williams hasn't shown up for work. We've waited an hour in case there was a delay or something but now we're worried.'

'Thanks, Penny, leave it with me. I'll be in touch.'

He put his phone down and noticed a Whatsapp notification. 'What the hell's that?' He tapped the app and two photos jumped out at him. 'Where did those come from. He looked closer and saw Williams ID and he tapped each photo in turn. It was the second one that caught his attention. Inside was a moulded box with rucksack type straps attached, but it was the labels he focussed on. A North Korean Flag and next to it the yellow and black international symbols for radioactive material.

'Jesus! Is that what I think it is. Shit!'

He closed the device but before he could take further action, his phone bleeped again. He picked it up and noted the caller. It was Agent Carrie Long. 'Yes, Carrie, what can I do for you?'

'Hunter, Tanya's missing and she's not answering her phone. She stayed over with Williams last night.'

'Shit!... sorry, Carrie. Was that her service phone you tried?'

'She left that at home. I tried her personal one.'

'Okay, Carrie. Williams is missing too. Lockdown that place and get yourself here asap. No, make it to Blacon Police Station instead. I'll see you there.'

'The kids, Hunter?'

'Second thoughts, Carrie, you'd best stay there. I'll keep you updated but it doesn't sound good.'

'Roger that, Hunter. Fingers crossed.'

He shut down the call and instantly dialled Inspector Newlove and when she answered he gave her no time to speak. 'Effie! This is

Hunter. '*Operation Trenchcoat*' is live. Get around and close that carwash and arrest anyone in it and do Williams apartment at the same time and search for traces of Williams and his wife Tanya. As before, Blues only and get armed back-up, and Effie! Don't go near that black container, it's a health issue, understood? Instead, warn SOCO to wear anti-radiation gear. See you at the carwash.'

'Err... Yes, but why?'

'I'll explain later. As promised do this before I call Special Branch.'

He closed the call and speed dialled Gus Thomas. He didn't waste time but laid out the full picture, to which Thomas replied, 'I'll inform 'C' and then standby for my helicopter.'

That settled Hunter grabbed his coat and on his way out blew a kiss to a sleepy Jacquie who was just coming into the kitchen.

'Can't stop, lass—Love you!'

———

Fifteen minutes later with blue LED lights flashing from behind the radiator grill, Hunter turned into Bourn Street. He was immediately confronted by two armed police officers standing by a Police vehicle parked in such a way that only one lane was clear and ignoring the LED's they stopped him. A tall female armed officer who looked competent with all the regulation gear on stayed back on alert while her male companion came forward and took Hunter's ID which he was holding up through the open car window.

Satisfied the officer handed the ID back. 'Thanks, Mr Hunter, your good to go.' He signalled his female partner who visibly relaxed and stepped back to let Hunter through and as he passed them he raised a hand in acknowledgement. Twenty metres further on he bumped up onto the pavement and parked behind a police car.

He didn't count the number of vehicles but he did wonder how many were left to keep up with the everyday jobs. He walked into the carwash and joined a small group including Effie who were watching and waiting for the SOCO operatives to investigate the container while on the other end of the wash a group of dispirited staff were being held ready to be transported to the cells.

He touched Effie's elbow, and said, 'Morning, Effie, how goes it?'

She looked around and seeing who it was stepped back from the group. 'Morning, Hunter. It's going okay, there are two tech boys in the container checking for radiation before the rest of the SOCO team go in and we're waiting for a bus to take the staff away but what happened and why the precautions?'

'Let's step back from the crowd, Effie and I'll fill you in.'

They retreated a few metres and stood by the low front wall and he told her about Williams and Tanya and showed her the pictures that Williams had messaged to him, '...and because of those nuclear warning symbols we can't take chances, though I'm told that radiation is low from these devices until they are triggered. Is there someone at the apartment?'

'Yes, Farmer is and what he's found is quite worrying. It looks like she's been kidnapped?'

'What makes him think that?'

'Her clothes are still there but the bedroom is upside down like there was a disturbance and the duvet is missing. That Boris is in custody.

'This does not sound good, Effie. I haven't told SB yet and I won't until SOCO has finished as I want to see what we've got. Here we go, the techy guys are out.'

They walked over to join the SOCO team and while the two operatives were stripping off their protective clothing Dr Kerr joined them.

'Hunter! Inspector! The container is clear. Whatever radiation was in there has dispersed but I am sad to tell you that there are traces of blood on the floor. We are going in now to do a proper crime scene investigation. Put overalls and overshoes on and join us but there's not much to see.'

They retrieved the necessary gear from Effie's car and followed the team into the container that was now floodlit. Dr Kerr was right as there was only two trestle tables down the centre and nothing else but these were the centre of attention as the blood was plainly visible. They mutually agreed there was nothing they could do when one of the operatives kneeling by the end wall called them over. He was holding up a smartphone between two gloved fingers.

'I've got something of interest.'

Dr Kerr took it off him and brought it over to Hunter and Effie. 'It's one of yours, Hunter.' He turned it over to show them the WD mark.

Hunter eased his device out of his pocket and after a bit of fiddling, he dialled a number and instantly the smartphone sprang to life. Hunter closed the call, and said, 'It's Duncan's. How soon can we have it, Doc?'

'Don't worry, Hunter, I'll get one of the team to fingerprint it and give it the once over in the van and you can have it in the hour.'

'Thanks, Doc.' He turned to Effie. 'While we're waiting let's go to the flat and see what they've turned up.'

'Okay, Hunter, there's nothing here. I'll have a word with the team and I'll be right with you.'

As they left the container a faint familiar odour wafted over him. 'Hang on, Effie, won't be a tick.' He ducked back into the container and stood in the middle of the floor and took a deep breath, and, 'Yes,' there it was. Discernible hints of carnations, jasmine and cinnamon. A memory from his youth. 'Old Spice,' an aftershave he would never forget and one that was still in his cabinet.

Outside Hunter stripped out of his protective gear and joined Effie who was organising the rest of the squad and on a nod from him, she went to her car and followed Hunter around to Williams flat where parking was first come first served and they had to settle for a space a hundred metres down the road.

Effie was first through the door and DC Farmer was there to meet them.

'What have you got, Farmer?'

Farmer acknowledged them, and said, 'Inspector! Mr Hunter! Put your gear on and come and see the flat where that Boris guy lived.'

They put overalls and shoe covers on and followed Farmer upstairs. At the top, they put gloves on and went into what can only be described as a single man's pit.

'There's not much to see, boss, but over here in the corner is CCTV recording gear. I've only had a brief look but it shows Agent Williams and his partner plus someone we think is the leader of the outfit.'

'Effie,' said Hunter, 'I want those tapes or should I say we both want them and let's view them asap before you interview the guy and I want a picture of that leader fella.'

'Farmer!' said Effie, 'bag them up. All of them and we'll take them. Let's take a look at Williams place.'

Farmer spoke to one of the SOCO ops before leading the way downstairs to the flat. He stood to one side and let Hunter and Effie go in. At first sight, it was obvious that something had happened as the furniture was disarranged in a manner that suggested it had been pushed aside to allow easier passage. Walking through they went into the sleeping area and Effie stopped in the doorway and took a deep breath before stepping to one side and letting Hunter in.

'There's been a ruckus here, Hunter, which like Farmer said suggests kidnapping.'

'You're right there, Effie. There's not much we can do, let's talk to Boris.'

In the hall they stripped off their protective gear and Farmer gave them an evidence bag with some videos in it.

'Well done, Farmer. Stay here until they're finished.'

Outside they stripped off their protective overalls and Effie said to Hunter. 'See you at Blacon HQ.'

'Okay, lass, can I get you anything from the canteen while I'm waiting?'

'I'll be there before you but you can call into the local *Tesco Express* and get me a proper latte.'

'Will do.'

Effie and Hunter stood in the corridor outside Interview Room 2 looking in through the one-way window watching a disgruntled Boris. 'We're getting nowhere, Effie. He's time-wasting and this bastard does speak English. Have we nothing from his flat yet?'

'No.'

'Effie, can you go and check with your lot and get onto SOCO. I'll wait here.'

'Are you sure? I may be awhile.'

'I'll be alright. Do me a favour, lend me your cuffs.'

'What for?'

'My dad taught me a trick when I was a kid, and I want to see if I can still do it. I'll pass the time.'

She gave him a curious look and reached under her jacket and pulled the cuffs from the waistband of her trousers and with some uncertainty handed them over. 'Don't do anything stupid, Hunter.'

'And the key.'

She gave him the key and he dropped it into his pocket with the cuffs. 'I won't, I promise. Be as quick as you can.'

Effie scooped up her briefcase, and said, 'Do you want the file?'

'No, you're okay. I'm going to the loo.'

He turned to walk to the end of the corridor and Effie went the other way out through the swing doors. As soon as the doors closed behind her Hunter walked back to the cell and went in. The young police constable stood up as he went in and Hunter, said quietly, 'Go and have a coffee, Hendry, I'll take over. She knows.'

'Thanks, sir, I was dying to spend a penny.'

'Off you go. Close the door.'

As soon as the heavy door clunked shut Hunter walked behind Boris and unseen took the cuffs from his pocket. Before Boris could so much as blink Hunter reached forward a grabbed an arm and snapped the cuffs on and then wrenched his other arm back and clamped that. Leaning forward he said to Boris, 'I don't have much time, you chump, tell me who your boss is and what you are doing here.'

'I tell you nothing,' uttered Boris.

Hunter reached under his jacket collar and withdrew a safety pin, a leftover from Remembrance Day. He straightened it out and placing a hand on one side of Boris's head he pushed the pin slowly into the firm grisly flesh his ear lobe on the other side.

Boris screamed and cursed in his mother tongue.

'English you bastard. Tell me what I want to know.'

He jabbed a bit harder and Boris like most people who dished it out was not good at taking it, yelled. 'Stop! Stop! What you want?'

Hunter kept the pressure on. 'Your boss?'

'He Colonel.'

'Colonel what?'

'I don't know.'

Hunter jabbed the pin piercing the ear and going into the neck.
'More, you bastard.'

'Fabianski!'

'What's his real name?

'Fabianski!'

'Where is he?'

'Not know. He left last night and I not know where.'

'Where is Ivan Andrejev?'

'He not come home last night.'

'His wife?'

'She his wife?'

'Yes! Where?'

'Not know.'

Hunter withdrew the pin and Boris let out a sigh of relief before
he jerked upright again as it was thrust once more into his ear but
this time nearer the entrance.

'More! Boris.'

Another jab.

'Stop! Stop! She taken in car by Petrov.'

'Where to?'

'Not know. She drugged. Maybe 'Starlight'.'

'What's that?'

'Not know, I only housekeeper.'

Hunter had his doubts but he withdrew the pin and quickly
unlocked the cuffs and as the door opened he rammed a handkerchief
over Boris's ear and Effie stepped in.

'What are you up to, Hunter, and where's PC Hendry?'

'He went to spend a penny.'

She nodded towards Boris. 'What's wrong with his ear?'

'He had an itch and scratched himself.'

'I bet.'

There was a light tap and the door opened and Hendry stuck his
head in.

Effie said, 'It's okay, Hendry, wait outside.'

She sat down opposite Boris and switched on the tapes while
Hunter leaned against the wall behind her visibly toying with the
open pin. She pushed two photos over the table. 'Who are they, Mr

Volkov. It is Volkov isn't it?...' He nodded, '... we got them from your video.'

Boris glanced at Hunter nervously and pointed at him before he answered. 'I tell him.'

Hunter stepped up to the table and stabbed his finger down on one of the pictures. 'I know that face. Who is it, Boris?'

'He Fabianski.'

'Full name.'

'Colonel Fabianski.'

'Known to us as Fabianski.' Hunter pointed again. 'And him?'

'Alex Petrov.'

'Where does he live?'

'Next block from me.'

'Effie!' said Hunter, 'Get Farmer over there. We want anything mentioning Starlight.'

She stood up and left the room only to return two minutes later and take her seat. 'What's this Starlight, Hunter?'

'I don't know and neither does Boris, but he thinks that's where Tanya may be. Did you get anything else off those videos?'

'Only the comings and goings of the other residents who are co-workers in the wash.'

'Leave it there, Effie, question the others. I'm going to pick up my boss from the airport.'

Boris put the handkerchief on the table and Effie saw only a few small spots of blood and his ear had no obvious sign of injury. She shrugged it off but she knew something had happened in her absence. On that, she walked over to the door and called Hendry in and gesturing towards Boris, said, 'Take him down, Hendry, and bring the next one up and you can sit in as cover.'

———

Fabianski put his phone down and sat groggy-eyed going over the message he had just received. An SOS from one of the carwash employees telling of the news of the police raid. That put his new timetable in jeopardy and tired from a long night he was momentarily caught off his guard but a new plan leapt into his head. He grabbed for the phone and did a speed dial and he had only a couple of seconds to wait before Alex answered. '*Yes, Colonel.*'

'Leave Anna to look after the woman and come to my house now. I want you to help me dispose of the body and place this device. It won't take long but hurry and we fly out today all being well.'

'We fly out, Colonel?'

'Yes, bring your stuff you're coming with us. The device can be detonated from the U.S. now it's been modified.'

'Colonel, where are you?'

Fabianski read out his address and hung up and dashed to the bathroom. At the door, he stopped, turned and went back for his phone and tapped out a message and and hoped what he had asked for was possible. He would soon find out, he thought, as he made for the bathroom a second time.

———

As Hunter and Gus Thomas were leaving the airport they had to pull over to one side to let an ambulance through. It was moving slowly with its blues flashing but no siren and he thought nothing of it and they joined Effie at the Blacon HQ twenty minutes later. Intros over Hunter asked Effie for an update.'

'There has been progress,' said Effie, 'and you're just in time. We got Tanya's personal phone details from William's phone and traced it to Rossmore Business Park in Ellesmere Port. That's your patch isn't it?'

'Yes, what are we waiting for?'

'You, let's go.'

They grabbed their coats and Hunter called out, 'You're with me, Gus.'

'Hunter!' said, Effie, 'I've got the local uniform to close down the area but I've told them to wait until we get there.'

'It's blues and noise, Effie. Let's go and follow me. I know the quickest way.'

Before they turned into the Business Park, they eased themselves past a queue of irate Post Office drivers and their vans trying to clock off after a long day. Obliging Uniform PC lifted the blue and white tape and showed them the Starlight premises opposite the P.O. depot where an anxious Inspector awaited them by a car placed across the roller doors.

Effie flashed her ID. 'DI Newlove.'

'Nice to meet you, Inspector. My names Grey. Who are your colleagues?'

'These gentlemen are MI6, Inspector, and it's their case.'

He acknowledged Hunter and Thomas before advising them that the premises were locked up.

Hunter didn't waste time. 'Break it open, Inspector.'

'Have you got a warrant?'

'I'm sorry, Inspector, this is a National emergency,' said Hunter, 'I'll take the backlash if there is any.'

The Inspector called the two PC's who were leaning against the car. 'Get your tools and smash that door open.'

They duly obliged with a heavy battering tool. The lock wouldn't give and they had to smash the door frame from its mountings and they stood to one side and let Hunter in, followed by the others. The front office was tidy and gave up nothing but the work bay showed intense activity and what attracted Hunter was not just the faint perfumed odour but the medical gear scattered around and tyre tracks leaving the building. Stood just inside the door, he said, 'Better get the gear on, guys, and call SOCO, Effie.'

At that moment, Effie's phone rang. 'Newlove, What is it?...' She listened for a moment before closing down. '...Hunter, that was the tech guys. Tanya's phone is stationary at the north end of Hawarden Airport but they've traced her GPS which is on the move and over Ireland.'

'Effie! Leave Farmer here and tell him we want the CCTV from the Post Office depot over the road and any info from the adjoining premises. Are you with me?'

'Yes! Farmer will need my car.'

After a quick word with Farmer and with blue LED's flashing they set off with Gus Thomas in the rear and because both the Business Park and the Airfield were in proximity to the motorway they pulled up outside the airport security fifteen minutes at the same time as the tracker team. The ping led them to an ambulance parked in the small carpark between the airport buildings.

As they approached the vehicle Hunter put on some surgical gloves and opened the driver's door while Effie went to the other side but the search revealed nothing and together they went round to the rear.

Hunter loosened the Glock in its holster and carefully eased one of the doors open and he instantly grabbed and threw the other door open to reveal the prostrate body of Alex.

'We have a crime scene, Effie. I've got some overshoes in the car so I'm going in. Close the scene down and call the team and get the manager here.'

'Hunter! You can't.'

'I know, Effie, but that phone may lead us to her kidnapper not to mention Williams. I'll take the flak.'

Gus Thomas who had stood back until now stepped forward and had a word with, Effie. 'I agree with Hunter, Inspector. It doesn't happen very often but on this occasion, we must, as one of our operatives is in danger.'

Effie was about to say something but thought better of it and walked away towards the airport office talking on her phone at the same time while Hunter raced to his car and grabbed some overshoes and hurried back to the ambulance. Aware of Effie's worries about contamination he pulled down the access ramp and sat on it to put them on before he entered the vehicle. His first move was to check for a pulse and he quickly signalled, Thomas. 'Call for an ambulance, Gus, he's still alive but only just.'

He went through Alex's pockets and found Tanya's phone. He popped it into an evidence bag and retraced his steps off the vehicle and showed it to Gus. 'End of the trail, Gus, I was hoping for better.'

Gus pointed towards Alex. 'What about him and there's still her GPS.'

'That's on its way abroad and he'll be out of it for a few days. Let's speak with the duty manager.'

They were joined by Effie and the Airport manager. 'Hunter!' said Effie, 'this is Mr Albright, the manager here. I've explained the situation.'

'How do you do, Mr Albright. What can you tell us about this ambulance?'

'A Gulfstream G111 Air Ambulance landed at short notice earlier, Mr Hunter, and was met by this ambulance and a patient was transferred to the aircraft. There was a bit of fuss, what about I don't know. The flight departed and this...' pointing at the ambulance, '...was abandoned. We were on the point of calling the authorities when you turned up.'

'Where is that flight going?'

'The flight number is XY2296 and is logged in as going to Newark in the States via Reykjavik. That will be a fuel stop.'

'Oh! Shit! Can we stop him in Reykjavik?'

'You could try but it's been a while since he left and it's outside the European Zone. It would take too long to get the necessary paperwork.'

'Thanks, Mr Albright.' He turned to Thomas. 'Gus, can you get onto the 'firm' and put that in motion?'

'I'll try. Mr Albright—can I use your office and I need the flight details.'

As Gus and Albright walked over to the Airport building Hunter spoke to Effie. 'Anything from Farmer yet?'

'Only that we know the ambulance came from there and they have found two cars near the premises that belong to the perpetrators. We'll have to wait for the Post Office CCTV and a check on those cars and I've called in extra help to trace this vehicle.'

He checked his watch and looked up to see Gus approaching. 'Tell us the good news, Gus.'

'No can do, Hunter. That plane took off as we called.'

'Have you told the 'Cousins'?'

''C's doing that.'

Hunter cursed under his breath annoyed by the lack of action when Effie's phone tinkled. 'Yes,' she said, 'what is it?'

She listened for a moment before she replied, 'Get another team over there. We're up to our necks...' She kept the phone to her ear nodding her head while the conversation lasted until she finally found a gap, '...Why didn't you say that at the start? We're still going to need backup. Get on with it and we'll see you there. Where was it? Dunkirk Lane?'

She stabbed her finger down and swiped up in a fit of frustration. 'Hunter! We've got to go. A body has been reported and it sounds like Williams.'

They had a quick word with the manager to keep the area sealed off until SOCO, the Medics and the Police arrived before jumping into Hunter's car and setting off on the third emergency of the day. As they approached the gates a Medical First Responder arrived.

—

They turned off the 'B' road and a Traffic Policeman lifted the tape that sealed off the narrow lane taking them down into a small wooded copse and they parked the car behind other police vehicles. After fitting overshoes another Uniform directed them to follow the tape from the road towards the base of the bridge where an Inspector was waiting.

Effie flashed her ID. 'Inspector Todd...,' she introduced Hunter and Thomas, '...what have we?'

'Inspector Newlove! Gentlemen! A lady, who is giving a statement, was walking her dog when it ran into the copse barking like mad and wouldn't respond when she called so she went into the trees to investigate and the dog was licking the face of the body which is lying over there up against the bridge. She called it in and one of my constables first on the scene recognised what he thought was the missing person you are looking for.'

'Show me,' said Hunter.

'Doctor Kerr is there and I don't want to contaminate the scene any more than I have to, Mr Hunter, was it?'

'Call me Hunter, Inspector Todd, and after a dog licking and your lot I don't think we'll do much damage but just show me and I'll I.D. him.

Following the tape through the trees and the already crushed grass and scrub the Inspector lead him to where Dr Kerr was kneeling by the body. Hunter stopped. 'That's far enough, Inspector, I'll talk to the Doc.'

Inspector Todd left him and he moved forward to the shoulder of Dr Kerr. 'Is it him, Doc?'

'I'm afraid so, Hunter.'

'Let me see him.'

'It's not very nice, are you sure?'

'Yes, Doc.'

Dr Kerr reached forward and pulled the plastic sheet from the victims head to reveal Williams battered face with the puncture wound through the top of his nose and Hunter gasped. 'Oh, Jeezus! That's a Russian Mafia-style assassination.'

'Unusual in this country, Hunter, I must say, and he was alive when they did it although he would have died from the other wound anyway.'

'Doc, can you leave me for a moment.'

'Certainly.'

Kerr covered Williams and picking up his crime scene toolbag he joined the team back on the road while Hunter stood contemplating what was before him. He was not religious by nature but he said a silent prayer and then aloud, he said, 'I'll get the bastards, lad, and we'll look after the kids.'

As he made to recover his tracks in the fading light something caught his eye. On the top rail of the fence along the side of the railway tracks there were scrape marks like something had been dragged over and leading up to them was freshly damaged.

He shouted, 'Inspector Newlove!'

Effie replied, 'Yes, Hunter, what is it.'

'Bring some tape and a torch.'

A few moments later Effie arrived with the desired articles. 'Here you are, Hunter, what's it for?'

'I'm going over to that fence, Effie and I want to mark my tracks. He gave her the end, 'Here, hold this.'

Treading carefully and unwinding the tape behind him and making his own track alongside the others he went to the fence. He looked over and saw that the tracks continued through the grass on the other side towards the bridge. He tied the tape to the fence and climbed over the fence and treading alongside the tracks already there made his way to the bridge until they stopped where there was gravel underfoot.

He was moving forward slowly keeping close to the bridgework swinging his torch from side to side when he was startled by—

'HUNTER, A TRAIN!'

Instinctively he took a deep breath and hugged the stonework and his heart raced as the Chester–Birkenhead train braking for the nearby station thundered past blowing an angry horn and the back draft trying to suck him under the wheels. He breathed a sigh of relief when it had gone only to curse when he saw he was only two paces from a built-in safety alcove. But what was hidden in there was to cause him more anxiety. Before him lay the contents of one of the packages shown on Williams's phone and in the torchlight the yellow nuclear warning symbols stood out.

'Oh, shit!'

He was worried about a more serious contamination now. He returned to the fence and scrambled over and rushed to Effie's side. 'Effie, we have a problem.'

'Don't tell me,' she said, 'tell Houston.'

The joke relieved the tension and he gave her a gentle nudge on the shoulder. 'Nice one, Effie, but we need the bomb squad quickly. Let's get back up to the road and don't worry about the crime scene.'

They hurried up to the road and Hunter called Gus and the Uniform Inspector over. 'Sorry to break this to you, chaps, but we have a nuclear device under the bridge. Inspector Todd, call the bomb squad and tell them but don't inform the press whatever you do and get more back-up, you need to isolate the area.'

'How bad is it, Mr Hunter?'

'Very, but we don't want to spread panic. Gus—we need to call a meeting with the brass.'

'Very well, Hunter, but is it Williams?'

'Sorry, Gus, yes it is and while we're at it let the lab team in to collect him. This place is going to be swarming with troops shortly so forget the crime scene.'

'Mr Hunter?'

'Yes, Inspector Todd, what is it?'

'Should I evacuate the area it being a nuclear device?'

'That's not part of my remit, Inspector, that's up to your lot and the bomb squad but I suggest close the roads and get a team around the village and tell them to shut doors and windows and stay indoors. That includes the factories here, and stop the trains. If anyone gets too nosy it's an anti-terrorist exercise.'

'Got that. Thanks, Hunter.'

—

Five minutes past midnight and upgraded from the small operations backroom to a larger better-furnished stateroom, Local Controller Hunter stood with his back to a large screen and a whiteboard with Effie by his side. Facing him were the Chief Constables of Cheshire, Merseyside and Flintshire and an array of senior police officers including Inspectors Todd and Grey. To one side sat Lionel Drummond, Senior Agent Gus Thomas and 'C.'

Hunter pressed a button on the remote and the Google map of the area appeared with a large circular area of ten-mile radius highlighted the centre of which was Capenhurst train station.

'Ladies and Gentlemen, you are probably aware of the situation but if not here's a quick rundown. A nuclear device has been discovered under...' he pointed at the map '...this bridge. It is not the 'dirty bomb' we expected to find but a small nuclear device. It weighs 30 kilograms with a destructive explosion of about 1.5 Kilotons. It could be less and we think a one to two-mile radius would be the initial colossal damage area with major shock wave collateral damage out to the area marked. Add to that the radioactive fallout and we have a major situation. Mr Drummond will explain later. However! Because of International repercussions, we do not want to advertise our find. It must be kept quiet. My Commander-in-Chief will explain.'

'C' unwound himself from his armchair and walked to the front. 'Ladies and Gentlemen...' He went on to expand on what Hunter had said, and finished '...and there you have it and this will be disguised as an anti-terrorist exercise.'

A hand shot up instantly. 'Yes, Sir?'

'I'm sorry, but how do I address you?'

'Just plain, 'C' will do.'

''C'! Should we not under the circumstances be evacuating people out of the area?'

'That would take too long and cause panic and as I have already advised such a move would not be necessary in an exercise. Unfortunately, the device has been found to have a detonating device operated by mobile phone and although an anti-signal screen has been put around it, any delay could, and I emphasise 'could' be disastrous, as of course, it would be under any circumstances. We must rely on our Military friends to keep us safe and therefore we should come to some consensus about our actions.'

'Have you a time period for all this?'

'You cannot set a time for this but I can say that the phone detonator is a simple device but before they disable it they are checking for booby traps which I don't think it will take very long. Ladies and gentlemen, I will leave Mr Drummond to explain the different devices...' He looked across the room towards Hunter, '...Agents Hunter and Thomas—come with me, please?'

Outside in the corridor, they stood by a window overlooking the bright lights of Chester and 'C' was about to speak when his phone pinged. He took a brief look at the caller I.D. and answered, 'Yes, Major, good news I hope?' He listened for a short while, and finished, 'That's good, I'll pass that onto the meeting and you say it should be all clear by two 'o clock?' He nodded and shut it down. 'Well, chaps, good news. They've deactivated the bomb and all that a remains is to seal it into a container and ship it down to Aldermaston...' He nodded down the corridor. '...we won't tell that lot yet. Let 'em stew for a while. Where are you with the investigation, Hunter?'

'Agent Tanya Williams GPS is giving signals off the coast of Canada and tomorrow morning we are going to interview Petrov. Until then we're stuffed. What about Owens material?'

'He uncovered the 'October Legion' sleepers centred around Aldermaston who moved up here which includes that employment agency in Chester and you know the result. There is we believe still a sleeper in GCHQ and the team is working on that and hopefully, they'll find a connection in the States.'

''C', sir, I feel obliged to find Williams, killer. Can I follow it up?'

'Isn't that SB's job?'

'Williams has been my back-up and friend for a long time, sir, and I feel that I should give it my personal attention and they haven't been called in as our investigations are still ongoing.'

'C' deliberated for a moment before answering, 'Agent Hunter, you were hired on a temporary basis to cover because our books were full. However...' Hunter could feel the negative vibes before the verdict came, '...the case is more or less closed here in the U.K. and what is left can be covered by our current staff so I'm afraid your time is up. Thomas will take over and you are retired.' 'C' held his hand out, 'Thank you for your service, you did a good job but that is it.'

Hunter declined the handshake instead turned to Gus Thomas and shook his. 'I'm going to get some shuteye. I'll be in touch, Gus, and bring my files and other stuff. Maybe we can have a drink one evening?'

Pulling himself up to his full height Hunter walked towards the lift.

'Thomas and 'C' watched him and when he was out of earshot, Thomas said, 'That was a bit harsh, sir. I know how he feels about Williams. I would feel the same way. Can't we keep him on?'

'I've made my decision, Gus, and it stands. Let's go back.'

As they walked towards the stateroom, Gus continued, 'But, sir, I know very little about the investigation and if we are going to help the 'Cousins' we need to find out quickly and he's the chap to do it. He was planning to cross-examine the Russian tomorrow and if anybody can extract info, he can! Don't forget he's our connection with that Savitsky fella also.

'C' stopped and pulled Gus up by the arm. 'Gus! You are making a thing about this. Why?'

'Because, Sir, we need him. I know he can be a bit of a loose cannon but he does the job. I believe in him. He's better than you and me plus all those pipsqueak politicians in the Home Office put together and if you want that other bomb before it goes off you'd better get him back or should I say—persuade?'

'C' looked down at his shoes and scratched his forehead and then running his fingers up through his thinning grey hair, he said, 'You've made your point, Gus, but how do I get him back?'

'Leave it to me, sir, you're tired, it's late and like him, you're not getting any younger but that doesn't appear to affect him and you'll probably have to apologise sometime in the future.'

'Thanks, Gus, I'll leave it with you, I have a meeting at the Foreign Office with the Russian Ambassador.'

—

The text message was short and to the point: **SMS – Report to the Countess of Chester at nine sharp. Thomas.**

After he had poured himself a finger of whisky, he checked it again and, yes, it was from Gus Thomas. He had been expecting something but underneath a stubborn mindset was saying to him, 'Let 'em sweat!' but common sense prevailed as he would be able to follow up the investigation legally. He finished his whisky and not wanting to disturb Jacquie he settled himself on the sofa for what sleep he could get.

He was woken by the slimy rough tongue of Tess. 'Ugh!' He wiped his face with his shirt sleeve and pushed her away. 'Can't you let a man sleep you hairy monster?'

He was dragged further from his dreams by the synchronised voices of Iain, who took a picture with his smartphone, and Lesley, looking down on him from the other side of the coffee table. 'Morning, Dad!'

He pushed himself up on his elbows. 'What time is it?'

'Seven 'o clock,' said Iain, 'what are you doing there?'

Jacquie came in with a mug of tea. 'Stop moaning, Hunter and get your fingers around that.'

He took the mug and drank a little. 'Thanks, love, I needed that.' He swung his legs down to face them. 'It only seems like five minutes since I lay down.'

Jacquie hustled the kids from the room. 'Go on you two, get yourself washed and ready,' and then returned her attention to Hunter. 'What time did you get in?'

'It was after one 'o clock and I didn't want to disturb you.'

'It would have been okay, but thanks. What's happening?'

He gave her a quick rundown of events and finished... 'and in ten minutes I was sacked and reinstated. There you have it.'

'It was a full-blown bomb?'

'It sure was, and the one on the way to the States.'

'Won't they sort that out?'

'I hope so but I want the ringleader. He executed Williams and kidnapped Tanya. Which is another thing? Can we take on the kids at least until we have Tanya back? They're not going into care homes.'

'I don't see why not, ~~Jaqis.~~ ^H Get yourself ready while I do breakfast and we'll start things moving. Who's looking after them now?'

'Carrie, you know her. Have we enough room for her also?'

'Hunter! Go! We'll think of something. What time are you in?'

'Nine.'

He pulled himself up and gave her a quick peck on the cheek before dragging himself upstairs.

He stood with Jacquie on the doorstep and watched as Jamie drove off with the kids before he gave her a squeeze and they kissed unashamedly on the step. 'Take care, lass. I'll tell Thomas what we're doing and I'll arrange for Carrie to be rostered here.'

As he walked towards his Golf he realised what they had committed to. 'I'm going to need a bigger car.'

———

The banging on the bedroom door was both insistent and noisy which made Josef Bazarov nervy as he struggled out of bed and shuffled across the room while pulling on his dressing gown. He opened the door just as his aide was about to give it another battering. 'What is it, Captain, why the urgency?'

The Captain thrust some papers at him. 'This is a directive from the Kremlin. Comrad General, you must get yourself attired in full dress uniform and ready to travel immediately. There is a car waiting to take you to the airport at the front door.'

Bazarov struggled to open and read the papers without his glasses but he could see the Kremlin logo well enough. 'Wait here, Captain.' He closed the door and went over to his bed and put on his glasses and began reading. He didn't take long absorbing the directive and he took off his glasses and plonked the papers on the bedside locker when he felt the tugging on his nightshirt and looked around as his wife spoke, 'What is it, Josef?'

'A call from Nachal'nik. I must fly to Milan immediately.'

'Why Milan? Does he say why?'

'Ours is not to question, my sweet, but he is at the Asia – Euro Conference there. Stay in bed and I will call you. He leaned over and kissed her. 'Lyublyu tebya, sladkaya.'

He went to the door and opened it slightly and instructed his aide to prepare for the journey while he got himself ready.

—

Thankful for air-conditioning Josef had been sitting in an ante-room off the main conference hall for almost two hours before there was movement in the corridor and his Nachal'nik was shown in. A gentleman to the end as Josef stood he walked across and they shook hands and greeted each other in the traditional Russian manner. 'Welcome, Josef, sorry to be so late but these delicate things cannot be rushed...' He turned to the entourage which had followed him in. '...Please leave, all of you.'

Muttering amongst themselves they filed out of the room until only his personal bodyguard, a large beast of a man was left behind. 'You too, Brutus.'

Brutus was about to speak but thought better of it and grudgingly left the room and together they went over to a cocktail cabinet. The Nachal'nik poured two vodkas and as they raised their glasses they simultaneously, said, '*Zazdarovje*' took a small sip and protocol over they sat by a coffee table close enough to talk without being overheard.

'Colonel Bazarov,' said his host, 'The U.K. plot has been foiled and our London Ambassador and the U.K. Foreign Office have informed me about the discovery of a Field Nuclear Bomb. Not a 'dirty bomb' as planned, but a genuine 1.5kt bomb. Fortunately, the device has been disarmed but the situation demands that we act promptly. Therefore, cancel 'Operation Upstart'. Recall your men and material and our field exercises have already been stood down. Apologies and the offer of help has been made to the U.S. and the U.K. with the promise of an internal investigation. Who is responsible for those devices. Find out! They will be punished and, Colonel—your head is on the line here.'

Josef's let out a deep sigh as he summoned the strength to pass on his bad news and realising his situation and that he had nothing to lose he sat up, and said, 'Colonel Fabianski has gone feral. He has his own agenda and is or has killed those around him that don't play ball. That was not the plan. We don't know where he is as he dropped off our radar in Canada.'

Josef was shaking internally as he watched the red tide rising above his host's collar and the familiar stare and stern expression took over the domicile features that he showed to the world. For ten seconds there was silence and then he spoke. 'On the assumption that Fabianski will stick to the target in New York tell me where it is and I will inform the authorities. I will give them some bull about a mole in our midst and that our internal investigation has uncovered it.'

'It is an abandoned Sylvania Nuclear warehouse in Hicksville on Long Island.'

'Good, find those responsible for swapping the devices. We are finished.'

He pressed a device in his pocket and Brutus came in and was visibly relieved to see his Nachal'nik was in no danger. 'Brutus! Call my staff and show Colonel Bazarov to his car.'

He stood up and crossed to the drinks cabinet and poured himself a glass of Irn-Bru. Summarily dismissed, Josef followed Brutus from the room.

In the car to the airport, he sent messages and arranged an 'Upstart' meeting for midnight.

A weary General Bazarov sat at the top of the table and looked around the assembled committee. He let them talk amongst themselves for a few minutes before he called out. 'Gentlemen, before we get down to the nitty-gritty of this meeting there is something both dissatisfying and deeply disappointing I must do.' He rapped the table twice with his glass and instantly the door opened and a troop of armed FSB heavies entered. They lined up down either side of the room and as soon as they were settled, Josef spoke. 'Comrads Krilov and Zablonsky! Stand up!'

The nominated pair looked at each other but no sign passed between them and they did as they were bid. As they did so, Josef nodded to the Troop Commander, and shouted, 'TAKE THEM AWAY!'

Four men stepped forward and each took an arm and forcibly marched Krilov and Zablonsky out of the room while the remainder of the troop stood on alert waiting for a reaction. Non came and

Josef, said, 'Gentlemen! Our comrads will be questioned and you all know what that means so if anyone has any knowledge of the mini-plot they hatched help us now to avoid repercussions. Anyone?'

No one responded but looked at each other nervously and Josef continued, 'Very well, gentlemen we will go on with our meeting...' He nodded to the Troop commander who ordered his men to leave the room and when all was settled Josef offered them some liquid relief, '... single malt gentlemen?'

There was an audible sigh as the tension dissipated but no one made to take up the offer. Josef went to the table and helped himself and the three remaining members followed. Conversation was subdued and their observations were aimed more at the weather than the serious business of 'Upstart' until Josef ordered them to take their seats. When his depleted committee was settled, he came straight to the point.

'Comrads! 'Upstart' is over. I will not discuss the failure of our two compatriots other than to say what they did has caused the breakdown of the plan. From now on we have to reverse our earlier decisions and make this look like we are trying to preserve world peace. Comrad Kryuchkov! You arranged the smuggling of the device into the States?'

'Yes, Comrad, General.'

'What was the target destination?'

'An abandoned warehouse in Long Island, New York.'

'That was our planned destination was it not?'

'Yes, Comrad.'

'You have not heard of or planned a back-up?'

'No! Why?'

'Good. If you had you would be joining our friends. Colonel Fabianski has taken things into his own hands and diverted from the plan. Get on to your contacts and have them intercept Fabianski. We know he was in Canada and must assume he is coming in from a new direction. If your contacts run into the U.S. authorities they must help them. Do that now.'

'Yes, Comrad General.'

He gathered his things and left the room.

—

Hunter greeted a tired Thomas in the corridor of the HDU unit with a cheerful, 'Hi, Gus, a long night was it?'

'Morning, Hunter, what are you so cheerful about?'

'After last night, Gus, I'm not so sure. Any updates?'

'Yes, that bloody aircraft switched off its ADS transponder just off Nova Scotia and the Yanks are going apeshit but we still have Tanya's GPS signal which says it turned right and went inland and is in a place called Fredericton. That is not the destination it registered.'

'Have you told the Yanks this?'

'It's out of their territory but we are doing our best to wake up the Canadians but I can't imagine why when the U.S. is the logical place to copy what they tried here.'

'That plane is a decoy, Gus, I think they plan to smuggle the bomb overland. They probably transferred it to a vehicle and are on their way already. Let's see what Petrov has to say.'

They showed their I.D. to the armed uniform outside the ward and after giving a light tap entered only to be stopped inside by the specialist nurse. 'You have ten minutes, gentlemen. No touching or raised voices. He is stable but he did lose a lot of blood and is very weak.'

'Thank you, nurse, we won't be long and we think he wants to help us.'

She tidied up the sheets and left the room and Hunter and Thomas stood on either side where he could see them without strain.

Hunter held up his I.D. 'You are Alex Petrov?'

Alex nodded and mumbled, 'Yes.'

'Tell us what happened and what is happening. Take your time.'

'We put girl in aeroplane and I tell my Colonel when moving the ambulance that it is not a dirty bomb but a real nuclear bomb and I no like so we argue and he shoot me and run away.'

'Do you still want to stop it?'

'Yes. I put GPS with the girl to help.'

'Why have they not found it?'

'I touch her in a bad place and put it inside her when Anna the nurse, she go to toilet.'

'Do you know where they are going?'

'They not tell me. Only say America. I was supposed to stay here and explode English bomb but they have a mobile phone on it now and can do it anywhere.'

Hunter thought for a moment mentally tossing the question, "Should I tell him or not?" and decided, "If he's telling the truth he should know where it is."

'Where is the bomb, Alex?'

Thomas went to speak and Hunter held his hand up.

'Under a railway bridge near a nuclear factory.'

Hunter was satisfied. 'Alex! We have found it and it is safe.'

Alex visibly relaxed but took a deep breath and his eyes showed fear when Hunter said, 'Did you shoot, Ivan?'

Alex shook his head. 'No! No! My Colonel, he did it. He always killing.'

'Okay, Alex, think hard. Where in the States?'

'New York.'

'Why New York and was it the State or City?'

'I not know. I hear it one time when Colonel on phone.'

'This Colonel. Is that Fabianski?'

'~~That is English name. Real name is Fabianski~~i.' Yes'

That confirmed what Boris had said in the interview and Hunter stepped back. 'Have you anything to add, Gus?'

The nurse entered the room and Thomas shook his head and motioned they should leave.

'Good timing, nurse, we were just leaving,' said Hunter, 'do you think he'll be in here long?'

'No. He'll be taken to a private room tomorrow and should be out in a week maybe.'

'Okay, thank you, nurse, much obliged.'

As they stepped out into the corridor Hunter's phone buzzed and after a quick glance he answered it. 'Hello, Effie, what can I do for you?'

'We have ID'd the cars from outside that 'Starlight' place. One is the Russian chap in hospital but the other is a hire car on loan to a chap called McRae and the address is not far from your Garden Centre. We are going there now.'

'Where exactly...' he listened for a moment, '...see you there, and Effie! Look out for anything to do with New York.' He shut down, and said, 'Come on, Gus, we might have a lead.'

Fifteen minutes later, they parked behind Effie's SUV in the small residential close in a suburban area made up of a modern mixture of premises and after donning the compulsory overshoes and overalls they entered and bumped into Effie who was stood in the tiny hall.

'Hello, Effie, found anything?'

'Greetings, Hunter, Mr Thomas, we've only been here a few minutes but the living room seems to have been the centre of activity, come through.'

They followed her from the hall into the lounge and found all the furniture pushed back around the walls with a trestle table set out down the middle.

Underneath the table was what looked like an electricians tool kit and scattered on the floor were bits of 5 amp coloured wires and a flat metal box with two push button switches. On the table were the remains of a micro sim card.

'I don't know about you, Gus, but methinks this is where the push button field switch was replaced by the Wi-Fi phone detonator.'

'I'm not a bomb expert, Hunter, but I'm inclined to agree with you. Is there anything else, Inspector?'

'DC Farmer is going through the bedrooms. He's passed his Sergeants exam, by the way, Hunter, did you know? I'll go and fetch him.'

While she was out of the room Hunter began poking around in the sideboard draws while Thomas pulled apart the draws and paper compartment of the coffee table but apart from a 2010 AA road map probably belonging to the bungalow owner there was nothing. Their search was interrupted by Farmer with a laptop under his arm and Effie, who said, 'Find anything, Hunter?'

'No—how about you, Farmer?'

'We've got this laptop which looked like it was left behind in a hurry as it was under the bed but apart from that, we know whoever was here liked his women. There are traces of at least three different ladies in the bedrooms.'

'Are you any good with computers, Farmer?'

'Not bad but I'm not a specialist.'

'Okay, Farmer. What's your first name again?'

'Kevin, Mr Hunter.'

'Okay, Kevin, plug it in and see what you can find. Is that alright, Effie?'

'That's good by me. Take it into the kitchen, Farmer and try it?' As he left the lounge she turned her attention back to Hunter. 'How are we progressing, Hunter?'

'Whoever was here, Effie has left the country and is probably in Canada. Because of action taken by who we think was second in command we have tracked our kidnapped agent to Canada also. I say that but it's quite possible that it's only the device and not still with her.'

'What's the plan, Hunter?'

'I was going to discuss that with...' he nodded towards Thomas, '...my colleague. How about we three retreat to my office in the Garden Centre and talk about it over coffee?'

'Lead the way, Hunter,' said Thomas, and Effie also gave the affirmative. 'Just give me two minutes to tell the guys what's happening and they can get down to a big search and I'll be right behind you.'

———

Hunter and Thomas were sat at a table in the Garden Centre when Effie joined them. Ever the gentleman, Hunter stood up. Thomas made a half-hearted attempt and sat down again.

As he sat down, Hunter said, 'I've ordered your usual, Effie, is that okay?'

'Thanks, Hunter, I'm ready for that. Now, what have you pair got planned?'

'We're getting nowhere here, Effie, so it's been decided that head office wizards sift through Owen's stuff again and I have a deep chat with our ex-Moscow police defector. Meanwhile, Gus is going to chase up the Canadian authorities and try and find out why that plane diverted and what happened to the passengers.'

'What do you want us to do, Hunter?'

'Keep on the case, Effie, and dig up anything related to the

'October Legion' or 'Operation Upstart or Wyskochka. Our Agent Carrie Long, will be along shortly.'

Thomas interrupted, 'She's here, Hunter.'

Hunter stood up as athletic Agent Carrie Priya Long approached, her short black hair enhancing her golden skin and she had the most beautiful eyes he had ever seen.

'Welcome, Carrie, can I get you anything?' he said.

'Yes, please, Hunter, I'm good for a medium mocha.'

He dragged another chair over. 'Right Carrie, You know Gus Thomas, get to know, Inspector Newlove while I get your coffee. She'll be your contact with the police.'

He wandered over to the restaurant and returned a few minutes later with Carrie's mocha. 'Here you are, lass, now where were we?'

Thomas brought them up to date, and ended, '...when we've finished here, Hunter and I are leaving. Did Farmer get anywhere with that laptop, Inspector?'

'Hang on, I'll call him.'

She stood up and walked a little distance away and made the call and came back with the call on hold. 'I'm afraid that we're locked out of that laptop. What should we do with it?'

Hunter was quick to jump in. 'We'll take it with us. The boys at the 'firm' can have a go. Gus and I will nip round there and, Effie, after I've been home and picked up some gear we'll be off. Is there anything else?'

They all looked from one to the other and after a shake of heads, Hunter finished, 'That's it then. One more thing, Effie. If you have problems contacting Carrie call, Jacquie, she is still part of the team. Do you have her number?'

'No.'

He gave Effie a card. 'That's her service phone and Effie, nothing goes to the press. If anyone asks it's as we said at the time, an anti-terrorist exercise.' He pushed his chair back and stood up and Thomas followed suit. 'Thank you everyone and fingers crossed.'

Hunter handed Thomas his car keys, 'Gus, give me two minutes to say goodbye to, Jacquie, and I'll join you in the car park.'

~~~~~~

Part 3

CLOSURE

Chapter 16

From the street, the Camden safe house looked like two semi-detached Victorian properties but inside they had been modified into one. It had three floors and a basement with a walled rear garden that stretched back to the railway tracks and was conveniently close to Camden Town, the Parks and Primrose Hill with access to the Northern Line.

Inside there were three apartments. The top floor was a hi-tech room with recording devices etc... and the housekeepers, Mrs Amy Archer and her ex-SAS husband. The two apartments on the first floor were for guests of SIS or Agents like Hunter who were staying over.

The basement was a separate entity comprising two prison cell-like rooms with toilet facilities and a large open undecorated space with a few chairs and a table that was used for more questionable activities. It had seen little action since the end of the cold war.

Savitsky had been brought up from Salisbury on his own and Hunter chose to interrogate him in his designated flat instead of the basement facility hoping that the relaxed atmosphere might ease out forgotten information. When they had settled down with a beer each and with the original statement that Alexei had given his interrogators he started, 'Alexei, welcome, I'm sorry about the circumstances but I have called you here to think hard and fast of the drunken conversation you had before or in the car with your colleague, Serov. This is important as something has happened and we have come to a dead-end in the investigation. I want you to go over your conversation bit by bit and see if you can expand on what he said about the States. A word, a place, anything; it is vital.'

'Comrad Hunter, it is a long time ago and this old brain has big gaps.'

'Okay, Alexei, let's go back to the time we met. You said a diversionary bomb in the U.K. and America and you didn't like it.'

Alexei stood and began walking around talking to himself and rubbing his chin, occasionally he would stop and with little hand signals muttering at the same time go over something in his mind and he did this for a good five minutes before he stopped and pointing at Hunter, said, 'Silver... silver something. Shit! What is it?'

He continued walking backwards and forwards across the room gesticulating and talking to himself when he suddenly stopped and clicked his fingers. 'That's it. Sylvania or something like.'

'Did he say where?'

'America, I think.'

'It doesn't sound American. Let's Google it and see what turns up.'

Hunter got up from the sofa and went to the computer desk which was wedged alongside a writing desk in a corner. After making himself comfortable and cursing at the slowness of an out of date system while going through the rigmarole of start-up and passwords he finally got to the Google home screen. 'Here we go, Alexei, what was it you said,? Sylvania?'

'Yes! Comrad.'

'We'll add the U.S. and see what comes up.'

He typed it in and after a few seconds, he said, 'Wallah! The Wall St. Journal - Waste Lands. America's forgotten nuclear legacy. It's an abandoned Nuclear Storage depot.'

Alexei came over and looked over his shoulder. 'That's good, Comrad, but what has it to do with our case?'

Hunter read further and sat back. 'This site stored uranium and thorium according to government records. The government also says it cleaned up this site in the 1960s under the Formerly Utilized Sites Remedial Action Program which means it is a possible source of radioactivity to add to what was supposed to be a 'Dirty Bomb. Alexei! I think we've cracked it and according to this aerial shot it's in Hicksville in the centre of Long Island.'

'That's good, Comrad, can I go back to Malika now?'

'Yep! I'll fix it. I've got to go. You stay here until they come for you. First I've got to print this lot.

He took some screenshots and printed them off before closing the computer down and collecting his jacket. 'I'm off, Alexei and take care. We'll get around to having that night out one day.'

—

Back in Vauxhall House the not so secret offices of MI6 he showed Gus Thomas the evidence he had accrued but expressed some concern and said he needed to double-check it.

'How do you plan to do that, Hunter,' said Thomas, 'we haven't got much time. They're twenty-four hours ahead of us.'

'If I can use your phone, Gus, I'll call Inspector Newlove and she can go with Agent Long to chat with Petrov.'

Gus pushed the phone over the desk and when Hunter picked up the handset, he said, 'Don't you think it would be better to use 'Whatsapp' someone might be listening?'

'I'm hoping there is, Gus, and maybe realising we know they might call it off.'

'You're putting Petrov's life on the line, Hunter.'

'He should have thought of that when he signed up.'

He dialled a number and sat back and waited for a good half-minute before someone answered. 'Hello, this is MI6 Local Controller can you put me through to Inspector Newlove, please?'

Thomas looked skywards and shook his head, 'Why doesn't he put it on Facebook?'

Hunter looked at his watch and made a note of how long it had taken before anyone came back to him. 'Yes,' he said irritably. He listened for a couple of seconds before replying, 'Okay, find her and tell her to get in touch with Agent Long asap.'

He put the phone down and shrugged. 'She's been called out on a stabbing incident. I'll chase up Long.'

This time he used his service smartphone and she answered immediately. 'Yes, Mr Hunter?'

'Carrie, get to the Countess Hospital and put these questions to Petrov...' He read out a list to her '...and then get straight back to me. Inspector Newlove should be with you shortly. Fill her in and she will help. It's nothing personal but she's had more experience at that sort of thing, Carrie.'

He slid his finger up the off app and stood contemplating his next move and then out of nowhere, he said, 'Gus! Call the driver of the car taking Savitsky home and tell him to turn around and go straight to the heliport. I'll meet him there. I'm going to con Petrov, I hope.'

'How do you mean, Hunter?'

'Petrov doesn't know Savitsky and as a genuine Russian, I'm hoping Petrov will think he's from the Russian Embassy on a Peace mission and open up. It's worth a try as we're going nowhere at the moment.'

'I just hope our funds can cover it, Hunter,' said Gus.

'It's off the cuff, I know, and we'll worry about that later.'

'After that last spat 'C' will take it from your wages...' Thomas picked up his service phone and sent a message through to the driver and a positive reply was instant, '...you've got twenty minutes to get to the Heliport, Hunter. Do you want me along?'

'It's okay, Gus, can you chase up Fabianski's laptop. I'll come straight back after we've done. Notify Newlove and Long, I'll be at the hospital in a couple of hours.'

———

Standing some distance from the security guard outside the private ward where Petrov was being held Hunter gave Newlove and Long a rundown on their deception plan. 'Alexei here is going to pretend he's from the Russian Embassy with instructions from the Kremlin in the name of Peace to nip this illegal bomb plot in the bud and they want names and places in the States to stop it there also. Any questions?'

They glanced at each other and mutually agreed there was no problems and Newlove and Long stood back while Hunter and Savitsky went forward to enter the ward and as Hunter put his hand on the handle while acknowledging the police guard, he said, 'Put your hat on, Alexei. It makes you more official.'

Savitsky obliged and they went in to be greeted by Petrov who was enjoying a cup of coffee courtesy of the NHS. 'Hello, Mr Hunter, who is your friend?'

'Mr Petrov, this is Mr Savitsky from your London Embassy. He wants to talk to you.'

Savitsky held up his wallet showing his old retired MUR I.D. He was careful not to get too close so that Petrov was unable to discern the details but he flopped back on his pillows with a crestfallen look on his face. 'What can I do for you, Comrad Savitsky?'

Savitsky replied in his native Russian, 'We can speak our own language Petrov...' he nodded towards Hunter, '... This way you understand and he doesn't, okay?' Petrov nodded. 'Good, firstly I have a directive from our President. In the interest of Peace, this illegal plot 'Wyskochka' must stop. The leaders of the plot in Moscow have been apprehended and they want you to work with the authorities here and in the States and give any information you think may be helpful like targets etc...'

'Comrad Savitsky, I have told them everything.'

'I know, Petrov, so they tell me and the U.K. part of the planned operation is over but what do you know about the U.S.? Think hard man. Place names. You were going to be part of the U.S. plot and to save world Peace we must act quickly and it will do your defence a lot of good. Colonel Fabianski has his own agenda. Where is he planting the U.S. bomb?'

'Before I try to stop him, Comrad Savitsky, we were flying to Newark in New Jersey and by road into New York. I heard a name something like Sylvania but that is all. He told us nothing more. What I know I overhear.'

'That's a start. Comrad.'

Hunter's phone buzzed at the same time as Savitsky took out his phone and walked across the room and stood by the door and made a pretence of calling and talking to the Russian Embassy. Hunter cancelled his call so that Savitsky was not disturbed as he emphasised the names and places he had been given before, with the appropriate Russian protocol, he finished his call and turned to Hunter. 'Mr Hunter, my people have instructed me to tell you what he said. First, they go to Newark and then into New York to a place called Sylvania if that is indeed a place. They are passing the info onto Moscow who I assume will tell the CIA.'

'Thank you, Alexei but Newark is out. They diverted to Canada but we will follow up on the other names and hope it's just that, a diversion.'

'One minute, Mr Hunter, I will have another quick word with Petrov.'

'Ask him if he has contact with the 'October Legion' in the US?

Alexei pulled a chair closer to Petrov and leaning forward

whispered into his ear, 'Comrad Petrov! If you are sent back to Moscow your sentence will be severe but...' he gestured towards Hunter, '...he tells me he will put a good word in and you can stay here in the U.K. after a short prison sentence in an open prison and believe me English prisons are a good life. Is there anything more you can say? Names, anything?'

Petrov sat rubbing his chin and mumbling in Russian for a few seconds before he answered, 'I overhear two English names like Baker and Wallis during a phone conversation but I think my Comrad Colonel was talking about suppliers for the 'Starlight' business.'

Savitsky patted Petrov on the shoulder. 'Well done, what about the 'October Legion' in the States?'

'I only know about the U.K....' Petrov grabbed Alexei's arm. '...Do you know what has happened to Anna, Comrad?'

'Who's, Anna?'

'She's my girlfriend.'

'One moment...' he turned to Hunter. '...he wants to know about Anna.'

'We don't know. She went with Fabianski.'

Alexei returned to Petrov. 'Did you understand that?' Petrov nodded. 'Good, now was there anything else, like anything personal about Fabianski?'

'He hates homosexuals. Other than that he is always obsessively smartly dressed and clean-shaven.'

'That will do. Besides that, are they looking after you here?'

Petrov nodded the affirmative, 'Yes, Comrad Savitsky, I could not get better. Why do they not have this NHS in Russia?

'Another story my friend. Get some rest and we will see you soon.'

They assembled in the corridor and before anyone could speak Carrie Long jumped in. 'Mr Hunter! Thomas has been on and said to tell you that the GPS is moving West inside Canada but the signal is getting weaker. The good news is that the Canadian authorities are on to it.'

'What does that mean?' said Alexei.

'Alexei—I haven't told you. Agent Williams is dead and your Colonel Fabianski has kidnapped his wife and it is from her we are getting GPS signals so we know their whereabouts but not where they're headed but from the info you got today and what you already told us New York is the target and that doesn't make sense. We'll have to chase up this Sylvania and while we're searching hopefully the Mounties can cut them off.'

'One more thing, Mr Hunter. Petrov mentioned a Wallis and Baker...'

'...Hunter! Sorry to butt in,' said Effie, 'why haven't they been pulled in already.'

'Good question, Effie. We have been over twenty-four hours behind all the time. There was a reception for them in Newark but the plane diverted into Canada and they had cleared the airport in Fredericton before the Mounties were alerted. Now the GPS is doing a tour of Quebec that means they have sussed it and it is a decoy.'

Carrie who had been an onlooker chipped in, 'That's assuming of course New York is still the target.'

Hunter was about to answer and stopped with the first consonant on his lips and paused momentarily before, he said, 'Carrie, you're damned right as I think the Russki's are using old info. Here's what I suggest. Effie!—your number one murder suspect has done a runner but book our Mr Petrov as an illegal and accomplice before SB step in. Carrie!—assist Effie and continue as our go-between. What about William's kids?'

'We've moved their stuff to your place and a taxi has been arranged to pick them up from school and that nice Jamie is looking after them until I or Jacquie get there.'

'Good! Alexei and I are going to see Jacquie before we head back to London and hopefully, by then they will have checked up on this Sylvania. Take care and I'll be in touch. Come on, Alexei, let's not keep madam waiting.'

———

The next morning Hunter knocked on the door of Thomas's office and didn't wait for a reply before he pushed in with his obligatory cup of coffee.

'Come in, Hunter, why don't you,' said, Thomas.

Hunter raised his coffee and gestured towards Thomas. 'Mornin', Gus, before I sit down, do you want one?'

'Nice of you to ask, Hunter, but I've recently had one. Sit down while I give you the bad news.'

Hunter put his coat on the hook behind the door and plonked his cup on the front of the desk and sat opposite Thomas and placed his briefcase by his feet. 'That doesn't sound good. What's happened, Gus?'

'The Mounties have traced the GPS to a Motel courtyard outside Quebec.'

'And?'

'Tanya is dead. It looks like an overdose of Propofol. We will know more after the autopsy.'

Hunter stood up and started walking around the room. 'SHIT! THE BASTARD!,' he cursed, 'WHY?'

'You know what they're like with whom they consider traitors, Hunter. They've had her marked for thirteen years now and they never forgive.'

Hunter sat down again but Thomas could detect a change in his demeanour. 'You're right, Gus, I was being hopeful. Did you follow up that Sylvania?'

'Yes, it seems to be the target. As you said, it's an abandoned nuclear storage facility belonging to the Sylvania Nuclear Corporation which like Capenhurst would have added more radioactive material to the 'Dirty Bomb' which we both know is not going to happen.'

'Gus—would it be a good idea to send someone to the U.S.? We know who we're dealing with and the target.'

'No, Hunter, I spoke to 'C' and he's adamant that the Yanks can deal with it themselves. We've cleared our mess up and that's that. It's a diplomatic thing now.'

'So I'm retired?'

'If 'C' had his way, yes, but I want you to stay on as local controller at least until it's all done and dusted and while we're at it, SB tells me there's a dispute with the local police about who is charging who.'

'That's a difficult one. The leading suspect has left the country and the others are just illegal fodder on the other hand they are part of the 'October Legion' and therefore spies. I'm passing the buck on that one. Meanwhile, I've got two kids to rehouse so if there's nothing else I'm going.'

'Are you taking on William's kids, Hunter?'

'My next job.' He grabbed his briefcase and his coat and as he left the room, he said over his shoulder. 'See you, Gus.'

Thomas didn't reply. Deep down he had an idea Hunter was going awol.

Hunter didn't leave the building but went instead to the document forgery department in the basement where he was greeted by a portly happy lady with purple striped long grey hair and the biggest pair of red glasses he had ever seen.

'Morning! Hunter isn't it?' she said brightly.

'Yep!'

'Right Hunter, what can we do for you?'

'I want passports and U.S. visas for...'

'I know—Byewater...'

'...No, Jilly, he's *persona non grata*'. How about Drinkwater, a retired headmaster? Brian Drinkwater!'

'Sounds good, when do you want them?'

'Tomorrow? Oh! I want credit cards and a bank account for him also.'

'It's pushing it.'

'Bombay Blue Sapphire was it, Jilly?'

'Tomorrow, Hunter.'

'Just one more favour, Jilly, look up the nearest Flight Centre store on your pad can you?'

She fiddled about with her i-pad for a moment and held it out for him to read, 'The nearest is in Convent Garden, Hunter, is there anything else?'

'Send those docs to the Camden safe house?'

'Consider it done, now bugger off and let me get started.'

Outside he flagged down a taxi. 'New Row, Covent Garden, please.'

Back at the safe house, he helped himself to a single malt instead of his usual lager and he was in the process of sending two text messages to contacts in the U.S. when he was interrupted by a call from Gus Thomas. 'Yes, Gus, what is it?'

'Hunter, you're good to go. The Home Secretary has been onto 'C' and she wants Williams killer deleted. They just don't want to know-how. It's not official, you do it and put your expenses in when you get back. Best of luck. That's it, let me know if you need anything.'

'It's already set-up, Gus and I'm leaving on a flight at midday tomorrow.'

'I thought you might.'

Hunter put the phone down and swallowed the last of his whisky, poured another and said a silent toast to Williams. 'To you, lad, I'll get the bastard,' but before he retired he had an inkling and Googled, *Wallis and Baker,* U.S. and his search revealed '*Baker and Wallis' Warehouse, New York,* another site in the forgotten nuclear legacy and located in the heart of the Chelsea District of Manhattan.

—

The messenger arrived as Hunter was finishing his breakfast and returned with a gift-wrapped package for Jilly and as he finished the last of his coffee he wondered should he ask Penny Farthing to be his back-up. He thought better of it and prepared himself for his flight to New York.

~~~~~

Chapter 17

Jilly had done a good job and his passage through U.S. immigration at New York JFK was swift and waiting for him with the compulsory cheroot hanging from his lips was his old pal, Hank, waving a card with the name Drinkwater in large letters.

Hunter walked over to him, dropped his bag and they embraced and as Hank held him, he said, 'Twice in one year, there has to be a celebration here.'

'Hank, old pal, it's great to see you again but celebrations must wait. Have you heard from a guy called, Demyan?'

'Sure have, is he Russian or something?'

'Is he here?'

'He's keeping low and waiting in his apartment with his wife at the residential hotel I got for us. Is he legit, Hunter?'

'Hank! How should I say this? He has a colourful background and I've only known him for six months but I trust him. Old soldiers, veterans, you know albeit different armies.'

'I get ya! If you like him he's good for me...'

Their conversation was interrupted by a public announcement. 'Will Mister George Hunter just arrived from London please go to the 'Customer Services' desk. Thank you.'

'What have you lost, boss?' said Hank.

'Nothing, they have something for me.' As they walked across the large arrivals Hall Hunter enquired of their lodgings. 'Where are we staying?'

'I booked one single apartment and three doubles with free breakfast. Is that okay?'

'In the Chelsea district?'

'Sure thing, it's only four blocks from the address you gave me and my C.O. likes it and wants to move in permanent.'

'Do what you like when this is over. Let's go! The sooner we get there the quicker I get some nosh, I'm starving.'

At the Customer Service desk, Hunter showed his ticket and I.D. and was handed a small canvas briefcase.

'Thank you. Do I give it in here when I return?'

✗ 'No, Mr ~~Hunter~~, you give it into the flight desk of your airline.'

'Thank you.'

He rejoined Hank and they made their way out to the Taxi rank and five minutes after leaving the airport their taxi pulled off the main drag and into a semi-industrial area of converted warehouses and older apartment blocks and stopped outside a sleazy low life Bar called the *Blue Lotus*.

After paying off the driver, they waited on the sidewalk until the cab had disappeared and then walked to the next block where Hank had parked his car. Before they drove off Hank pulled a package from under the driver's seat and threw it into Hunter's lap. 'Your usual, Boss.'

'Thanks, Hank but I won't be needing it. I'm legal.'

Hank glanced sideways at Hunter but said nothing as he drove off. An hour later they swung into the underground parking area of the *'Maritime Residents Inn'* in the Chelsea District an area still undergoing modernisation from an industrial area into an upper-class hotspot popular with the gay pride society.

Forty-five minutes after checking in Hunter joined Hank and Demyan in the *'Early Bite Diner'* next door to their hotel and after introductions were over and they had a drink in front of them Hunter gave them a burner cell phone each before bringing them up to date on the situation as was...

'...and now I'm on an assignment to both stop an international crisis and settle a score. Hank—I want you as my eyes, guide and number two, while you, Demyan, owing to your situation I want you to keep low and be my interpreter and researcher and contact each other with those cells and use *'Whatsapp.'* Is that okay?' Both Hank and Demyan nodded and Hunter continued, 'The CIA are on the job focussed on what they think is the target but on my intuition we are going to concentrate on West 20th Street...'

The waitress came over and delivered Hunter's chilli beef burger and while he took his first bite Hank chipped in, '...Where did you get this info, Hunter?'

'It was the casual mention of two names in an overheard phone conversation but now that this Colonel Fabianski has gone feral it is the target I think he'll prefer as it will cause the greater amount of damage and it's the centre for the gay community which he hates intensely. Demyan—You know the Russian mindset, what's your twist on this?'

'Unlike you, Hunter, we don't go on intuition. If we make a plan we go for it which is sometimes our downfall. How should I put this? A bit like a team plan in a football match which is not working but we insist on sticking to it.'

'This is the concept the CIA is working on but if you as a player have already changed the plan on the field to suit yourself would that alter things?'

'Yes, because that is your plan and you stick to it. This intuition? How good is it?'

'As good as the one in an old social club in my home town six months ago...' Demyan nodded his head in acknowledgement. '...and to top it all,' Hunter passed a photo across to each of them, 'I Googled those names and I came up with this. The government says it has cleaned up this site under the Formerly Utilized Sites Remedial Action Program, whatever that is. It's a sixties aerial photo but it does mean it is or was a source of radioactivity to add to what was supposed to be a 'Dirty Bomb' and according to this shot it's here in the Chelsea District on W20th Street right by the Hudson.'

'Four blocks away,' said Hank, 'and much improved.'

'Hank—you and I will take a stroll there tonight. Demyan— what do you know of the 'October Legion'?

'Very little.'

'After dinner, Demyan, I want you to go to Brighton Beach and mix with the locals and see what you can pick up. I want to locate their source or HQ here and that seems a good place to start. How you do it is your affair but don't put yourself at risk.'

'Not a problem, Mr Hunter, we used to call it 'Little Odessa' when I lived there and I still have contacts.'

'Even better. Anyone like another drink?'

Never one to miss a freebee Hank nodded and answered with a brief, 'Yup,' while Demyan a fitness fanatic gave it a little thought, and said, 'Just a small beer.'

Hunter gave the order to the waitress before turning to Hank.

'Did you fix up that chopper?'

'Sure did, Hunter, it will be on the Hudson landing stage by W30th Street at seven 'o clock in the morning.'

'Your son is the pilot?'

'Sure is. He has his own Heli charter company and I'll be upfront with him.'

'Where's he staying?'

'At his place, the less he knows the better.'

'Tell him he needs a flight plan for Fredericton International. We're going to Canada, while you, Demyan, keep digging.'

'How long have we, Mr Hunter?'

'Just call me, Hunter, Demyan, but to answer your question—I don't know and I'm assuming that he will be using a cell phone connection as a detonator like he did in the U.K. so while he's in the area we're safe but we have to find him first. We should be back tomorrow evening Demyan. We'll keep you in touch. Are you okay with that?'

'Not a problem, Hunter,' said Demyan, 'My wife and I will see you at dinner tonight.'

'What have you done with the kids?'

'They're with grandma.'

He got up and collected his jacket and left them to it. When he'd gone, Hunter said, 'Hank—we could do with some female company on our walkabout to make us less conspicuous. Would your wife mind.'

'No problem, Hunter.'

'Okay, see you later. Is Aaron good for dinner tonight?'

'It's all set up, Hunter. I'm off now to do a recce of W20th. What are you doing?'

'Catching up on my sleep.'

———

Enjoying the mild October evening like many New Yorkers, Hunter, Hank and Audrey his wife strolled along 10th Ave. At the junction of 10th and W23^{rd,} they stopped. Hank pointed to a low bridge crossing over W23rd.

'Let's take a stroll along there.'

'Lead the way, Hank, can Audrey manage the steps?'

'There's an elevator and on W20th we go down steps.' He put an arm around Audrey's shoulder. 'Are you fit?'

'Try me you old crank.'

'See what I have to put up with, Hunter? Come on.'

When they reached the bridge they crossed over to the elevator and in moments were standing on a paved pathway studded with seats winding its way through scattered flower beds, grassy knolls, shrubs and small trees.

'Wow!,' said Hunter, 'this is a surprise. What do they call it?'

'This is the High Line. It's an old industrial rail track that closed down in 1980 and over time it became overgrown with wild growth so they converted it to a green walk for the benefit of the citizens. Nothing here has been planted by hand it all grew naturally. We built the boardwalk around it and the seats and you can still see the old rail tracks in places. An overhead park if you like.'

They turned south and joined the mixture of tourists and locals enjoying the mild early fall evening and Hunter was impressed at the way an industrial rail track had been turned into a green belt through the maze of what used to be a manufacturing and meatpacking area.

At W20th they went down to street level and turned west under the footbridge. 'Cross over, Hunter and we get a better look at the target.'

On the other side, they walked past a Jehovah's Witness Chapel and what used to be the *Wallis and Baker* warehouse but only the ground floor appeared occupied as the top six floors were boarded up but there were multiple aircon boxes attached at every level.

'The premises on ground level, Hunter, are art galleries until you come to those roller doors in the last quarter. Behind the last one is parking for the staff of the businesses in the street the first rollers are the delivery and office of the business on the upper floors and the middle one is the business outgoing orders exit. Next door to the car park complex you see another Art Gallery but that only goes back twenty feet. Beyond that is waste ground which can be accessed through the garage.'

'How did you find that out?'

'I went in this afternoon enquiring about parking and they showed me around. It's an 'L' shaped space with a fire escape door leading out the back.'

'I take it, Hank, like now, it's closed at night?'

'Yes, but if you pay for parking they give you a fob to operate the doors.'

They walked to the junction and turned north along 11th Ave and back into W21st St and joined Aaron and Demyan with Esther and Elena fifteen minutes later in the *Astor Court* restaurant on the corner of 10th and W20th.

When introductions were over Hunter apologised to the ladies and gave Aaron a quick rundown of their mission, and he finished, '...And so Aaron once more it is work that brings us together with the addition of Demyan who by the way has a free pass to the best golf clubs in Florida. He's pretty good too.'

'Thanks, Hunter,' said Demyan, 'how's your handicap?'

'My biggest handicap, Demyan, is me but I'm very much the same as when we last played.'

'Excuse me,' interrupted Aaron, 'Golf aside, you mentioned in your intro the 'October Legion', who are they?'

'In the UK, Aaron, it's an underground organisation of sleeper Russian agents left over when the USSR crumbled and some of whom were revived for this operation. I'm assuming that they exist in the States. As I mentioned, Demyan is using his connections in Brighton Beach to dig them out.'

'Hunter, I may be of use here. I'm going to a convention of religious leaders in the Holocaust Memorial Park in Sheepshead Bay. I have friends in the Orthodox Church of America and many Russians attend. I'll ask around and see if they can help.'

'Aaron, before you go I'll give you a photo of our suspect on your phone. Keep this low key but if anyone queries impress on your friends that this mission has the official support of the Russian government and the CIA to bring this feral mission to a peaceful conclusion or we may have a ginormous holocaust on our hands here in New York. One last word and then dinner. Hank, I'll go alone tomorrow you get that unlocking tab for the garage and duplicate it. Can do?'

'I'll sure as hell try. Let's eat!'

—

Glad that the introductory speeches and convention protocol was over, Aaron picked up his glass of green tea and looked around and saw a group of Priests from the Orthodox Church of America stood in the middle of the floor one of whom was his friend Michal and he wandered over to join them.

Before he spoke to Michal he acknowledged the Elder and the group, 'Good morning, gentlemen, how's it going. It does get better as you well know.'

'Good morning, Aaron,' replied the Elder, ' now that the boring stuff is out of the way things are much better.'

'That's good,' he turned to Michal, 'Michal can I speak to you in private. It won't take long.'

Michal took him by the arm and lead him away to a quiet corner of the room. 'What is it, Aaron, how can I help?'

Aaron gave him a rundown of the situation and finished, '…and I wondered if you had heard of this 'October Legion' or noticed anything unusual lately?'

'Funny you should mention that Aaron, but a friend has been acting strangely for a few days now. He's more or less become a recluse and won't acknowledge calls or messages. He should have been here, in fact, he never misses these get-togethers.'

'What does he do, Michal?'

'He runs 'Isis Five Star' the upmarket online women's clothing business from a warehouse over in Lower West Side Manhattan. Near 10th Ave I think. He's doing very well too.'

'Can you recall anything else?'

'He's been like this since the day before a large black SUV arrived.'

'Is that unusual? Maybe he's bought a new one.'

'He's normally a comfy limo man. His latest one was a Jaguar.'

'Oh… I see. I won't keep you anymore, Michal. Keep this under your hat and I'll be in touch but a social call next time.'

On an impulse, Aaron took out his phone and showed him the photo. 'Is that his visitor?'

The elder looked closely. 'Yes, I believe it is. The hair is different but I'm convinced that's him. Does it mean anything?'

They shook hands and Aaron made for the exit and outside the hall, he walked through the Memorial Park until he found an unoccupied bench. He sat down and sent a short message: **SMS: Hunter - Have a possible lead. A.**

—

They were approaching Fredericton Airport when Hunter got the message and he sent texts to Demyan and Hank to meet up with Aaron and set up a watching brief and he would be back asap.

He closed the phone as they were approaching the landing pad and he waited until the arrival protocol was over before he spoke. 'This will be a quick meeting, Landon. Get fuelled up and something to eat and we'll be going back. For a bunch of oldies, we're working pretty fast.'

'You sure are, Mr Hunter. Dad always said you were quick. Don't worry I'll have it all sorted by the time you get back.'

RCMP Inspector Paquin welcomed Hunter, who was in his official mode, in the Staff canteen airside and after checking Hunter's papers and ordering coffee Paquin opened the conversation. 'What can we do for you, Agent Hunter?'

Hunter took out his notebook and after a cursory glance replied, 'Flight number XY2296. What can you tell me about it, Inspector?'

Paquin opened a file. 'The airport got an emergency call for permission to land from the aircraft. When permission was given they requested we call...' he looked in the file, '... this phone number.' He passed it over to Hunter. 'Which we did and on landing an ambulance turned up. When we asked what the emergency was, they said, and I quote, "Low cabin pressure causing life-threatening trauma" unquote. She apparently has an inoperable brain tumour and is returning home to her local hospice. Our doctor examined the patient and he Okayed it so permission was given to transfer her to the ambulance and the rest of the journey to the States would continue overland.'

'What happened then?'

'A doctor and a nurse from the plane were cleared through immigration and they left with the ambulance.'

'And the aircraft?'

'The aircraft was a genuine air ambulance and after the crew had their required rest they went to another call out which was probably already on their flight plan and that was in New Jersey.'

'My, my, it was well planned. So, Inspector, you were oblivious of the goings-on until MI6 got in touch about the GPS signal?'

'That's right. We were on it straight away and as you know we found the abandoned ambulance with the victim.'

'She was kidnapped at the same time as her husband was killed. Is that all you have?'

'Only she died shortly after leaving here and the crew abandoned the ambulance and were picked up by a car with false Canadian plates so there must have been another contact enroute which we don't know about.'

'Have you any photos.'

'We have CCTV pictures taken at passport control.'

He withdrew two photos from the file and passed them over to Hunter. 'This is the doctor and his nurse.'

Hunter flashed up the photos on his phone and compared them. 'That's them. What name did he use?'

'Doctor Alistair McRae with an impressive string of letters after his name and his documentation was good.'

'Okay, Inspector, we'll have to leave it there and tell your medics there was nothing wrong with that woman, just the opposite.'

They stood up and as they shook hands Inspector Paquin, said, 'I'm sorry to hear about your agents and we will be following up on this. Good luck, Mr Hunter.'

'Thanks, Inspector. You have my contact details?'

'Yes, and if anything turns up you will be the first to know.'

Back on the tarmac, Hunter strapped himself in and as Landon slid the throttle of the Bell 407 chopper into the flight position and pulled back on the collective he had an overwhelming feeling of *déjà vu*. He was taken back to the time when, Hank, Landon's father, had rescued him from the *'Pathet Lao'* way back in 1966. Aaron was part of the same exercise and had been airlifted out by a medical Huey helicopter.

He arrived back in New York in time for the evening de-brief and joined Hank and Aaron just as they were ordering in the *Light Byte*. Once settled with a cold beer in front of him Hunter enquired where the girls were.

'They're enjoying the freedom and uptown at some show on Broadway,' said Hank.

'And the latest news, Aaron?'

'Luck was involved, Hunter. I saw my friend from the Orthodox Church at the Convention and dropped a hint about the 'October Legion' and he mentioned that a close friend of his was behaving out of character. He has more or less shut himself off and all enquiries are met by a stranger. The man in question is the owner of *'Isis Five Star'* who has a warehouse in—you tell him, Hank.'

'W20th, the very building we've been sussing and Demyan is on watch at this chaps house now.'

'We'll have to arrange a shift pattern,' said Hunter, 'has he got cover?'

'And how! Tell him, Aaron.'

'Michal, my friend lives almost opposite this guy and he and another friend are right into this thing. They volunteered to help and are rotating with Demyan who also has his wife with him and watching from the spare bedroom of Michal's house. Demyan's wife is right behind him and I get the feeling she is relieved to see him working for us instead of his former vocation.'

Their meal was served and as they got stuck in, Hunter said, 'If they can keep watch that end let us cover the warehouse. Did you get a duplicate entry fob, Hank?'

'Yep!'

'Can we access that business?'

'The staff use the car park facilities and there's a code to unlock the door but I think we can swing it. They start work at six in the morning.'

For the next five minutes, they concentrated on eating and when he had finished Hunter pushed his plate away, and said, 'Do you know what? I think our Colonel Fabianski has been ill-advised.'

'Why's that?' said Aaron.

'He's working on the concept that that building is still a radioactive minefield. It can't be otherwise nobody would be working there.'

Hank put his knife and fork down, 'Hunter! Do you think this device you mention is already in there? I mean, he's had this guy under closed doors for nearly a week now.'

'That's a possibility, Hank, but the battery life on the detonator is only about three days at most. Just enough for the perp to get away and he's still here isn't he?'

'Good point.'

'It could be stored there.'

'Hank—can you use your connections in the NYPD and get us a Geiger counter?'

'Hunter,' said Aaron, 'can we not just inform the CIA?'

'The place would be surrounded by SWAT teams and the area evacuated which would scare Fabianski off and goodness knows where he would dump it then. I want him to think that this target is not on the radar.'

'I'll get on to it now, Hunter.'

'Tonight if possible.'

'You don't want much.'

He got up from the table and went to the washroom while Hunter said to Aaron, 'Tell your friends to get themselves burner phones and we'll keep this thing to ourselves.'

They chatted about old times for what seemed an age but was only a few minutes before Hank came back and sat down and plonked his phone on the table. 'It's no go, Hunter, the best he can do is tomorrow lunchtime and he says can you give him more notice.'

'That's okay, Hank, I was being hopeful. Did he ask why we wanted it?'

'Yup, he was curious but I gave him some bullshit about you being into cold war historical investigations and you were curious about us having radioactive material in town. I said it was safe but you want to see for yourself and we were going into the car park to check.'

'Did he seem happy with that?'

'Yup, anything for an old pal but can we get it back tomorrow night. I said the day after and he was okay.'

'Okay!' Hunter put his phone on the table. 'This is the master phone which we'll keep on site. Aaron!—Hank and I are going to do a recce and then start the rota. I want you to call your friends and give them this number and if anything happens to call it immediately which will alert whoever is on watch here. Leave a message for the girls also. We'll do two hours on and four off and you do the last shift and don't worry if you fall asleep as the phone will be set on loud and it will wake you in time. If you leave the car carry the phone. Hank—we'll use your car on site and yours, Aaron as the shuttle. Is that okay?'

Hank and Aaron looked at each other and shrugged and spoke at the same time. 'No problems there, Hunter. You're the boss.'

'Okay, drink up and let's get started. One last thing. When you arrive on-site call the number and whoever is on duty will open the door. Oh! Tool up. Can you do that, Aaron, there's no religious misgivings, is there?'

'No, and if there was our Lord forgives those protecting the world.'

—

Hank, wearing his old NYPD cap and blouson jacket, wheeled the car into the parking bay and Hunter, disguised with a navy blue cop type baseball cap and glasses leaned out and pressed the button on his remote. Although they looked battered and rusty the doors rolled up without a squeak and the garage lights came on as Hank guided the car in and chose a spot close to the exit.

Hunter made a note of the cameras while they waited five minutes for the lights to go out and gave it an extra ten minutes for everything to settle before they got out and Hunter thought it odd when the lights didn't come on. He shrugged it off and loosened his gun and torches lit he followed Hank over to the door that led into the clothing warehouse.

Shining his torch over to the left of the door, Hank said, 'There you have it, Hunter. One manual push-button locking system.'

'That's a bugger,' said Hunter, 'How do we get the code for that? Give it a try, Hank, but I think you'll need some luck. Try 1234.'

Hank tried and did a few more random numbers. 'Nothing doing, boss.'

'I didn't think we would, Hank, and with ten-thousand options, it's a no-no. If you get bored give it a twirl but tomorrow should be okay as our friend doesn't appear to be in a hurry.'

'Don't bet your life on it, Murphy's Law says he'll move now.'

'Right, Hank, let me out. You've got supplies?'

'And a four-pack as back-up.'

'Good thinking, I'll see you in a couple of hours. Your Indian summer is ideal for a walk along the High Line.'

———

It was just past six a.m. when the first of the *Isis Five Star* employees turned up. She parked her car and Hank followed her over to the door. She was about to punch the code in when Hank spoke.

'Excuse me miss.'

She took note of his NYPD cap, Navy blouson and the poised notebook before replying, rather sternly, 'Mrs.'

'I'm sorry, Mrs…?'

'…David.'

'Mrs David, have you seen anyone hanging around here lately. Someone reported his car was broken into yesterday?'

A small queue had gathered behind her and, she said, 'No! Look, I'm late. Gotta go.'

She turned away and punched the code in while Hank scribbled in his notebook and put the same question to the man behind her. He shook his head and was about to clock in when Hank asked him why the lights didn't operate with movement.

'We've moaned about that for about six months but they just don't fix 'em.'

'I see,' said Hank, 'thank you.'

Satisfied there was nothing more to be gained by holding them up anymore Hank returned to his car to wait the rest of his watch out.

———

Other than Hanks interviews with the workers the night had passed without incident and there was only one thing to report when they met up with Hunter in the '*Light Byte*' at eight-thirty.

'And what's that, Hank?'

'9381.'

'Is that what I think it is?'

'Yep! I checked it out a few times and that was the number they used.'

'Well done! Demyan has nothing for us so if that's it lads let's have some breakfast. Are the ladies joining us?'

'No,' said Hank, 'they'll do anything but early mornings are out.'

Hunter looked at Aaron who nodded in agreement. 'He's right, Hunter, it's a mid-season holiday for them and shopping comes high on the agenda. This could become a regular thing. Esther asked me why Jacquie wasn't here.'

Hunter shook his head. 'Nah! That's a no, no. I couldn't babysit and run a business.'

The master phone buzzed and Hunter picked it up and ran his finger up the app. 'Yes, Demyan?'

'A UPS van has just pulled up over the road and the two-man crew are taking delivery of a suitcase-sized heavy package. I say heavy but one man has just lifted it with difficulty. About 30kgs I reckon.'

'That sounds like we're on the move. The crafty bastards. Follow that van, Demyan, but it's probably going to the depot. Leave a watch on the house.'

'Copy that, Hunter.'

The phone went dead and Hunter put the phone down and looked at Aaron and Hank who were waiting expectantly. 'It looks like things are moving but not the way I was expecting. Where is the UPS depot, Hank.'

'I don't know. I've seen dozens of their vans but never knew where the depot was.'

He picked up his smartphone and began fiddling and after a few moments, said, 'It's on 50th Ave, Long Island, just over the East River from Lower Manhattan. Why UPS, Hunter?'

'If you wanted to plant a package without anyone questioning it, what would you do?'

'That's what they're doing?'

'Yep! Hank—At this moment UPS are picking up the package which is about the size we're on the lookout for.'

Aaron chipped in, 'And you think they are going to deliver it to the *'Isis Five Star'* warehouse, Hunter? What a great idea. They receive large boxes of dresses and material there all the time and no one would take any notice.'

'Got it in one but it will go to the depot first before distribution which gives us a couple of hours. Hank—collect the Geiger counter while Aaron and I do a watching brief on W20th.' He drank the last of his coffee and stood up. 'Let's go!'

Aaron stayed seated and looked at Hunter thoughtfully. 'Hunter, do you think they will detonate it while it's in transit or even in the warehouse?'

'No, Aaron, it's not likely. Our Colonel Fabianski, is not a suicidal maniac. He'll be well away from here before he pulls the trigger. I think we have twenty-four hours at least to disarm it. Call your friends and tell them to report anyone leaving and tail them until we get a relief to them.'

'I'll do that on the way round to the warehouse.'

—

Sat comfortably in the shade with newspapers and magazines, Hunter with mini-binoculars, and Aaron with his head stuck in a magazine watched from the High Line bridge over W20th when they were woken from their daydreams by the buzzing of the Master phone.

'Hunter!' He listened for a few moments before he rang off, and said to, Aaron, 'It's at the depot. It's late as they had a couple more pick-ups on the way.'

'Any idea how long it will be in there?'

'No, and we've no way of telling when it leaves. We'll just have to sit it out, chum.'

'Okay, Hunter, I'm going for some coffee. Americano black is it?'

'Get some doughnuts, Aaron, I'm starving.'

Aaron stood up and stretched before going down to street level and a modest stroll to the coffee shop on 10th Ave while Hunter buried himself in a newspaper for the umpteenth time while cautiously watching W20th below. He hadn't settled for more than half a minute when the phone buzzed again.

'Hunter!' This time he listened longer before, he replied, 'Yes, Demyan, stay with it but don't stop if and when it arrives here. Return to base and watch for Fabianski leaving or his vehicle. The team there have had instructions.'

He checked his watch and began gathering their baggage wishing Aaron would hurry up at the same time. After fifteen minutes he was getting anxious and contemplating going down to street level at the same time doubting this action as they could miss each other. He stood up and gave up the bench to an elderly couple looking for respite when Aaron's head appeared above floor level a step at a time smiling at the discomfort of the normally calm figure awaiting him.

'He must be getting old,' he said to himself.

He stopped alongside Hunter and shoved a pot of coffee into his hand and held up a packet of doughnuts. 'What's the matter, Hunter, you seen a ghost?'

Hunter looked at the laid back priest beside him and deciding any rebuke would be wasted flicked the lid off his coffee as he shook his head and plucking a doughnut from the bag, he replied, 'Nothings amiss, Aaron, our bomb is due here any minute, where've you been?'

'Blimey, that's quick. You sure?'

'Nothing definite, Aaron, but the same van that picked it up left the depot ten minutes later and headed for the Queens Midtown Tunnel which is in our direction so it seems likely.'

'It takes about half an hour, Hunter, on a good day.'

Hunter checked his watch again. 'That gives us about ten minutes. Let's get below and stroll the street.'

'Sorry I'm late, Hunter. I'd have given up on the doughnuts had I known. There was a queue.'

'Don't worry, matey, I should've called you. Let's go!'

As they turned to walk to the steps, Hunter said, 'How many nuts did you get?'

'Four, two jam and two custard.'

'Huh! Is that all?'

On the street, they walked back as far as 10th Ave crossed over W20th and began to stroll back down the warehouse side. They stopped under the footbridge in the shade and sipped their coffee and as they were doing so the UPS van pulled into the street.

'Come on, Aaron, I want to get a close-up.'

They began walking at the same time Hunter switched on the video app of his phone and watched as the van stopped outside the delivery door of the warehouse and the driver went into the building only to come out a moment later with a young helper.

They were thirty yards away when the driver flung the van doors open and together with the helper manoeuvred the heavy package onto a two-wheeled handcart and trundled it inside ignoring Hunter and Aaron videoing the scene as they walked past.

They walked to the junction with 11th Ave and crossed over in time to see the van drive off.

'That looks like it, Aaron. Now we have to sit out the next eight hours until we can get in there.'

'Hunter,' said Aaron, with a hint of concern in his voice as they wandered along, 'shouldn't we tell the cops?'

'I understand your unease and that's a worry I have, Aaron, but I'm more concerned at what the Fabianski reaction would be if he saw the swarm of armoured vehicles, swat teams not to mention cops closing down New York. He'd take a chance being twenty miles away and do it there and then and I want him, PERSONALLY!'

Aaron held Hunter back by his arm. 'Hunter, do you know how to disarm this damn thing?'

'Gleaned from the info given to me, because of the type of detonator and the low voltage there is no anti-handling set-up just two very thin wires coming from the phone to the device trigger itself.'

'Hunter, I wish I had your confidence. Let's rejoin, Hank.'

———

They went back to the *Light Byte* and were halfway into their coffee when Hank carrying a rucksack joined them. He eased the rucksack off his shoulder and lowered it to the floor with a sigh and sat down.

'Phew! I'm getting too old for this. There it is, Hunter, he wants it back first thing in the morning.'

'No probs, Hank, if all goes well tonight.'

'It's in there?'

'It sure is. Okay! Here's what I want to do. Hank—I want you as my bagman. Aaron—I want the girls safe so take them out to friends in Sheepshead Bay. That's about twenty miles isn't it?…'Aaron confirmed it with a nod. '…stay in a hotel if you have to. Join up with Demyan but he'll be stalking Fabianski if and when he moves. Hank and I will do a watching brief on the warehouse to make sure the bomb doesn't leave and then at nine o'clock, we'll be going in. If you don't hear a big bang you know it's gone well or if there is any snags we'll let you know. I'll warn Demyan you're coming. Is that okay?' Aaron looked a bit despondent and raised a hand. 'Yes, Aaron?'

'Hunter, as part of the team I would like to play a bigger part. Why are you sending me away?'

'Nothing personal, Aaron, but I want your calming influence with the ladies if anything goes wrong and your Church connections to help them afterwards, also, to act as a go-between with your friends. I will be talking to Jacquie later and I want you to stay in touch with her. I'll also send you a message to give to the CIA explaining the situation and relieving you and Hank of any blame.'

'I get you, Hunter, I didn't want you sidelining me because of my way of life.'

'That's, okay, Aaron, believe me, if I thought there would be any trouble you would have been included. As it is there'll be no one near the damned thing only Hank and me, I hope.'

Aaron stood up and picked up his coat and Hunter walked around to him and shook his hand vigorously. 'Take care, Aaron.'

Hank did likewise and Aaron left them to plan the rest of the day.

———

It was a few minutes after 21^{00} hrs and almost dark when Hank parked the car close to the wall and close to the exit doors. They waited for the lights to die before they clambered out in their bogus NYPD outfits. Hank used his old NYPD gear while Hunter's was a bodged up cap and jacket in the right colour.

Hunter gave Hank some surgical gloves, 'Wear these the whole time, Hank, and make sure you leave nothing behind.'

They kept close to the wall with Hank in the lead the Geiger counter slung over his shoulder and Hunter following carrying a small holdall. At the door, Hank held the torch in such a way that only a slim sliver of light shone on the keypad and he quickly punched in the numbers and was relieved to hear the click as the lock released. They slipped inside and closed the door and Hank didn't waste any time setting up the Geiger counter. He hung the strap around his neck so that it lay across his stomach and he wore the headphones over one ear which meant he was hands-free to operate the detector module and use a torch.

Because of the industrial complex of the building, the staircase that faced them was wide, steep and long and both of them were breathing heavily when they reached the top.

'They must be a fit lot that work here,' said Hunter.

'It didn't show in that bunch I spoke to,' replied Hank, 'in fact just the opposite. Typical Macdonald statistics.'

'Tut! Tut!, Hank. Come on let's go.'

They were on a long landing with two large lifts one marked incoming and the other outgoing and at the end a wide entrance covered with hanging plastic draught excluders. Hank waved the detector into both lifts with no result and they made their way to the entrance into a large warehouse complex divided into two and filled with rows of clothes and more lifts to upper floors. At the far end was a large roller door.

They worked their way around both halves with no signal and moved on to the roller door.

'Looks like some sort of warehouse, boss.'

'Okay, Hank, stand clear and I'll open it up.'

There were two buttons at the side and he pushed the green one and was relieved that the maintenance was up to date as it rolled up with barely a squeak. He stopped it when it was head height and they stepped inside and they were faced with shelf upon shelf and row upon row of multi-coloured materials.

Hunter let out a long sigh. 'Just what we needed,' he muttered, 'should've brought two detectors.'

Together they went through the maze. Hunter in the lead looking underneath with his torch and Hank following listening and watching. They were pressing on too quickly Hunter thought but time was of the essence. They finished the last line and worked their way around the wall where many boxes were stacked but not a bleep.

'Next one, Hank. Are you fit?'

'I'm good boss.'

They went up to the next floor and in the poor light, they could see this one was also divided but one side was rows of benches with stacks of flat cardboard boxes and wrapping paper between them and the other half was rows of loaded movable clothes racks. Among all this were printers, computers and sticky tape and everything else that went to make up parcels. By each lift was a clear space with a mixture of loaded pallets and a hand-operated fork loader

'Look like the online section, Hank.'

'It sure does, and Aaron was right when he said it was a big business.'

'Okay, Hank you search amongst the racks and I'll go through the benches.'

Twenty minutes later they met by the lifts. Hank didn't wait but pushed the up button and prepared to move on. The next floor was a copy of the third floor but with an e-tech room filled with computers and wi-fi equipment at one end. Hank got a reading but they wrote that off as all the technology in the room and went up to the fourth floor.

This was the high-class department where all the clothes were of superior quality and everything was widely spaced and the boxes and wrapping were top line and across one end was the office.'

'Hank—do the office. I'll check out here. Make sure you do every alcove and cupboard.'

'Copy that, boss.'

They had only been searching a couple of minutes when Hank joined Hunter. 'What is it, Hank?'

'I've got a signal.'

'Get to it, Hank, I'm right behind you.'

Hunter closed the office door behind him and noticed it was the only part of the warehouse that had windows and the city lights enabled them to move around without torches. Hank led the way over the main office and into a more lavishly decorated personal office and in the corner was a large mahogany cupboard that Hank had left open and Hunter didn't need a torch to see what was in it stood on its end. A large leather case with straps and locks.

Hunter shivered. He was looking at something that could sink

Manhattan. He wasn't religious but he looked heavenwards and sent a silent message to Jacquie. *'Love you. Jacquie.'*

'That's it, Hank, a copy of the UK bomb. What's the reading?'

'Ten, boss, about the same as my CT scan.'

'Okay, Hank, let's get it out.'

Hank ditched the Geiger counter and Hunter his holdall and reaching into the cupboard they gently eased it forward and as it came out they tilted it back until it laid flat. An inch at a time they gently moved it into a clear space and set it down. Hunter looked at it and smiled. Apart from UPS stickers there were others like, THIS WAY UP or DO NOT STAND ON END. If they only knew.

'Hank—you can leave now and I'll give you an hour or we can get this thing done.'

'I'm good to go, boss, I'm with you.'

They did a knuckle handshake and Hunter called Hank around to his side. 'Shine your torch on those locks and I'll get to work.'

He unbuckled the straps and pushed them to one side and opened his bag and plucked out a key ring with a selection of lock picking tools and went through them one at a time until the locks opened. With mental fingers crossed he eased open the lid and lifted it slowly and when it was open a few inches he signalled Hank to lower his torch and he bent down to check for attachments of any sort. Nothing appeared untoward so he pushed the lid wide open.

Inside was a metal cased package similar in shape to a packed rucksack complete with shoulder carrying strap with the international Nuclear signs stuck on it. Glued on the top was a basic cell phone with two fine insulated wires extending from it.

'There you have it, Hank. A 1.5Kt nuclear bomb which would sink most of Manhattan.'

'Jeezus! Hunter, how did he get that here?'

'It's a long story but very clever, in fact so clever even his own country are panicking. Let's get started.'

Hunter traced the wires and they went into the device through a couple of tiny rubber-lined holes cut into one edge.

'Here's the fun part, Hank, I have to get the back off that phone.'

'You can't just cut the wires?'

'It may be smart wired, Hank, so if you chop one the current is activated and goes down the other. They may be earthed inside the casing making a circuit. I've got to get the sim card out to stop the signal. Doing it this way he could set it off twenty miles or thousands of miles away.'

He delicately held the cell device with a thumb and a finger and tried moving it but it was stuck firmly. He took a torch off Hank and bent down level with the base of it and he could just see a smear of super glue.

'Superglue, Hank. Nothing for it but good old WD40.'

'Will that work?'

'It's worked before albeit removing glue from my fingers.'

From his bag, he took out a small can of WD40 and tickling the push top went carefully around the base.

'Take a break, Hank. We'll give it three or four minutes.'

Three minutes seemed like a lifetime and Hunter couldn't wait. He reached into the bag and took out a scalpel and on his hands and knees began sliding the tip under and along the length of the phone. He could feel the glue softening and using the screwdriver blade of his Swiss Army knife as a lever as he cut with the scalpel, millimetre by millimetre, he was able to tilt the phone until he finally scraped away the last sticky bond.

He waited anxiously for half a minute before examining the back of the phone. It was one of the later ones with a clip-on back and he inserted the screwdriver blade into the small gap at the end and gradually with his fingertips eased the back off.

'We have a slight problem, Hank.'

'What's that, boss?'

'The bloody battery has to come out before I can get to the sim card. Hank! You can hop it now or we go for it. What do you reckon?'

'Hunter, I'm repeatin' myself. Get it done man.'

'Okay, here goes.'

He put his thumbnail into the slot alongside the camera and holding his breath flicked the battery upwards and out. They both held their breath and counted. Nothing happened and they went—
'Phew!' simultaneously.

'That solves the power problem but low and behold the crafty bastard has fitted a twin sim cell. It's no good without the battery though.'

They were marked 1 & 2 and he fiddled them out. From his bag he retrieved a burner phone and inserted card №1.

'Have you got a spare sim slot, Hank?'

'Sure thing. My Smarty is a doubler.'

Hunter gave Hank sim №2. 'Stick that in it.'

They waited while Hank fiddled with his phone before, Hank said, 'Why've we done that boss?'

Hunter gave Hank the burner. 'Fabianski has made mistakes before and I'm hoping when he rings to detonate this thing he will give away his position. If he does, Hank, get your contact to track the number.'

'Will do, boss.'

Hunter looked at his watch and saw that they had been in the building for almost three hours. 'Okay, Hank, let's get the hell out of here.'

'What do we do with this, boss' said, Hank.

'Leave it. Second thoughts, we'll take it with us. Go get one of those trolleys while I tidy up here. That way nobody here will be any the wiser and we won't alert Fabianski who hasn't made a move yet.'

Hank pushed himself up on a nearby desk and stretched before making his way out to the lifts while Hunter snipped the wires freeing the cell-detonating device. He dropped it into his pocket before closing the lid and locking and fastening the belts. He eased himself up and closed the cupboard when Hank returned and stood by the door.

'Get as close as you can. Hank.'

'It's too big to get between desks, Boss. We'll have to carry it.'

'Not a problem. Take one strap and I'll take the other.'

They eased the bomb up onto its side and between them managed to get it onto the trolley. They did a last check around before locking the door and making their way to the lifts.

Inside the lift, Hunter enquired, 'Is there a way into the garage, Hank?'

'No, boss, it's down the stairs.'

Hunter reached for the buttons and paused for a second before realising there was no 'G' button and pushed №1 instead. He leaned back. 'They don't do Zero's just like the bloody Romans.'

On the ground floor, they manhandled the trolley over to the head of the stairs leading to the garage and through the heavy steel doors where they were able to descend by holding onto the handrails and do step-by-step level with each other. Another fiddly manoeuvre into the garage and with a collective sigh they stopped by the car and got their breath.

Both were fit for their age and in a minute they were ready to lift it into the trunk.

A quick glance at his watch and Hunter was surprised how time had flown by. 'Two-thirty, Hank, let's go and snatch some sleep.

'What do we do with the what's it?'

'We're stuck with the same dilemma. I don't want to alert Fabianski so we'll hang on to it and when he moves we give it to the CIA.'

'Is it safe in the trunk, boss?'

'Yep! The radioactivity is low so it won't affect passers-by, but don't use the car. Hang on! Didn't you say there was waste ground out the back?'

'Sure is.'

'Can we get out to it?'

'Yep! Over in the far corner is a door.'

'We'll leave it there.'

They carried the neutralised bomb over to the door and after a moment fiddling with the lock Hunter had it open and they dragged it through into a builders wasteland.

'That's weird, Hank, why didn't they use this patch?'

'Your guess is as good as mine but I can only think this is where the heaviest radiation may have been.'

'You're probably right. Okay, put it here by the wall and let's get the Hell out of here.'

'Sleep you said, boss? Let's go!'

———

When they met in the *Light Byte* and the waitress had filled Hunter's coffee for the second time when he called Demyan.

'Morning, Hunter, what can I do for you?'

'Morning, Demyan, anything happening?'

'Nothing yet, in fact, it is strangely quiet.'

'We've disarmed the bomb, Demyan, he's got to move now. Have a car ready.'

'You disarmed it, Hunter? How?'

'Pure talent, man, and good luck.'

'What next?'

'The battery in the detonator would only have three days life, Demyan, which means Fabianski has got to move anytime soon.'

'We're on it, Hunter. Aaron and Esther are set to go in one car and Elana and me in the other. Hunter! You have to make it up to these people. It has been like a second life to them and they're keen not to mention how they looked after us.'

'I'll see what I can do when it's all over. Give them my regards and tell them it's much appreciated.'

'Copy that, Hunter.'

Hunter put his phone down and took a swig of cold coffee. 'It's all quiet there so it's wait and see. Hank—Is your lad on standby?'

'Yep!'

'Good, but right now I'm going back to the apartment. Four hours sleep does not go well with me.'

'I'll join you or rather I'm going back to my place.'

———

It was turning one 'o clock when Hunter rolled off the settee and looked at his watch and couldn't believe he'd been asleep that long. 'Bloody hell, I'd better get a move on.'

He nipped over to the bathroom dropping his clothes as he went and jumped in the shower. He shaved as he was showering and was towelling himself down when his phone buzzed in the lounge. He quickly wrapped the towel around himself and dashed over to the phone noting it was Demyan as he slid his finger up the app. 'Yes, Demyan?'

'He's on the move. A taxi has just pulled up and Fabianski and that nurse are leaving. They have hand luggage only. Aaron is following now and we'll be swapping over intermittently as we go.'

'Thanks, Demyan. Keep me posted.'

He put the phone down and hadn't completed one-step when it buzzed again. This time it was Gus Thomas in the UK. 'Yes, Gus, what can I do for you?'

'Hunter! We've just received a text from the girlfriend of Petrov on his mobile.'

'Petrov, Gus, remind me.'

'You're getting old. Hunter. The guy that was shot in the ambulance. She went off with Fabianski as a nurse.'

'Got it. What did she say?'

'I quote—HELP. On move. Follow number.'

'Send us her number, Gus. We can trace it from here and she's right. They are on the move.'

'What about the bomb?'

'Sorted but no one knows but us. Give it a couple of hours and you can tell the Yanks. It's behind the *Baker & Wallis* warehouse.'

'Got it. Keep us posted.'

Hunter dropped the phone, and said, as he dashed to the shower room, 'Better get a shift on, Hunter, things are moving.'

He stopped suddenly and nipped back for the phone and made a quick alert call to Hank before finishing his preparations for the day.

Ten minutes later there was a knock on the apartment door and Hank joined him. 'Is it happening, boss?'

'It sure is, the latest from Demyan is that our target is on his way north towards Manhattan accompanied by the nurse so for now we sit tight. Get your lad fuelled up, Hank, and over to the helipad.'

'I'm onto it.'

Hank took his phone from his shirt pocket and speed dialled a number which was instantly answered. 'Yes, Dad?'

'Landon! Are you ready?'

'Sure am, Dad, and fully fuelled.'

'Things are moving, get over to the helipad and standby.'

'Wilco, Dad.'

The phone went dead and Hank gave Hunter the thumbs up. 'He's up and running, boss.'

'Thanks, Hank,' and just then an SMS buzzed onto his phone. He picked it up and after a few moments, he said to, Hank, 'They're entering the Battery Tunnel now.'

'Do you don't think he's going to inspect the bomb?'

'Unlikely. Newark airport maybe?'

'That's expensive.'

'Would you like a coffee, Hank?'

'Sure do. This is nail-biting.'

Hunter went into the kitchen area and switched on the percolator when a call came through from, Gus. 'Yes, Gus.'

'Hunter—the last message was just, 'TUNNEL' and I've put a call divert directly to your phone.'

'She's right, they've entered the tunnel under the East River and are coming towards us.'

'Okay, Hunter, it's in your hands. Best of. Bye.'

He poured two cups and rejoined Hank who was pacing up and down. 'Thanks, boss.'

'Stand by the phones, Hank, I'm going to get tooled up. I got a feeling I may need it.' He took his cup into the bedroom and left Hank to his nervous patrolling.

Meticulous with his armoury he stripped and cleaned his favourite Glock 17 and loaded it with one up the spout and he had stripped down his small back-up Walther PPK when Hank called from the other room. 'Hey, Boss, we got something!'

Hunter stopped what he was doing and went through to Hank. 'What is it, Hank?'

'Aaron has set up a group video link and we are following the cab. Come see.'

Hunter looked over Hank's shoulder and watched as the cars weaved through the afternoon traffic. 'Where are they?'

'They're going across town and are onto Greenwich Street. Hang on, they're turning onto King Street. Hey, Boss! I reckon they're heading for Penn Station.'

'What makes you think that?'

'After thirty years with the NYPD, I've got the city routes imprinted in my brain. He's following the road plan.'

'Keep watching while I finish what I was doing.'

Three minutes later Hank popped his head in the door. 'It's definitely Penn, boss. They've turned north into 6th Ave. I bet they're into West 31st already.'

He glanced down at his cell and then held it up for Hunter. 'They're cruising across 7th and will be turning into 8th for the main Amtrak entrance.'

'Okay, Hank, tell Aaron and Demyan to keep tabs on them and we'll be in Penn asap.'

———

Traffic was heavy and it was twenty minutes before Hank dropped Hunter off before disappearing into the vehicle crush to find parking. Hunter, carrying an overnight bag and a briefcase wound his way through the continuous crowds milling around the upper concourse of the station and found Demyan and Elana waiting under the destination board.

'Hi, Demyan, What's happening?'

'Too late, Hunter, their train was called ten minutes ago and is probably on its way.'

'Do we know where too?'

'Yes, Elana got close up behind them at check-in and overheard everything. They're booked on the overnight Silver Meteor Amtrak to Miami and have a reserved deluxe bedroom.'

'Do we know the route?'

Demyan handed Hunter a timetable map and after a moments scrutiny, Hunter said, 'It stops at Washington DC. We have a little over four hours. Demyan, Miami is your area isn't it?'

'The other side of the peninsula, but, Yes!'

'You have twenty-five hours. Can you and Elana fly down and cut him off?'

'Wilco, Hunter, and what are you going to do?'

'With a little luck, I'll be on the same train.'

'One other thing, Hunter. Fabianski had a firm hold on that nurse almost dragging her...' and pointing across the concourse, '...and over by the escalator he threw a smart cell into the rubbish bin.'

'That figures, she's been sending guiding signals to us and he's sussed her. I'll have to stop him before she gets it as well.'

Demyan struck Hunter on the shoulder and stuck a hand out. 'Take care, Hunter, See you soon and I'll treat you to a game of golf at my place.'

They shook hands and Hunter turned to Elana. 'It's been a pleasure to meet you, Elana. Keep an eye on him and I'll take him up on that golf.'

'My pleasure Mr Hunter, you must bring your wife over.'

'I have four kids now Elana, you want that?'

'I'm sure they'll get on fine with our two. See you.'

As Demyan and Elana moved away Hank and Aaron pushed their way through the crowd. Breathing heavily, Hank said, 'Sorry I'm late, there's a bit of a crush on parking today. It was never like this when I was with the NYPD. Hunter—Aaron's got something to tell you.'

'What is it, Aaron?'

'I've had a call from our watchers in Sheepshead Bay. They were disturbed by the fact that the house was quiet. Blinds and curtains still down, no movement and their guest had left leaving the SUV so they went across to check and found the bodies of the family inside. They had been shot and the cops are in attendance.'

'That changes things. Aaron—rejoin your friends and tell them that you and they were hired as watchers and know nothing else and if anyone mentions Demyan, he was hired as an interpreter and he's left. Hank—you were hired as my chauffeur and you supplied me with those tools from your contact because you thought I was doing this historical bullshit thing. If the cops ask tell them we are veteran Army pals from the Vietnam War. They're big on that here. Was there anything else?...' Both Aaron and Hank looked at each other and shook their heads simultaneously, and Hunter continued, '...Good! Hank!—call Landon and tell him to get ready to fly me to Washington and then pay off the hotel. I'll settle later.'

'What are you going to do?'

'I'll get a taxi to the Heliport and on the way, I'll call my CIA contact and tell her about the bomb. Aaron—help me book an overnight ticket on the Silver Meteor service from Washington to Miami tonight.

Hunter made a move towards the booking offices when Aaron stopped him. 'Hunter, give me your smart cell.'

'What for?'

'It's easier to book online and keep it on your cell and just show it at the office in DC and they'll print it off for you.'

Hunter dug deep into the side pocket of his bag and pulled out another cell phone. 'What's wrong with the one you've got,' said Aaron.

'I've changed my name, Agent Hunter is staying in New York.'

'Who are you now?'

'Brian Drinkwater!'

Aaron busied himself on the phone and was having quite a stern conversation with whoever was on the other end, when he said, 'Hold it there, I'll speak to my customer...' Hunter, I can only get you a deluxe bedroom, everything else is booked up.'

'That'll have to do, Aaron.'

'It's expensive.'

'I'm worth it, go ahead.'

Aaron continued, '...Hello, sorry about that, we'll take it. Card number, one sec...' He waved at Hunter to give him his credit card and then read it out. '...Yes, it's English and it's a gold card.' He waited and pushed a few buttons and handed Hunter his smart cell. 'All done.'

'Thanks, Aaron. Take care, it's been great working with you and I'll organise a get together when this is all over.' They shook hands and he took Hank by the shoulder. 'Come on, I've got a train to catch.'

Like all good cab drivers, this one knew the shortcuts but Hunter still had time to make the critical phone call and he could almost smell the panic as they weaved through the traffic. He was greeted at the heliport by Landon. They shook hands and Landon, said, 'How long have we, Mr Hunter?'

'The trains at 19^{25} hrs from DC.'

Landon looked at his watch. It was ten past four. 'We're good, it'll take one hour-forty or so. Two hours at most depending on the wind and the taxi from the Helipad to Union Station is only twelve minutes.'

'It's as close as that?' Like most visitors to the U.S. Hunter thought Washington was much further. An hour into the flight he got the message that two attempts had been made to detonate the bomb.

—

Wearing a quilted cardigan over a blue striped business shirt and cavalry twill trousers, his disguise enhanced by colourful framed glasses, at precisely 18^{30} hrs he plonked his hand luggage down with his suede jacket and placed his cell phone on the counter of the Washington Amtrak check-in.

The clerk responded, 'Yes, sir, what can we do for you?'

He held the cell up, and said, 'Hi, my colleague says to show you this and you have my reservation.'

The clerk studied the cell and responded by clicking away on his keyboard and immediately reached under the counter and withdrew some tickets. 'Here you are, sir, I see you have our Viewliner Bedroom Suite service?'

'That's all that was left in the sleeper section.'

'In that case, you get the real deal,' he pushed the tickets across, 'the train's running late, sir, so you have a whole hour and some to relax and have complimentary drinks on us…' he pointed over to his right, '…in the Acela Lounge over there, sir, between gates D & E. Enjoy the rest of your day, Mister Drinkwater, sir.'

Hunter scooped up his ticket and bent down for his bag and as he was about to step off he turned back, and said, 'If I want to break my journey say in Savannah, can I do that?'

'Yes, sir, and you can catch a later train but you will lose your Bedroom but get First class seating and service.'

A plan was forming but he would have to wait and see what the circumstances were first.

—

Standing on the spot allotted on the platform for sleeper passengers he was feeling much refreshed as the train pulled in ten minutes late. He declined the offer by the Coach Attendant to carry his bags but followed her down the corridor between the Roomettes to his Premium bedroom suite and as she stepped aside to let him in he slipped her a few dollars.

'Thank you, sir, I'll call you for dinner. Would you like any pre-dinner refreshment, sir?'

'No, love, but I would like a nice bottle of red with my dinner.'

'I'll bring you our drinks menu, sir. Why did you call me, love?'

He laughed and ran a hand through his hair. 'Oh, dear. As you've probably guessed I'm English and in the U.K. it's a North country term of endearment. A local habit, nothing detrimental.'

'I like it, makes me feel, I don't know, warm. I'll get you that menu.'

Moments later as the train pulled away from the platform there was a gentle knock on the door. 'Your menu, sir!'

He flipped up the catch and opened the door and she handed him the menu. 'Pick what you want, sir, and give it to the waiter in the dining room. It will be about half an hour or would you rather dine here in your room, sir?'

He winked, and said, 'Thank you, love, but I like company.'

She laughed and he could see a darkening of her cheeks as she turned away. He closed the door and dropped the catch and made a note of the lock workings before he sat down and pulled out the folding table and opened his overnight bag. From a side pocket he took out a list and a quick glance told him what he wanted to know and he unzipped the bag and from a numbered pocket took out a roll of twine. He unwound two metres and snipped it off with the scissors of his Swiss Army knife and tied a small single knot at either end to stop it unravelling. He went to the door and tied one end around the catch and let it dangle before he opened the door and took a quick look along the corridor. It was clear and stepping out he slid the door shut with the string dangling outside. With a steady downward movement, he pulled on it and it stuck. He had a quick look around before he opened the door and tilted the locking lever slightly. He tried again and the lever moved but not enough to lock him out. He went back inside the compartment and undid the twine, wrapped it around his hand and put it in his jacket pocket.

Next from the bag, he picked up a keepsake from his SAS days. An issue Fairburn-Sykes combat knife that he strapped to his left forearm. He'd put a bit of weight on since he had last used it and he had to fiddle with the straps and release catch. Satisfied with its comfort he made sure it didn't show below his shirt before lifting from the bottom of the bag an ankle holster. Ignoring protocol he put his foot on the chair and fastened the holster onto his left ankle and then tested it with a pocket-sized .32 ACF Walther PP. It was good so he popped a pill up the spout, cocked it, set the safety catch and put it in place hidden by his sock and trousers.

The next bit was easy. He stripped off his cardigan and from under his left armpit, he pulled out his old faithful Glock 17. He gave it a quick once over and from his bag, he took out a silencer and clipped it onto the weapon. With the silencer fitted he would have to wear his jacket and as he went to take it from the back of the chair there was a knock on the door.

'Dinner, sir.'

'Thank you,' he called out, 'I'll be right there.'

He hid his bag on the ledge under one of the seats, slipped on his jacket and gave himself the once-over in the mirror. Satisfied, he followed the other passengers through the three sleeping cars and joined the queue to the dining room. When it was his turn the Dining Room Attendant took his ticket, and said, 'Mr Drinkwater, as a Premium passenger you can have a table to yourself or would you prefer to share?'

'I'll share.'

'Certainly, sir, and thank you. It makes it easier for us. Come this way.'

He followed the attendant and was only two tables in when he sensed a familiar aftershave. He made a mental note and continued down the car and he was offered a seat with three women travellers. One, in her mid-sixties, sat next to him was headed to Miami to rendezvous with her new boyfriend that she reconnected with at their 40th high school reunion. Of the other two, one was rather quiet but they were friendly, conversant and all-around pleasant table-mates. They chose the 'grilled' salmon and rice but Hunter went mad and had the 'Amtrak Signature Steak' followed by his favourite profiteroles.

Conversation was at a minimum during the meal and Hunter took the chance to suss out table two. It was Fabianski with Anna who did not look happy. He apologised and took his cell phone from his inside pocket. 'Excuse me, ladies, I think I've just seen a colleague from my Army days.'

He flicked through his photos and compared the image of Fabianski with the real Fabianski and had a welcome little smile to himself. 'Got Ya! You bastard.'

'What was that?' said the lady next to him.

'Oh! Sorry, I'm right, he's an old Army pal. I'll get a bottle of bubbly and join him later.'

They had coffee and immediately the quiet one left while Hunter and the other ladies shared another bottle of wine and nattered on.

During their banter, Hunter called the Attendant. 'Yes, sir!'

'That chap on the second table. He's an old army pal and I want to have a surprise reunion. Do you have champagne?'

'We only do half bottles of sparkling wine, sir.'

Hunter slipped him twenty dollars. 'Two bottles of that and I don't suppose you know his Sleeper number?'

'Not on me, sir.'

He rejoined the conversation and a couple of minutes later the attendant delivered his bubbly and a folded note was slipped into his hand. 'There you are, sir, enjoy. That will be thirty-three dollars.'

Hunter gave him forty and told him to keep the change and as he tucked his wallet away he saw Fabianski holding Anna by the arm get up and have a curious look in his direction as he wheeled away to leave the diner.

Hunter, happy with the company continued for a few more minutes before he too threw in the towel and after some vigorous hand-holding and hugging, he said, 'Goodnight,' and went back to his compartment checking on Fabianski's bedroom in the carriage before his.

He threw his glasses on the bed and gave himself a last-minute check over and put one of the half bottles of bubbly in his jacket pocket and waited fifteen minutes. He put on some surgical gloves and slid the door open, paused and eased his head forward to check the corridor and listen.

His was the end compartment and satisfied it was clear he closed the door behind him and treading softly moved forward past the double bedrooms A & B to the first bend in the corridor that took him to the centre aisle through the twelve closed Roomettes. He negotiated this quickly taking extra care past the attendant's compartment and safely into the next car past the store cupboard and to the front of Bedroom 'H' which was reserved for wheelchair users. Next was Fabianski's room and he stopped outside. The curtains were closed so they couldn't see him and after a glance either way and working on the theory that Fabianski was as naive to Amtrak methods as he was he took a deep breath and knocked on the door.

He heard a thump inside as feet hit the floor and a muffled voice said, 'What is it?'

Hunter drew his Glock and with his best American accent, he said, 'Tickets, please. Last check before Miami.'

There were shuffles and grumbles before the lock clicked off and the door began to slide open. It had barely moved an inch when Hunter pushed his fingers into the gap and heaved it wide and he was confronted by Anna. He placed his hand on her breast bone and pushed and with his gun at the ready he stepped inside and swept the door closed and clicked down the lock.

As he straightened up his aim was at Fabianski's head who stood with his back to the window but Hunters push had placed Anna into his arms and he was holding her around the neck with his Makarov aimed at Hunter.

'Come in, Agent Hunter. So, they're sending pensioners now.' His mood changed, and he said aggressively, 'Throw down your weapon.'

'Try me you Russian scum bag. I'll take an eye out before you can take a breath.'

Fabianski's reaction was to pull Anna closer and he rammed his pistol into her head. 'Drop it, Hunter, or she gets it.'

Hunter had a dilemma. While Fabianski shot her he could kill Fabianski but did he want her to die unnecessarily. He pondered his position and threw his gun onto the nearest bed.

Fabianski gestured with his gun, 'On your knees, Hunter. Move!'

Unsure what Fabianski would do next he made a show of easing himself down with his left hand close to his leg when the steady drone of the train suddenly changed to a roar as they entered a short tunnel under a highway. Fabianski flinched and his attention was momentarily diverted. It was enough for Hunter. His left hand swept down and flipped off the holding strap on the leg holster. He slid the Walther out and in a smooth choreographed arc clicked the safety off and pulled the trigger the sound of the shot muffled by the low calibre and the noise of the train. A hole appeared above Fabianski's nose and his head jerked back before he sank to the floor with his pistol dangling from lifeless fingers dragging Anna down with him just as the train left the tunnel and continued its normal humming passage through the pristine Virginia countryside.

Hunter picked up his Glock at the same time he grabbed Anna's arm and pulled her to her feet. 'Clean yourself up,' he said, as he took the bottle of bubbly from his pocket and opened it. He splashed some wine on the floor, grabbed a glass and poured some in and put it on the folding table.

'Anna! Give me a hand to put him to bed.'

Hunter stripped the bedclothes back, wrapped a towel around Fabianski's head to stem the spread of blood and between them they manoeuvred him into bed and covered him with just the top of his head showing.

Hunter stepped back and looked around when there was a knock on the door. 'Who is it?' he called.

'Attendant, sir. We heard a noise. Is all okay?'

'One moment,' Hunter replied. He kicked Fabianski's gun under the bed and picked up the bottle and glass and whispered to Anna to dim the lights and pretend to tuck Fabianski in. He made a show of unlocking the door and slid it open a few inches and with a drunken slur in his voice, said, 'Yes, sir, how can I help.'

'Someone reported a strange popping noise, sir, and a bump, what was it?'

Hunter nudged the door open wider, and said, 'That was me, sir. When we hit that tunnel the sudden noise change made me jump and I dropped...' he held up the bottle, '...this and the cork blew out. That's all it was.'

'Was there any mess?'

'Just a little on the floor but we mopped it up with a towel.'

'You need a clean towel, sir?'

Hunter shook his head. 'No, you're alright. They can manage.' The attendant looked across at Fabianski. 'Your friend is in bed?'

'Yep! He celebrated too much and felt a bit iffy so we helped him into bed,' He took a swig of wine, 'and I'm going to my bed now. I'm just around the corner.'

'Okay, sir, but why are you wearing gloves?'

'I have a psoriasis rash and I didn't want any skin flakes dropping in the drinks or anywhere for that matter.'

'Oh! I see. Have a good sleep and we'll see you at breakfast.'

'No problem,' said Hunter, and he closed the door and leaned his back against it. 'Right, Anna, here is what we do. Make up an overnight bag. Have you got money?'

'No, Mister, what is your name?'

'Call me, Hunter.' He pointed at Fabianski. 'Have a look in his wallet.'

She went to a jacket hanging on a coat hanger and took a wallet from the inside pocket and opened it and began fingering notes.

'How much is there?'

'Twelve hundred dollars.'

'He carries a lot, leave forty and take the rest. Credit cards?'

'Two. One is a debit.'

'Do you know the numbers?'

'The credit card, yes. I watch him in New York.'

'Take that, and have you all your documents including your U.K. right to reside?'

'Yes.'

'Good, make up your bag and then we'll lock him in. Oh! And bring both your tickets.'

While she was packing he tied the length of twine to the door catch and tilted it slightly of the vertical. Five minutes later she was ready.

'Okay, Anna, follow me and be careful. We're only going back one carriage but we're right at the far end.'

He slid open the door and took a quick look right and left before he called her out. She waited while he closed the door and gently pulled down on the twine. When he felt the click he cut the twine as close to the door as possible and with the screwdriver element of his knife eased the end back in between the door and the jamb.

He held a finger to his lips and signalled Anna to follow him down the corridor into the next carriage between the Roomettes. He breathed a sigh of relief when they passed number 12 and around the corner out of sight of anyone coming into the carriage and as the suites didn't lock from the outside they were inside quickly. He removed the gloves and pushed them into a side pocket of his bag and then helped Anna set up a second bed.

'Right, Anna, you sleep on that one. Don't sleep in the clothes you're going to wear.' He looked at his watch, 'we have about five hours before we get off so grab what sleep you can and we'll have you back with Alex soon if all goes well.'

'Thank you, Mr Hunter, I'm sorry for Fabianski and what he did. He kill too much, that is why I try to help you.'

'We were watching, Anna. He probably would have killed you. He's gone now, grab some sleep.'

—

'Anna! Wake up.' Hunter shook her, 'come on, time to go.'

'Ooh! What time is it?'

'Four-fifteen. Come on, wakey-wakey, you've got half an hour.'

She rolled over onto her back and looked up at Hunter who was holding a cup of coffee ready. She reached up and took it and lay back against the head of the bed getting her bearings until the caffeine did its stuff and disregarding Hunter she swung her legs off the bed and made her way to the toilet and shower cubicle in her underwear.

Five minutes later she returned and began getting dressed and while she was doing her hair, she said, 'What is the plan, Mr Hunter?'

'We are going to play it by ear, Anna. Have yours and Fabianski's tickets handy for when we get off. They're in the name McRae aren't they?'

'His is, he has used that name since we left the U.K. He used my real name.'

Hunter raised the curtain on the platform side and saw they were entering the suburbs and looked at his watch. 'By my reckoning, we should be there in five minutes. Have you got everything?'

'I think so, Mr Hunter. '

Hunter hadn't added Amtrak delays into his reckoning and they pulled into Charleston twenty minutes late. The attendant's cubicle was at the other end of the carriage but they took no chances and slipped quietly out of the Suite. Hunter did his trick with the twine and treading carefully they nipped around the corner to the last exit door of the train. Conscious of CCTV everywhere Hunter put on a Yankees baseball cap and his glasses and as the train came to a stop he released the door and waited for the steps to lower. He went down first and then held his hand out for Anna.

They were walking briskly towards the exit when the Platform attendant waving his arm hurried towards them. Breathlessly, he said, 'Phew! I was not expecting arrivals. Are you breaking your journey?'

'Yes,' said Hunter, 'The motion was making my partner queasy.'

'That's okay, give me your tickets and I'll mark them up for you so you can carry on at your leisure. You will lose your Bedroom though.'

'That's okay. Anna give him the tickets.'

Anna took the tickets from her bag and handed them over and after making his mark the Attendant said, 'How long will you be staying Dr McRae?'

Hunter wanted to hurry things along fearful that his Car Attendant might be disturbed and he looked anxiously towards the open carriage door. 'It depends if her tummy settles. About twenty-four hours maybe. Are there hotels close by?'

The Attendant gave the tickets back to Anna. 'Yes, you can walk to most of them but there is a cab outside he'll know the best one.'

'Thank you, sir, we'll see you tomorrow.'

The Attendant crossed over to the door and closed it while Hunter urged Anna to hurry off the platform and through the exit and they found one solitary cab waiting. They had to knock on the window to wake up the driver and after listening to a few recommendations they made their way to the 'Extended Stay America Hotel' close by the airport.

Using his Drinkwater I.D. he wangled Senior Citizen rates and they got a One Bedroom suite with 'grab and go breakfast' paid for with Fabianski's contribution. At precisely six o'clock Anna threw herself on the Queen sized bed and mumbled through her arm, 'I don't want breakfast just let me die, I'm tired.'

'Okay, lass, we have a few hours.'

He dropped into an armchair, put his feet on a stool and dozed off into neverland with her.

It was three hours but it felt like minutes when he woke up. He took advantage of the free coffee while he smartened himself up and took the cash from Anna's bag and left her asleep and went down to the Restaurant and grabbed something to eat from the free grab and go facilities.

Refreshed he went to Reception and called Enterprise Car hire on the landline and read the local press while he waited. He didn't have long to wait before the car hire rep arrived and drove him down to their office where he introduced himself as Drinkwater.

'Let me check Mr Drinkwater, you want the SUV for a week and you want a one way to Miami. There is an extra charge?'

'I'm aware of that but my partner became unwell on the train so a gentle car ride will be better.'

'No problem. We have a RAV4 in the yard, will that be okay?'

'Perfect. Is it ready? I'm paying cash and I want to be on the move by midday.'

'Cash, huh! That's a new one. Let's go and have a check on it.'

Twenty minutes later he pulled up outside the hotel and went upstairs to drag Anna from her dreams but she was waiting for him as he went through the door.

'Where have you been, Mr Hunter. I worry you leave me.'

'I left you sleeping but my bags are still here.'

'I see that, but I still worry.'

'Okay, lass. Grab your stuff and you can have a snack downstairs and we go on our way. In reception draw some cash on the credit card.'

'How much?'

'The daily allowance. I've spent a lot on the car.'

'Oh, we have a car?'

'We sure do. Let's go.'

—

Satnav pointed them up the Interstate-95 and it was an easy drive. Hunter didn't hurry and stopped after two hours at a roadside cafe in a small town.

'Pay with the card, Anna.'

'Such a small amount?'

'Yes, you'll get the logic.'

They did this twice more before they drove into Lafayette N.C. and Hunter saw a sign for the Travelodge Hotel just off the I-95. 'That'll do,' he said, 'I stay in those at home.'

They booked a twin bedroom and paid cash as they did for their evening dining and drinks in the restaurant. The next morning they didn't eat in the hotel instead went to a nearby burger joint and used the card. As they were finishing their coffee and burger he had Anna write the PIN on the back of the card alongside Fabianski's signature and then he sent Anna into the local supermarket to buy a throwaway cell phone and anything else she fancied and get some cash back.

'Not the full allowance, about fifty. When you come out, Anna, drop the card near those yobs hanging around outside and hope they don't call you. If they do say 'Thanks' and go back.'

Hunter's instinct proved correct and they didn't call Anna but waited until they had driven onto the Highway and continued their journey north.

'What was the idea behind that, Mr Hunter?'

'I assume that card will be tracked and those simpletons are now having orgasms because we left the PIN which I hope will make the authorities think the card was stolen in Charleston and is being used locally while we go north instead of south.'

'Mr Hunter, you are crafty. Is that the right English?'

'It'll do, lass.'

'Mr Hunter?'

'Yes.'

'Thank you for not trying to take advantage of me in the hotel.'

'No worries, I'm old enough to be your father, besides you're technically under my authority as there is an arrest warrant out for you.'

'Have you arrested me?'

'No, I'm trying to get you back to the UK where questions will be asked but a lot better than here in the U.S. where a long prison sentence and repatriation to Russia awaits. Answer me one question?'

'What is that?'

'Did you know of the bomb plot?'

'No, my parents were part of the 'October Legion' and I grew up in England and I thought I was just part of and helping the Russian Society living in the UK until Fabianski tricked me. Alex was also innocent to the plot but he was threatened by Fabianski if he didn't help.'

'No, Anna, Alex knew of the 'dirty bomb' plot but came clean when he found out about the big bombs. We'll leave it there and hope I can wangle it. Meanwhile, we have to dodge the CIA because I'm wanted to.'

'But you stopped Fabianski.'

'It's a long story, Anna, I've been here before.'

She didn't reply but uprated her opinion of him while on the horizon Washington loomed.

Negotiating the many Exits and diversions leading into downtown Washington from the I-95 to the Embassy Area the satnav got them onto Wisconsin Ave NW, across Massachusetts Ave NW which lead to Embassy Row and on to the West of the Naval Observatory. Progress was slow as mid-afternoon traffic was heavy and it was with sweaty palms that Hunter eventually turned into the Park America car park.

Rush hour had not started and there were only a few spaces available but with a little bit of nifty manoeuvring, he wiggled the car into a corner on the third floor. He knew he couldn't remove all traces but he gave the interior a good wipe down and kept his fingers crossed that no one would find it before Enterprise Rentals. Satisfied there was no more he could do they made their way to the street level.

Getting a cab was something else and it was ten minutes before they managed to grab one for the five-minute drive to the British Embassy and they made it with fifteen minutes to spare. Hunter flashed his I.D. and was directed to a side room which compared to the rest of the Embassy was quite bare.

It was after four 'o clock before an official and his assistant entered and crossed over to Hunter who stood up with his hand outstretched. They shook hands, and the official said, 'Good afternoon, Agent Hunter, I understand you have a problem?'

Hunter showed his I.D. again. 'Yes,' he said, 'who am I speaking to?'

'Oh, sorry, I'm Isaac Carter and this is Mary Jones.'

'Mr Carter...' he pointed to Anna, '...this is Anna, she is Russian with dual nationality and she has a British passport. She is wanted by MI6 and Special Branch in connection with the International plot to move and use illegal nuclear devices. We must get her to the UK before the Yanks get their hands on her. Can you organise diplomatic immunity and smuggle her out?'

'I'm afraid not, Mr Hunter, we have a working relationship with the U.S. concerning all security matters and we must tell them.'

'Mr Carter! We need to question her first as she is a prime witness in this incident. If the U.S. get their hands on her we will never get the chance or even see her again.' He took his wallet out and gave Carter a card. 'Call that number in the UK. It is the Head of the SIS who has a direct line to the Home Secretary. Meanwhile, can you give her safe sanction and don't tell anyone?'

'I'll need to speak with the Ambassador.'

'Do that, Mr Carter. I'm sure your forgery department can fix it. Meanwhile, have you any facilities and a diner of any sort? We're both weary. We've been on the road all day.'

'Yes, we can do that.' He turned to Jones. 'Mary can you organise that while I go and have a word.'

'Mr Carter, when you make that call mention Operation 'Upstart,' 'Operation Trenchcoat' and Agent 'Silvanus.' He held out his Drinkwater passport. 'and while you're at it get me a 1st class ticket on the first BA Red Eye flight out of here.'

'First-class!'

'Yes, and add a 'Sir.' That way the checks are less stringent.'

'You are asking a lot, Mr Hunter.'

'The Home Office will be asking a lot more if I get stopped.'

'I'll see what I can do. Meanwhile, Mary will show you to the annexe where you can rest and snack.'

Two hours later Carter rejoined them and sat in an easy chair opposite and opened a file. 'Agent Hunter! It appears like you said to be a matter of urgency…' he threw an envelope onto the coffee table, '…here are your flight tickets and boarding documents. You will be given VIP treatment at the airport. Miss Anna here will be staying in the Embassy until we can get the appropriate documents, which should be in about twenty-four hours. She will have an escort, obviously. Was there anything else?'

'Just one thing.' Hunter opened his hand luggage and took out a canvas wrapped bundle. 'Put this in your diplomatic bag when you ship Anna over.' He left it on the table and picked up his tickets. 'And now I need a store where I can buy stuff to top up my hand luggage and buy a clean shirt. It would look a bit odd if I didn't have any.'

'There's a diplomatic car on standby, Mr Hunter. You can stop off on the way to the airport.'

A savvy Chauffeur made a quick diversion into the Tysons Corner Center Shopping Mall and a quick shop in a major store and Hunter not only changed his shirt and topped his hand luggage up but bought himself a new suit, a fashionable cream coloured Trenchcoat and new shoes. At the airport, Hunter asked the chauffeur to dump his old clothes and tipped him generously and feeling dressed for the part looked forward to his VIP treatment.

His last action before boarding was a message to Demyan and another to Enterprise Cars before he dropped the throwaway cell phone into the nearest scrap bin.

~~~~~~

Chapter 18

The constant ringing of the telephone by his bedside shook Hunter awake and through half-open eyes, he looked at the time. 'Midday, give a chap a break.' He rolled out of bed and stretched before he answered the phone. 'Hunter!'

'Hunter! Get yourself over here. 'C' wants a debrief.'

'Is that you, Gus?'

'Yep!'

'I'm having brunch first and I'll be right there.'

'Okay, I'll send Penny for you.'

The phone went dead and Hunter put it down and wandered over to the bathroom. 'Nice to be back,' he muttered.

—

An hour later as Penny drove them from the Camden safe house, Penny asked him, 'How did New York go this time?'

'Pretty good. You know Hank and Aaron, from the last time...' she nodded, '...they looked after me well and rather enjoyed it, especially, Hank. He was getting bored in retirement and he really got stuck in and his contacts were good.'

'You should have called on me, Hunter. I was all ready to go.'

'Sorry, Penn, I did consider it but after the stories that went around last time I decided against it.'

'I don't blame you.'

She swung the car into the main gate and showed their I.D. and accelerated over to the entrance. 'See you later, Hunter and you can tell me all about it.'

'Bring a takeaway from the Chinese Restaurant of yours and we'll have dinner together. I'll get the wine.'

—

Hunter hung his leather jacket on the hook behind the door and sat down opposite Gus Thomas who as usual was surrounded by a mass of files and paper. Gus scribbled something and threw the note into the out tray before pushing back from the desk. 'Right, Hunter, what have you got?'

'Where's 'C'?'

'He's been called to the Home Office and he's asked me to debrief you. So! What have you got to tell us?'

'It was straightforward, Gus, I was prepared to go awol to get Williams killer when I got 'your blessing' to do it legally so to speak and I carried on with my original plan and organised my friends. I didn't fraternise with the CIA and as I suspected they went for the most obvious site while I stuck with mine which proved right.'

'What actually happened, Hunter?'

'It was like this...' He went on to explain the whole episode, '...until Fabianski did a runner with the girl in tow and the rest is history.'

'You disarmed a nuclear bomb. Why didn't you call in the proper authorities?'

'It was only sim cards but that was something I was asked the whole time and I'll repeat myself for you, Gus. Had I told the Yanks they would have been swarming around the place with their SWAT teams and the whole town locked down and door-to-door TV coverage and Fabianski would have responded by pushing the button. I couldn't allow that, think of the mayhem that would have caused and I would not have had the chance to avenge Williams's death or Tanya's, not to mention his kids.'

'I hear you've taken them under your wing?'

'I think they would rather have Mum and Dad but I will do my best for them. That's my full-time job now.'

'Just to let you know, Hunter, the Yanks as you call them, are looking for you. You're not planning on going back by any chance?'

'Yes, the team are planning a family get together but I'll wait until the political hoo-haa has died down. I hear the golf's good there.'

'Lie low. They still want a chat about that Irish guy's mishap earlier this year.'

'Was I there then? That was Byewater wasn't it?'

'Bugger off, Hunter, and give my regards to Jacquie. When are you going home?'

'Tonight! I'm catching the ten past six direct.'

Gus stood up and shoved a hand over the desk. 'Good luck,

Hunter, and well done.'

'Thanks, Gus, keep in touch. Oh! One more thing, I'll send the bill in as soon as the team get their act together.'

'Best of luck with that one, Hunter.'

'I was given an open check, remember?'

Gus remained silent as Hunter closed the door.

———

Iain and Lesley hit him at the same time as he walked through the barriers at Chester Station. He gave them both a big hug and with one on each side walked across to Jacquie waiting with Williams' children Emery and Zara who were stood by her looking rather solemn.

Hunter sympathised with them and his first reaction was to lower himself in front of Zara, and say, 'Hello, Zara …' and pointing to Iain and Lesley, '… are these two treating you okay?'

Zara smiled, and said, 'Yes, Mr Hunter, we are in the same class at school and we have the same i-pad.'

He turned to the young lad and held his hand out and Emery responded by shaking hands. 'And how about you, Emery?'

'Hey, Dad,' Iain interrupted, 'Emery is teaching me Russian and I've got him into rugby.'

Emery was smiling now. 'We do great, Mr Hunter.'

Hunter gave him a man tap on the shoulder, stood up and stepped backed to look at Jacquie who was dressed in skin-tight jeans with knee-high boots and topped by her Gucci jacket draped across her shoulders. They kissed regardless of onlookers. 'It's great to see you, lass, you look fantastic, as always.'

'And you look knackered, Hunter. Let's get home and fix you up. Have you eaten?'

'Not since lunch. I tell lies, I had a kit-kat on the train.'

'Okay, kids, let's go, Hunter's hungry.'

Hunter held her hand as they left the station, and whispered, 'That was tactful love.'

'It's difficult, but I try to keep it family neutral and I better warn you. Russian is a new language in our house. They both speak it fluently and are teaching our two so we don't know what they're up to.'

'One set of secrets for another. I can't get away from it.'

Outside the station, as they walked across the car park he stopped, and said, 'Where's the car, Jaq's?'

'That's it over there.' She pointed to a shiny black Land Rover Discovery. 'We've got a big family now so I swapped mine for a seven-seater which was a waste of time because they all crowd together in the main seat.'

He stopped to admire it. 'We are going upmarket. Is it new?'

'It's classified as used but has no mileage.'

'You sold a tree or something?'

She gave him a nudge on the shoulder. 'Come on, you old bugger, get in and let's get some supper.' She pressed her key and the boot opened by itself. 'All the bells and whistles, Hunter, chuck your bag in if you can find room behind those seats and while we're talking about cars a Mrs Jenkins from Upton left you a message. Something about you being interested in her husband's car. I told her you would contact her when you get back.'

'I know what that's about and I'm getting rid of the Golf. I'll do it tomorrow.'

Bag in, he jumped in the front passenger seat and as predicted the four kids squashed into the back ignoring the two extra seats in the rear and he sat back and admired the way Jacquie handled her new toy.

Back at the house as soon as the door was opened the kids dashed in and seated on the bottom few steps took their shoes off and coats and turned to nip upstairs when Jacquie said loudly. 'Stop! Hang your coats up.'

They turned and picked up their coats and hung them on hooks down the hall before dashing upstairs jabbering something which Hunter didn't understand. He looked at Jacquie and they both shrugged, and she said, 'I told you, Hunter, and don't ask me how they picked it up so quickly. I knew they were smart, but that? Come on, let's get you sorted.'

He followed her down the hall and into the kitchen and sat on a stool as she put the kettle on and set about preparing something for him to eat, she said to him. 'Okay, tell me all about it and which bit of young stuff you took this time. Wasn't Penny was it?'

He held his hands up. 'Not guilty. I had the option to take her as backup but I declined. I couldn't stand the agro, instead, it was all down to the oldie gang plus Demyan.'

'Demyan? He was willing?'

'Yes, and a great help he was amongst the Russian community.'

'I'm surprised after what he was up to previously.'

'It's an old soldier thing, Jacquie. We became colleagues at the club shoot out, remember? We shook hands and he took photos of me lying allegedly dead. He got his money for that too.'

She put a plate down in front of him. 'Chilli burger and salad?

'Yep! Is there any lager in the fridge?'

'Is there a time when there isn't?' She went to the fridge and pulled out a pint bottle of Stella. 'Anything else, sir?'

'Come here you.'

She walked over to his side and he put an arm around her waist and pulled her closer. 'Give us a kiss.'

She swung around onto his lap and they kissed vigorously until she pulled away breathlessly.' Enough, Hunter, eat your burgers while they're hot.'

'I rather eat you while you're hot.'

'Burger, Hunter, while I get the kids to bed or at least into bed.'

—

It had been an amorous night during which they had talked about adopting Zara and Emery and he slept late. By the time he wandered into the kitchen, Jacquie had gone to work and Jamie had taken the children to school but it was when he read Jacquie's love note stuck on the kettle he felt the oppressive cloak of the last weeks slide off and it determined his future.

He walked the two miles to what had been his Parish Church before they had moved and it was a little after eleven o'clock when he entered and sat in a pew in the centre of the colourful and airy atmosphere brightened by the sun coming in through the stained glass windows and the many vases of fresh flowers. It was much like his previous visit and he found it, relaxing, was not the word he was looking for, more, tranquil, soothing and it added to his feeling of being removed from the pressures of his working life. Today was a new start.

Although his religious views were still atheist he leaned forward in his seat and quietly asked forgiveness for the people who had caused the travesty which had overcome the Williams family and although he didn't feel any guilt for the killing of Fabianski he asked forgiveness for himself.

The calming voice of the Reverend John Fraser awoke him from his deliberations. 'Good Morning, Mr Hunter isn't it. Can I be of assistance?'

Hunter sat upright quickly, 'Good morning Reverend.'

'What has brought about your visit today?'

'A close comrade of mine and his wife were slaughtered by a renegade faction of the Russian underground and I wished for forgiveness for their killer and in my hunt for him, I lost my conscience and I asked for a little salvation for delivering that same killer to the depths of Hell.'

'This sounds not too dissimilar to your last visit. Did you feel any guilt at all?'

'No! This man deserved it. He orphaned two children, which he knew about'

'Were the authorities aware of this?'

'I'm sorry, Reverend, but I can't talk about that. You know my circumstances.'

'Mr Hunter, the Lord and myself cannot condone killing but even I can see that you dealt out justice where none would have been forthcoming. Join me in a little prayer and seek forgiveness and repentance for those who follow the path of evil.'

The Reverend knelt in the pew across the aisle from Hunter and recited a short prayer. When he had finished they shook hands, and Hunter said, 'I have finally retired from my profession, from now on I'm set to look after not only my children but to adopt the children of my dead colleague and give them the life they deserve. It's going to be some job. All four are more intelligent than me.'

'Best of luck, Mr Hunter.'

~~~~~~

THE END

Printed in Great Britain
by Amazon

77659680R00153